W9-ARG-948

"Featuring a charming hero with a mysterious past and mission, *Lady in the Mist* brims with tension, intrigue, and romance."

Julie Klassen, bestselling author of *The Silent Governess* and *The Girl in the Gatehouse*

"Laurie Alice Eakes pens another novel that keeps the reader turning the pages with her expert knowledge of the time period and her skill with language. If you want to read a historical novel with romance, intrigue, and mystery all rolled into one, *Lady in the Mist* is a book you won't want to miss."

Golden Keyes Parsons, author of *In the Shadow of the Sun King* and *Prisoner of Versailles*

"I loved, loved, loved this book. Laurie Alice is a master storyteller. Her book grabbed me by the heart and held on. I loved the characters and the plot, which was full of delicious romance and dark mystery. Authentic historic details brought the setting alive. I can hardly wait for her next book."

Lena Nelson Dooley, author of the McKenna's Daughters series and *Love Finds You in Golden, New Mexico*

"*Lady in the Mist* is not to be missed. Secrets, suspense, and a sweetly told love story make this a highly rewarding read."

Cheryl Bolen, Holt Medallion–winning author of *One Golden Ring*

"Tabitha had lost everything dear to her, but just when she thought her heart might mend, two men vie for her feelings. Two men with pasts as gray as the turbulent sea."

DiAnn Mills, Christy Award–winning author of *Breach of Trust*

"Laurie Alice Eakes tackles an era in our country's history about which little has been written to craft a fascinating story of redemption and sacrificial love. Her absorbing novel captivated me from the first page. *Lady in the Mist* boasts a fresh plot, impeccably researched prose, and realistic characters. Readers are sure to have their hearts stirred as Tabitha and Dominick learn to trust one another and their heavenly Father's plans for them.

"I hated to leave these characters behind when I finished the story. I'll be eagerly awaiting book 2 in the Midwives series."

Ann Shorey, author of At Home in Beldon Grove series

The
MIDWIVES
BOOK 1

LADY *in the* MIST

A NOVEL

LAURIE ALICE EAKES

Revell
a division of Baker Publishing Group
Grand Rapids, Michigan

Valley Community Library
739 River Street
Peckville, PA 18452-2313

11/15/2012 DONATION

© 2011 by Laurie Alice Eakes

Published by Revell
a division of Baker Publishing Group
P.O. Box 6287, Grand Rapids, MI 49516-6287
www.revellbooks.com

Printed in the United States of America

All rights reserved. No part of this publication may be reproduced, stored in a retrieval system, or transmitted in any form or by any means—for example, electronic, photocopy, recording—without the prior written permission of the publisher. The only exception is brief quotations in printed reviews.

Library of Congress Cataloging-in-Publication Data
Eakes, Laurie Alice.
Lady in the mist : a novel / Laurie Alice Eakes.
p. cm. — (The midwives ; bk. 1)
ISBN 978-0-8007-3452-7 (pbk.)
1. Midwives—Fiction. I. Title.
PS3605.A377L33 2011
813′.6—dc22 2010031561

Scripture is taken from the King James Version of the Bible.

Published in association with Tamela Hancock Murray of the Hartline Literary Agency, LLC.

This book is a work of fiction. Names, characters, places, and incidents are the product of the author's imagination or are used fictitiously. Any resemblance to actual events, locales, or persons, living or dead, is coincidental.

11 12 13 14 15 16 17 7 6 5 4 3 2 1

To the ladies of the His Writers group, for your prayers, your encouragement, and your dedication to history. You all inspire me.

But he was wounded for
our transgressions,
he was bruised for our iniquities:
the chastisement of our
peace was upon him;
and with his stripes we are healed.

Isaiah 53:5

1

Seabourne, Virginia
May 1809

"I'm sorry." Tabitha Eckles dared not look Harlan Wilkins in the eye. If she witnessed even a flicker of grief, the floodgates of her own tears would spring open and drown her good sense in a moment when she needed all of it. "I did everything I could to save your wife."

"I'm sure you did." Wilkins's tone held no emotion. He stood next to the dining room sideboard with the rigidity of a porch pillar. Candlelight played across the lower half of his face, sparkling in the crystal glass he held to his lips without drinking, without speaking further.

"The baby came too soon . . ." Tabitha needed to say something more to a husband who had just lost his young bride of only six months, as well as their son. "After the accident—"

"Did she regain consciousness?" Wilkins lashed out the words. The amber contents of his glass sloshed, sending the sharp scent of spirits wafting around him.

Tabitha jumped. "No. I mean, yes. That is—" She took a breath to steady her racing heart and give herself a moment to think of a safe answer. "She mumbled a lot of nonsense."

At least Tabitha hoped it was nonsense, the ravings of a woman in terrible pain.

"The blow to her head must have made her crazed," she added for good measure.

Wilkins's posture relaxed, and he drained the liquid from his glass. "Thank you for trying. You may collect your fee from my manservant."

"Shall I send the pastor?" As much as she wanted to, simply taking her fee for attending a lying-in and leaving Wilkins alone unsettled her as much as had the disastrous night. "I pass his house—"

"Just go." The whiplash tone again, an order to depart with haste.

Tabitha spun on her heel and trotted from the room. The door slammed behind her. A moment later, an object thudded against the panel. The tinkle of broken glass followed.

So his wife's death moved Harlan Wilkins after all.

Trembling, Tabitha collected her cloak from a cowering maid and her payment from a stony-faced manservant. She struggled for words of comfort over the death of their mistress, but her throat closed and her eyes burned. With no more than a brusque nod, she fled into the dawn.

Mist swirled around her, smelling of the sea and the tang of freshly turned earth, muffling the click of her heels on cobblestone and brick pavement. Trees appeared out of the gloom like stiff-spined sentries guarding her way along the route she had taken since she was sixteen and her mother had deemed her old enough to begin learning the family business of midwifery. The trees would shelter her journey if she turned left off of the village square and headed home past the houses of the townspeople.

She hesitated, then continued straight toward the sea. She needed the tang of salty mist on her lips, the peace of the beach at low tide, the extra walk home to calm her spirit, before facing Patience—her friend, her companion, her maid of all work—and admitting she'd failed to save a patient's life.

To her right, the church with its bell tower looked like a castle floating in the low clouds. But castles meant knights in shining armor riding out to rescue maidens in distress. Maiden though she was, Tabitha faced her distress alone. She enjoyed no husband to await her return, unlike her mother, grandmother, great-grandmother, and so many generations before. In fact, no one knew for certain when the women of her family began the tradition of practicing midwifery from Lancashire, England, to the eastern shore of Virginia. But Tabitha defied the convention that unmarried women didn't practice the art of delivering babies. She adhered to the wishes of her mother, who had died too young, followed by her grandmother, who had died too recently, and carried on the family business to support her small household. A husband would have made work unnecessary. She loved her work most of the time, and one too many young men had sailed into the mist never to return or to come back with a different bride. One man in particular had vanished mere weeks before their wedding. Now that she was four and twenty, Tabitha's chances of finding a husband seemed unlikely.

Except in her imagination.

Walking alone through the stillness between night and day, Tabitha held loneliness at bay, imagining her fiancé returning to make her his bride, or someone else materializing from the smoky light to claim her heart and hand so, at last, every baby she held wouldn't belong to another woman.

This dawn, more than her empty arms weighed down Tabitha's spirit—so much that she felt as arthritic as Grandmomma had been at the end. She trudged past the church and out of the village square. The sea beckoned, a constant taker and giver of life, ebbing and flowing, ever changing, yet comforting in its power.

If only the sea held enough power to wash the night's events from her mind and heart. The drip of moisture from the trees and the distant murmur of the retreating waves reminded her of Mrs. Wilkins's muttered ravings. Fact or nightmare?

"No, no, no," seemed to be the predominant words, common protests of a woman in labor who thought she could bear the pain no longer. Disjointed phrases like "in the cellar" and "must ride" made little sense. No one in the swampy climate of the eastern shore dug cellars, and to Tabitha's knowledge, the Wilkinses owned no riding stock. But another repeated word rang in her ears—"pushed."

Tabitha shivered in the damp air and drew her cloak more tightly around her. She should have gone the shorter way home. All a walk along the shore would do was give her a chill rather than clear her head. Too late now. Trees fell behind, then houses vanished in the gloom. Cobblestones gave way to soft sand and, finally, the hard-packed leavings of the ebbing tide.

"No one could have pushed her." Tabitha paused at the edge of the high tide line, inhaling the familiar scents of fish and wet wood, seaweed and brine. "I saw no bruises except for the one on her head. I'd swear to it."

That bruise was the sort one would receive from falling down steps. Tabitha had suffered one herself in the past. And no one save for the manservant and maid had been home at the time of Mrs. Wilkins's fall. They could have shoved their mistress down the steps, but servants who did that wouldn't fetch help at once; they'd run away, knowing the consequences of being found out would be as severe as whipping or worse. Mr. Wilkins had been at the inn, drinking with some friends. His behavior was reprehensible, leaving his expecting wife alone like that, but not criminal. Yet why would Mrs. Wilkins make such a claim? Even women in labor due to accidents didn't lie during their travail. Part of Tabitha's responsibility as a midwife was to get truth from laboring women when the occasion called for it.

She'd gotten no truth from Mrs. Wilkins. Now, poised on the edge of the beach, she wondered if perhaps she should tell the sheriff or mayor of what Mrs. Wilkins had claimed in her ravings. Tabitha should have told the husband. But no, a man who had just lost his wife didn't need to know she'd died in terror as well as pain. She would tell the mayor later that morning. He could talk to his friend.

Decision made, she resumed walking parallel to the sea. Though less than fifty feet away, the ocean's roar sounded farther off, muffled, nearly still. No lights bobbed on the surf, not an oarlock creaked to indicate a fisherman passing.

Shoulders slumped and head bowed with the weight of losing a patient, she considered giving in to the temptation of weeping without inhibitions.

"Childbirth is dangerous for women," Momma had told her from the beginning. "We can only do our best and leave the rest to the Lord."

Momma and Grandmomma's best had been to save more than they lost. In the two years she'd been working on her own, Tabitha had followed in their footsteps until tonight, when her efforts to ease suffering had been in vain. She had failed.

If just one of her dreams had come true, she would have given up midwifery right then. If loss was inevitable, she didn't want to continue. She wanted to live like other young women—with a husband, children, a proper place in the community. But God ignored her pleas, and she'd given up asking for anything to change.

That didn't mean she'd given up wanting things to change. Crying had made her want a shoulder on which to rest her head, arms to hold her. She'd wasted too many tears alone in her room, her garden, walking along the shore, praying for God to send her someone to share her sorrows along with her joys. She would neither weep nor pray now.

But as she turned and crunched her way along the hard-packed sand toward home, she couldn't stop herself from slipping into the hope, the dream, of a beloved striding out of the mist to greet her, take her hand in his—

Lost in her imagination, she blundered straight into a person standing on the beach. He grunted. She reeled backward. Her heel caught in the hem of her skirt. Her other foot slipped on the wet sand, and her posterior struck the ground with a splat like a landed fish.

The person moved, looming over her. "What do we have here?" The quiet voice was real and male, deep and unmistakably English. "Are you all right?"

He sounded friendly, even warm, and not threatening. Yet no one should be about on this stretch of beach in the wee hours of the morning. No Englishman should be about on the Atlantic coast, where young men disappeared with regularity, unless he were—

"Press-gang." The word burst from her like a curse, and her heart began to race. Her mouth went dry, tasting bitter. She tried to scramble to her feet. She needed to warn the village men to stay inside. But her cloak and skirts tangled around her, holding her down.

"Let me help you." Still speaking in an undertone, he stooped before her. She caught an exotic scent like sandalwood, saw no more than a shadowy outline and dark hair tumbling around features pale in the misty gloom.

Listening for others moving about on the beach, Tabitha waved him off. "No, thank you. I can manage myself." She tugged at her skirt and nearly toppled sideways.

"You don't look to be doing such a good job of it." Laughter tinged his words. The hand that clasped hers was masculine, strong, and too smooth to belong to a fisherman or sailor. "Perhaps you can get to your feet if I help. Do you have feet? There does seem to be something trailing behind you. Perhaps it's a tail. Are you a mermaid?"

Tabitha snorted and tried to wrench her hand away. Flirtation would get the stranger nowhere with her. The instant she regained her feet, she would run back to town and warn the sheriff or mayor that the English were at it again, stealing young American men to serve aboard their ships in their endless war with France.

If the man let her go. At that moment, he gripped her hand with a firmness suggesting he would not.

"I'm not certain whether or not that noise you made was human." He closed his other hand over hers. "But this lovely hand hasn't any scales on it, which argues on the side of human. On the contrary, it's as smooth as silk." He rubbed the tip of a finger across her knuckles, and the skin along her arms felt as though lightning were about to strike. "What's a human female doing out so early?"

"Going home." Her voice emerged hoarse, sounding unused. She swallowed to clear it. "What's an Englishman doing in Virginia?"

"President Madison hasn't managed to rid these shores of all of us yet."

"A pity."

"Ah, a hostile mermaid."

His words pricked her conscience. She was being rather rude to someone who, although in a place where he had no business being, acted kind enough to deserve a modicum of courtesy in return.

"I'm not hostile. I'm cautious and worn to a th-thread." Her voice broke.

"You must have been swimming against the tide." Speaking with a tenderness that drew all-too-ready tears to her eyes, despite her contrary efforts, he rose, drawing her to her feet with him. "No, not a swim. Alas, a fatigued female human. That's a cloak, I see, not a tail. Forgive the mistaken identity, But I'd expect to see a mermaid out here before I'd think to find a . . . lady."

"An understandable error." She used the edge of her cloak to dab at her eyes. "I wouldn't be out here if I weren't a midwife."

"Indeed?" His tone spoke of disbelief. His hand lingered on hers, that errant fingertip tracing the third finger on her left hand.

She didn't need to see his face or have him speak the words to understand he sought a wedding ring. She snatched her hand free and tucked her ringless fingers inside the folds of her cloak. "Indeed."

"Then it's the last proof you're human, since surely mermaids are hatched in the bottom of the ocean." He curved his hand over her forearm. "Then allow me to walk you home, Madam Midwife."

"I'm not going—" She glanced around her.

A hint of sun glowed along the line between sea and sky, turning the sand to a silvery gray and the mist to tendrils of gauze. Other than the stranger, her, and the usual flotsam thrown up by the tide, the sand lay empty. If he'd had cohorts, he'd managed to distract her long enough for them to get away. By the time she found someone in authority, he would have vanished too. She couldn't even identify him with any certainty. He stood with his back to the light, a tall, broad-shouldered silhouette with hair tumbling from his queue.

"It's not necessary," she said instead. "I'm perfectly safe, especially now that daylight is nearly here."

"I insist." He released her arm but headed in the direction of her house. "You were going this way."

"I was, but if someone sees me walking with a man . . ." She sighed and hastened to match her stride to his. "I depend on my reputation to make my living secure, sir."

He continued up the beach but slowed. "Ah, I see. If someone sees you with me, they will think perhaps you had an assignation rather than a duty."

"Only my good name allows me to move about freely at night without being accosted," she affirmed.

"Then I'll leave you here, before we're in sight of the village again." He stopped, took her hand in his, and bowed as though they were attending a formal reception. "Have a care, Madam Mermaid Midwife."

He released her hand and retraced their footprints in the sand, his head bent, his hands clasped behind his back.

Feeling as though flotsam filled her shoes, weighing them down, Tabitha trudged toward home. Images of the Englishman filled her head, tingled along her fingers, danced down her spine. She despised the way she thrilled to his flirtation, his touch. She feared his presence on her normally empty beach.

In the past year, she knew of a dozen young men along the eastern shore who had disappeared. One had returned with the information that he'd been press-ganged aboard a British war ship and escaped when the vessel came afoul of a reef in the Caribbean. His story made all Englishmen along the coast suspect. Not satisfied with taking American sailors off of ships at sea, the British apparently decided to steal them from the land, as they did in their own country.

So an Englishman standing on the beach in the dawn hours appeared suspect at best, outright criminal at worst. Yet he hadn't seemed in the least alarmed when she ran straight into him. None of his words or actions spoke of a man guilty of wrongdoing.

And he'd distracted her from thoughts of Mrs. Wilkins's pain and death, from her husband's coldness then burst of anger, better than had any of her hazy dreams of knights riding out of the mist. He was flesh and blood and no doubt a danger to the community she served and loved.

She reached her garden gate and paused, her hand on the latch, reconsidering going back to town. But the man was gone and she would awaken Mayor Kendall for nothing. She would stay with her original plan and go into town later, after she slept.

The idea of sleep suddenly the most important thought in her head, she pushed open the gate and froze. Her nostrils flared, catching a scent familiar and out of place, a sharp tang piercing through the subtle richness of newly turned earth. To her right, fabric rustled.

She started to turn. "Who's—"

A hand clamped over her mouth. "This is a warning." The voice was sibilant, muffled, as though he spoke from behind a kerchief. Something sharp pricked the skin of her throat. "Keep silent about this night if you don't want to swim with the fishes."

2

Dominick Cherrett finished sharpening the last of the kitchen knives and removed his own blade from its sheath inside his boot. He hadn't cut anything with it since having to slice up the rock-hard beef aboard the merchant brig that had carried him into exile. But rusty stains marred the perfection of the steel blade, and he wanted the weapon sharp, ready for action at any time.

And whetting knives made an excellent excuse for coming in from outside at six o'clock in the morning instead of stumbling down from his cupboard of a chamber at the top of the Kendall mansion. It wouldn't do for his master to discover Dominick had spent the night outside of the village. He hadn't earned that kind of trust in his two weeks as a servant to the mayor of Seabourne.

He shuddered at the notion of donning the ill-fitting uniform and powdering his hair like some English butler of the previous century, gave his knife one last swipe along the whetstone, and held it up to the light. Sunshine breaking through the mist sparkled and shimmered along the blade. Not a speck of rust, not a hint of a nick marred the steel. With a nod of satisfaction, Dominick slipped the knife into its sheath and gathered up the kitchen utensils.

The kitchen door sprang open behind him. "That's what I like to see, a man willing to work before his breakfast."

Dominick faced the tall cook whose thinness belied the

fact that her culinary arts rivaled the best he'd eaten in any nobleman's home. "I figured it was the best way to get a fine breakfast if you could slice the bacon thick and the toast thin."

"Yes, and you want me to cook your egg as runny as tree sap." Letty Robins shuddered. "But that's not cooking and I won't have it in my kitchen."

"Please." He gave her his most engaging grin. "I already make my own tea so as not to offend the sensibilities of you Yankees."

"I'll soft-boil your egg." Letty spun on the heel of a sturdy brogan and stomped back to the kitchen.

Laughing, Dominick followed with the knives. Coffee he could abide, with a generous dollop of cream applied. Eggs cooked until they resembled the beef served aboard ship, turned his stomach.

Letty stood before the fire, pouring water from a bucket into an iron kettle suspended over the flames. Despite her height, she appeared too scrawny to heft the five-gallon pail.

Dominick took it from her. "Kendall would have been better off buying my indenture to make me your assistant here than to answer his front door."

"He's the mayor." Letty picked up a basket of eggs. "He needs to maintain an appearance of importance."

Dominick managed not to snort. "And now that you mention appearances," he said, "I'll just go up and change into my livery."

"Yes, that coat you're wearing looks like you slept in it." She narrowed her eyes so they skewered him like emerald blades. "Next time you sneak out at night, at least remember to tie your hair back before you come home."

"Why, Mrs. Robins," Dominick drawled, giving her a wide-eyed stare, "I have no id—"

"Don't try to bamboozle me with those pretty brown eyes of yours."

"Pretty?" Dominick's cheeks warmed.

"With those lashes, yes, but handsome if you prefer. Handsome is as handsome does, and if you're playing the tomcat and get caught, your lady won't find you so good-looking with the stripes of a whip across your back."

Dominick flinched. "No tomcat acts, I assure you, ma'am."

But there had been a lady, a lady who would likely wield the whip herself for nothing more than his country of origin.

"I needed air," he added.

"Then take it in the garden." Letty returned to her eggs. "Mr. Kendall is a kind and generous master if we do our work and mind his curfew. But if we break the rules, the law is on his side to do about anything short of killing one of us."

"Perhaps I should have risked life on my uncle's Barbados sugar plantation instead of here."

Dominick spoke the truth. Life in the Caribbean sounded harsh, even deadly, but there he'd have been a free man. Free so long as he didn't set foot in England. But here, his signature marked papers that made him little more than a slave to Thomas Kendall for four years. Still, he was in America, where he could do the most good and make up for, if not clear, his name.

"But I'm here now." He injected cheerfulness into his voice. "No sense regretting what I can't undo."

"Hurry yourself up. If you're down in a quarter hour, I'll have time to powder your hair for you."

"Thank you, madam." Dominick bowed, then raced up the back steps with such a light step, his feet barely made a sound on the treads.

He'd practiced the art of flying up and down stairs with

little noise since boyhood. He and his brothers entertained contests to see which of them could sneak out of the house most often without getting caught. He won every time. Francis, older by three years, grew broad in the shoulders but without Dominick's height, and never mastered the ability to skip every two steps. Percival, the eldest, with Dominick's height, possessed no grace at all.

Second nature to Dominick now, the skill had served him well the night before when he made his first move to abide by his uncle's dictates. No one else had noticed his departure. Of course Letty would, sleeping in a room off of the kitchen as she did.

Next time he'd be more careful. Next time he'd exit somewhere else. And when he prowled the beach, he'd keep an eye out for mermaids who weren't watching where they were going.

Not that he could wholly blame her for running into him. Gazing into the mist as though he could see England floating on the edge of the horizon, he'd paid no attention to anything else but the ache in his heart. For those few minutes, he'd forgotten four years of banishment, loved ones left behind, and a mission that could make him wish for a whip as the least of his difficulties.

She wasn't a charmer. Her very lack of artifice appealed to him after five years of parading through the drawing rooms, dining rooms, and ballrooms of London, sought after as an eligible bachelor to even out numbers at a dinner table, and provide shy young ladies with dance partners and bold women with someone to boost their self-assurance. She didn't seem to care what he thought of her. She was forthright and unique, if she truly was a midwife and her lack of wedding ring proclaimed an unmarried state.

He didn't know if she was pretty in face or form. She had

been as shadowy to him as he must have been to her. But he did know that she possessed the most elegant hand he'd held since the last time he saw Mother alive.

And he knew the lady in the mist could prove dangerous to him if she talked.

He leaned against the closed door of his room, the only place in the chamber where he could stand up straight, and scowled at the dormer window so fiercely the glass should have cracked. He had only himself to blame if she discovered his identity and told Kendall. Midwives and mayors didn't travel in the same circles in England, but who knew what social starts the Yankees practiced. Kendall certainly thought nothing of inviting Dominick to sit and talk with him on those evenings when he didn't have guests. It was a practice that discomfited Dominick while at the same time pleased him. The rest of the indoor servants were female and not the sort of companionship he needed or wanted.

But Madam Midwife . . .

Dominick began to slip the buttons on his coat out of their holes one by one. He should hurry if he didn't want to trust Dinah or Deborah, the maids, with powdering his hair in time for him to serve Kendall his breakfast, but he couldn't move faster with the lady on the beach occupying his thoughts. Part of his brainbox suggested he ignore her from now on and hope good sense would prompt her to say nothing of their encounter. He should have kissed her. That would have ensured her silence to avoid a scandal. But he hadn't been that much of a rascal, alas. Still, it would have been far nicer than any threat.

A threat was likely the wrong course to take with the mermaid midwife. Foolish to have considered it for a moment. Any pudding head should recognize a threat would send her in the opposite direction.

If he weren't a sap skull, he wouldn't be tugging on indecently tight knee breeches in deep blue and silver braid, and a matching coat. The silk stockings and leather pumps didn't allow for him to carry his knife strapped to his calf, so he tucked it down the neck of his shirt. Although he felt as though he needed the sort of insurance Lloyd's of London could provide, the knife was the best he could manage in his current position.

His tread stiff now, he descended the steps at the pace of a man three times his five and twenty years, and entered the kitchen. The other two house servants sat at the table cutting their spoons into those spongy eggs, and eating pallid toast with cups of black coffee. Still chewing or sipping, they faced him, their identical blue eyes sweeping him from head to toe as though he were the next course.

"I'll go make your toast the way you like it, Mr. Cherrett," Dinah cooed.

"I'll put your egg in the water to boil." Deborah leaped to her feet. "Three minutes exact, right?"

"Yes, thank you, but first—" He glanced toward Letty. "My hair?"

"I'll do it," the twins cried.

"A pity you have to powder it," Deborah added. "It's so thick and shiny and—"

"Return to your breakfast," Letty commanded. "You're making the boy blush. Dinah, that bread's too thick. Come into the yard, Dominick." She gathered up the pomade pot and powder box.

Feeling like an actor about to step onto stage, he submitted to Letty's ministrations. She possessed as deft a hand with his hair as she demonstrated with a pastry.

"Does the man think imitating an English nobleman will get him out of Seabourne and into Richmond?" Dominick asked.

"Not anything so unimportant as Richmond." Letty laughed. "He wants to get to Washington. He thinks Senator Kendall sounds fine."

"To vote against my countrymen?"

"Yes. His nephew got shipped aboard an English vessel last year. Cover your face." Dominick drew over his face the edge of the holland furniture covering he used to protect his clothing when Letty dusted his hair with powder like a cake being frosted with sugar. "So the English Navy doesn't care if they're rich men's sons or not, eh?"

"Seems that way, unless the young men around here are just taking themselves off after—what is it, Dinah?"

Dominick peeked over the edge of the cloth. Dinah stood in the doorway, her cap askew, revealing guinea-gold curls, her eyes streaming. Behind her, smoke billowed toward the door. The reek of burned toast spilled into the garden.

"Not that crispy," Dominick muttered.

"It fell into the fire," Dinah cried. "All four pieces."

Letty sighed. "No more cooking, girl. Open the window and don't open the door to the rest of the house."

Dinah vanished into the smoke like the mermaid midwife had slipped into the mist.

These thoughts of the woman had to stop. Dominick fixed his gaze on a fat, red-breasted bird the Americans called a robin but was surely a thrush. It perched on the branch of an oak, whistling tunelessly and preening. It was a cheerful sound, but not nearly as happy as that of the red cardinal. Dominick had spent so much time in London to avoid his father in the country, he hadn't noticed much about birds. He liked them. A man could distract himself from females by watching birds, as long as the creatures didn't go about courting and flirting. Now that spring had arrived, courting and flirting permeated the avian population.

Dominick shifted his shoulders. "Is it possible to run out of powder or have it get damp? Perhaps you could give that instead of bread flour to Dinah."

"Old Mrs. Kendall ordered it by the ton, I think." Letty chuckled. "If we run out of the white, we have the pink and blue."

"If you dare . . ." Dominick twisted his head around to see the end of the queue.

It was white, powdered thickly enough that not a strand of the original dark brown showed through. Revolting.

"Can I bear four years of this?"

"You'll have to, lad." Letty whipped off the holland cover. "Unless those fine relations of yours can find the wherewithal to buy your indenture."

They could. His brothers' quarterly allowance alone provided them with more than enough. The question was, would they? The answer to that was simple—no. To have him out of the way for four years would have them all returning to church to count their blessings.

His uncle, on the other hand, had promised to free him if the mission succeeded. Prancing about a rich man's house like a Bond Street beau, instead of what he'd imagined—working hard outdoors, spending time along the shore, associating with the sort of young men disappearing from the coastal villages—made success appear unlikely.

"I think you'll have to suffer with me for four years, Letty." He rose. "Thank you for playing coiffeuse. Do I get my breakfast—" A bell rang inside the house. "No, no breakfast for me. The master calls."

He strode into the kitchen and picked up the tray of coffeepot and cream pitcher that one of the twins had prepared. The stench of burned toast stung his nostrils, and he didn't mind missing breakfast quite so much. It wouldn't be the first morning meal he hadn't partaken of in his life. Since leaving for Oxford at seventeen, he'd more often than not been sound asleep when food was available. Never in those lazy days of indolence did he imagine he'd be up before the birds to serve someone else.

"Justice," he reminded himself, and shoved open the door between the kitchen and dining room.

Thomas Kendall sat at the head of a table for twelve, a newspaper spread out and a Bible open before him. Sunlight shimmered off his hair, turning the thick locks to pure silver, which emphasized the bronze of his complexion. At Dominick's entrance, Kendall turned a pair of pale blue eyes in his butler's direction. "Good morning, Cherrett, you're looking fatigued. Didn't sleep well?"

What about not at all?

"No, sir, I'm still getting used to things here."

"It's a different life from the one you're used to, I'm sure." Kendall moved the newspaper aside so Dominick could serve the coffee. "But you've taken to it well. It's a good thing. In another two weeks, we'll be entertaining some important guests and I'll hire extra servants to help. You'll be responsible for them."

Father would have an apoplexy laughing if he saw his younger son responsible for anything.

"Will you be up to that, Cherrett?"

"Yes, sir. I'll fetch your breakfast now."

He retreated to the kitchen for the plate of bacon, eggs, and sconelike roll the Americans called a biscuit, though it wasn't sweet. Once the meal lay before Kendall, Dominick withdrew to a place by the door to wait for orders to retrieve more coffee, butter, a handkerchief. Some mornings he never stood still. This morning he stood like a part of the wainscoting while Kendall munched and read, grumbled over the newspaper, and smiled over the Scriptures.

Dominick began to nod. His eyelids drooped. Visions of mermaids danced between shafts of sunlight and his eyelashes. Mermaids with pretty hands and caustic—

The front door knocker sounded.

Dominick's head shot up and smacked the wall. "Ah!" He rubbed the back of his head.

The knocker pounded again, going right through his skull.

Kendall's glance bored through his eye sockets. "Go get that, Cherrett, if you're able."

"Yes, sir." Dominick tripped over his toes as he exited the dining room by its second door, the one leading into the entry hall.

He reached the front door as the knocker banged for a third time. He wondered if the brass pineapple was difficult to break. Or perhaps he should apply it to the head of the early morning caller.

He hadn't taken the time to speculate as to what sort of person would call at that hour, but if he had, he knew from his experience of the past two weeks that it wouldn't have been the female who stood on the porch. Old ladies called on the mayor in groups. Elderly gentlemen called on him singly and in pairs. Businessmen of all ages arrived to petition him for favors, and widows brought gifts as excuses to gain entrée into his presence so perhaps they could attract him into making one of them the next Mrs. Kendall. Not once had a young female arrived on the doorstep—until now.

Dominick had read about heart-shaped faces in sentimental literature but never before believed any female possessed such a visage. The evidence stood before him wearing a plain dress and pelisse the same blue-gray as her eyes, and an unadorned straw hat perched atop auburn tresses. No fashionable curls obscured the breadth of her cheekbones. The severity of her hairstyle emphasized the wide brow bisected by a widow's peak that looked like a nice place to plant a kiss.

He cleared his throat as though that would clear his head. "May I help you?"

"Yes, please. I need to speak with—you." One hand flew to her lips. Her eyes widened.

Dominick thanked God for something for the first time in many years—that he hadn't eaten breakfast. The flip his stomach gave at the sound of her accusing tone on the "you" would not have improved upon toast and a soft-boiled egg.

He gripped the door frame with one hand and the handle with the other. "Yes, the last time I looked in a mirror, I was me. Is there a difficulty with that, madam?"

"Only if Mayor Kendall approves of his manservant prowling about the beach in the middle of the night. His English manservant."

She pronounced his nationality as though it was a felony offense. Then again, to her, it probably was.

The skin along his back crawled, feeling the bite of the lash. "Not prowling. Merely a lark." He gazed down at her through his lashes. "Mermaid hunting."

A hint of pink tingeing her pale skin assured him she was not immune to his wiles.

He smiled. "Surely you won't tattle on a lad who needed some sea air."

She set one hand on a hip. "Considering I'm here to inform him of Englishmen wandering about at night, yes, I will."

"Please don't." Abandoning flirtation, he stepped onto the porch and closed the door behind him. "It could cause unnecessary trouble."

"And I think it already has caused unnecessary trouble for me." She tilted back her head and raised one hand to where a thin red scratch ran above the collar of her pelisse, marring the creamy perfection of her throat. "Tell me, Mr. Englishman, do you own a knife?"

3

Tabitha had never seen a man with such beautiful eyes. The rich, deep brown of coffee, they sparkled with pinpoints of gold light behind a fringe of lashes that would have made them feminine if not for his strong cheekbones and firm jaw. The powdered hair, ridiculous as it was in Seabourne, created a striking contrast to the dark eyes and sun-bronzed complexion.

As she looked into those extraordinary eyes, she found herself going soft like butter left too close to a fire. Soft in the head anyway, for asking him if he had a knife. Even if he had a motive for holding her at knifepoint and commanding her to say nothing of the night's activities, before pushing her forward hard enough to make her fall to her knees—as the man had in her garden—he wasn't about to admit he had a knife.

"Never you mind me asking that." She gave him the gentle smile she bestowed on frightened young mothers. "I don't want you to feel you need to commit the sin of lying to avoid trouble."

He laughed. "Oh, my dear Madam Mermaid, my sins are so numerous, lying is the least of them. But thank you for the reprieve, as I wouldn't wish to give you cause to accuse me of doing this." He traced his forefinger along the scratch.

Tabitha's knees turned to oatmeal porridge. Nonetheless, she made herself meet his gaze. "You recognize it for what it is, the work of a knife, and you have reason to want me to keep my mouth shut."

"I expect a number of persons have cause to wish you to keep your mouth shut." He smiled, with his lips, with his eyes. "You know the secrets of this town, don't you, Madam Midwife?"

"I am often a confidante," she answered with care. "But I've never been threatened before."

"Before you ran into me." He propped his shoulders against the polished oak of the front door and crossed his arms over his broad chest, as though preparing for a long chat. "Then I am in a pickle."

"You'll be in more of one if you keep denying me access to the mayor."

"All too true." He didn't move. He said nothing else. In the village square beyond the fence surrounding the front garden, wheels rumbled on the bricks of the street and two men exchanged greetings. Inside the gates, birds set up a choral symphony in ode to the bright warmth of the morning.

Tabitha's and the Englishman's gazes clashed. Tabitha set her hands on her hips and compressed her lips. It was the look and stance she applied to husbands who thought she was too young to know what she was doing. Most of them backed down, crept meekly away to pace the floor, or left to cause trouble for someone other than her.

The Englishman laughed. "You're rather beautiful like that."

"Flattery will get you nowhere with me."

"I'm rather impervious to that glare of yours too. But I do concede I can't keep you standing on the front steps all day." He straightened and half turned to the door. "I'll show you in. He should be finished with breakfast by now. You may tell him what you like, but I doubt he'll thank you for informing him that his perfect English butler has been a naughty lad. He'll have to punish me for form, if nothing else. Then I wouldn't be able to wear my livery, and he has important guests coming in a fortnight."

Speech delivered, he opened the door and stood back with a gesture for her to precede him.

She glided over the threshold and he closed the door behind her. After the sunshine, the entryway seemed as dim, chilly, and quiet as the spring nights—or a tomb. The soles of the Englishman's shoes resounded like bass drum beats on the marquetry floor as he strode toward a door at the far end of the hallway.

Tabitha shivered. When she left home and set out for the sheriff's to report the assault on her person, doing so seemed like a sound idea. No one should dare threaten the midwife. Gathering information came with her work, and if men threatened her for coming across something they didn't want her to know, she couldn't serve the community. And the community needed her. She was the only person with medical knowledge of any kind within twenty miles.

But after meeting Mayor Kendall's new manservant face-to-face, she couldn't outright accuse him in the event he was innocent, as he claimed. The townspeople said Kendall was proud of having a proper butler. Tabitha had thought nothing of the talk when she met him that morning. Indentured servants tended to come from the lower ranks of society. They spoke with bad grammar and nearly incomprehensible accents. They did not affect a manner of speaking she'd heard only from educated persons. The men she'd met who talked like that tended to come from England—scholars traveling to observe the peculiar Americans or military officers. If this man was an indentured servant and an aristocrat or gentleman, he'd fallen on terrible times and didn't need worse to befall him.

Ahead of her, the man paused and glanced over his shoulder. "Please, Miss—" His color heightened. "I forgot to ask your name."

"Tabitha Eckles."

"Ah, then, Miss Tabitha Eckles, please say nothing."

"I'll take it under consideration."

With a sigh, he turned his back on her and knocked. "Miss Tabitha Eckles, sir."

"Well, send the girl in. Bring her some coffee." Mayor Kendall's voice boomed into the entryway.

Tabitha started forward. Her feet dragged, her shoes leaden. And at the end of the hall, the Englishman held the door open for her, holding her gaze with his beautiful eyes. If she could have done so without making a fool of herself, she would have turned back and not spoken with the mayor then and there. But she was committed now, so she entered the dining room and slid onto the chair the Englishman pulled out for her. She started to speak.

Mayor Kendall waved her to silence. "Fetch a fresh cup and pot of coffee."

"Yes, sir." The butler trotted from the room. A door opened, sending the aromas of bacon, bread, burned toast, and coffee wafting into the dining room. Then the door closed.

"This is a pleasant surprise, Tabitha." The mayor smiled at her. "How may I help you?"

"It's not for me." She took a deep breath while the Englishman was gone and she could breathe properly. "Well, I suppose it is. I went to the sheriff first, but he was gone already."

"That concerns me." Kendall pushed his plate and newspaper aside and gripped the edge of the table. "I hope nothing too awful has occurred to take him out so early."

"Maybe he's fishing?" Tabitha smiled. "He does like his boat."

Kendall chuckled. "Yes, indeed. He missed his calling, staying on land. But what was so urgent it took you to the sheriff this early, then back here to me?"

To give herself more time to decide on her course, she began, "You may wish to know, before I mention the other matter, that Mrs. Wilkins went to the Lord early this morning. She fell down the steps, and I was called—" Her throat closed and a tear formed in the corner of one eye. "Forgive me." She drew a handkerchief from her reticule and dabbed at her face.

"Of course, my dear." Kendall went white around the lips. "You're too young to have to manage this sort of thing on your own. I don't approve of an unmarried midwife, you know, but you're all we have, and I know you did your best."

"I hope so." Tabitha swallowed. "Sir, I wouldn't think anything of this if too many of our young men weren't disappearing from the coastal villages." Once started, she couldn't stop, not even when she heard the kitchen door creak open. "There were strangers about last night. English strangers."

China rattled behind her.

In front of her, the mayor's eyes widened. "Where?"

"The tide was out, so I walked along the beach when I . . . er . . . ran into them."

"How many?" The words emerged like two hammer blows.

"I—I don't know."

She sensed the stillness of the Englishman behind her. Her hand went to the scratch on her throat.

"It was dark," she plunged on, "and I was understandably distracted."

"Of course." The mayor frowned. "And it was misty."

"Yes. And, sir—"

Valley Community Library
739 River Street
Peckville, PA 18452-2313

Kendall raised one hand. "Why are you just standing there, Cherrett? Come serve Miss Eckles some coffee."

"Yes, sir. I beg your pardon, sir." He sounded subdued as he approached Tabitha and set the tray on the table. "Cream, Madam M—Miss Eckles?"

"No, thank you." She didn't look at him as she continued to address the mayor. "Whoever it was let me go on my way, but when I reached my garden"—a shudder ran through her—"someone threatened me at knifepoint."

"Threatened you?" Kendall half rose from his chair. "What are you saying?"

Tabitha accepted the cup the Englishman—Mr. Cherrett—shoved in front of her and wrapped her hands around the smooth china. Despite the warmth of the day, her hands felt like ice.

"He held a knife to my throat and told me to keep my mouth shut about the night," she blurted out on a single breath.

"It was this same Englishman?" Kendall nearly shouted.

The silver serving tray struck the floor with a resonant clang. Tabitha jumped, slopping hot coffee over her fingers. She gasped.

Mr. Cherrett groaned. "I am so sorry, miss. I'll fetch you a cold wet cloth." The kitchen door creaked.

Tabitha stared at her reddened fingers. She'd questioned the man's guilt when looking into his eyes. But now, with Cherrett's noisy reaction to the mayor's raised voice, she wondered if she'd allowed herself to succumb to a pretty face and charming manner while the threat had indeed come from the Englishman.

Raleigh Trower feasted his eyes on the whitewashed cottage before him. From the neat hedge of flowers keeping the beach away from the front garden to the green door and window frames, from the smoke curling out of the chimney into the clear blue sky to the scent of baking bread, from the roar of the ocean across the dunes to the sundry birds chorusing in the trees, nothing about the Eckles home had changed in the two and a half years since he'd last laid eyes on it or its youngest lady inhabitant.

"Tabitha." Her name burned on his lips. Her face swam before his eyes.

Swaying, he grasped the top rail of the gate. He probably should have stayed home long enough for a good night's sleep. But the promise of seeing Tabitha again kept him going through the hardships of the past nine and twenty months, kept him alive, when dying would have been easier. Now, on sufferance from a British captain, he was nearly free to return to his life, his fishing boat, his family, his Tabitha.

"If you'll be my Tabitha again."

One bit of news he'd gleaned, while Momma had stuffed him with food and his sisters fluttered around him like finches in a field of grain, was that Tabitha was still unmarried and the town's only midwife.

"The only thing we have for a healer," Momma had added. "Her mother died right after you disappeared, and now it's just her."

"Is she courting anyone?" Raleigh asked.

She should have been married. She would have been married if he hadn't betrayed her out of selfishness, out of fear.

"The men are all scared of her." Fanny, his younger sister, giggled. "I mean, she knows everything that happens around here. Last year, when Rachel Goodwin got herself into trouble, Tabitha made her tell her who the father was before she'd deliver the baby."

"That's the law." Felicity still affected the haughty tones

of a plantation mistress rather than the daughter of a mildly prosperous fisherman. "She's required to ask that when the woman is in—"

"Girls," Momma snapped, "this isn't proper conversation." She turned to Raleigh. "She knows too much about what the young men get up to, now that her mother isn't here to protect her from some of the . . . er . . . more unpleasant parts of her work, so they're afraid she's heard tales."

"They wouldn't need to fear her if they were acting as they should." Raleigh realized he sounded smug, hypocritical. His conscience might be clear where behavior toward females went, if he discounted jilting Tabitha. Yet he lived a lie that should keep him away from any decent female.

Now he opened the gate and strode up the flagstone path to the front steps, to the door, to the knocker in the shape of a dove. The golden metal bird gleamed in the morning sunshine, and its flesh-and-blood counterpart cooed from a pine tree at the corner of the yard, as though encouraging him to seek entrance.

He let the knocker fall once, twice, three times, then a fourth for good measure. He kept his hand on it, the other one on the door frame for support, and waited. He heard nothing from inside the house.

"Bobwhite. Bobwhite," a bird of that name chided from a cedar around the side of the house. "Bobwhite. Bobwhite."

Quick, light footfalls sounded on the other side of the door. Raleigh straightened, lips curved into a smile, heart racing.

The door opened. A woman twice Tabitha's age, a full head shorter and half again as wide, stood in the opening. She looked familiar, but he couldn't recall her name. "May I help you?" she asked.

"I'm—" He swallowed. "I'm here to see Tabitha. Miss Eckles, I mean."

She narrowed her eyes as though she too recognized him. "Is this an emergency?"

Oh, yes, he needed to know right away if Tabitha had forgiven him. Or at the least, if she could.

"Not an emergency." He had to be honest about some things after all. "I—I'm an old friend. Raleigh Trower."

"Are you?" The woman's round face tightened, her green eyes grew cold. "I can't be sure she'll be wanting to see you."

Raleigh looked down his nose at the woman. "That's for her to decide, isn't it?"

"It is, and she isn't here." The woman started to close the door. "You'll have to come back later."

"Please." Raleigh stuck his foot over the threshold and smiled. Suddenly the woman's name came to him and he added, "It's Patience, isn't it? Patience Neff?"

"Well, fancy that." Patience stuck her own nose in the air. "You couldn't recall you was engaged to Miss Tabitha, but you remember my name."

"Oh, I remembered." Raleigh closed his eyes, recalling every detail of Tabitha's lovely face. "I made a mistake."

"And now you come back to pick up where you left off?" Patience set work-reddened hands on her hips. "Well, young man, she's had her heart broke once too often and I don't want to see it happen again."

"I know about her family."

The mother and grandmother who had never been quite as welcoming of the engagement as he would have wished, for Tabitha's sake.

"That's why I thought she might be kind enough to see me," he continued. "She might like to know I'm not dead."

"And I can tell her, or she'll learn in the village." Patience sighed and pulled the door wide. "All right, come in and wait.

The parlor's clean and I was just making some coffee." She waved him forward.

He entered the tidy parlor, with its open windows allowing the sea air and sunshine inside, and a braided woolen rug on the floor. He wanted to pace while waiting for Tabitha. He wanted to stride in circles around the house, waiting for her to arrive across the beach or from town, as he had waited many times in the past. With Patience's bright eyes on him, he chose a chair facing the parlor door, perching on its edge so he could spring to his feet the instant the front door opened or she came down the hall from the back of the house.

He expected Patience to leave him alone to stew in private. A maidservant would have. But Patience was much more to the Eckles family and had been since the grandmother, Mrs. Nottingham, had bought the woman's indenture mere months before Raleigh left. Now that Tabitha was alone in the world, Raleigh expected Patience had taken on an even more protective role.

"Is she truly well?" he decided to ask.

"As well as a woman of four and twenty and still unwed can be." Patience pierced him with her eyes the green of the sea before a storm. "You're talking like an Englishman. Did you go back to your sainted mother's people?"

"Not by choice." He made himself focus on the old lady. "I was on a merchantman bound for China. A British frigate hauled me aboard and asked me a lot of questions."

Lantern light had hung in his face so he couldn't see the officers except for the occasional glint of a blade. They'd struck his head when hauling him out of his boat and onto their deck. He'd been dizzy, cloudy of brain, sick in body.

"I made the mistake of telling them my mother is from Halifax. That made me English enough in their eyes to justify tossing me into the stinking coffin they call a man-of-war, and made me—" His fists clenched on his thighs. "I've tried everything to get away, to get back to Tabitha."

"Before or after you were pressed?"

Raleigh swallowed and dug his knuckles into his thigh muscles. He couldn't meet Patience's eyes. "After."

"And now you've managed to—what?—desert, and you want to renew your relationship with Tabitha?"

"You're rather forward for a redemptioner," Raleigh retorted.

"I'm free now and I'm all she has—me and Japheth, the outdoor man. Someone has to see to her welfare."

All she had were two servants who would be free to leave her in a matter of years.

Raleigh hung his head. "I want . . . her forgiveness. I've prayed for two years to see her again."

"Praying's more than she does these days." Sorrow filled the woman's voice. "When your wedding day passed without a sign of you, then her mother died of a fever she contracted from a patient, my mistress stopped praying."

Sickness roiled inside Raleigh's belly. He should have been there to be a husband to her, a helpmeet, someone to support her—even guide her—in her spiritual life, not contribute to her turning from the Lord.

"Maybe if she can forgive me—" He broke off on a sigh to loosen the tightness in his chest. He didn't deserve her forgiveness, but oh, how he wanted it. If Tabitha would give him her heartfelt mercy for what he'd done to her, the risks he took would be worth it. If they could start again, renew their friendship, their love . . .

"I don't know if you'll get forgiveness, Mr. Trower," Patience said. "The hurt runs deep inside her."

"Maybe if she knows—"

Footfalls sounded on the walk, swift and light. Raleigh

shot to his feet, then stood motionless, not knowing whether he should wait for Tabitha to enter the house or if he should rush out to greet her. His heart raced, and he feared if he didn't move, it would burst right from his chest.

He took a step toward the door, stopped, glanced at Patience. "Should I wait here or—"

The front door burst open. Warm air smelling of the sea swirled through the room. Carried on the breeze like a schooner under full sail, Tabitha swept into the parlor. "Patience, it's so terrible. Three young men disappeared last night. They left the tavern in—" She ceased on a gasp. Her hand flew to her throat, and color drained from her face. "Raleigh!"

4

A long scratch marred the pristine surface of the silver tray where Dominick had dropped it onto the floor. He intended the incident to distract Miss Tabitha Eckles, the mermaid midwife. Instead, it drew too much attention to himself, not to mention the hour he was spending in the stuffy confines of the butler's pantry, rubbing out the scratch with emery grit that stuck to his fingers, his sleeves, his nose.

"I should have gone to Barbados," he grumbled to his reflection in the glittering surface of the tray.

At least in the Caribbean all he would have to worry about pertained to simple matters like yellow fever and field worker uprisings. Unlike the eastern shore of Virginia, where disaster could land on his head at any moment—literally.

"At least a bash to the skull would knock off the powder."

He grimaced at the quantity of white froth adding its detritus to the emery grit. The pallid color aged him, making his skin appear sallow rather than lightly bronzed from the sun. Not attractive, whatever Letty told him and however the other female servants flirted with him. He didn't need their approval.

He needed Tabitha Eckles's approbation.

"I'll get that when Barbados gets snow." He shook his head, sending a shower of powder onto the nearly polished silver.

His yell of frustration brought Letty stomping into the doorway. "What are you grousing about, laddie? You were the one to drop that tray. You have to be the one to polish it up again."

"And I'm the one ordered to wear this . . . flotsam on my head." He yanked at a curl tumbling from his queue. "It's utterly ridiculous."

"It's charming." Letty tucked the errant strand beneath the ribbon.

"It gets over everything."

"It wouldn't if you didn't stamp around here like an angry bull." Letty softened her admonishing tone. "Dominick, you're likely going to be here for at least four years. You may as well resign yourself to the fact and do your work with good cheer."

"Sensible advice."

"That you don't intend to take."

"I understand the gentlemen who settled this colony—"

"State."

"It was a colony then and will be again, if my country has its way." He flashed Letty a grin. "But as I was saying, the gentlemen who settled in this blighted place two hundred years ago were just that—gentlemen. They didn't intend to work. They intended to get rich off of the land."

"And most of them ended up dying of starvation." Letty removed the tray from Dominick's hands. "You're going to rub right through the silver if you go about polishing thatta way. Be gentle."

She demonstrated a light, circular motion with the cloth against the tray. The rasp of grit against metal sounded like harsh breathing in the tiny pantry, the grating breaths of a runner, someone fleeing.

No, someone chasing. He was there to chase, to catch, to stop a villainous character, not run away.

And perhaps chase someone else to keep himself safe.

"There now." Letty returned the tray to the table with a clunk.

Dominick jumped. "I should have asked you to help from the beginning."

"It's not my job. It's yours, and you're perfectly capable of carrying on if you don't woolgather."

"How can I do anything else when I look like a . . . er . . . woolly lamb?" Dominick picked up a clean cloth and removed the last of the grit from the tray. "I shouldn't have dropped it. Why don't you simply remind me of that?"

"I can't think how you came to do that." Letty cocked her head, waiting to hear.

"Miss Eckles distracted me." Dominick shrugged. "She was talking about strangers around on the beach. I seem to be the only Englishman in town, and in light of some more of your young men disappearing last night, I don't wish to be accused of having aught to do with it by virtue of my nationality."

"There is another English person in Seabourne," Letty said. "She's Tabitha Eckles's servant."

"And highly likely to be running about at night stealing men from their tavern haunts."

"Their fishing boats." Letty's tone held a hint of ice. "And you were running about last night."

"Not on the water." Dominick shuddered hard enough to make the tray rattle as he slid it onto its shelf. "I never went past the beach."

"That narrows your wanderings down to twenty miles or more."

"Letty, are you accusing me of something?" He gave her a wide-eyed stare.

She laughed and backed from the pantry. "I'll wager you got away with everything using those eyes like that."

ith my nursemaid and mother." Dominick gri- ouldn't be here if I could charm my own sex into umbing to my charms."

"And here I thought it was charming the fair maidens that was amongst the things that got you here." Still chuckling, Letty returned to the kitchen and her pots of savory dishes bubbling over the fire.

"If only it had been fair maidens," Dominick murmured.

He returned the canister of emery grit to its shelf, applied a boar's hair brush to his coat, and followed Letty into the kitchen. Dinah and Deborah sat at the worktable peeling potatoes. He hoped the young women's presence would prevent Letty asking him questions or making further innuendos about either his activities of the night before or the circumstances that sent him bucketing across the Atlantic. Tabitha Eckles had put him through enough of that agony already this morning.

Did he have a knife indeed. What a thing for a lady to ask a gentleman.

Except she wasn't precisely a lady. Nor was he a gentleman any longer.

Social standing aside—this was America after all, where those sorts of things weren't supposed to matter—nothing changed the fact that she had asked. Her asking signaled one fact—she believed he was responsible for cutting that long, slender throat of hers.

Nodding to the kitchen maids, he strode through the back door and headed across the garden to the laundry. His fingers twitched with the desire to stroke away any pain that cut might cause her. Marring her skin was a crime worse than the act of threatening her at knifepoint. He didn't understand the drive that compelled some men to violence or greed. His previous sins stemmed from nothing as ambitious as the wish to conquer or gain great wealth. And now his contrary ambitions threatened to make a manipulative, unconscionable monster of him.

He retrieved a stack of table linens from the worktable, where the laundry maid had left them for him to collect. Before stacking them in the sideboard, he must inspect each piece for wear or tear, fray or stain. Kendall expected his tablecloths and serviettes to be as pristine as his shirts and cravats, as white as his butler's hair. Dominick had never known his parents' stiff-necked butler to stoop to such menial tasks—he probably gave the chore to his army of footmen. Dominick didn't possess such a luxury.

Of course, Dinah and Deborah might oblige. They greeted him with enthusiasm when he returned to the house.

"I'll get the door for you, sir." Dinah bounced to her feet, allowing a shower of peelings to cascade onto the floor.

"I'll pull out the drawers for you." Deborah followed with a little more decorum.

"You will return to your chairs and finish scraping the vegetables," Letty commanded. "Mr. Cherrett, you will see to the linens yourself."

Did the woman read his mind?

"But I was so hoping for some company in my lonely task."

"It must be lonely, being the only manservant in the house," Dinah said. "Surely I can help, Letty. It'll take only a few minutes."

"It'll take less time if you both help," Dominick suggested.

"No, you will do your own work," Letty admonished. "Alone."

"And here I thought the butler directed the servants." Dominick sighed gustily enough to flutter the serviette on the top of the stack.

The scent of starch wafted into his face stronger than the stewing game, and he screwed up his features in an effort not to sneeze.

"I've been here longer." Letty wiped her hands on her apron and took two cloths off the top of the stack. "I'll need these to wrap the bread rolls for dinner. Mr. Kendall is entertaining, if entertaining a newly widowed man is the right term."

"Newly widowed?" Dominick arched one brow in query. "Mr. Wilkins, is it?"

"Aye, so you know of that."

"I heard through the dining room door when Miss Eckles told Kendall of the loss."

"The poor man," Dinah cooed. "All that lovely money of his, and he's without a wife to enjoy it."

"Or heir to inherit it," Deborah added.

"He won't be looking to either of you for solace," Letty snapped. "Get your minds off of men and onto your work. You're both too young for Harlan Wilkins."

"He's no more than thirty," Dinah pointed out. "That's young to be a widower."

"Isn't the midwife a bit too young to be a widow?" Dominick asked.

"She's not a widow," all the women chorused.

"The women in her family have been midwives for generations," Letty explained. "She used to simply work with her mother and grandmother, but when they died, Miss Tabitha took on the work alone. She's the closest medical person we have since the apothecary died last year."

"Then the death of a patient must be even harder on her." Dominick gazed through half-lowered lids at the bundles of herbs hanging from the ceiling. "I wonder if she needs comfort."

"She's so old," Dinah and Deborah protested.

"All of four and twenty." Letty banged a lid onto a pot. "And you steer clear of her. She's had enough grief in her life, and Harlan Wilkins may make more for her."

"Will he blame her for his wife's death?" Dominick asked.

"Most likely. He'd never think it has to do with his neglect of that poor young lady he married."

"You have a poor opinion of the man," Dominick mused.

"No less than I have of any gaming male." She gave Dominick a pointed glance, then yanked open the door of the oven set into the hearth. "I expect you gambled your way into servitude."

"I didn't gamble away my future," Dominick shot back, then, for a chance at honesty in an existence that owed little to truth, he added, "not like you think."

Gaming establishments hadn't been his downfall. No, he'd taken a different sort of gamble and won at a price he still didn't know if he could pay.

"You don't fool me." Letty stalked to the table and began to inspect the vegetables the girls had peeled. "Nothing else brings a gentleman down like the cards or the dice or females."

"Not me." Dominick shot her a smile and headed for the dining room. "Though you're mighty presumptive that I'm a gentleman."

The dining room door swung shut behind him before she could respond, which was good. The cook was, after all, right in that. He was a gentleman, destined from birth to become a clergyman. Third sons of Cherretts always became clergymen. If no third son existed, then the honor and living went to a male cousin. Second sons became Army officers.

Cherretts did not become redemptioners in lands barely developed out of the wilderness.

He set the linens on the table and began to inspect each piece. If he'd been an obedient son, if he'd been interested in being a politician vicar instead of a man serving God, Dominick would be sorting altar cloths for imperfections instead of serviettes. But from the moment he'd set foot in Oxford, he'd determined to destroy any of his father's hopes that the third son of this generation would step into the role of vicar.

He'd considered himself a success until his downward trajectory flew out of control and he found himself facing a scandal that hurt his family. He chose exile to spare them. More than exile—a chance at redemption.

As he spread a cloth over the table and arranged serviettes and silver for two diners, he wondered if he could bear four years of servitude and no hope of redeeming himself, rather than take the next step in his plans. Acting as a butler-cum-valet was proving onerous. Less onerous than all the things his uncle said he might have to do to accomplish his mission. But he'd agreed. He'd practiced with his knife, the only weapon he could get away with as an indentured servant. If his life depended on it, he could use the slender, Italian blade.

But he couldn't use it on a female.

No, now that he knew more about the lady, Dominick Cherrett made other plans to ensure Tabitha Eckles, the mermaid midwife, didn't speak out of turn where his activities were concerned.

Tabitha crouched beside a bed of roses, breathing deeply of the heady scent. Weeds grew in too much profusion around her precious herbs, and she should be pulling them up to protect the stock that produced necessary medicines for her work and other ailments for which people came to her for help. But the roses held her attention with their deep red hues and fragrance like the oh-so-precious vanilla bean. Only the most perfect, most succulent petals would she pluck to create her favorite treat, the indulgence she allowed herself other than walks on the beach—candied rose petals. The previous month, she had plucked and preserved the violets. Already, she tasted the aromatic sweets on her tongue, the best medicine in the world for perking up the spirits.

Except her spirits shouldn't need perking up. God, apparently, had listened to her after all. Raleigh had come home. He was too late for their wedding, too late to comfort her through the deaths of her mother and grandmother. Yet not an hour earlier, he had stood in her parlor, as large as life.

Larger than life. Years of hard labor aboard a British naval vessel had developed his physique. He stood no more than average height, but his arms and shoulders bulged beneath the confines of his coat as though the muscles strained for freedom. His skin glowed a healthy bronze, while gold streaks lightened his oak-colored hair. With his bright blue eyes, the entire effect pleased Tabitha's eye.

Her heart remained still, cautious, dried at the edges like a rose petal left too long in the vase.

"I've come home," he'd announced with his grin that created a dimple in one cheek.

"To take up where you belonged?" She knew her tone held no warmth of welcome and didn't know how to change it. "Were you not happy with a life of freedom, wandering the world?"

His smile wavered. "I wasn't happy with being alone on my travels. I thought of you every day. And aboard the man-of-war was worse. I wished I'd stayed behind. I plotted every day to get here, to you."

"I expect so." The ice broke through, cutting with every word and the sharpness of her tone. She needed it to keep herself from laying her head on his broad shoulder, asking him to hold her.

Of all days for him to return, this one was the worst. She needed companionship, a distraction. Yet if she succumbed to the relief of seeing her fiancé again, she would regret it in moments.

He didn't deserve a friendly welcome back into her life.

"Life aboard a British naval vessel is unpleasant at best," she said, pressing home her point. "Of course you'd regret leaving me then. Maybe you should have stuck by your commitments to avoid getting caught by the British."

"Once they learned my mother was from Canada, they wouldn't let me go. They said I was English."

"But you changed their minds and finally were able to come back?" The weakness to seek his comfort fled. Tabitha straightened her shoulders and made herself meet and hold his piercing blue eyes. "You think you can dance back into my life after deserting me practically on the eve of our wedding and expect nothing to have changed?"

"No, but I can hope for forgiveness and go on from there."

She read the hope in his face, in the way he leaned toward her with his hands clenched at his sides.

"Will you forgive me for leaving?"

"I . . . don't know."

It was the only thing she possessed to offer him—the truth. She didn't know, not this soon, not this easily. "You have had weeks, maybe months, to think about your return. This is a shock to me. Maybe you should leave now and give me some time to accustom myself to the new circumstances."

"All right, but I'll not give up on you." Raleigh departed with a last, longing glance back.

She fled into the garden, with the sunshine, the scent of roses, mint, chamomile . . .

And the lingering memory of another, elusive scent that had warned her of someone's presence in her garden.

She touched a forefinger to her throat, where her fichu hid the scratch. She knew two men who had reason to threaten her into silence regarding knowledge of the night. If Wilkins had something to do with his wife's injuries, he might fear what she had said in her delirium. But surely he understood Tabitha couldn't divulge what she heard during a lying-in, except for the identity of the father in the event of illegitimacy.

As for the Englishman . . . At the least, a bondservant shouldn't have been out and about after curfew. The greatest of his crimes could be that he, an Englishman, had been directly involved with the three men's disappearance the same night.

Yet the Englishman had been miles from the abduction scene when Tabitha met him, possibly too far away to have gotten there without a fast horse. Tabitha had noticed no horse on the beach.

She had noticed only the man, noticed so much she recognized him in an instant when she came face-to-face with him at Mayor Kendall's house. She knew enough to have told Kendall that his manservant, the only stranger in the village, had been prowling the beach at dawn.

And she would have seen that manservant whipped.

She shuddered. Even if he had threatened her, she couldn't be the one who reported him. If he continued his nocturnal wanderings, he would bring punishment on himself. Yet if he were the culprit who had taken the young men away, he would strike again. More families would live without sons and brothers and husbands to support them. More young women would live without prospective husbands because the population of males had dropped below that of females.

And perhaps she should make certain of his guilt before she spread damaging tales about him. It wouldn't be the first time she'd kept her mouth shut about words she'd overheard or been told directly while tending a patient, or even traveling home. She could do so for the Englishman—for a while—rather than see him hurt. Like a doctor, she was compelled to do no harm to a living creature.

Surely that reasoning—not a pair of long-lashed brown eyes that sparkled with gold lights in the sun—stopped her from confiding in the mayor. She would never be that foolish.

She would never be foolish over a man again, as much as she yearned for a family of her own. Once upon a time, she'd fallen for a man with beautiful eyes. Blue eyes. Deep blue eyes she thought she could drown in.

They seemed bluer now in his bronzed face. Yet any depth they held didn't hold a reflection of her soul, of her heart. He claimed he'd come back to her, but she wouldn't believe him any more than she'd believe the Englishman had been on the beach for nothing more than an early morning stroll.

The Englishman. So attractive. So flirtatious. So nervous in her presence, stealing her attention from the man she should forgive and let herself love again.

Raleigh should consume her thoughts. Or perhaps Mrs. Wilkins and whatever had gone wrong with the lying-in, or the condemnatory rumors Mr. Wilkins might spread about her. Not an Englishman, who looked at her as though—

"Ah!" She jerked her hand away from the roses. Blood speckled her palm where she'd gripped the stem of a bush hard enough to drive the thorns into her skin.

"Stupid, stupid." She wrapped her hand in her handkerchief and scrambled to her feet. She needed to get a comfrey poultice on the punctures immediately. She couldn't afford to injure one of her hands. Her hands were her livelihood.

"Patience," she called to the maid in the kitchen, "get some water boiling."

"Oh, Miss Tabbie, you've never gone and hurt yourself." Patience poked her head around the frame of the open door. "What if someone's about to deliver and you can't use your hand?"

"No one's about to deliver." Tabitha slipped into the kitchen and plucked a bunch of comfrey leaves from a jar.

"That's what you was thinkin' last night." Patience swung the water kettle over the hearth and built up the fire. "You thought you'd have a peaceful night of it, and look what happened."

"It's not likely to happen again," Tabitha said, spooning leaves into a teapot and bracing herself for the rotting garbage odor of the healing herbs.

At least she hoped it wouldn't. She wished to avoid nights where patients died and strangers wandered her beach.

A shudder ran through her, the chill of a cool breeze on a hot, sunny day. Her hand shook, and she spilled the leaves across the table and onto the floor. First the thorn punctures, now a mess to clean up. If she wasn't careful, the man would have her walking into the ocean instead of along the tide line.

If she saw him again, which was unlikely. As small a village as Seabourne was, she rarely dealt with the mayor and consequently not his servants. She and Letty met while marketing. They exchanged friendly greetings, but Tabitha wasn't a servant, even with her position as a hireling. She was a professional for all she was a woman, and Letty, with her Old World ways, disapproved of hobnobbing between classes.

And Mrs. Kendall, were there to be a Mrs. Kendall, would never have passed the time of day with Tabitha unless she needed her medical care. Tabitha often felt caught in the middle, neither fish nor fowl, but far too much alone. If she had a husband, women would know where to place her, how to fit her into their gatherings and entertainments.

After cleaning up the spill, she snatched up a cup and dipped water from the simmering kettle to pour in the pot on the table. The rank stench of the comfrey rose on the steam, smelling of anything but an herb possessing its soothing and healing powers.

"I'll return to the garden until that steeps," she said.

"Are you avoiding me?" Patience fixed her with an unwavering stare.

Tabitha arched her brows. "Why would I do that?"

"Huh." Patience plucked onions from a basket and snatched up a knife. "You don't want to talk about Mr. Trower coming back."

"I don't know what to say." Tabitha traced the punctures on her palm with a forefinger, then gave Patience a sidelong glance. "But I'm sure you do."

"I do." Patience sliced through an onion as though she needed to kill it. "I know you want a family, a real family, not just me and Japheth, but I'd make sure that man intends to stay for real before I tumbled head over heels for him again."

"Never fear that." Tabitha laughed. "I'm happy he's still alive and well, but I'm not ready to repeat the kind of mistake I did with him."

Like trust him to be faithful more than she did anyone, including God.

Patience set down the knife with a clatter. "You got to trust someone if you want a family, child."

"It won't be Raleigh, not for a long time."

"You're sure of that?"

Tabitha nodded. "I'm sure."

Because, as she returned her attention to the punctures

on her palm, she couldn't hold Raleigh's face in her mind's eye, though he had left her house less than an hour earlier. She saw dark eyes surrounded by powdered waves and a cocky grin.

And that frightened her more than the idea of giving her heart back to Raleigh Trower.

5

"I tell you, the woman should be jailed for murder." Harlan Wilkins's voice rose through the study door and slammed against Dominick's ears.

Dominick paused on his way to perform the ignominious task of emptying the mayor's chamber pot and waited to hear more.

"I told you that two days ago and you've done nothing," Wilkins continued to rave.

Told Kendall what? Dominick frowned. He should have listened in on that dinner between the mayor and the merchant.

"And I told you two days ago, Harlan," Kendall responded in a calm voice, "that neither the sheriff nor I have any evidence of murder, certainly not caused by Miss Eckles."

Dominick's fingers closed over the newel post. He scarcely dared breathe for fear of missing a single word.

"According to my servants," Wilkins ground out, "my wife took a little tumble. Even if the babe came too early, my wife shouldn't have died."

"Now, Harlan, Miss Eckles said Mrs. Wilkins was out of her head and—"

"Of course she'd say that." Something crashed inside the book-lined room.

Dominick drew his brows together. Anger over a wife's death was surely understandable, but to blame the poor midwife seemed wide of the mark.

"She should be removed from her occupation before anyone else dies," Wilkins commanded. "She's a heathen anyway."

A heathen? Dominick cocked his head, making certain he'd heard correctly. He didn't think anyone in the civilized parts of America was a heathen.

"That's a grave accusation, Harlan," Kendall said. "And even if it were true, it wouldn't support accusations of incompetence at her profession."

"She hasn't gone to church in a year," Wilkins pointed out. "And we shouldn't have someone without a Christian faith delivering our young into the world. Maybe if she'd prayed, my wife would still be alive."

"And maybe," Kendall said with a tone of steel, "if you'd been home praying instead of at the Fisherman's Tavern, your wife would be home and well right now."

"Why you—you—" Wilkins spluttered to a halt.

Dominick sprinted into the parlor across the hall just in time to avoid being caught eavesdropping, as the study door burst open and Harlan Wilkins surged into the entryway.

"You'll regret taking her side," he tossed over his shoulder, then slammed out of the front door.

"Some men must blame others for their misfortunes," Kendall said from the library doorway. "Have you found it so, Cherrett?"

"Sir?" Dominick emerged from the parlor.

Kendall chuckled. "Next time you choose to eavesdrop on one of my conversations, don't stand on the bottom step. It squeaks."

"I beg your pardon, sir." Dominick grimaced. "I didn't notice." He'd skipped over it the night he sneaked out of the house.

"I did. But no harm done. If you happen to encounter Miss

Eckles while on your errands, do warn her that Wilkins is speaking against her."

"Yes, sir. I will consider it my duty to do so, sir."

He saw the midwife Thursday morning as he followed Letty around the vendors who gathered in the square most mornings, selling fish and early produce, butter and cream. Carrying a basket like a common footman, he espied Tabitha Eckles choosing her own wares. Once, he caught her eye and coaxed a smile from her. Another time, he saw her lingering over a stall of used goods, fingering the spine of a worn volume. Such a look of longing etched her delicate features, he had to stop and speak to her.

"My mother loved that book."

She jerked her hand away as though the leather had turned to hot coals, but she smiled at him. "My mother brought it home to me from a patient once, but my father said it was silly and wouldn't let me read it. He made me read things other than novels."

"I haven't read it either." He picked up the book, casting the seller a frown to keep him from protesting. "*Evangeline* sounded like something a female would read. But I miss—"

"Dominick, where are you?" Letty called.

He sighed and returned the book to the shelf. "I hope to see you again soon. I have something I have to tell you, but not here in public. If we could meet—"

"It wouldn't be appropriate."

"But—"

"Dominick?" Letty sounded impatient.

"I'll make a way to talk to you," Dominick promised.

Tabitha didn't respond, but a glance back told him she watched him stride away.

He smiled. The midwife liked to read. If only he could

purchase the book, he could take it to her, lend it to her. But he had no money and thus no excuse to seek her out.

He didn't see her for what remained of that week. But snippets of overheard talk told him Wilkins was speaking against her. No one seemed to hold much credence in the censure of her skill. Still, she needed to know, for her own sake.

For his own sake, Dominick feared that, if he didn't find her soon, Kendall's guests would arrive, and Dominick would have no free moments to slip away until they departed. By that time, he feared she would have forgotten him. Of course, if she did, he would have no reason to pursue her, to persuade her he was the kindest, most gentlemanly of men . . .

He didn't like the notion of having no reason to seek her out, but only because he thought a flirtation with the midwife would ease the tedium of his work, the frustration of being away from the home in Dorset he had rejected and now missed enough to dream about, as though his school holidays had been an endless succession of joyful activity.

School was where he'd found joy, the books he'd read in secret so his classmates wouldn't harass him, the schoolmasters who'd encouraged him while keeping his secret. If he had showed academic prowess, his father would have believed himself correct in sending his youngest son into the church.

Of course, if Dominick had known of another vocation acceptable for a man of his station in life, he might have been able to persuade Bruton, his father, to allow him to head in that direction. Unfortunately, Dominick hadn't known anything other than getting himself out of a life as a vicar.

Now that he knew what he wanted, however temporary, it eluded him. She eluded him. Seabourne lay in peaceful mourning over the loss of more young men, without a clue to their whereabouts, and the midwife had vanished from

Dominick's presence like the mist she'd stepped out of on their first encounter.

Meanwhile, he played his role of butler, preparing for the important guests due to arrive the following week, and chafing under the dullness of his existence. So far, in the nearly three weeks he'd resided under Kendall's roof, he had served only one guest at a time, and those infrequent. Kendall dined out at the homes of others more than he remained at home. But, at last, he announced that the minister and his family would be coming home with him after church on Sunday.

"His wife is related to the Lee family, and the niece coming with them is a Lee. So make certain everything goes well," Kendall admonished Dominick.

"Yes, sir," he responded with a calm outward demeanor.

Inside his uniform, his skin crawled at the idea of serving a minister. The last man of God with whom he'd come face-to-face didn't want the kind of favor Dominick was prepared to give—his life.

"Thank you, Lord," Dominick muttered on his way back to the kitchen. "You have a droll sense of humor, making me wait on one of your servants."

Dominick didn't know who the Lee family was but presumed they could help advance Kendall's political ambitions. He wondered how the minister felt about being invited because of his wife and not because the mayor wanted spiritual advice. Not that Kendall seemed lacking in his faith. He read his Bible along with the newspaper every morning. For all Dominick knew, the minister liked political connections as much as did the mayor. The vicars whom the Marquess of Bruton appointed to the livings he controlled tended in that direction. The dozens of other vicars whom Dominick had made a point of meeting preferred other distractions to keep them from serving God.

Perhaps Sunday should be the day he acquired a case of the ague or broke a leg. He disliked the idea of bowing and scraping to men who traded favors for advancement in their profession, when they were supposed to have thoughts of a spiritual nature.

"I believe I'll direct the serving from in here," Dominick told Letty Sunday morning. "I'd rather not serve the dinner."

"It's your job to carve the meat for guests," Letty said. "Carry the roast to the sideboard and lay a slice on each plate. Deborah or Dinah will take the plates to the guests, and they'll pass around the removes."

"I know how a dinner is served," Dominick responded. "But I've never done the actual work. That is . . ." He eyed the hunk of meat glistening under a glaze of juice. "I have no idea how to carve."

Letty sighed. "Whatever got a gentleman's son into a situation like you're in, if it wasn't females or gaming?"

"Stubbornness. Now show me what to do."

She showed him on a ham. Preserved in salt, it needed a swift, hard slice of the knife to break through the surface, but he managed to make credibly even and straight wheels of meat. He didn't think about the tenderness of the roasted beef presiding on its china platter.

Deborah and Dinah carried the bowls of crab soup to each guest. All Dominick had to do was stand at the sideboard and fill the bowls from a tureen. Trying not to yawn, he watched the guests from beneath his lashes and realized halfway through the first course that one of the guests watched him in return.

She was the minister's niece, a golden-haired beauty with eyes the color of spring grass. From beneath her own long, dark lashes, she gazed at Dominick and ignored her food and her aunt's frowns. When their eyes met, she smiled and looked away.

Dominick pretended not to notice. Flirting with the guests was certainly not acceptable for him. Flirting with a servant was not acceptable for her, and he would never be the cause of a lady getting into an awkward situation, however unwittingly.

He picked up the now empty tureen and headed toward the kitchen.

"Do tell us about your manservant, Mayor Kendall," the young woman said as the door swung shut behind him.

Dominick thudded the basin onto the table. "That young lady needs some lessons in decorum."

"She's got an eye for you." Deborah nearly doubled over laughing. "Never saw the like, a lady flirting with a servant."

"She recognizes quality." Dinah tossed her head. "But Reverend Downing would be well served to marry that one off again soon."

"Again?" Dominick paused. "She's a widow?"

"Two and twenty and recently out of mourning." Letty spooned gravy into a bowl. "She was downcast, so her parents sent her here to the seaside for the summer."

"The only thing she's cast down," Deborah said, "is her handkerchief for Mr. Cherrett."

Dominick's cheeks grew warm. "Don't be absurd, Deb."

"Stop gossiping about the guests and take in the next course," Letty directed.

Dominick lifted the roast and carried it into the dining room. The niece tried to catch his eye again, but he kept his own gaze downcast and set the meat on the sideboard.

"When do the senators arrive?" Reverend Downing was asking.

Apparently talk about the butler had been brief. Dominick doubted that would have been the situation if Kendall knew how his butler ended up in Virginia.

Dominick picked up the carving knife.

"Tuesday or Wednesday," Kendall answered. "If the fine weather holds. But I'll see they come to church on Sunday."

Dominick steadied the roast with a fork held in one hand and positioned the knife in the other hand for the first cut, the well-done end piece that would go to Mrs. Downing, as she preferred her meat nearly burned, according to Letty.

"Why doesn't your midwife go to church?" Mrs. Lee asked. "I hear talk she's a heathen."

Dominick stood still, knife poised above the roast. He was glad the woman had chosen to talk of someone besides him, but asking about Tabitha surprised him into waiting for the answer.

"She's lost a number of important people in her life over the past few years." Kendall spoke slowly, as though thinking over each word. "She stopped going after her grandmother died year before last, leaving her alone in the world except for her servants."

"The poor woman," Mrs. Lee murmured. "You should invite her to dinner, Uncle."

"You're right, Phoebe." Reverend Downing cleared his throat. "I get so busy with my regular parishioners, I can often neglect others in the town in need. Dinner it is."

"Speaking of dinner . . ." Kendall's chair creaked. "Are we going to enjoy any of that roast, Mr. Cherrett?"

"Yes, of course, sir." Ears hot beneath his powdered hair, Dominick fixed his attention on the roast. Picturing the ham, he jerked the knife downward into the tender roast. The blade struck bone, deflected, and drove the point into the palm of his other hand.

6

Blood spurted. He gasped and dropped his utensils with a clatter.

"My apologies," he managed with all the stoical training life with his father had taught him. He grabbed a serviette from the sideboard, wrapped it around his hand, and exited the now silent dining room with his back straight and head up.

In the kitchen, he collapsed onto a chair and fought a wave of nausea. "I'd be better at farming than butling."

"Mercy." Letty dropped her stirring spoon. "What have you done?"

"Added a bit of my claret to your fine roast." Dominick grimaced. "And possibly ruined everyone's appetites."

"Let me see." Letty took his hand in both of hers and unwound the cloth.

Blood welled from the gash.

"That's a bad one, not big, but deep." She pressed the serviette to the cut again. "Deborah, remove the roast. They'll have to do with just the fish. Dinah, run for Miss Eckles."

"Miss Eckles indeed." Dominick lowered his head to his uninjured hand and started to laugh.

"He's gone all over funny," Deborah cried. "Should we make him lie down or something?"

"I'm all right." Dominick forced himself to be quiet.

He could never explain to the girl how hard he'd been trying to see Miss Eckles, how he'd joked with himself about breaking a leg or catching a fever. He should have simply cut himself earlier and been done with the matter.

"I doubt Miss Eckles will want her Sunday dinner interrupted." He smelled blood, not Letty's excellent cooking. His stomach churned.

At least this time the blood belonged to him and not some misguided defender of the guilty.

"Your roast is too tender, Letty," he said to keep his mind off his throbbing and bleeding hand. "I cut it too hard like the ham."

"You weren't distracted by Mrs. Lee?" Deborah tossed over her shoulder as she snatched up the fish platter and headed for the dining room.

The aroma of shrimp stuffed with crab meat wafted past Dominick's nose. His nostrils flared, and his stomach came close to rebelling. "She's one to talk," he grumbled.

"You're not flattered?" Letty brought a clean serviette to wrap around his hand.

"Of course I'm flattered." Dominick managed a smile. "I'm human. But I am not in America to commence a liaison with an inappropriate female."

Except he was a liar. Of course he would start a liaison with an inappropriate female if it served his end.

"And what sort of female would be appropriate?" Letty held his gaze for a moment, then left him to draw a pie from the oven.

Dominick welcomed the distraction from his throbbing hand, if not the topic.

"'Appropriate' would be my social equal, of course." He injected as much flippancy as he could into his tone.

Letty snorted. "Haven't you worked it out yet, laddie? Deborah and Dinah are your social equals here."

"But I won't be here—" He broke off. He didn't know how long he would be there. Not permanently, that was for certain, and he wouldn't take an American-born lady back to England with him, even if he had to serve out his four years. He'd already dishonored his family enough.

"Kendall's likely to send me to a plantation to weed tobacco, or whatever the crop is," Dominick finished. "I've just made amok of his precious dinner with a concession to the Lee family, whoever they are."

"Never you mind about that." Letty returned with a cloth soaked in cold water. "This might help. And about Mrs. Downing, she doesn't care about her family connections. She serves God with her husband, not politicians."

"How peculiar." Dominick grimaced. "I've rarely met—"

The dining room door swished open and Deborah swept through. "Everyone is concerned about you, Mr. Cherrett. Shall I tell them you are in good hands?"

He would be. Soft little hands with long, narrow fingers. If she ever got there. If she got there before the spots in his eyes turned to total blackness.

It was just a little cut. A little cut with a lot of blood and even more pain. After all his knife throwing with his uncle, he'd cut himself on a mere carving knife.

But the sight of Tabitha Eckles striding through the doorway made the injury worth every throbbing moment. She wore a plain blue gown and white kerchief around her shoulders. Her hair shone beneath a cap with a single frill to adorn it, softening the angles of her face.

And he still wanted to kiss that point of hair in the center of her forehead.

He smiled. "See the lengths I go to so I can see you again, Miss Eckles?"

"You can't have too serious an injury if you can talk such nonsense, Mr. Cherrett." Her tone was brisk. She glanced around the kitchen. "You're in the middle of serving dinner, I see. I'll take your manservant into the kitchen garden."

He'd have suggested his room if he thought he could climb the steps. But just rising from the chair proved difficult. He gripped the edge of the worktable with his good hand and hauled himself up. Dizzy, he swayed, waiting for the room to stop spinning.

"Are you all right, sir?" Deborah asked. "You've gone as pale as my apron."

"Perfectly fine. I should be back in time to serve the pudding." Dominick managed a smile.

"Your brains are the pudding if you think that." Tabitha slipped her forearm beneath his. "Has he lost a great deal of blood?"

"Apparently enough." Letty began to slice into the pie, sending the aroma of raisins and cinnamon around the kitchen.

Dominick leaned on the midwife's arm. "I don't like blood, especially when it's mine."

"Then we'll stop it," Tabitha said.

She proved to be a strong woman, easily steadying him on their way outside into the warm sunshine and fragrant herb garden. A puff of air smelling of the sea blew into Dominick's face, reviving him like a whiff of hartshorn.

He sank onto the bench. "I apologize for interrupting your Sunday dinner, ma'am."

"It isn't the first time a meal has been interrupted." She settled beside him and took his hand in hers. "It won't be the last."

"This town needs a surgeon or apothecary."

"I'll still be getting interrupted." She began to unwind

the makeshift bandage. "Babies don't wait until I'm done eating."

"A pity."

For what, he didn't know. Air struck his wound and pain shot up his arm. As she probed the gash with fingers as gentle as breaths, he fixed his gaze on what he could see of her face—the smooth, creamy brow with that intriguing peak of hair that lent her features their heart shape. The way her golden brown lashes shielded her eyes when her head was bent. A wrinkle in the center of her cap, as though it had been ironed inexpertly or in a hurry.

A pucker formed between her winged brows. "The bleeding is slowing, but I need to stitch this. Can you bear the discomfort?"

"I did the last time."

"The last time?" Her head shot up, her blue eyes questioned him. "You've cut yourself before?"

"It wasn't a cut." And he wouldn't have said a word if he didn't feel so lightheaded.

"A gunshot?" she asked.

"You don't need to know to treat me." His tone was sharp.

She returned her attention to his hand, her cheeks flushing. "Of course not. Medical curiosity, is all." She set his hand palm up on the bench and reached for the satchel she carried. "This will hurt."

"But I'll get to see you in a week or so to get the stitches out?"

"Yes." She took several items from her bag. "Meanwhile, you should be able to continue your work, though I recommend you wear gloves if you have them."

"I have them." He shuddered at the idea.

"Good. Close your eyes."

He caught a glimpse of a needle and silk thread and obeyed. He braced himself for the bite of steel in flesh, but caught the odor of spirits first. The burning sensation on his cut made him long for the needle. Words not fit for a lady's ears surged to his lips. He clenched his teeth, swallowed, wished he could smell that springtime aroma he'd caught from her hair earlier.

Then the needle came. The muscles on his back jerked in sympathy. His entire body tensed, and behind his closed lids, he saw a cloudy day, cold and wet, a stable yard, fetid and dirty, blood soaking into the cobbles, washed pink from the rain. His blood, shed in such a humiliating way . . .

"Mr. Cherrett?" Tabitha gripped his shoulder, her fingertips resting on the scar, though he doubted she could feel it through his coat and shirt. "You're not going to faint on me, are you?"

"No." He opened his eyes to find her face mere inches from his. Her breath fanned his face, and he caught his reflection in her clear eyes. "I've humiliated myself enough for one lifetime. I won't add losing consciousness over a little blood and pain to the list."

"Good." She smiled and drew back. "I'll set a poultice on this, and you'll be back to your duties in a day or two."

"I have to be. Mr. Kendall is having important guests."

"That's right." She smeared a foul-smelling ointment on his hand. "You'll do well enough. Come to see me in two weeks and I'll remove the stitches."

"I'd rather see you sooner." He caught her gaze and held it.

She blinked several times, like someone suddenly exposed to strong light. "That isn't necessary, Mr. Cherrett, unless you pull a stitch or it goes septic."

"I could go for a walk on the beach with you."

"I like my walks early in the morning."

"How early?"

"Earlier than a bondsman should be about."

"Ah, a direct hit." He feigned a recoil as though from a blow. "You don't like me much, do you, Madam Midwife?"

"You're English. You were where you shouldn't have been the night three of my countrymen vanished."

"And I've been charged guilty because of a little walk on the beach and my country of birth?" He kept his tone light, playful, to mask the tension running through him, tension that had nothing to do with pain. "Is that any fairer than Harlan Wilkins accusing you of his wife's death?"

"Ah, so you've heard that talk." She curled her upper lip. "He's off drinking and gaming and thinks I did something to harm the poor creature."

"Will it harm your work, your reputation, Madam Mermaid?"

"Not likely." She shrugged, though her jaw hardened. "My family has served this community for three generations without a whiff of scandal."

"Would that I were so confident in my family name saving me." Dominick heaved an exaggerated sigh. "But I'm judged guilty for being the dreadful English."

"If I judged you guilty, Mr. Cherrett, I'd have told your master of your escapade."

"So why haven't you?"

She shrugged. "You were a bit too far from where the men were last seen. And we have no proof the British are involved, only suspicions due to your ships being in our waters."

"But not too far"—he raised his uninjured hand to touch her throat with a whisper of his fingertips—"to have done this to you."

She sat perfectly still as though his contact paralyzed her.

He didn't even know if she breathed until she drew in a ragged breath and pulled away from his caress.

"Whoever it was, I heed the warning. I'm used to keeping my mouth shut in my work." She bent her head over his hand, which she wound in a strip of bleached linen. "Keep this clean. I'll leave some salve with Letty. She'll find you fresh cloth for bandages."

After giving the bandage a final tweak to tighten the knot, she rose and turned toward the house.

Dominick stood too and rested his hand on her arm for a breath. "I can tell you it wasn't me, and you'll believe what you will."

"You have reason to want to keep your nighttime activities private, where no one else I know does." Her mouth pursed. "A whipping is painful."

Skin along his back crawled. "Oh, don't I know."

"Do you?" Her eyes narrowed, and he knew he condemned himself with that careless remark.

"I was an English schoolboy." He tried to recover from his slip. "You can imagine that I often gave my tutors cause to whip me."

"I doubt that's the same as what's doled out to a bondsman, so watch your step, Mr. Cherrett. I don't like tending to a back cut to ribbons." Admonition delivered, she strode to the house, her skirt swishing around her ankles, her low-heeled walking boots raising puffs of dust in her wake.

Dominick smiled despite his aching palm, despite what she'd intended as a rebuff of his flirtation. He would win her over. He had to. He had less than four weeks to complete his mission, before his uncle left the American patrol and returned to England—leaving Dominick stranded as a servant for months, even years, regardless of whether or not he completed his mission.

7

"Miss Eckles?"

Her thoughts back in the mayor's garden, Tabitha started at the sound of a soft voice calling her name. She turned to see an unfamiliar young woman trotting toward her.

"I'm so glad I reached you in time." Golden curls bouncing beneath the brim of a cream straw hat with lavender ribbons, the woman slid to a halt on the sandy path to the beach. "We could really use your services."

"Yes?" Tabitha waited for the woman to catch her breath.

She knew of no one in the area even close to labor except for Marjorie Parks, a sailor's wife, and to have two people be injured on a Sunday afternoon was unusual.

"It's the dog." The young woman turned the pink of a begonia as she spoke in a voice as sweet and slow as honey. "She's whelping. Or she's trying to, and something seems to be wrong. Can you help her?"

"I can try." Tabitha didn't smile. The request wasn't unusual, not common, but this wasn't the first time she'd been called to the lying-in of a creature that was not human. And a dog was a whole lot more pleasant a prospect than a pig or a cow, both of whom she'd helped through labor.

"Where is this?" she asked.

"Oh, I'm so sorry. I'm Mrs. Phoebe Lee, Reverend Downing's niece."

"Ah, Reverend Downing will do anything to get me near

his church." Tabitha smiled now. "What kind of dog is she and when did you notice she was in trouble?"

"I noticed her pacing around before church this morning and thought it might be her time." Mrs. Lee spun on a dainty heel, sending the flounce at the bottom of her lavender gown fluttering in the sea breeze, and headed back toward town with Tabitha beside her. "And when we got home from Mayor Kendall's, poor little Ginger was on her side in the garden, panting and whimpering. I saw you go past and thought maybe you could help."

"I usually can." Tabitha eyed the lovely young woman, who looked like she'd walked off the page of an English periodical rather than gone running after the midwife for the minister's spaniel. "Is there a servant available to help me?"

"No, Reverend Downing gives his servants the day off on the Sabbath, but I can help." Mrs. Lee smiled. "I'm a widow, not unmarried like the Downing daughters. They all ran inside at the first sign of the dog's condition, and Uncle is visiting a sick parishioner. That leaves me."

"Have you ever attended at a lying-in?" Tabitha asked as they reached the town square. "Or perhaps you have children of your own?"

"No." The curtness of the word was unusual in the sweet voice, then Mrs. Lee giggled. "But I've been around a number of cats and dogs in a similar situation."

"Then you can help me, if you like, but I suggest you change. I seem to already have blood on my dress."

Dominick Cherrett's blood, because she'd held his hand too tightly, too close over her lap when she'd tended to his cut.

"I saw Mayor Kendall's redemptioner cut himself." Mrs. Lee shuddered. "I'd have gone to help him, but my uncle said it was inappropriate. I didn't know helping a body in need was inappropriate, but then, I'm always being told—" She broke off and laughed. "Like talking too much. And there's poor Ginger."

Tabitha heard it too, a pitiful whining drifting from the parsonage garden. She hastened to go through the gate and straight to the distressed spaniel. Ginger, named for her spotted coat, lay on her side in a corner beneath the low boughs of a pine tree. Her sides heaved, but nothing happened where it should be happening.

"I'm here to help you, Ginger." Tabitha knelt by the dog's head and rubbed the silky ears. "We'll make things all better, me and Mrs. Lee here. Will you let us?"

Ginger licked her hand and panted despite the cool, fragrant bower.

"She trusts you," Mrs. Lee said, her voice full of awe.

"She knows me, don't you, girl?" Tabitha began to pat the dog down, smoothing the dulled coat over her ribs, then moving on to her distended abdomen. When she reached the hind end, she glanced up. "Will you hold her head? Even the sweetest dogs can get snappish at a time like this."

"Like some humans?" Mrs. Lee dropped down beside the dog and began to pet her with one hand while holding her muzzle gently with the other. "Ever been bitten?"

"Yes, and not by a four-footed patient." Tabitha probed with one finger, then two. "Ah, a puppy turned incorrectly. Let's see what we can do."

Dogs were difficult, being so small. But Tabitha's hands were small too, as had once been required of a midwife by law. With Mrs. Lee stroking and soothing, and Ginger alternately licking and growling, Tabitha managed to turn the puppy. In minutes, it slid into her hand. She set it under Ginger's nose. The dog struggled to rise, but Tabitha held her down.

"Easy, girl. You've got more in there."

Ginger licked the first puppy clean. Tabitha attended to the delivery of the second, third, fourth, and fifth, which came so rapidly they must have been waiting in line, anxious for their first and biggest brother to get out of their way so they could experience the light of day and a mother's love.

And she loved them. Tabitha and Mrs. Lee ceased to exist for the spaniel once her brood surrounded her, squeaking and clamoring for their first meal.

"I think they'll do just fine." Tabitha rose and grimaced at her hands and skirt. "Is there water anywhere?"

"There's a pail by the door." Mrs. Lee also stood and made a face. "I think this gown is for the rag bin." It was covered with birth matter.

"Try soaking it in cold water and salt," Tabitha suggested. "That works for me."

"I will, but no matter if it doesn't." Mrs. Lee shrugged. "It's still too close to mourning clothes for my liking. How much do I owe you?"

"Owe me?" Tabitha blinked at the rapid change of subject. "Nothing."

"Nonsense. You used your skills to help this dog. You should get paid."

"I . . . never think about the fee for anything but human babies." Tabitha rubbed her soiled hands against her worse-off skirt. "Farmers usually pay me with eggs and the like."

"Well, I don't have the like, but I do have money." Mrs. Lee's nostrils pinched at the mention of money, as though it smelled worse than the afterbirth.

"Then pay me what you feel is fair." Tabitha felt too warm inside her light muslin gown. "I don't have fees for a puppy delivery."

"Then I'll come by tomorrow. No, I can't. We're going fishing. I've never been on the ocean before. Have you?"

Tabitha smiled, her heart twanging. "Often."

Before Raleigh left.

"I think I'll like it, if I don't get ill. Day after tomorrow then." Mrs. Lee rubbed her own hands on her skirt. "Will that do?"

"Whenever it's convenient for you, ma'am." Catching sight of faces peering out of the windows, she bade goodbye and beat a hasty retreat home. The last thing she wanted was for the parson and his family to feel obligated to invite her inside their home. The last time she'd talked with Reverend Downing had been when her grandmother died. He'd tried to give her words of comfort, assurances that God loved her and was with her.

"I'd rather have a family alive than God's invisible, silent presence," had been her cold response.

And she'd never set foot inside the church again. It often isolated her. Women who might otherwise be friends with her stopped inviting her to their gatherings. She was unmarried, worked to support herself, and chose solitude in a town where activities centered on the church.

She wanted a life centered on a husband and children, not a church, not a God who had ignored her prayers for her father and mother, for her fiancé and her grandmother. Possibly for herself most of all, burdened as she was with the knowledge that she could surely have prevented her parents' deaths.

She hadn't realized that at the time. She hadn't known her father, never strong, would go seeking birds' eggs for his students. She could have gone to the patient's lying-in in her mother's place.

But she had stayed home with her own occupations both times, and now her house felt too big and quiet with Patience off visiting friends, and Japheth, the man of all outdoor work, presumably doing such, or crabbing. It was a house her great-grandfather Eckles had built for a family, with a kitchen big enough for everyone to gather around the table, two parlors, and four bedrooms above. Her mother and grandmother, though midwives too, had been married and were mothers by Tabitha's age. She had lost one prospect after another to the sea until Raleigh had vanished altogether.

Now that he had returned, she didn't know if she wanted to see him. She didn't trust him not to leave, and seeing him felt too dangerous, too likely to lead to the wish to renew their relationship, their plans.

Being alone was safer. Being alone gave her the freedom to come and go as she needed or pleased. But sometimes the silence grew intense. She spent a great deal of time reading—the heavy tomes her father had loved, the herbals from her mother and grandmother. She practically had them memorized.

How she'd wanted that novel she'd seen in the market. How thoughts of the novel made her think of Dominick Cherrett. He gave her the impression he liked to read too. Mayor Kendall's study contained books only on politics and money, Adam Smith and Edmund Burke. Dull stuff.

The temptation to lend him her father's volumes of Shakespeare's works grew within her. She had thought about getting to know him better, to discover if he was up to no good. She needed to look at his hand to ensure it was healing well.

On Friday, she packed a volume of Shakespeare into her satchel and walked into town. Dominick was just emerging from the laundry with a pile of linens. He glanced up at the creak of the back gate, and his face reddened.

"You find me in the ignominious work of laundress," he greeted her. "I, apparently, am the only one unoccupied enough to take on the chore."

"It's not good for your hand." She hastened forward and took the wet sheets from his arms. "What was Letty thinking? Sit down. Let me look."

"If it brings you to fuss over me, I'll do this more often." He grinned at her.

She reminded herself he was English to minimize his effect on her. She reminded herself he was a patient. "I'll help you hang these. Where is everyone?"

"At a farm purchasing the finest of produce and meats for Kendall's guests." Dominick held one end of a sheet. "These, apparently, were put away less than dry and smelled too musty for company."

"But—never you mind that. How is the hand?"

"It started aching the instant I saw you. Surely it needs your tender ministrations."

She couldn't help but laugh. "I'm pleased it's healing well."

And the banter continued, nonsensical, ridiculous, and making the task of hanging the heavy sheets fly by.

When they finished, she examined his hand, pronounced it healing well, then, cheeks warm and eyes downcast, she drew out the Shakespeare volume. "I thought you might enjoy this."

"Oh, I would." Reverence filled his voice. "*The Tempest* is my favorite. Yours?"

She glanced up. A tempest inside her warned her to flee.

"I rather like *Twelfth Night*," she said past a dry throat.

"Hmm, a midwife who reads Shakespeare." He rested his thumb on her chin. "My dear, you intrigue me."

"Right now, I'd better leave you. That is—" She sprang to her feet. "I have work waiting."

He followed her to the gate. "When will I see you again?"

"A week. I'll remove your stitches."

"Too long. I've looked for you in the market and on the beach in the morning."

"I'm only out in the morning if my work demands it."

But if he was on the beach early, when he shouldn't be, maybe she should join him there—keep him from, if not learn, what mischief he was up to, if any. She must give him the benefit of the doubt about his dawn activities. He could be innocent of wrongdoing. Yet if she met him by more than chance in the early morning and someone saw him, her reputation would surely suffer.

How she would enjoy discussing books again. She hadn't done so with anyone since Grandmomma died. And this man sounded educated, intelligent . . .

"Tell Letty you can't get that hand wet," she admonished him, and fled.

She arrived home to the news that she was needed for a woman on the other side of the cape.

"They want me to go to a lying-in in Norfolk," she told Patience. "We'll leave early Monday."

She disliked leaving her community for long periods of time, but sometimes it couldn't be helped. She went where and when she was needed, mostly out of a sense of duty, partly out of financial necessity. She had a household to support, and the Belotes were going to pay her well for what seemed to be a routine lying-in.

On Monday morning, she woke before dawn, only to find Japheth and Patience already in the kitchen with breakfast going.

"It's going to be hot today," Japheth said. "Thought we should get an early start."

"I'd like a walk before we leave." Tabitha inhaled the aromas of coffee and frying ham. "But some breakfast would be good. Why don't you meet me in the village, Japheth. If I'm going to ride twenty miles in a wagon, I'd like a walk along the beach first."

"I wouldn't do that, Miss Tabitha." Patience flipped over the ham slices. "It ain't safe."

"The press-gangs aren't going to take up a female." She touched her fingers to her throat. Though she might see an Englishman.

Patience and Japheth argued. Tabitha ate her breakfast in silence and thus quickly. She grabbed a shawl from a hook by the door, picked up the satchel she liked to keep with her at all times, and departed with a brisk, "I'll meet you and the wagon in the square."

Warm, damp air swirled around her as she left her garden. She crossed the dunes and headed along the tide line. The breeze picked up and turned cooler, lifting the spring mist from the water and creating odd shadows along the brightening horizon. Waves pounded against the land, suggesting a storm out to sea.

Watchful, Tabitha headed south to where one of the numerous small waterways cut into the land to form a haven for fishing boats and well-worn paths on which to lengthen her walk to town. Halfway there, she paused at the Trowers' inlet. Their jetty stretched into the stream. Raleigh could be coming into it with his father and their boat at any time. She couldn't avoid him forever in a village like Seabourne. But neither did she have to make their next encounter look deliberate. With a sigh, she turned away from the sea and toward the nearest path over the dunes, through the sea grasses to where the trees began and the village lay beyond, sheltered from ocean storms.

A creak and rumble drifted to her ears over the muted roar of the sea. She paused and turned back. Wind lifted the veil of mist to display a golden pink line between dark sky and darker sea.

And against that sliver of light, as sharp as silhouette cut-outs, a three-masted vessel bore down on a fishing boat.

"No," she shouted, as though she could stop the inevitable. She ran toward the sea.

"No," her voice echoed.

No, not an echo—another protesting cry, lower pitched than her voice. Footfalls followed, pounding the hard-packed sand toward the edge of the water.

"Don't!"

Light flared across the water, glittering in the waves. Arms wrapped around her and dragged her to the sand as the concussion of a cannon blast surged toward the land like a tidal wave.

8

Tabitha gasped for breath. She lay on her back on the sand packed as hard as rock, staring at stars fading into streaks of lavender, and wondered if the air driven from her lungs would ever return, or if the blast of gunfire had caused irreparable damage.

"Miss Eckles, are you all right?" Dominick Cherrett asked.

"You," she gasped. "You . . . oaf. You . . ." She ceased speech in favor of a struggle to sit up.

"Let me help you." He slipped an arm beneath her shoulders and raised her to a sitting position.

He didn't remove his arm. He knelt beside her, his head bent over hers, his hair falling soft and free of ribbon and powder to caress her cheek.

Breathing continued to prove difficult, though the effects of her fall—the numbing jolt to her torso—had already faded. She lifted a hand to brush away his soft waves, and he clasped it.

"I'm so sorry I hurt you." The pale blur of his face hovered near hers, his breath brushing across her lips. "I acted without thinking."

"I doubt that's the first time." She tugged her hand free of his but made no move to elude his supporting arm. "The first time you've acted without thinking."

"In truth, Madam Midwife, I rarely act without thinking.

But I usually don't have a ship of the line firing so close at hand."

"The ship." She jerked out of the circle of his arm and surged to her feet so she could look out to sea. "How could I forget it?"

Easily. She wasn't thinking with Dominick Cherrett so close to her, smelling of sun-dried linen and heady sandalwood—an expensive fragrance for a bondsman, and hauntingly familiar.

She peered into the lightening sky. The ship appeared as nothing more than a curved dark hulk against the horizon, while the fishing boat swooped toward shore like a dolphin fleeing a net.

"They got away." She spun toward Dominick, heart soaring. "They didn't get captured."

"It looks that way." He caught hold of both of her hands. "For once."

"Indeed." She started to yank her hands free, felt the bandage wrapping his left palm, and hesitated. "Mr. Cherrett." As much as she wished to be free of his hold, she didn't want to hurt him. "Please let go of my hand," she said.

"Which one?" Teeth flashed in a grin.

She ground her teeth. "Both of them."

"Ah, if you insist." He drew his fingers away, the tips grazing her palms, stopping. "What is this?" He traced the scabbed-over marks where the rosebush had punctured her palm.

"A disagreement with a rosebush."

"I have been so distracted by your lovely face I didn't notice before now. I am sorry. It must have been painful." He lifted her hand and pressed his lips to the palm. "Better?"

"No, worse." She'd rather have a hundred thorns driven into her flesh than to feel the jolt of heat rushing through her, stealing her breath as though she'd been knocked to the ground once more. "You shouldn't do that." Her voice sounded breathless.

"Probably not." He released her hand, remaining close to her. "But be assured I didn't do it without thinking first."

"Why would you—"

Tackle creaked above the hiss of the retreating tide. She glanced toward the sound and caught sight of the fishing boat heading toward shore, hull down with its night's catch, and she understood.

Dominick Cherrett, the Englishman, wanted to distract her from the incident of the frigate firing upon that single-masted craft.

She faced him, eyes narrowed. "When threats don't work you resort to—to—flirtation?"

"I have no idea what you're talking about." He sounded bored. "Does a man need a reason to kiss the hand of a lovely lady?"

"I am not lovely and I am not a lady," she snapped. "And you, sir, are once again on the beach at an hour when you're supposed to be in your master's home. And, once again, we have a British vessel invading our territory at the same time you appear on the beach. Coincidence? I think not."

"Neither do I."

His calm reaction to her accusation left Tabitha speechless.

"I came out early in the hopes of seeing you. I hoped to waylay you to inspect my hand."

"In the dark?" She snorted. "Unlikely."

Up the beach, the fishing boat entered the inlet and lowered its sail in preparation for tying up to a jetty. Other men in proximity—American men—lent Tabitha a sense of security. Dominick Cherrett wouldn't harm her with others so near.

Her hand still tingling from his kiss, she doubted he could

harm her at all. When she encountered him under other circumstances, she believed him to be as innocent as he claimed. On the beach at dawn, with a British vessel vanishing over the horizon after firing on a fishing boat, she believed him capable of anything dastardly.

She touched the healing mark on her throat. "You don't need to see me regarding your hand, Mr. Cherrett, unless it's gone septic."

"Alas, it is healing very well, thanks to that vile ointment you left behind. What's in it? Kitchen waste?"

"Comfrey." Her lips twisted into a reluctant smile. "Its foul odor is only outweighed by its healing properties. But if you don't need me for your hand, why are you here?"

"For you." He drew a knuckle along her cheekbone. "I said I would join you on your early morning walk one day."

"I should report you for being here," she thought aloud.

He took her arm and started walking toward the edge of the wave-flattened sand. "But you won't. You enjoy my company, despite your suspicions."

"I believe I have reason for my suspicions." Though she hadn't seen anything that could be construed as a signal. "I won't tell about this night's work either, since your mission has failed and the boat got away."

That boat had reached the jetty, a quarter mile down the beach. Men's voices shouting directions to one another drifted toward her. One sounded familiar, and her stomach contracted.

"But it's for my own reasons and not for any of your enticing tricks," she clipped out, then scrambled for an explanation to have ready when he asked the inevitable.

He picked up her bag from where she'd dropped it on the sand. "If I don't charm you, and you don't like Englishmen in general, even ones more charming than I—if that's possible—I wonder why you'll hold your peace this time, without the fear of a threat."

Tabitha couldn't help herself. She laughed at his outrageous speech. "You're incorrigible."

Dominick laughed in response. "That's what my tutors at Ox—" He stopped, as though slamming a door on revealing something about his past. But Tabitha, daughter of a schoolmaster, knew about tutors and Oxford, and her skin tingled with curiosity—with more suspicions—regarding a well-spoken Englishman who'd attended Oxford University, living the life of a redemptioner. Intriguing. Disturbing. Definitely on the wrong side of usual.

"I suppose all English butlers attend Oxford?" she probed with a smile.

"Only those of us who excel at our studies." He glanced over his shoulder toward the sea. "The rest become gentlemen."

Tabitha laughed. "You don't seem to think a great deal of your countrymen either."

"I try not to think of my countrymen at all." His voice dropped to a tone as warm as a caress. "Especially not when I'm with you. You make me forget that I miss home."

"Mr. Cherrett—" She stopped, at a loss for words under his onslaught of teasing and flirtation.

Further along the beach, the fishermen's voices ceased.

"They've noticed us." She hastened her steps toward town.

"And they mustn't recognize us." Dominick matched her stride. "You're protecting me again. Do tell me why so I may use it in my favor for future expeditions into fresh sea air."

"I don't approve of men being treated worse than animals, locked up or whipped if they stray."

"You have a kind heart. I wish I'd known from the beginning. I wouldn't have distressed myself fretting over you tattling on me."

"Somehow, Mr. Cherrett, I don't think you were fretting in the least."

"I have been." His voice sobered. "Your dislike of my countrymen is blatant. I wonder why."

"You all stole my fiancé." She spoke harshly, lashing out against his appeal to her senses, her female vanity. "His mother is Canadian and was staying with family when he was born, because his father was on a long voyage, so the Navy claimed he was a British subject."

"I'm so sorry." He took a few more steps and paused at the edge of the dune, where the grasses waved in the rising dawn breeze. "Did he die?"

"No, he's returned after two years in your Navy, but—" She hesitated to admit it was too late. She wasn't certain of that. Most of her hoped it wasn't. If Raleigh settled there, fishing with his father, he would make a fine husband and wouldn't interfere with her work. She could have her own children and companionship by the fire. They would lack for nothing.

"War changes men." Dominick stepped back so she could precede him up the path toward town. "My father fought in a war, and my aunts say it changed him from a carefree youth to the despotic tyrant I knew."

"What war was that?" she asked, though she knew the answer.

"The one that gives you more cause to dislike me." Dominick let out a humorless laugh. "Your revolution."

"Of course." She studied the ground at her feet, careful not to entangle her ankle with a trailing length of sea grass. "Was he wounded?"

Should she be asking so many questions of this man? *Oh, yes, every bit of it and more. Be friendly. Gain his trust.*

"Not a scratch. But he lost many friends."

"Loss makes the soul sick."

Her father, when she was only sixteen. Raleigh and her mother, when she was only two and twenty. Yes, her soul still felt sick, curled in on itself like a body with a wasting disease.

"Has Harlan Wilkins caused you any trouble?" Dominick asked abruptly. "There's a man angered by loss."

"He's talking against me, yes." Tabitha bit her lip, glad she was going to be gone for a week at the least, possibly two.

"He wants the mayor to have you arrested. I should have warned you sooner, but I am always a bit distracted in your presence."

She tilted her head to look up at him. "And I suppose you're going to tell me that's why you're out this early? You suddenly remembered?"

"No, I won't tell you such a fib." He set down her bag and tucked one finger beneath her chin. "I have been concerned about you, though. Wilkins is a powerful man."

"I'm not without influence."

Or a secret or two of which she wouldn't hesitate to remind more than one councilman if necessary. She wouldn't let Harlan Wilkins ruin her livelihood, even if, at times, she would prefer to be a normal female, attending parties and receiving callers rather than delivering other women's babies.

"Reverend Downing will vouch for me," she added.

"Even though you're a heathen?" Dominick smiled into her eyes.

She blinked against a warmth, a brightness in her eyes that owed little to the rising sun. "Why would you call me a heathen?"

"That's what Wilkins called you. You never go to church."

"I'm not a heathen." She sighed with the old frustration of this conversation. "Neither am I a hypocrite. I don't have any more time for God than He has for me."

"Yet the reverend will vouch for you?"

"We have mutual respect for one another's work." She smiled ruefully. "And I may agree to go to church when I return, for the sake of appearances, of course."

"Church isn't about appearances. It's about worshiping God—at least it should be."

"I knew that . . . once." She tried to look away and failed. "I must go, Mr. Cherrett, and you should too. Don't risk coming out here again."

"It's worth the risk to see you again."

"I wish I believed that." The words emerged before she stopped herself from uttering something so foolish, so . . . inviting of further flirtation.

"May I see you when you return?" He glanced toward the fishing boat. "Perhaps where and when I won't risk trouble?"

She wanted to say no. Voices from the fishing boat that came too close to getting stopped by a British frigate, and Dominick Cherrett just happening to be in the vicinity, compelled her to take the risk.

"If you like. I'm certain you'll know when I return."

"Thank you." He pressed a hand to his chest. "My heart rejoices enough to make my burdens of labor light."

"You're absurd." She smiled at him anyway and started walking toward the village.

"I'm not absurd." His voice rang with sincerity. "I'm just beginning to understand a thing or two about my father."

"Indeed?" She kept walking, guessing he would follow with her satchel.

He did, his long legs catching him up with her. "He made it through your war without so much as a cold in the head in the four years his regiment was stationed in the colonies. Spent most of his time in New York City in relative comfort and safety."

"How fortunate for him." Tabitha tried to sound disinterested, though she wasn't.

"It wasn't fortunate," Dominick said in a voice so quiet he might have been talking to himself. "It gave him time to fall in love with an American girl."

Tabitha snorted indelicately. "To believe you've fallen in love with me is more than I can swallow, Mr. Cherrett."

"Of course it is, but I see how easily it can happen."

"And having your loved one go away can happen just as easily." She tasted the bitterness of her words and tried to soften them as she paused at the trees. "Did he have an unhappy experience?"

"She refused him because he was English."

Tabitha faced him. "Then take heed of his heart wound and have a care you don't lose your heart to an American lady."

"Perhaps I already have." His smile flashed, bright and warm in the rising sun. Gold lights gleamed in his velvety eyes, all the more intense for the veil of lashes.

An alarm clanged in her head and she stiffened. "Then I pity you, Mr. Cherrett. I have no balm to heal that kind of hurt."

"We'll see about that, Madam Mermaid," he murmured.

Then he kissed her.

9

Raleigh Trower tugged so hard on his end of the net, the ropes parted and silvery fish slid onto the deck of the boat.

"Trower, you oaf," Rhys Evans bellowed. "There's half the catch to collect again and time's wasting."

"You can't rush fishing." Rhys's younger brother Lisle spoke in a gentler voice.

"This morning proves it." Rhys grabbed a bucket and began to scoop the catch into it. "If we'd stayed out an hour later like I wanted to, we wouldn't have encountered that British frigate at all."

"It all came out well in the end." Lisle joined his brother in gathering the fish. "Raleigh has a silver tongue in that head of his."

"Telling a pack of lies," Rhys grumbled.

"It wasn't lies." Raleigh began to gather up the edges of the seine, knotting ropes to repair the portion he'd broken.

"Right you are." Rhys guffawed. "Maybe we are a lot of half-wits, risking our skins against the English scum to get a night's catch."

"I never said we were half-wits." Raleigh frowned over the lines he knotted.

He wouldn't have lied. He was a sinner, breaking too many of God's commandments to feel truly forgiven and redeemed—despite what the ship's chaplain told him—but lying wasn't one of them. Or at least nothing as barefaced as that of which Rhys accused him.

"I just kept saying we're Americans," Raleigh reminded his companions.

"Like you didn't understand what he was yelling at us." Rhys wiped silvery scales onto his canvas breeches. "Which made you sound like a half-wit."

"And we just kept pretending like we was mute," Lisle added.

Raleigh grinned in spite of himself. "That poor lieutenant was getting frustrated, wasn't he?"

"Especially when the first lieutenant came along and told him to let us go," Rhys said.

Raleigh's grin faded at the knowledge that the officer had said to let them go because he knew Raleigh, knew he was free to be home.

For now.

"The other lieutenant sounded like some lordling," Raleigh explained. "There's a lot of them who don't approve of impressing Americans, just like they wouldn't fight against us in the last war."

"This isn't war," Lisle said. "Not if President Madison can stop them from taking our men."

"We can't fight the greatest Navy in the world." Raleigh looked out to sea to where he thought he caught the merest hint of the frigate's topsails against the bright horizon. "Or the most powerful country."

"Then let's stay out until after daybreak next time," Rhys admonished. "They seem more inclined to steal us in the dark, like the criminals they are."

"All right," Raleigh agreed. He had accomplished what he needed to and had seen Tabitha. He'd seen too much.

Raleigh dropped into the hold and began to work the net

free of the hatch hinge it had caught on. He let the brothers talk, Rhys venting his spleen on Raleigh to ease the tension of those moments beneath the prow of a man-of-war, Lisle soothing like one of Tabitha's healing balms.

Except what he'd glimpsed from the boat felt more like she'd rubbed salt or lye on an open wound. He saw his lady, his love, talking to another man.

He was a stranger. Or at least a stranger to Raleigh. A big man with hair longer than most men wore theirs nowadays and a confident way of holding his head. Raleigh heard laughter floating on the sea air, the man's deep and husky, Tabitha's light and young.

As she had laughed with him so many times before the lure of the sea tugged him away like the undercurrent of an ebbing tide during the full moon. Now she laughed with another man.

She had more than laughed with him. Though the distance was great enough that they had become little more than doll-sized at the edge of the village, Raleigh saw the man's head dip toward Tabitha's. Quickly. Briefly. Not so briefly he couldn't have kissed her in that time. And Tabitha made no move to shove the rogue away from her.

You pushed me away the first time I kissed you. Which made him think this wasn't the first time for these two. *No wonder she's been avoiding me.* Raleigh jerked the entangled ropes so fast, he slid on fish scales and landed hard enough on the deck to see stars—red, shooting stars from the burning heat of anger.

"Easy there," Lisle called down. "You're making a mess of things."

"What's got your back up?" Rhys kicked at the tangled net. "You're the one who wanted us to come in now so's we met up with that ship."

Raleigh sighed. "Never you mind me." As fast as a comet streaking across the heavens, the outrage passed. He couldn't blame Tabitha for seeking someone else. He'd left her without an explanation. She was so lovely, of course another man would court her.

Yet his mother said Tabitha remained unattached. Tabitha confirmed it. And the predawn rendezvous on the beach held a clandestine appearance that set the hairs rising along the back of Raleigh's neck.

The man must be unsuitable for Tabitha. Who in a village like Seabourne would be unacceptable to her?

Bracing himself on the bulkhead for support as he clambered to his feet, Raleigh determined to find out who the man was. Somehow he must keep him from Tabitha, or tear him from her if necessary. If she wouldn't fall in love with Raleigh again, nothing he had done, none of the steps he risked, would be worth the danger into which he'd placed himself to win his freedom from the British Navy.

He finished untangling the lines and gathered the edges of the net together for hauling on deck. It was a good catch. They would divide it into three equal parts and take some to the market and the rest home for preserving in brine. Once he would have taken a basket to the Eckleses. Now he wasn't welcome, maybe less welcome than he first thought.

His body tensed at the memory of that scene with Tabitha and another man, the man's head bent so low over Tabitha's his hair formed a curtain around their faces. Raleigh's stomach knotted like the hauling seine.

"Lord, this can't all be for nothing," he cried aloud once Rhys and Lisle went to their own cottage further up the shore. "I can't be risking all this for nothing."

Somehow he must succeed so he would be in a position to make up to Tabitha the hurt he had caused her. Somehow he must make himself worthy of God's love and forgiveness by undoing the damage to Tabitha's faith to which he had contributed. Somehow—

If she'd found interest in another man, Raleigh was too late.

He hauled home his catch in a two-wheeled handcart. Father greeted him at the cottage door, dressed and ready to take the bulk of the fish into town.

"Looks like a good night's work, son." Father smiled, deepening the lines around his eyes and mouth. "Good to have you home. I got some sleep for once."

"I'm glad I can do that for you, sir." Raleigh released the cart. "It was a good night's work."

"But a risky one." His father glanced at the swells of the sea sparkling in the sun. "We heard gunfire."

"Yes." Raleigh's mouth tightened. "The British were out, but they left us alone."

"Maybe that's a good sign. If they don't stop taking our men off our boats, there'll be war."

"That's what the Evans brothers were saying. President Madison would be a fool to get us into that. We couldn't possibly win."

"We'll see about that." A muscle in Father's jaw bulged. "I'd better get going. We'll go crabbing later today."

"I'd like that."

So many boyhood memories lay in crabbing with his father, learning about the different sorts of sea creatures and birds. More memories of Tabitha filled his head. He'd shown her how to fish, to crab, to handle a sail and tiller. He'd shown her living sea creatures, for her own father—a schoolmaster with weak lungs—possessed little energy to teach his daughter about the true sea, the one outside of books and a few withered specimens he'd collected in his younger days.

Raleigh's heart squeezed with sorrow for the girl of ten or so years he'd met as she wandered alone on the beach, while her father drowsed in the garden between lessons most of the time, and her mother and grandmother tended patients. She thought they'd notice how useful she could be too, if she brought home a basket of clams, but she was trying to dig at high tide and came close to drowning in waves taller than she.

Raleigh smiled. "I'll take a couple of baskets of these fish to Momma and the girls to preserve."

"You do that." Father nodded. "Never too early to start preparing for winter."

He departed for town with the cart, and Raleigh, a basket of shad in each hand, rounded the house to the kitchen garden.

The sight of his mother and sisters ready for him with knives and a barrel of salt gave him an idea he realized he should have thought of at once. Momma and the girls knew everything that went on in Seabourne.

"You had faith in my ability to still seine," he greeted the three ladies awaiting him on the back porch. "And rightly so."

"What is it?" Fanny asked.

"Shad."

She wrinkled her pert nose. "Ew. All those tiny bones."

"It's good eating." Momma grabbed the back fin of a fish. "Let's get to work, girls. What was that gunfire we heard, Raleigh?"

"A quarrelsome British frigate." Raleigh made his tone light. "But we pretended not to understand their accents, and they let us go."

"I'd say it was my prayers." Momma began to scale. "Can't have you getting taken up again when you're finally home, just because we were born in Acadia. Now go change out of those clothes in the barn. I've left fresh ones and water in there for you. And get yourself some breakfast. It's waiting on the hearth. Then get some sleep."

"I'd rather stay and help you all." Raleigh began to clean another shad. "I've missed you all so much, and sleeping just takes me away."

"But you look tired," Felicity pointed out. "I don't think you sleep more than four hours in a day."

"The training of the British Navy." Raleigh grimaced. "And it's a bit too quiet here after two years on a ship."

"I couldn't do it." Slowly, with obvious reluctance, Fanny began to strip heads, tails, and fins from the fish. "The noise. The smell. Nothing but water around you." She shuddered.

"But all those men." Felicity chopped off a fish head with unnecessary force. "There aren't any for us females here on land with the British Navy stealing them from us."

"We don't know the British are responsible," Raleigh pointed out.

"No, there's just a British ship around every time someone vanishes." Felicity smacked the shad into a barrel. "I'm two and twenty and don't even have an escort for the Midsummer Festival."

"The Midsummer Festival?" Raleigh's head shot up. "It's still going forward?"

"Of course it is," Fanny and Felicity chorused.

"Many a young couple gets themselves—" Momma stopped, her face stricken.

"Engaged there," Raleigh finished.

He and Tabitha had three years ago. He'd departed six months later.

"You should take Tabitha this year." Felicity spoke Raleigh's thoughts aloud. "Surely she'll have forgiven you by then."

"I hope so." Raleigh bent low over his work, suddenly nauseated from the odor of fish. "I understand she rarely goes to church nowadays."

"She prayed you'd come home," Momma confirmed. "We all did."

"But we didn't lose faith," Fanny added.

"Her mother died at the same time." Raleigh felt the need to defend Tabitha's absence from Christian fellowship. "But maybe my return will help bring her back."

"It's all in God's perfect plan," Fanny agreed. She gave her sister a pointed look. "Including finding us husbands. Either the men will get brought home, or new ones will come."

Raleigh set down his scaling knife. "That reminds me. Are you certain there are no new men in town? I thought I saw—" He hesitated. He didn't want to admit he'd seen Tabitha with a man on the beach. It could ruin her reputation, which would make her an ineligible wife for him, if he wanted to rise to more than just another fisherman in the community, someone worthy of Tabitha. "Someone," he finished lamely. "We don't get many strangers about."

The girls exchanged glances.

"I can't think of anyone," Momma said. "No one except for farmers and fishermen who find themselves here for market or even Tabitha's care."

"Except for Mr. Cherrett," Felicity murmured, her eyes half closed, her knife poised in midair.

A glance at Fanny told Raleigh she too was poised as though caught in a dream. Hairs along his arms rose as they had when he saw the man kiss Tabitha.

Raleigh jabbed his knife through the next shad. "Who is Mr. Cherrett?"

"No one appropriate," Momma snapped. "You girls shouldn't think about him."

"But he's so handsome," Felicity crooned.

"Those eyes," Fanny added in a similar tone of adulation.

"Handsome is as handsome does," Momma clipped out. "Only a terrible deed like gaming debts or worse would get an Englishman with his breeding trapped as a bondsman."

"A bondsman?" Raleigh set down his knife and put his hands on his hips. "An English bondsman of good breeding? You're certain?"

"I met a few English aristocrats in Halifax," Momma pointed out. "I know the accent when I hear it."

"He has a beautiful way of talking," Felicity fairly hummed. "So clear. So crisp."

"It's possible it's not his fault he's a redemptioner." Fanny gazed into the sun still hovering over the ocean. "Maybe his father lost the family money."

"And maybe you girls had best get back to work," Momma admonished. "We've bread to bake once this is done. You get to work too, Raleigh, if you aren't going to sleep. Why the interest in strangers?"

Raleigh shrugged and set to work again. "As I said, I thought I saw one. What does this Cherrett fellow look like?"

The twins sighed.

"You shouldn't have asked." Momma cast her daughters a half-annoyed, half-amused glance. "He's too good-looking for the peace of mind of any mother in Seabourne or mistress of a female servant. A few inches taller than you, but not as broad in the shoulders, and he wears his hair long. He's serving mainly as Mayor Kendall's butler, so he wears his hair powdered."

"He's so elegant," Felicity proclaimed.

"Like a cavalier out of a story," Fanny added.

The man's hair hadn't been powdered that morning, but Raleigh didn't doubt for a moment that the man he'd seen kissing Tabitha was the bondsman about whom his mother spoke and over whom his sisters were moonstruck. A bondsman strolling freely on the beach before the curfew for bondservants ended.

Raleigh began to smile.

10

"You are either very clever, my boy," Dominick addressed his reflection in the tiny scrap of mirror that had to serve him for shaving, "or you are the biggest fool who ever walked the earth."

He'd been acting like a fool for the past seven years, seeking his own ends regardless of who got hurt, since he only intended that person to be himself. But he couldn't help thinking that kissing Tabitha Eckles was not one of his less intelligent actions.

At least it didn't feel unintelligent an hour later, as he prepared for a day of standing about waiting for Kendall's guests to arrive, wasting time if the primitive tracks this blighted country called roads hindered their progress. Kissing lips as soft as the rose petals she smelled like could never be a mistake.

A thrill ran through him at the memory, and he drew the razor away from his throat before he slit it.

Shaving himself was one more thing he had to get used to. Until his disgraceful actions came to light in a scandal with the impact of a broadside from a seventy-four-gun ship of the line, Dominick had enjoyed the luxury of a valet who shaved him, kept him supplied with starched neck cloths, and cut his hair. He was getting used to doing these things for himself, except for the hair. That he left to nature.

And consequently Kendall's powder.

He grimaced at his reflection, knowing the dark locks would soon be pale from Letty's ministrations with the powder pounce. An hour ago, he'd used his hair to shield Tabitha from view of the three fishermen as he'd touched his lips to hers with no more pressure than a feather fallen from a white heron's wing.

The action left her speechless, not angry, as Dominick had feared. It left her dazed, judging from the way she didn't smack him, and the way she picked up her bag and headed for the village without a word, her cheeks as rosy as the sunrise, her eyes misty.

It left Dominick far more shaken than he expected.

Than he wanted.

Wooing her to encourage her to step onto his side was a matter meant for the good of many. Finding himself drawn to her more than he was ever drawn to any pretty female looked like danger to him.

"Though not as dangerous as that frigate." He scraped the last of the foaming soap from his throat and pressed a cloth steeped in warm water against his face and neck. "It shouldn't be this close in."

But he'd heard of ships sailing right into bays and up rivers to inspect American vessels and take men aboard. The fishing boat seemed to have gotten away, lucky fellows.

Too lucky.

Dominick removed the towel from his face and frowned at his reflection. "I don't like it one bit."

One week, three men disappeared, while a British naval vessel cruised off the coast. The next, three blithely sailed away from a frigate that had looked determined to stop them at all costs. The fickle Navy? One British captain scrupulously honest and another one not?

Dominick needed to learn the identity of the men aboard

that fishing boat. That should be a fairly easy task. He knew the location. Others would know whose jetty lay there. And Tabitha had been in the vicinity two weeks in a row.

He flung the towel into the basin and began to don his hateful uniform. Even though Tabitha Eckles had been on the beach this morning when the frigate fired and two weeks ago when three young men disappeared, that was not reason enough to think she could possibly be involved. She was a midwife. She traveled about at all hours of the day and night. And she hated the British.

Or claimed to.

Claimed too much dislike too openly?

"Now you are being a fool." Dominick stamped his foot into shoes that looked more suited to a ballroom than a seaside village mayor's house. But he liked the stockings Kendall provided for the visit. Instead of plain lisle cotton, they were silk—rather expensive accessories for a merchant and small plantation owner to provide for a mere servant, and a bondservant at that. Kendall's land and business must be prosperous.

Or he received money from a less legitimate source.

"You're suspecting everyone these days. And that's no way to find real answers."

He had less than three weeks to find those answers before the first scheduled rendezvous with his uncle's messenger. That could mean only sixteen more days as a servant. He must, must, must get answers, not mere suspicions if he wanted away from servitude and a return to a life of—what? He'd achieved his goal of escaping from the church. What came next didn't matter if he couldn't complete his mission.

Dominick tugged on his coat and ran down the two flights of steps to the kitchen. Halfway down the second stairwell, he smelled burned toast.

"Not again," he groaned.

He would have to start eating plain bread. That's all there was to it. Dinah and Deborah couldn't toast bread that was cut as thin as he liked it, regardless of how much they wished to impress him. But untoasted bread didn't work so well in his coddled egg.

Resigned to going hungry again, he pushed open the door into the kitchen.

"Deborah burned it this time," Dinah declared. "She was pretending you were dancing with her at the Midsummer Festival."

"Dinah, that wasn't nice to tattle," Letty scolded.

Dominick glanced at Deborah's scarlet face. He should either offer to dance with her at some festival or tell her why he was a redemptioner. The former would get her toes smashed enough to quell any romantic notions, and the latter would give her an outright disgust of him. Likely, it would give everyone such a disgust of him they'd send him inland to Kendall's plantation to pick whatever these colonists grew.

No, they weren't colonists *now*. Or was that *yet*?

"I don't dance." He bowed to Deborah. "Or I'd be honored to take a turn with you at this fete about which I know nothing and am probably not welcome."

"But you are," Deborah burst out. "We all are. The ticket money goes to a fund for widows of sailors and fishermen, so anyone with the admission price is admitted."

"A good cause. But how, pray tell," Dominick asked, "does a bondservant get money?"

"He takes on extra work that pays." Letty scooped an egg from a pot boiling over the hearth. "Three minutes and I'll make the toast."

"Deborah and I've been taking in sewing," Dinah explained. "We want new dresses."

"Alas, I have nothing I can do to earn my fee." Dominick feigned disappointment, but it was no jest. He would love the money to take Tabitha. Nothing like convivial company and moonlight to make a lady trust him.

So long as this lady didn't get called away to a birthing or a broken skull.

"You'll get tips this week if you do well." Letty slid pieces of thinly sliced bread onto a toasting fork. "Mayor Kendall's friends are as generous as he is."

"That's because they are paying us not to gossip." Dinah giggled.

"They talk politics, like this." Deborah whispered. "Like it's treason they're planning, but I never heard any sed— anything bad against the government."

"Sedition, I believe you mean." Dominick seated himself at the table and picked up a spoon to break the top of his egg. "Perhaps I'll manage the fete after all. When is it?"

"June 21," Letty said.

Dominick hit his egg too hard, shattering the shell and sending soft-boiled egg oozing across his plate. "My apologies." He snatched up a piece of bread and used it to mop up the runny egg.

The twenty-first day of June indeed. Surely, for this cause, he could gain permission to be out after curfew, which would make meeting his uncle's messenger that much easier. Especially if Dominick escorted a lady.

"Whom will you escort?" Both girls gazed at him with their big blue eyes.

"Neither of you." Letty slapped the toasted bread in front of Dominick. "He'll keep his affairs out of this household."

"I don't have . . . inappropriate relationships, Letty. Do please believe me."

Guilt twanged his innards. Kissing Tabitha was probably inappropriate. It was wrong, calculated, intrusive . . .

"You'd best get your hair ready." Letty broke into his musings. "I have to get dinner started. Can you carve a chicken with that hand bandaged?"

"I doubt I can carve one with my hand unbandaged." Dominick rose. "Let's get the powdering over with. I have . . . er . . . politicians to charm."

They arrived in plenty of time for Letty's dinner, three men from the state legislature and their wives. Between serving at the table, fetching and carrying for the male guests and, more often than not, the servants they had brought with them, Dominick found little time to think about Tabitha or even overhear snippets of conversation. With ladies present, the men didn't talk politics at the table. Afterward, when the ladies withdrew, they sent Dominick and the other servers out of the room and kept their voices so low that an ear to the dining room door allowed Dominick to catch only an occasional word.

He did catch the tone of the rumbling voices, though. Anger. Frustration. Hard determination to do . . . something. President Madison's name seeped through more than once. Whether or not they supported the new president, Dominick couldn't gather before Letty and the girls warned him of someone approaching the kitchen door.

"All right." Dominick heaved an exaggerated sigh. "I can't hear a thing anyway."

"What were you hoping to hear?" Letty gave him a speculative glance. "Secrets?"

"Sedition, of course. You know, extort my way to freedom." Flashing her a grin, he ducked into the butler's pantry, where a pile of newly washed silverware awaited his polishing cloth. One or two of the knives appeared in need of emery grit through the K carved into the handles. Grumbling, he removed the can of the polishing substance from a high shelf.

"Mr. Cherrett," Deborah—or perhaps it was Dinah—called. "You have a visitor."

Dominick's heart leaped. Perhaps it was Tabitha. She'd come to tell him her journey had been canceled and she wanted to give him a smack on the face for kissing her.

He was smiling when he entered the kitchen to find a stranger standing in the doorway. Sunlight behind him cast his face in shadow, but the breadth of his shoulders and bulging muscles of his arms spoke of a laborer or sailor. Nothing about him struck a chord of familiarity with Dominick. Judging from Letty's and the girls' faces, they found the stranger baffling too.

"May I help you?" Dominick asked in his best lord-of-the-manor accent.

"Are you Kendall's redemptioner?" the man demanded.

Dominick winced. Put neatly in his place by a laborer or sailor. Served him right for forgetting his lowly status and acting the arrogant lordling he most certainly had no right to be.

"I am." He inclined his head. "Did you need something from me?"

"Aye—yes." The man's hands balled into fists. "I'd like to speak with you alone."

Letty caught Dominick's eye. "The rooms in the house are all filled up with guests, but there's that bench in the garden."

Which was too far from the kitchen door for Dominick's comfort. He didn't like the looks of this man, and those clenched fists boded no good.

"If you're here because you've got a grudge against the English," Dominick drawled, "I'd rather not ruin my uniform by engaging in fisticuffs. Do please allow me to change. And be warned. You're likely to get powder in your eyes."

"It's words I want to exchange, not blows," the man said, "if you'll talk to me."

"Of . . . course." Dominick strolled toward the door, his steps slow, deliberate.

Ahead of him, the man turned on the heel of a thick-soled boot and marched to the center of the kitchen garden. A man of his brawn didn't fit in the center of strawberry bushes, but he didn't seem to notice. He set his hands on his hips and thrust out his jaw.

Now, in the sunlight, that jaw shone hard and firm beneath lean, bronzed cheeks and a thin mouth. Deep blue eyes met and held Dominick's gaze without so much as a blink of the stubby, dark lashes.

Dominick stopped a yard away. "Who are you?"

"The name's Raleigh Trower."

Dominick waited for more. The name meant nothing to him. The accent sounded too quick to belong to someone native to the region, and too lazy to be British. But that hint of an English accent set Dominick's senses on high alert.

"I'm a friend of Tabitha Eckles," Trower announced. "An old friend."

"I expect she has any number of friends." Dominick's bored tone hinted at none of the strain tensing every nerve in his body. His hands balled into fists, his left protesting around the cut.

"We were going to be married," Trower continued, "until you British stole me off my ship simply because my mother is from Canada."

Dominick stiffened his face to stop from reacting to this useful bit of information. Suspicious information, with Trower standing right in front of him, obviously a free man.

"Ah, the vanishing fiancé," he murmured.

Too late, he realized his error. Trower rose on the balls of his feet, and Dominick prepared to block a blow.

"So it was you." Trower didn't strike, but his arm quivered hard enough for Dominick to see how hard the man strove not to. "You were with Tabitha on the beach this morning."

Dominick realized now that his danger didn't lie in Trower's hamlike fists, it lay in his knowledge.

"I saw you kiss her." Trower took a step forward.

Dominick held his ground. Nothing to do but brazen this out. "Dear me. How crude of me to kiss a lady without ensuring we didn't have an audience. But it was quite ungentlemanly of you to watch."

"Quite ungentlemanly to watch? You talk to me about not being a gentleman, you—you—" Trower spluttered to a halt. A white line formed around his mouth, and he took a deep breath through his nose, a nose that appeared to have been broken and reset with a bit of a list to one side. "Mr. Cherrett, you are a redemptioner. You have no business even talking to Miss Eckles, let alone . . . touching her."

"Indeed." Dominick gave the man a little bow of acknowledgment. "Did she send you to defend her honor?"

"She didn't send me—that is . . ." Trower's gaze slipped away from Dominick's for the first time, and he flattened his palms against the legs of his breeches. "Tabitha has suffered enough in the past few years. She doesn't need a roué like you winning her affections and leaving her behind."

The softened tone, the sincerity in the other man's face, nearly undid Dominick's plans. He struggled to maintain his blasé demeanor.

"I'd say that decision is hers, Mr. Trower. Now, if that's

all you have to say, I must return to my duties." He started to turn away.

Trower shot out a hand and grasped Dominick's arm. "It's not all I have to say to you."

"Indeed." Dominick glared at the broad, calloused fingers gripping his forearm.

He'd never thought of himself as a spindly fellow. On the contrary, he could outrow, outride, outspar the best of his friends. But beneath that brawny hand, Dominick's arm felt like a sprat in the maw of a shark. In a fight, Dominick doubted he'd come out the winner. But he had words, and they made great weapons.

"Do tell me what you want before you ruin my coat," Dominick said on a sigh.

"If you stay away from Tabitha," Trower said, "I won't tell Mayor Kendall you were out during curfew."

"How generous of you." Dominick lifted his eyes to the other man's. "And if you don't tell Kendall I was out early this morning, I won't start asking questions about how a man born in Canada got released from the British Navy in less than two years. If," he added with a curl of his lips meant to only feign a smile, "the good citizens of this town aren't harboring a deserter."

11

Dominick had kissed her, the rogue, the blaggard, the unmitigated reprobate. Brief though it was, Tabitha still felt the pressure of his mouth against hers—warm and soft, though firm—four hours later, as Japheth, following the directions given in the summons, drew up before the Belotes' house on the outskirts of Norfolk. Instead of the raisins and walnuts she'd eaten to sustain her through the journey, she tasted the tannic edge of strong tea Dominick must have made himself before leaving the house. Instead of the smell of the Chesapeake Bay and spring flowers, she inhaled the heady aroma of sandalwood. His hair, long and loose, had fallen around her face like a silken curtain.

She'd walked away with her head whirling as though she'd been turned upside down and spun like a child's toy. Not until she got on the rough track of a road did she realize she should have broken her personal code, going against everything she had been taught and come to believe in herself, and slapped him. She should have left a mark so big and red he would have had a difficult time explaining it to Mayor Kendall. Let every finger mark show so his master would guess that his bondsman had been acting improperly.

And what about her? Surely she was no better than he. If she hadn't been gazing up at him as though every word he spoke were important, he wouldn't have seized the opportunity to take a liberty with her.

And all the while she sparred and flirted with Dominick Cherrett, her countrymen narrowly escaped capture by the British Navy. And she narrowly missed capture by a British adventurer.

"You're the one who thinks you can learn something from him."

She didn't realize she'd spoken aloud until Patience faced her. "Beg pardon, miss?"

"Thinking aloud." She glanced at the house. "It looks like no one's there, but pull around to the stable or barn, Japheth."

"Yes, miss." He turned the horse up a tree-lined lane leading from the road to the stable yard.

A youth, his hair the color of the straw stuck between his teeth, ambled out of the barn and took the horse's head. "Go-on-in." The directive came out as all one word around the makeshift toothpick. He flushed a bit and pulled it out. "I'll bring your bags in, miss, if your man can take care of the horse."

"I can do that." Japheth jumped down and held up his hands to assist Tabitha then Patience to the ground.

"I'll take my satchel." Tabitha hefted the bag and led the way along a flagstone path to a front door painted as green as the countryside. A knocker in the shape of a pineapple glowed against the wood. She lifted it and let it fall with a resounding bang.

A slight girl with dusky skin and a red turban opened the door so quickly Tabitha suspected she'd been standing with her hand on the latch.

"I'm the midwife," Tabitha announced. "Is anyone at home?"

"Yes'm." The girl giggled. "Where would they be going with Miss Sally as big as—"

"Abigail, let them in," a strident voice called from another room. "You know better than to chat with the guests."

"Yes'm." The girl bobbed a curtsy and spun on her bare heel. She led the way through an airy hall from which the stairway rose and into a dimly lit parlor. "The midwife, Miz Belote."

"Very good." The speaker rose to an impressive height and held out her hand. "So good of you to come all this way."

"I go where I'm needed." Tabitha held out her hand to grasp Mrs. Belote's. She saw a streak of grime across the back of it and returned it to her side. "My apologies, ma'am. Travel is so dirty. Perhaps my companion and I could wash first?"

"Of course." Mrs. Belote raised her voice. "Abigail, come show Miss Eckles and her companion to their room and serve her some refreshment."

"Yes'm." The maid reappeared. "Do I set her a place in the dining room with you?"

"Serve them supper in her room, or the kitchen if they prefer," Mrs. Belote responded.

Tabitha's ears grew hot beneath her hat. She'd been snubbed often. A midwife didn't rank even as high as a governess to many people, but never so bluntly, and not usually in Seabourne. After all, she'd had breakfast with the mayor. Not as company, but he had invited her to sit and join him.

Where she should have told him about his recalcitrant bondsman.

Thoughts of Dominick with his incorrigible spirit lent Tabitha the audacity to stand up to this bossy, arrogant woman. After all, if her daughter was as close to her time as the woman believed, she wasn't about to send Tabitha away or refuse to pay her for her services. She wanted a midwife from twenty miles' distance for a reason.

"Before I eat," Tabitha said in a cool manner, "I would

prefer to meet my patient. Does she live with you, or do she and her husband have a separate house?"

Mrs. Belote's entire face turned a color of crimson that clashed with her rather carroty hair. Her mouth opened and closed several times before she managed to speak in a hoarse, halting voice. "My daughter . . . has no . . . husband."

"I beg your pardon." Tabitha bowed her head. She should have guessed that was the reason for sending for a midwife from far away. They didn't want someone local who would talk.

"We have a number of ways you and your maid can occupy yourselves before Sally's time comes." Mrs. Belote gestured toward the windows shrouded in heavy, dark draperies. "We have outdoor servants, but perhaps you know more about gardening than they seem to."

Tabitha exchanged a half-irritated, half-amused glance with Patience. "Quite a bit, ma'am."

She understood clearly that she was to make herself useful, rather than amuse herself, sit about resting, and eat their food for nothing.

If Tabitha prayed anymore, she would have asked the Lord to set the unknown—and unmarried—Miss Sally Belote into labor sooner rather than later.

If Tabitha had prayed that prayer, she would have been disappointed in the lack of an immediate response. Which was why she didn't vex herself with praying and expecting answers. God simply didn't listen to her.

Nor did any of the Belotes. Tabitha discovered that she was supposed to remain invisible to the family, including the patient she was intended to deliver of a healthy infant—presumably. The girl seemed to be confined to her bedchamber. Mr. Belote owned several coastal trading crafts and spent most of his time cruising from New York to Baltimore to Norfolk. He was home, but Tabitha caught only glimpses of a slight, quiet man with a pinched face that should have been darkened by the sun if he were a typical man of the sea, but which appeared pale. Tabitha suspected he was ill, but she couldn't treat him if he didn't request it. Perhaps he used the services of a man in town for himself but not his disgraced daughter.

So, while Tabitha fretted at being away from home for so long, leaving her patients without a medical person close, and while no doubt her own plants grew weedy, she and Patience worked in the kitchen garden, weeding and harvesting herbs and vegetables. They earned remarks of gratitude from Abigail, the maid of all work, and her mother, Cookie, a chubby, cheerful woman who looked too young to have a daughter of at least sixteen. The women made better companions for meals than Tabitha suspected the Belotes would have.

Two days into their stay, Tabitha spotted Reverend Downing strolling along the beach, his head bowed and his hands clasped behind his back. Despite grass stains around the hem of her plain gray gown, she straightened her straw hat atop her coiled hair and headed in a path that would intersect the pastor's out of sight of the house.

He glanced up at her approach, noisy through the tall sea grass, and smiled. "How good to see you, Tabitha. I arrived a bit ago and am sorry you're being treated like . . ."

"One of the slaves?" She shrugged. "Abigail and Cookie are lovely women, and Patience is more my friend than my paid servant. I don't in the least mind remaining in their company." She fell into step beside the pastor. "But I'd like to see my patient, examine her to see if she truly is ready to deliver."

"She is." Downing looked out to sea, his face a bit flushed above his stiff collar. "She knows exactly when . . . er . . . it must have occurred, and her mother has calculated from there based on her own experience."

"Then she's probably right. Still . . ." Realizing Downing wasn't comfortable discussing a female condition with a young woman, she turned to less physical aspects of the situation. "So they sent for you from afar, as they sent for me?"

"They're trying to preserve the family honor and hers." Downing scowled. "I suspect more for the Belote shipping interests than . . . Well, I suppose I shouldn't speculate on that score."

Her own conclusions running along the same lines, Tabitha let the matter drop. "Are they keeping Miss Belote confined?" she asked instead. "Or is she remaining secluded voluntarily?"

"I'm afraid they're keeping her confined." Downing's jaw hardened. "Mrs. Belote says they will until she tells them who the father is."

"They don't know?" Tabitha's heart sank. "Sir, you know I have to find out before I can assist with the delivery."

"Yes, I know. I've explained this to Mrs. Belote and to Sally." He stopped and faced her. "And have been praying."

Tabitha said nothing. She kept her face blank.

"You think that's useless," he said.

"Maybe not for you, sir. For me . . ." She shrugged. "God abandoned me a long time ago."

"God never abandons us, Tabitha." Downing's voice held a note of sorrow. "But we too easily abandon Him."

"I didn't." She allowed an edge to sharpen her tone. "I prayed every day for six months for Raleigh to come home. I prayed every day and night and in between for my mother to live."

So she wouldn't have to feel the guilt of her own responsibility for her mother's illness.

"I prayed for Grandmomma to be relieved of her pain," she continued ruthlessly. "And she died."

"Where she is free from her pain." Downing gave her a gentle smile. "And Raleigh came home."

"And my mother is dead." Tabitha's throat closed. "I had to work instead of getting married like every other girl my age."

"But you were experienced enough to take care of Seabourne when the apothecary died so unexpectedly last year."

"So I get to tend the hands of impudent bondsmen and deliver other women's babies while being treated like a redemptioner myself."

"And what would have happened had Raleigh gotten his desire to wander after you married? And he's back now, just as you prayed for, and from what he says so openly that I'm not breaking a confidence, he's had more than enough of the sea except for fishing."

"But I can't trust him now." Tabitha turned on her heel and began to stride toward the house.

Downing easily fell into step beside her. "Can you trust any suitor not to leave you?"

"Probably not."

Which was why she needed to stop waking in the middle of the night with the memory of Dominick's kiss in her head. On her lips. If any man would leave her, he would. She was nothing more than a diversion, an excuse to be where he shouldn't be. In four years, he would sail back to England.

"Then how do you expect to have the husband and children you want?" Downing cast her a warm smile. "If you can't trust God, you can't trust anyone, and if you can't trust anyone, you can't enjoy their love."

"I trusted God once upon a time."

"Good. Then you can trust Him again."

"I . . . doubt it."

They reached the front door and Tabitha bade good day to the pastor. She wouldn't go in by the door used for guests again.

Later that night, while trying to sleep and not see Dominick's velvety brown eyes every time she closed her lids, she pondered her conversation with the pastor. Perhaps matters were reversed. If she could, for example, trust Raleigh again, she could renew her childhood relationship with the Lord. The best way to trust Raleigh again was to spend more time with him. Of course, that could make it awkward to spend time with Dominick to find out what he was up to, if it was indeed no good for America.

She would have a bit of extra time on her hands. Summer didn't see the birth of as many babies. Too many men were gone oystering on the Chesapeake or fishing in the autumn. Spring and autumn proved her busy time due to long winter nights and summer weddings. She could manage two suitors, if suitors they were.

An unexpected thought crept into her head right before she finally slept—maybe this year she would go to the Midsummer Festival.

A wholly inhuman shriek woke her. Her feet hit the floor and she had her dress half over her head before her eyes opened. She knew that kind of cry.

Sally Belote was in labor.

Unless she was a complete coward or in a weakened condition, she was well along in labor.

Tabitha took the steps two at a time and followed the

cries to the girl's chamber. For once, the door stood open. Cookie, Abigail, and Mrs. Belote circled the bed, the first two looking like they were praying, the latter wringing her hands.

Golden-blonde hair soaked with perspiration and blue eyes dull, Sally writhed on the bed.

"Why didn't someone call me sooner?" Tabitha demanded.

"You weren't needed." Mrs. Belote turned on Tabitha. "How dare you question my actions?"

"It's my responsibility to do so." Tabitha approached the bed. "Everyone out of here. I need hot water and strong soap and all the cloths you've prepared for the baby."

No one moved.

"Now." Gently she nudged Abigail away from the bedside and clasped Sally's hand. "I'm the midwife. I'm here to help you, but you're going to have to help yourself too."

"I can't do this." Sally's fingers squeezed Tabitha's hard enough to crunch them together.

Ignoring the pain she'd felt more than once in her career, she smoothed damp hair from the girl's brow. "I'm afraid you'll have to, child. You got yourself into this fix, and now you're the only one who can get yourself out of it."

"You shouldn't talk to her that way," Mrs. Belote protested. "She's frightened."

"Of course she is." Tabitha gave the mother a hard stare. "I didn't have time to prepare her or examine her to ensure things were going well. Now leave the room so I can do so."

"You'll bully her." Though her tone was harsh, her chin quivered.

So the mother was scared too.

Tabitha softened her tone. "Ma'am, I have to find out who the father is. It's required of me. But I promise to go about it as gently as possible. Now, if you please, get the things I need."

"Don't just stand there," Mrs. Belote snapped, turning her anxiety on the servants, "do what Miss Eckles ordered."

The maid and cook fled.

"Now you, Momma," Tabitha said with a smile.

"But . . . my baby."

"Will be in good hands, Mrs. Belote," Reverend Downing said from the doorway. "Tabitha has delivered more babies than you've probably seen in your lifetime."

"And the last one di—" Mrs. Belote slapped her hand over her mouth.

Tabitha felt sick. Even this far away Wilkins had managed to malign her skill.

"Sally will be—" A shriek from the girl drowned out Downing's words.

Hands to her ears, Mrs. Belote charged for the door. From the color of her face—a pea green—she looked as though she might be better off keeping her hands over her mouth to hold in the sickness.

Downing slipped out behind the mother and closed the door.

"Whew." Tabitha heaved a sigh of relief and gave her patient her full attention. "As soon as they bring me hot water so I can wash my hands, I'll give you a thorough examination. That means I'm going to . . ." She proceeded to explain exactly what she was going to do to see what was going on with Sally and the baby. Some of her explanations had the girl staring bug-eyed and gasping instead of screaming as her womb contracted.

"That's . . . that's . . . indecent," she croaked.

"Not at all." Tabitha tried to keep her tone light. "I'm specially trained. Women in my family have been midwives for generations." Tabitha frowned. Labor was intense, but this looked worse than usual. She feared a breech. If she couldn't turn a breech, few babies and nearly as few mothers survived.

But you're good at turning babies, she reminded herself.

She began to manipulate Sally's belly through the sheet since she hadn't yet washed her hands, a stricture passed down through the generations of Eckles women. From what she could feel externally, all was not well.

"Sally," Tabitha asked, "when did your pains start?"

"In the morning. Right after breakfast. It made me sick."

Tabitha glanced at the clock on the mantel. Nearly twenty-four hours ago, and no one had thought to tell the midwife.

Please, God, don't let anything go wrong because—

Realizing she was praying, she stopped and, her hands on Sally's belly, looked her patient in the eye. "Who is the father, Sally?"

Sally closed her eyes.

"You have to tell me."

"No." Sally's abdomen contracted, and the girl cried out. "Help me."

"I can't until you tell me who the father is."

The girl called her a rather rude name.

Tabitha set her jaw. She'd been called worse by laboring mothers and husbands alike.

"Who is—"

Cookie slipped in with a copper can, steam rising from the top. Abigail followed, her arms loaded with clean cloths.

"I'm to stay and help," Cookie said. "Abigail be too young to watch."

"Go away," Sally bellowed.

"Do you want me to stay, Miss Eckles?" Cookie asked Tabitha.

"Please. I need help washing my hands."

Abigail deposited the cloths on a chair near the bed, and Cookie hefted the copper can over the washbasin.

"Wait." Tabitha left Sally's side. "Pour it over my hands."

Cookie did so. After repeating the process, Tabitha returned to the bed and the wailing girl.

"I'm going to examine you now." Tabitha lifted the sheet.

Sally snatched it from her. "No."

"Cookie, will you take her hands, please?"

While Cookie kept the girl from hindering Tabitha, she made a thorough examination, then straightened to look Sally in the eye between contractions.

"The baby is breech. You have to tell me who the father is, or I can't turn the baby and help you."

"He'll die," Sally sobbed.

Not sure if she meant the baby or the father, Tabitha said, "Then you'll be responsible."

The names Sally applied to Tabitha had Cookie's eyes widening to twice their normal size.

"You hush that," Cookie scolded. "Where'd a nice girl like you learn such talk?"

"Or end up like this," Tabitha murmured. She watched as another contraction brought more blood than she liked. "Tell me now, Sally."

"All right, all right!" Sally screamed.

12

"Today's reading is from the eighteenth chapter of Matthew." The sonorous quality of the pastor's voice reached the servants' gallery without apparent effort. "'Then came Peter to him, and said, Lord, how oft shall my brother sin against me, and I forgive him?'"

Dominick squirmed on the hard, backless bench. He knew that chapter. One of his Oxford tutors had reminded him of it as Dominick began his campaign. But Dominick, like the forgiven servant, had gone out and forced payment from those who owed him—in a manner of speaking.

Others got hurt because of his hardened heart. No doubt they suffered torment too, possibly worse than his, all because he couldn't forgive one time, let alone seven or seventy, and claimed his actions were for the good.

How did a man pay a debt when he was locked away? Dominick always wondered how, when someone he knew ended up in debtor's prison. If he couldn't work, if he couldn't oversee his property or investments, he couldn't earn the money necessary to discharge his debts.

Most of Dominick's debts weren't monetary. On the contrary, at the moment he felt more comfortably off than he had since the day his father threw him off of the family estate, broken, bloody, near to penniless. Kendall's guests proved to be generous with their vales, and he now possessed the equivalent of two pounds, more than enough to go to the fete with Tabitha.

Not enough to discharge his debt to the society of his homeland, to his family, or now to Kendall. What he needed was information, and when those same generous guests had taken up so much of Dominick's time without divulging a snippet of good information in front of him, he'd gained nothing.

If only he could contact his uncle before June 21. He would admit failure and go to Barbados. At least he would have freedom of a sort there, could come and go as he pleased, could be a guest at the table instead of serving.

Although it might increase his family's wealth, however, going to Barbados would never redeem him. For that, he must, must, must suffer torment and come out the victor, all debts paid.

He rubbed his palm where the stitches itched. If Tabitha didn't return soon, he would have Letty remove them, though he'd much prefer Tabitha's feathery touch against his skin.

Next to him, Letty gave him a poke in the ribs with her elbow, reminding him not to fidget like a schoolboy.

Clamping his hands between his knees, he scanned the congregation. The Trower fellow sat halfway back amidst three females and a man who looked enough like Trower that he must be his father. The women were likely his mother and sisters, again bearing a family resemblance, all tall and stately and pretty. Trower appeared intent upon the sermon. The girls looked disinterested.

Trower. True believer or hypocrite? He'd been ready to fight Dominick for Tabitha. Not very Christian behavior, but he had restrained himself, which was. But the extortion, the threat, set Dominick's hackles rising. If he hadn't been suspicious of Trower's release from the Navy, Dominick would not have had a chance to win in a battle of words.

Those suspicions still teased his mind. The British Navy

wasn't in the habit of releasing men once they felt they had a good enough reason to keep them. Raleigh Trower's mother being a Canadian, Raleigh being born in Canada—regardless of the citizenship of his father—was enough cause for the British Navy to hold a man until he died in battle, was maimed too badly to be of use aboard ship, or grew too old and feeble. Unless, of course, his ship had been paid off. Not likely with the war going far too strongly and the British not doing well since their defeat in Spain in January. Even the citizenship of Trower's father could be made suspect by the British. The man had been born in America before their revolution.

The way Trower had backed down from their contretemps convinced Dominick that Trower had deserted.

Most Americans wouldn't care. In fact, most would consider him a hero for defying the enemy, for depriving them of one more man. That didn't concern Dominick. That Trower had gotten away from another British frigate last Tuesday morning made Dominick wonder, speculate, suspect.

He needed to get word to his uncle before the twenty-first of June. That was all there was to it. He needed to ask him if he could learn something about Trower. Doing so could take weeks, even months, so the sooner the better. If Dominick could get a message to one of the frigates or schooners cruising around the American coastline, they could contact his uncle.

The risk would be great. The captain might not believe his story of who he was and might take him aboard as an able-bodied seaman.

Feeling as though he were about to suffocate in the tight, airless confines of the gallery, Dominick ran a finger around the inside of his collar.

Letty grasped his arm as they rose for the final hymn. "You are the worst congregant in history. If you were a child, I'd send you to your room with bread and water after a thrashing in the stable yard."

"It wouldn't be the first time, m'dear," Dominick responded.

The skin on his back crawled. At that moment, his room with bread and water sounded like as much as his belly could take in.

"This balcony is worse than the hold of a ship," he added. "Let me out of here before I do something womanish and swoon."

He spoke louder than he intended. Although the service had ended and the congregation began engaging in conversations, several of the females in his vicinity must have heard him, for they gave him indignant glances.

"Servants don't have time to swoon." Deborah stuck her pert nose in the air. "That's for arrogant English aristocrats."

"Weak ones, more like," Dinah added.

"Who says I'm an aristocrat?" Dominick feigned annoyance. "It seems an unkind retort to my unintentional insult to you ladies."

The girls giggled along with several other servants waiting for their betters to leave the church so they too could file out.

"Senator Lee says you talk like one," Deborah said. "I heard him asking Mayor Kendall how you managed to get yourself stranded here."

"And what did the mayor answer?" Dominick's tone held as much ice as the chill crawling down his spine.

"He said you probably gambled away your inheritance or were running away from a female," Deborah said.

Dominick laughed, relaxing. "Would that I'd enjoyed myself that much. And now we may depart from this oven.

Letty, have you considered bringing your bread rolls up here to bake during the service?"

"Dominick Cherrett," Letty scolded, "you are the most irreverent man who ever lived."

"I've heard that before too. Now, may we leave? I can scarcely breathe."

They filed out of the gallery and down the narrow staircase. Outside, again they had to wait to leave until their betters departed, while congregants milled about the yard, talking and laughing and greeting one another as though they hadn't met for a year. Light breezes off the ocean lifted frills on the hems of the ladies' gowns and fluttered the ribbons on their hats, catching the eye and creating a flower garden of temptation. Like bees drawn to those flowers, the men, young and old, swarmed around the females, and a number of them left the churchyard in pairs.

Dominick rolled his eyes. "Church as Almack's."

"Where?" Letty asked.

"A private club in London whose primary purpose is to make matches. A sort of marriage market."

"I can't believe you failed there," Dinah said from his other side.

"Failed to get a wife there?" Dominick laughed. "My dear girl, I failed to get accepted into such august halls of society. By the time I might have been interested—" He broke off.

Across the church yard, Mrs. Phoebe Lee was looking at him. A man several years her senior stepped between her and Dominick. Though the man's back was to them, Dominick recognized Harlan Wilkins.

"Looking for his next wife?" His tone dripped contempt.

"With Mrs. Downing's approval." Deborah grimaced. "His

wife not in her grave three weeks and he's escorting that young woman home."

One of Wilkins's brawny arms went out. Mrs. Lee grasped it in her tiny, white-gloved fingers, and they headed for the parsonage.

"The poor girl," Dominick murmured.

"Poor?" The other servants stared at him.

"I hear tell she's quite wealthy," Deborah said.

"I don't like him." Dominick gazed after the retreating pair and the rest of the Downing family. "He's trying to make trouble for Miss Eckles."

"That's mean-spirited," Deborah declared.

"We shouldn't talk about our betters like this," Letty admonished them.

"Harlan Wilkins is hardly my—" Dominick made himself shut up. Right now, everyone there considered a merchant superior to a mere redemptioner.

Dominick's good suit of clothes chafed as though made of the cheapest of wools. He wished to tear off the coat at the least and dive into the cold waters of the Atlantic—dive deep and swim far.

He trudged back to Kendall's house, his heels kicking up puffs of sandy soil in the rising heat of mid-June. Kendall and his guests were dining at the home of some local landowner, so Dominick was free the rest of the day, Letty informed him after their dinner. He could go where he liked.

"But see you're in at sundown," she reminded him.

"Yes, ma'am."

He changed his clothes for the casual garb of a country gentleman, laughable under the circumstances. But the Hessian boots and buckskin breeches gave him far more freedom of movement than his servants' garb, and he needed the ability to stride along the dunes until he reached a certain cove. His uncle wouldn't be there for nearly two weeks, but perhaps he would have the foresight to send a boat in the event a message lay in their agreed-upon place.

Standing at the edge of the cove not much bigger than a village pond and nearly as still at low tide, Dominick doubted his uncle would take the risk of sending one or more of his men ashore. Even trusted men might be tempted to fly. If they didn't succumb to temptation, they might be caught. A house lay on the other side of the nearest dune. Its occupants could too easily walk in this direction for fishing or viewing the sunrise, though it was in the opposite direction of the village. If more dwellings spread along the coast, the occupants might have business that could bring them—her—in the cove's direction.

No one stirred on the hot Sunday afternoon. Even the sea merely rippled and swirled on the surface with wavelets no bigger than what a cat's paw would produce as it speared a fish.

Certain of not being observed, Dominick pulled the note from his pocket. Oiled paper protected it from the elements to some extent. Unless the tide rose unusually high, a pile of rocks like a cairn would provide the rest of the protection and keep the message from flying away. Without much hope of anyone finding the message before June 21, Dominick slipped the note inside the pile of rocks. It said little, but that little could alert the wrong party of interference close at hand, for Dominick needed to use a name to begin the process of gleaning information.

"And if I'm not too much of a sinner for you to listen to me, God," Dominick said aloud, "don't let the information about Trower take the months it could to get to England and back."

He held out little hope that God heard him. He was too

busy taking care of the good people in the world, like Dominick's second-eldest brother with the Army, or the eldest one, the heir, helping their father run the family estates. They were good men, devout in their worship of God, strong in their faith.

Dominick didn't think he would have been suited for the Army either. He feared he was doing a poor job of spying. At least he had done something by asking for information on Raleigh Trower's release from the Navy.

Still tempted to dive into the inviting coolness of the water, Dominick turned away and headed back toward the village. If he got home before sundown, no one would suspect a thing about him taking a long walk on a Sunday afternoon. He hadn't seen another soul since leaving the paved streets of Seabourne.

But he saw someone now. She stood at the edge of the water, wavelets teasing her bare toes and threatening to soak the hem of a faded blue gown. Tied back with an equally faded blue ribbon, her auburn tresses hung in wildly curling abandon to her waist.

Dominick swallowed the groan that rose in his throat. His fingers ached to reach out and bury themselves in her hair, gather it to his nose to see if it smelled like lavender and roses, rub it against his cheeks to feel its silken texture, press it to his lips . . .

"A mermaid indeed," he said in a voice no louder than the muttering surf.

She cried out and jumped as though he'd shouted in her ear. One of her feet slipped in the loose sand at the water's edge, and she flailed her arms for balance.

Dominick leaped forward and grasped her around the waist. He drew her to more solid ground.

"I am sorry." He continued to hold her, noting even through

the stays she wore beneath her gown that she trembled. "I didn't mean to frighten you."

"No, you simply make a habit of sneaking up on unsuspecting females." Her voice and the breath that followed quivered too. "Now, if you please, release me."

"I'll release you." He did so. "Even though doing so does not please me."

"Mr. Cherrett." She sighed again and turned to face him.

He caught his breath.

Her eyes looked like someone had struck them, so dark were the bruises of fatigue around them. Their clear blue-gray now resembled a misty morning, and the whites shone with red veins. Her creamy skin held no hint of color, and her wide cheekbones stood out above hollowed cheeks.

"What's wrong?" Dominick pressed the back of his hand to her brow. "Are you ill?"

"No." She took a step away from him. "Thank you for asking. My health is good."

"If you don't object to me saying so, Madam Midwife, your health looks anything but good." He'd felt no fever, but all was not right. "Tabitha—"

"I haven't given you permission to use my Christian name." The words should have been snapped, especially when she interrupted him to utter them, but her tone remained quiet, neutral.

Dominick smiled and touched a forefinger to her lips. "You did when you didn't smack my face for kissing you." He half expected her to do so now and be done with it.

A delicate pink tinged her pale skin and she dropped her lashes over her eyes. "I have never struck anyone in my life, Mr. Cherrett. Even if you deserved it, I am a healer, not a person who harms others for my own satisfaction."

"Then I can kiss you with impunity." Dominick grinned at her.

Her lips compressed. "I don't recommend you do so."

"Not even after I take you to the fete?" He hadn't meant to invite her now, but no time like the present one. "You will go with me, will you not?"

"The fete?" She looked vague. "Oh, you mean the Midsummer Festival?"

"I do indeed."

He gave her a hopeful smile.

She said nothing, simply gazed out to sea.

"Or am I too presumptive in asking you, being a bondsman and all."

"No, I'm not much more than a servant myself, but . . ." She bowed her head and rubbed her temples. Her hair cascaded around her face like a curtain, but not so much that he couldn't see her switch from massaging her temples to massaging her eyes.

"Tab—Miss Eckles?" Dominick brushed her hair back, finding it every bit as soft as he'd anticipated. Above the aromas of salt water and seaweed, he caught a hint of rose petals. His toes curled inside his boots.

He swallowed. "Let me walk you home. You can claim you're well, but you don't look it."

"I'm not ill," she insisted, then lowered her hands and offered him a half smile. "I would just do well with a good night's sleep."

"Was your journey difficult?" He took both her hands in his and began to chafe them as though the day were cold instead of sultry.

"No, we returned last night, but I haven't slept since Sal—" She bit her lip. "I must be tired if I was about to tell you something about my patient."

"Then let me escort you home. Even mermaids need rest."

"If I can sleep."

"Were things difficult?" Remembering Wilkins and his threats, he felt his heart skip a beat. "The baby didn't . . . die, did it?"

"No, it's a healthy boy. But there were circumstances . . ." She drew her hands free. "I should be going. It's time for supper."

"I'll still escort you."

She didn't object, simply headed up the beach. He fell into step beside her, watching the way her toes flexed and extended in the soft sand above the tide line, the way her skirt swirled around her ankles. He wanted to ask her if she'd forgotten her shoes but feared he would embarrass her.

"Can you tell me anything about your journey?" he asked instead of inquiring about her lack of shoes.

"I prefer the seaward side of the eastern shore to the bay side. But then I've grown up near the Atlantic, so maybe I'm simply used to it." She glanced up at him. "Did you grow up near the sea?"

"The English Channel. I never saw the Atlantic until my fortunes"—he laughed—"or should I say, my misfortunes, brought me here."

"Never saw the Atlantic." She shook her head, sending her hair flying in a quickening wind. "Did you never leave your village?"

"Often. I went to the east and north and not the west. London, Ox—"

"Oxford. You can say it, Mr. Cherrett. I know what it is. My father was a schoolmaster educated at Princeton because William and Mary had lost its charter during the revolution. He could have taught anywhere, but ill health brought him back here to the seaside, where he met my moth-ther."

With her hair flying about, Dominick couldn't see for certain, but he thought a tear glistened on her cheek. He hadn't mistaken the hitch in her voice on the word *mother*.

"Tabitha—Miss Eckles—dash it all, I'm not calling you Miss Eckles when you don't slap my face for kissing you and you are trotting alongside me in bare toes with your hair down like an urchin."

She stopped, glanced at him with red-rimmed eyes definitely glazed with tears, and emitted a throaty laugh. "All right, Mr. Cherrett—"

"Call me Dominick."

"I can't. You don't have bare toes."

"But I do have my hair down."

They shared eye contact and a smile that felt far more intimate than that brief kiss. His innards turned the consistency of syllabub cream.

"I miss my mother too," he said gently. "She died when I was ten." And was spared the shame he brought onto the family.

"I was twenty-two. She was a skilled midwife and healer, but she couldn't stop herself from contracting the patient's fever." Her voice broke.

"I'm sorry."

"Not as sorry as I am. I should have gone to that lying-in instead of her. She was so tired from working . . . and I no longer have her counsel when I need it—like now."

"Because of what happened on your journey?" Dominick laced his fingers through hers and headed in the direction she'd been going. "You need a colleague to talk to."

Raw pain crossed her face. "I had one, before my mother then my grandmother died. The midwife in Norfolk is too far away and not highly respected."

"You could always take on an assistant."

"I will when I have a daughter. Until then . . ." She sighed. "We are sworn to uphold the sanctity of secrets divulged to us when a woman is in her lying-in, except for one circumstance."

"What is that?"

"If the name of the child's father is in question."

Dominick took a moment to understand her meaning. "Because she's unwed."

"Yes."

"And you have a patient who told you who the father of her child is."

"Yes."

"But you can't tell me?" he pressed.

"If things go badly with me before the council tomorrow, I can't tell anyone."

"You're going before the council?"

"Wilkins's doing." She grimaced. "My qualifications have been called into question after all these years."

"And you're losing sleep over it." Dominick slowed their pace. He saw the house now, a neat white cottage with a walled garden to protect the plants from the sea. The trees cast shade over house and wall, looking cool and inviting, but he didn't want to reach the gate. Even if she invited him into her home, her servants sat behind those walls, and he wanted Tabitha to himself for a few more minutes.

Tabitha didn't slow with him. "Come inside. I'll remove those stitches."

"Wait." He stopped, still holding her hand.

"I don't wish to discuss it further." She faced him. "I've already said more than I should."

She'd certainly said enough for him to work things out and know her very real danger.

"I don't want to discuss your patient." He smiled and

brushed a lock of hair from her brow. "I want you to say yes to accompanying me to the fete."

"I don't go to the festival anymore." She avoided his eyes. "It holds . . . memories."

"Of Raleigh Trower?"

"What do you know of Raleigh?"

"Know of him?" Dominick chuckled. "We've met. But I'll let him discuss that encounter. Far be it from me to be a tale bearer. But don't let it be far from me to have you come with me, if it won't be a disgrace for you to be seen with a redemptioner."

She released his hand and folded her arms across her chest. "I suppose I don't need to ask if you have the price of the tickets."

He straightened his shoulders. "Of course you needn't ask. I do and then some."

"Will you go if I do not accompany you?"

He studied her face for a moment, trying to judge how he should answer. Certain he caught a twinkle in one bloodshot eye, he said, "No, I couldn't."

"All right then. I'll go with you." Answer given, she turned on one bare heel and marched toward her gate.

He followed. "What changed your mind?"

"The idea of an Englishman contributing to the welfare of American sailors." She laughed, a sparkling fall of notes in the still afternoon.

Dominick laughed too. If she only knew.

13

Tabitha wished she had bitten her tongue rather than make such an outburst in front of Dominick. At the present, spouting her distrust of God's motives for her life was not a wise action, especially to the man who worked for the mayor, who was bonded to the mayor.

"Remember that bit of it," she muttered to herself as she wiped a few bread crumbs off of the kitchen table and spread a clean towel over it. "His loyalty lies with the mayor."

Or England.

At that moment, his loyalty to the mayor concerned her more than his loyalty to England. She must remember not to trust him, that he wasn't a friend, however much she must pretend to like him.

She wished she pretended to like him. She'd wanted to burrow into the sand like a crab when she heard his voice behind her on the beach. He'd seen her with her hair down and her toes bare like some slovenly maidservant.

Yet his eyes had expressed admiration, then concern.

That concern had nearly undone her. Only years of her mother's training had stopped her from resting her head on his shoulder and weeping from fatigue and fear and frustration.

He was just another one of God's cruel jokes upon her life—a man she could let herself care about, if he weren't a bondsman who would leave as soon as his indenture ended, and an Englishman who couldn't be trusted.

The time had come to encourage Raleigh's courtship.

Except she'd said she would go to the festival with Dominick. What had she been thinking?

Tabitha slapped a bowl of water onto the table hard enough to make some slosh over the edge. She wiped it up and fetched another clean towel from the linen press in the hall, then poked her head around the edge of the back door to find Dominick talking to Japheth about her aging horse.

"I'm ready for you," she called.

He shook hands with the older man and strode toward her with his easy grace. "Your nag looks as tired as you do."

"At least you didn't tell me I look like the horse." She smiled and took his hand in hers. "Come to the table. I'm going to wash and inspect the wound."

To her surprise, sand was caked in the stitches and beneath his normally spotless fingernails.

She glanced at his face. "What have you been doing? Digging for clams?"

"No, but I'd like to. Do you go crabbing?"

"Often. But tell me how your hand got so dirty when the rest of you didn't."

He shrugged. "Just looking at some rocks on the shore. Will you take me crabbing one day?"

"Maybe." She plunged his hand into the bowl of water. "You'll need to be more careful with this wound in the future. It's healed well, but not completely."

"And what a pity it would be if I had to come back and have you care for me." His fathomless brown eyes gazed into hers in a way that made her pulse skip more beats than was healthy. "It would be an excellent excuse to see you if you won't go crabbing with me."

"You may have better luck crabbing with me than getting medical treatment from me, after tomorrow." Tabitha rubbed gently at his palm to ensure no sand would creep into the minute holes left behind by the removal of the stitches. “Wilkins is angry about his wife’s death and wants me to suffer by taking away my livelihood.”

“Is it just his wife’s death he wants you to pay for?” Dominick caught hold of her hand to keep her from concentrating on his wound. “Is there more?”

“I can’t tell you.”

Which, of course, told him too much.

“I don’t mean regarding your patient. I mean, do you know things that could harm his reputation, so he has to harm yours first?”

“I don’t talk about my patients.”

The now faint mark across her throat burned all of a sudden, and she recalled the knife, the sting of the blade, the warning not to speak of the night. Wilkins? Could it have been?

No, he knew as well as anyone else in town that she kept her mouth shut, as her mother and her grandmother had. If Mrs. Wilkins had said anything that made sense, which she had not, Tabitha would not have repeated it. No, Wilkins had begun his campaign against her in an official capacity, with the town council, soon after she’d received the summons to cross the peninsula, for that was information she might have to divulge, if Sally’s family wanted him to make reparation for his promise, his seduction, his abandonment. But a midwife discredited by a town council would not be called to testify in a lawsuit.

“It’s not over his wife at all.” Tabitha resumed work on Dominick’s hand. She snipped through the threads in their neat line across the flesh of the palm between thumb and forefinger.

“The men of the council are good men,” Dominick said.

"This is going to hurt." She tugged out the first stitch to stop him from discussing her situation further.

His breath hissed through his teeth. "You're a cruel—" She tugged out the second stitch. "Ah!"

"One more." She gave him a cheerful smile.

"You'd better not break your word to go—" His teeth snapped together.

"Almost done." Tabitha spread more foul-smelling comfrey ointment on his palm, then wrapped a strip of linen around his hand. "That should do. Keep it clean and come to me if the redness doesn't go away or spreads. That is—" Her throat closed.

"Oh, my dear." Dominick shoved back his chair and rose. "Don't be so distressed over this." He rested his hands on her shoulders.

He stood a full head taller than she, and the temptation to lean her head against his chest and let him hold her nearly knocked her off balance. Her body ached for affection, for comfort, for security, as she faced the possibility of having her freedom, her livelihood, taken from her.

Security she would never receive from Dominick Cherrett, bondsman, Englishman.

She stepped out of arm's length, allowing his hands to fall to his sides. "I'll stop being distressed if God remembers I exist and takes care of matters. Now you'd best be going. Your master wouldn't like me being the cause of you getting in after sundown."

He flinched as though she'd struck him. In a way, she had with her reminder of his servant status. She might often be treated as no better than a housemaid or perhaps respected housekeeper, but she was a free woman. Pointing out that he was not free to come and go as he pleased set a barrier between them.

"Yes, ma'am." His voice was cool and so very English. "Shall I have Kendall send your fee? I do presume a bondsman doesn't have to pay for his own care."

"Mayor Kendall will pay me." Though she knew doing so was unkind, she added, "He's always done so with his redemptioners."

"Then I bid you good evening." He spun on his heel with military precision and stalked to the door. When he opened it, a blast of mist-laden air swirled into the room, cold and smelling of the sea and her garden. She expected him to simply walk out without another word, but just before he closed the portal behind him, he flashed his beguiling grin. "You've still promised to go to the fete with me . . . even if I am low company for you."

The door closed. Tabitha remained where she was, her gaze fixed on the panel as though she could see through it, could see his retreating form tall and straight as his long legs ate up the distance to the gate.

The gate where someone had waylaid her with a knife.

She pressed her fingers to her throat. It should be him. She wanted it to be him. Anyone else who might fear some knowledge she could have unwittingly gleaned from being about that night was someone she'd known all her life—a neighbor, a friend, a patient.

But blaming Dominick without proof wasn't fair. She was merely struggling against her attraction to him, warning herself to break off all contact. Yet how else could she work out what he was up to along the shore if she didn't spend time in his company? If matters went badly for her with the council, she would need a way to restore her good name, her reputation, her position of respected woman in the community. If she could find out who lay behind the disappearances, if Dominick truly was a participant who could lead her to answers and a way to stop the abductions, no one would listen to Harlan Wilkins.

From the moment Tabitha walked into the town hall, her back straight, her head high, her knees wobbling, to present herself before the council, she knew the men had been listening to Harlan Wilkins a great deal. Only Mayor Kendall, residing at the head of the long table, did not look upon her with censure. He rose, drew out a chair, and set a glass of water before her, though a manservant—not Dominick—hovered nearby to perform these tasks for the council.

"We just need to ask you a few questions," Kendall said in a gentle voice. "You do understand why we've called you here."

"Yes, sir." She refrained from glaring at Wilkins.

He sat at the opposite end of the table, his dark eyes narrowed, his jaw bunched. If he'd been closer, she feared she would have lost her temper and thrown her water in his face. He deserved worse, but that wasn't her place.

"Mr. Wilkins has accused me of being unqualified to practice my profession," she continued. And dared not take her to court for fear of what she might testify about his actions. "He wishes to have me censured from practicing."

"What do you have to say for yourself regarding these charges, Miss Eckles?" Kendall asked.

"You've said it all right there." Wilkins surged to his feet. "She is Miss Eckles, not Mrs. Eckles. She shouldn't be allowed to deliver babies when she hasn't borne one herself."

"Many women who have never borne children are midwives." Tabitha spoke those words calmly, out of practice. She'd been challenged on her status since taking over her mother's work.

"We should have sought for another apothecary to come when Teagues died," another council member declared. "A female this young? It's bound to cause trouble."

"Many women are not comfortable with a man attending—" A hubbub of voices interrupted Tabitha's explanation. From the exclamations, most of these men didn't care if their wives were uncomfortable or not.

"It's the safety of the mother and the child that matters," Mr. Lester, the postmaster, said in his soft voice. "I understand that doctors can use implements that help the birthing process and have saved many lives."

Tabitha clenched her fists beneath the shelter of the table. The man was right. Doctors held the monopoly on the use of forceps. From what she'd read, many mothers and their babies had been saved by this instrument, as it was thinner than even slender hands like hers and could aid the baby's entrance into the world.

"In Norfolk," Wilkins declared, "women are happy to use a physician's care."

"Not all of them." Tabitha caught and held his gaze and smiled.

His face reddened. But he held all the cards in this game, if he persuaded the others to go along with his scheme of discrediting her. If Sally sued for support of her child and called Tabitha to testify, Wilkins's lawyers could bring her testimony into disrepute by claiming she merely wanted revenge.

Oh, you are a clever man.

All she could do was attempt to discredit him now.

"You've accused me of providing poor care to your wife on the night of her accident," Tabitha said. "But you weren't with her, so how would you know what sort of care I provided her?"

Most of the men frowned at her. None gave Wilkins the

glances or murmurs of disapproval she would have expected at the least.

"What man wishes to be about when his wife is in travail?" Lester shuddered, and his spectacles slid down his nose.

Now the murmurs came—murmurs of assent to Lester's assertion.

Tabitha glanced from one to another and was almost glad she wasn't married. Almost. She knew these men, had known most of them all her life. She'd delivered a few of their children and had been present when her mother delivered still more. Most of them loved their wives, some even as devoted as bridegrooms. Their devotion led to a horror of hearing their wives suffering to bear the fruit of their union and affection. Most of them had stayed nearby, despite their terror of "women's things."

But Wilkins had left his young, new, and expectant wife alone even before her travail . . .

Which meant none of the men would blame him. He hadn't known until his presence was no longer necessary.

Tabitha compressed her lips to stop from biting them. She tried to catch the eye of each man present. Only Mayor Kendall, the one unmarried and childless man in the group, would return her gaze. "What qualifies you, Miss Eckles?" he asked.

Tabitha took a long, deep breath to ensure the steadiness of her voice. "I apprenticed with my mother for six years before her death. The women of my family have always started working with their mothers at the age of sixteen, whether married or not. So when Momma died, I took on the practice. And when the apothecary died last year—"

"You thought you could act like a surgeon at the least." Wilkins sneered. "Uppity for a female."

"Mayor Kendall's redemptioner owes a well-healed hand

to my care," Tabitha shot back. "If I hadn't cleaned it and stitched it—"

"Was that what you were doing with him on the beach yesterday?" Wilkins overrode her explanation, his upper lip curling. "Cleaning and stitching his hand, with your hair hanging down like a wanton?"

The room erupted into exclamations of outrage.

"Hair down in the middle of the afternoon?"

"And the Sabbath."

"Wasn't at church."

"And him a bondsman. Indecent."

Kendall called for silence. Once the men had complied, he turned to Tabitha, his eyes full of sympathy and concern. "Please wait for us in the entrance hall. We will call you in when we finish our discussion and vote."

"Yes, sir." Head high, back straight, knees too tense to wobble, Tabitha exited the council room.

In the hall, where meetings open to everyone and town-wide activities took place, she walked to the fireplace at one end of the room and gripped the mantel. Above her, a portrait of the town founder, Peter Bourne, hung in all his outmoded splendor of embroidered satin coat, lace jabot, powdered wig, and patch, beside a firm, unsmiling mouth. His dark eyes seemed to bore into hers, accusing her. *How dare you taint my town with your female incompetence.*

"I didn't do anything wrong." She pounded her fist on the carved wooden edge of the mantel. "She didn't die from childbirth."

As many times as she'd gone over that night in her head, she could find nothing wrong with her actions. Yet, if she were more experienced, had gone through her own lying-in, maybe she would have worked out something she was too young and naive to see.

And if she weren't so young and empty in her heart and her soul, she wouldn't have succumbed to the charms of a certain Englishman and let him hold her hand.

She glanced from the council room door to the front entrance. It stood open to the sunshine and crystal blue sky, washed clear of clouds after the previous day's rain. A long walk along the beach would do her good. She may as well leave. From the moment Wilkins divulged knowledge of her behavior the day before, she knew she'd lost. They would discredit her. She wouldn't be able to support herself or Patience and Japheth or assist Sally Belote in getting help for her baby.

"So much for God taking care of us," she muttered and started for the door.

"Miss Eckles," Mayor Kendall called from the council room entrance. "Tabitha, come back. We've reached our conclusion."

14

"We're going out in your boat?" Tabitha looked so dismayed, Raleigh wished he'd planned a day on the beach, fishing from one of the coves or digging for crabs.

"I thought you'd like to be on the water." He glanced from her white face to the open water. "It's a perfect day. Not too sunny. Not too rough, though the wind is kicking up a bit." He gave her what he hoped was a coaxing smile. "And you used to always like going out on the *Marianne*."

"That was before the men around here started to disappear."

"From land." He set his jaw. "The last five have been from land."

"Well, yes, but Raleigh—" She gazed at him from eyes that revealed she'd enjoyed too little sleep lately. "It's not safe for you. I wouldn't want anything to happen to you, for you to be taken up again."

The tenderness of her voice warmed his heart. She cared about him. She still cared. When he'd called Monday night, a time calculated to coincide with the city council meeting's aftermath, she had talked with him in the garden for half an hour, though she'd refused to discuss the council meeting more than to say no one was forcing her to stop her practice—yet. Before he left, she agreed to spend the following afternoon with him, as long as no one needed her care.

He prayed the only care she would give would be to him—

smiles to soothe his fears, words to heal his envy of that upstart bondsman, perhaps the touch of her hand to restore his soul to a state of a free conscience.

"Not even the British are crude enough to take up a woman," Raleigh said to reassure her. "Everyone who's disappeared has done so at night."

"And you came too close the other morning." Her look was direct, piercing despite the soft blue-gray of her eyes beneath the brim of her straw hat. "How did you do it this time?"

Raleigh's gut tightened. "What do you mean?"

"I mean, why would they let you go last Monday, if they didn't before?" She clasped her elbows and looked like nothing so much as a stern schoolmistress asking for an explanation of why his slate was empty instead of full of sums. "Your birth hasn't changed."

"Different captain." Raleigh shrugged and leaped onto the deck of the single-masted boat. "Some of them are decent fellows." He held out both his hands to her. "Now come on board. We're losing the ebb tide."

"All right." Her movements slow, appearing as though she still doubted the wisdom of their actions, she leaned forward, clasped his hands, and made the jump between jetty and deck.

Two years away from regular excursions on his boat hadn't ended the grace with which she leaped aboard. Of course, she might have been on other boats, sailed with other suitors.

He stifled the stab of jealousy. He had no right to feel envy for the men who had stayed at home and tried to win her.

Except for that bondsman.

Lips thinning at the thought of the Englishman, Raleigh sprang back to the jetty, released the painter, and bounded onto the deck before the gap between land and boat grew too wide.

Tabitha laughed. "I always admired how you could do that without falling on your face. But I always expect you to go splash one of these days."

"I expect I will." Her laughter eased his tension and gave him the courage to take her hand in his. "Thank you for coming, even if you are afraid of the British."

"I'm not afraid of the British." She lowered her gaze to the deck. "I'm afraid for your sake. You just returned. And the other day—" A shudder ran through her.

"Then there's hope, Tabbie?" He tucked his hand under her chin and urged her to meet his gaze. "Does that little speech mean there's hope for my suit?"

"There's always hope, Raleigh." She smiled. "For the time being, I'm a midwife and, due to lack of anyone else, a healer. One thing we learn with patients is that if they are still breathing, they have a chance of pulling through."

"Then your feelings for me are still breathing?" He stroked her jaw with his thumb, loving the softness of her skin. "And maybe there's a pulse somewhere?" He touched the pulse beneath her ear and heaved a silent sigh that it didn't feel the least bit accelerated.

Not compared to his.

"Yes." She smiled. "But there won't be if we don't get that sail up."

"Right." Laughing, he dodged across the deck and pulled the halyard to unfurl the single sail. "Get the tiller, will you?"

For the next quarter hour, he could pretend they were on that last sail together, working in harmony, as he raised and secured the sail and she manned the wheel, keeping the little craft headed away from land on the gentle swells of the outgoing tide. He didn't need to shout directions to her. She knew. She'd grown up on these shores too, sailed with him from the time they were old enough to go out on their own, and with others before then. Her light skirts fluttering around her legs and her hat ribbons hovering around her face, she bent and swayed with the roll of the deck to keep her balance. Sunlight stole beneath the hat brim and lit her features, washing away her pallor and dark circles of fatigue. And she was smiling.

"This is all worth it, God," he spoke to the opalescent sky. "Being here with her is worth every risk I've ever taken."

Lines belayed to the rail, Raleigh joined Tabitha at the wheel. "Have you been sailing since we went last?"

"No." She shook her head.

"You haven't lost your touch with the wheel." He stood behind her and set his hands on the spokes next to hers, encasing her in his arms. "But I'd better take over from here. You don't know where the sandbanks and rocks are now."

"No." He felt her go rigid from his nearness, and she snatched her hands away from contact with his. "If you'll just move one arm for a moment . . ." She pushed at him harder than necessary to break his hold on the wheel, as though his forearm was a barricade or a prison bar.

He released the spoke long enough for her to step away from him, leaving him cold where she'd stood. "We used to steer like that."

"That," she said with the hint of a chill, "was when we were going to get married."

Raleigh's insides felt as though the boat had twisted into the deep trough of a wave. "I'm sorry. When you came with me today, I'd hoped . . ."

"I came with you today because I want to rebuild our friendship, Raleigh." She gave him one of her direct, clear gazes. "I want to forgive you, and if we can be friends again, then maybe I can."

"Not forgiving harms you," Raleigh told her. "Sunday's sermon was on forgiving those who hurt us again and again and how not doing so harms our relationship with God."

"I don't have a relationship with God that can be hurt."

"Tabbie." He reached one hand out to her. "I could never forgive myself if I'm the cause of your damaged faith."

"Don't concern yourself about it." She smiled, though her eyes were sad. "I must not have had a good relationship with God in the first place, if it could be shattered so easily."

"Easily? You suffered a great deal." Raleigh returned his hand to the wheel and began to make a sweeping turn to take them up the coast. "I disappeared and your mother died. You'd already lost your father."

"Well, Grandmomma lost her husband when she had a small child to raise and then later lost that child."

"He brought me home." Raleigh turned so he could look at her. "I prayed every night to come home, and He finally answered my prayer."

Even as he spoke, Raleigh's conscience pricked him. If he'd trusted in the Lord to get him home, he wouldn't be in such a pickle. Yet he would tell Tabitha anything to bring her back into fellowship with the Lord.

"And I'm glad you're here." This time, her smile reached her eyes. "Let's sail out a bit further and drop anchor. I want to indulge in some real fishing for once."

For that smile, Raleigh would have sailed to Halifax. He tacked northeast, making a diagonal course from the land. Off the larboard quarter, the roof of Tabitha's house and her prized apple tree showed above the dunes. Along the beach, several children dug for clams in the hard-packed sand below the tide line. One or two adults watched over them, and a lone figure strode across the dunes—a man, judging from the clothes, with long hair blowing in the breeze.

Raleigh jerked the wheel. The fishing smack yawed, hit a wave with the starboard bow, and rolled over far enough to touch the larboard gunwale. The sail flapped, lost the wind, then caught it again with enough force they rolled in the opposite direction.

Tabitha staggered. Raleigh shot out his arm and caught her around the waist, drawing her to safety, drawing her close to his side.

"Hold on to me while I straighten us out."

When he felt her grasp his waist with her arm, he released his hold on her and returned his attention to the wheel and wind and waves. The smack dipped and twisted like a confused dancer, then caught the next wave beneath her prow and rose with the grace of one of the seagulls whirling and calling near the shore.

Tabitha released him as soon as the boat's pitch grew even enough for her to stand on her own. Far too soon for Raleigh. She didn't even look at him—she was looking at the shore. Too easily, Raleigh guessed what on shore held her attention, and he nearly sent the bow rolling beneath a wave again. With an effort, he said nothing. He wanted to, but feared mentioning his suspicions about the man would do him no good at the moment and probably would harm the day. Just mentioning his name would bring him aboard the boat. Later, when they were on shore, he would warn her to stay away from the bondsman.

Raleigh tacked again, heading further out to sea. The land fell away, its inhabitants too small for identification. And Tabitha seemed to lose interest. She made her way forward, to where poles and lines lay tethered to the deck.

"Did you bring bait?" she asked.

"Some rock crabs." Raleigh glanced at the horizon, the angle of the sun, and the now distant shore little more than a horizon itself. "I'll get the sail down, then you can help me with the anchor."

Raleigh leaped forward and furled the sail. Then, together, they spun the windlass and got the anchor dropped over the side and down to the sandy bottom of the clear blue water. The *Marianne* jerked like a large fish at the end of a line, then settled to rise and fall on the swells of the sea. Around them, sunlight sparkled off the waves like golden-backed fish. The rising wind tugged at Tabitha's hat ribbons and flirted with her frilly hem.

Raleigh paused in the middle of retrieving a pole from the canvas netting and gazed at her in wonder. She'd been pretty when he knew her before. Now, with the sun gilding her skin and her hair shining more red than brown, her looks held something more, something deeper than beauty—strength. He read it in her broad cheekbones and determined chin, the firmness of her mouth and set of her shoulders.

But was she strong enough to withstand the turmoil the next few weeks would bring upon her? Afterward, if she could no longer practice her profession, she would need even more strength to carry on.

Or a husband.

Baiting a hook, Raleigh smiled to himself. Yes, that was it. He would complete his commission and marry her.

Heart as light as the breeze, he handed her the rod. "Do you remember how to cast, or shall I do it for you?"

"I said I haven't been out on a boat." With a flip of her wrist, she sent the line spinning over the rail to land as light as an insect on the waves. "I didn't say I haven't been fishing. Remember that inlet near my house? I've caught a few things there."

"Alone?" he couldn't help asking as he baited his own line.

"Yes." She gave him a quick glance, then returned her attention to the bobbing cork on her line. "There hasn't been anyone else, Raleigh. I told you that."

What about that Englishman?

He clenched his teeth until the question dissolved on his tongue.

"The men of Seabourne are fools," he managed instead.

"If I agree with you, I'll sound rather self-centered, won't I?"

He smiled. "I suppose so. But Tabitha, please talk to me about what happened." He followed her along the side of the craft. "You used to always tell me about your troubles and dreams."

"Yes, I did." She turned on him so abruptly her pole collided with his, entangling the lines. "I told you I wanted to have a family, lots of children, at least one daughter to teach my trade. I told you about the way I would want to make the house bigger for my family and how I'd teach them from my father's books. I told you about wanting to sit with my husband by a fire on cold winter nights and read and talk and just be together. But you never told me you wanted to run away."

"I didn't run away." The pain on her face tore his heart in two. "I just wanted to see a bit of the world before I settled down to that hearth and—"

"You could have told me."

"I was afraid you'd end things between us."

"So you simply left me to mourn."

"Yes." He dropped the hopelessly snarled rods on the deck and rested his hands on her shoulders. "Yes, I did," he repeated in a voice no louder than the hiss of the waves against the hull. "I was a fool and a coward, and I want to spend every day of the rest of my life making that up to you. Please, give me a chance." He raised his hands to cup her face in his palms. "If you'll let me." He lowered his head.

An instant before his lips met hers, she twisted out of his hold and strode across the deck to the opposite gunwale. She grasped the rail, her back to him, her knuckles white.

She hadn't twisted away from the Englishman when he'd kissed her. She hadn't collapsed in his arms, but neither had she given him the slap he deserved.

The image of that contact burning in his mind's eye, Raleigh demanded, "Do you prefer an English bondsman who'll leave here in four years to a man who wants to spend the rest of his life with you?"

"I don't know what you're talking about." Her spine was stiff, her voice tight.

"I think you do." Raleigh joined her to face the nearly invisible shore. "You let him kiss you."

"I didn't let—"

"I saw it, Tabitha. You were on the beach with him at dawn, and he kissed you."

"I . . . he . . ." She sighed. "Yes, he kissed me. I didn't expect it."

"You didn't seem to dislike it."

Between collar and hairline, her neck turned rosy pink. "I was taken aback, is all. I suppose you'd be happier if I'd slapped him."

"I would be, yes."

"I've never slapped anyone in my life. I bring life into this world. I don't do anything that could lead to ending it."

"Which is why I love you so much." He braced his legs against an increase in the pitch of the deck and clasped his hands behind his back. "And if it were any other man, someone worthy of you, I wouldn't mind nearly as much. But Cherrett—Tabbie, he's English. He acts like a roué."

"You can't know that." Tabitha turned her back to the rail and gripped it with both hands. "He's usually a gentleman and—" She caught her breath. "Raleigh, we have company."

15

Compared to a frigate, the vessel was small, a mere two-masted sloop built for speed and boldly flying the Union Jack from its mainmast. It swooped over the horizon like a hawk stooping on a rabbit, and the *Marianne* might as well have sprouted ears and a furry tail.

Tabitha's stomach dropped to the pit of her belly. Her hands flexed on the rail as she waited for the explosion of the long gun mounted on the sloop's bow.

In front of her, Raleigh's face whitened and he spun. "The anchor." He sprinted forward. "Loose the sail."

Tabitha sprang to obey. She didn't take time to remind him she hadn't touched a belaying pin or sheet since he left two years earlier. Surely she remembered how to spring the knot free and let the canvas fall without sending it flapping from the spar like a broken bird wing. Surely . . . surely . . .

She grappled with the salt-stiffened lines, tugged at the belaying pin holding it fast to the rail. Rough hemp scored her palms.

Behind her, Raleigh took an ax to the anchor hawser. A loss for him, the anchor. Better than his life. Better than the fishing boat.

She kept her gaze fixed on the sloop. Every second drew it nearer, made it larger. She caught the movement of men on the deck, the flash of a telescope.

"How dare you? How dare you?" she shouted at them. "This is our country, our ocean."

She slammed her fist into the belaying pin. It sprang free and sailed across the water to disappear into the foam of a wave. A big, beautiful wave that lifted the smack and edged her toward shore. Of course. The tide had turned.

"We can do this, Raleigh." Tabitha grasped the sheet and raced across the deck, the sail swirling out behind her.

The *chunk*, *chunk*, *chunk* of the ax on a hawser as thick as a man's arm was the only reply.

"If I can sheet home, draw that line taut, and flatten the sail—"

A gust of wind caught the canvas and tore the line from her hand. With a shriek of frustration, she dove after it, tackling the trailing end against the rail. The sail sagged. The smack yawed, then dropped into a trough. Seawater splashed Tabitha's face. She coughed and blinked to clear her eyes, and held fast to the line.

"Help me," she choked out. "Raleigh—"

The sloop drew nearer, loomed too close, black-hulled and menacing.

Tabitha scrabbled for footing on the slippery deck. One of the discarded fishing lines caught on her ankle. She landed on her knees. But she held fast to the sail line, her front pressed to the gunwale, her legs entangled in skirts and fishing tackle.

Another chunk sounded a dull vibration through the deck, and the *Marianne* pitched and rolled, uncontrolled in the heightening waves of an incoming tide.

"Tabbie, the sail," Raleigh shouted. "If we don't—" He interrupted his admonition with something like a bellowed prayer. His footfalls pounded on the deck. He tore the line from her hands. "Got it. Hold on tight. I'll help you."

"No, the wheel. Get the wheel."

They swung and dipped over the waves like a mere bucket on the swells. And the sloop drew nearer, near enough for her to see faces of the men, mere blurs of white against the misty blue of the sky.

But the gun didn't fire.

"They're not going to fire on us," she announced with relief.

"They don't have to." Raleigh sounded breathless. He hauled the sail across the boom and slammed a belaying pin through the knot. "They'll just run us down."

"But why?"

"I don't . . . know." He stumbled over the fishing poles stretched across the tiny deck. "But they're chasing us or they'd have sheered off by now."

"The water gets shallow soon." Tabitha leaned on the wheel, fighting the waves, the current, the boat's lack of propulsion—besides the water—without the sail raised. "If we can get into shallower water than their draft can draw, we'll be safe."

"No, we won't." Raleigh fought with the sail, a single, too-small square of canvas in comparison with the vessel behind them. "We'll go aground and lose the boat."

Of course they would. Tabitha knew that. She had lived by the sea all her life. They didn't want to ground a boat, not even on sand.

And the sloop had guns. Only fourteen she could see, but that was fourteen too many, too dangerous, too overwhelming.

"Where?" She cried out, scanning the coastline. "Where should I—"

The smack jerked like someone stumbling over a rock on a path. A crack like small arms fire resounded over the deck, and the sail caught the wind, rode up the next wave, and settled into an even bow-to-stern pitch.

"Praise God," Raleigh shouted.

But the sloop still gained on them, faster, with more men to manipulate her sails.

"Head north by northwest," Raleigh directed, still struggling to secure the sail.

Tabitha glanced at the compass mounted above the wheel. They were headed due west, straight for shore, close enough now that she saw people standing on the beach to watch. As she leaned on the spoke to force the rudder around three degrees on the compass, she turned her head to view the sloop. In moments it should run aground.

Its commander wasn't that foolish. He too had adjusted his course and ran on a similar heading, parallel to theirs. With its greater speed, the sloop drew ahead of them, close enough for Tabitha to see the rude gestures many of the sailors on the enemy deck made, before the vessel dipped her Union Jack in an insolent salute, and she vanished around a headland, only her towering masts visible against the horizon.

"She's gone." Tabitha sighed with relief. "She was only teasing us. I wish I understood her game."

Raleigh joined Tabitha at the wheel, soaked with seawater and perspiration. "She's a bit close in, even for the British."

"Close in? Raleigh, you've been away too long. We've had British ships sail right up our rivers or into the Chesapeake and waylay our ships." She squinted against the brightness of the horizon for a glimpse of the sloop. "I still see her masts. She must have slowed."

"Or maybe she's coming about to make another pass." Raleigh's lips thinned into a hard line. "Something's wrong around here and has been since I got home."

"It's been longer than that." Tabitha stepped aside to relinquish the wheel to Raleigh. "Should we come about too, and head back to your jetty?"

"We can't." He tilted his head like a hound sniffing the wind.

Tabitha understood. The light breeze from earlier had turned to a brisk wind, clearing the sky of the earlier haze, but blowing from the south. Tacking into the wind with only two of them would be difficult.

"It was always a risk," Raleigh said. "Always is with only two people aboard. We'll sail into that cove north of your house."

The British sloop had headed in that direction.

She scanned the northern horizon but couldn't be sure if she saw masts there or simply a cloud formation. "I'm willing to try."

"No, it'll risk hurting your hands. I can fetch the boat home with the Evans brothers or my father later."

"But we don't have an anchor."

"Plenty of rocks." Raleigh squinted at the compass. "We'll tie up to one of those."

"All right." She laid her hand on his arm. "I'm sorry you lost your anchor."

"Just another black mark against the British." Raleigh covered her hand with his and smiled at her. Wind ruffled his sun-streaked hair, and his eyes were as blue as the sea around them. He looked young and carefree and so much like the youth she'd fallen in love with that her heart began to soften toward him.

"I'd like to come out with you again," she said before she lost her courage.

"Tabbie." He raised one hand as though he intended to touch her face.

A wave caught the starboard quarter, lifted the smack, and sent it slamming into a trough of the next wave. The bow yawed and the sail flapped. Their course altered too close to the shore.

"Never court a lady while in command of a vessel." Raleigh laughed, a rich, heartfelt rumble in his broad chest. "Good way to go aground."

He turned his attention to the navigation. Tabitha watched him for a minute and absorbed what he'd said. Courting. Yes, he was courting her and she encouraged it.

She mustn't let herself be confused by his looks—enhanced by the two years away and hard work aboard a man-of-war—and his entreaties to her heart. She mustn't let her attraction to another man scare her into Raleigh's arms.

Her mouth hardened as she narrowed her eyes against the glare of the horizon. White-capped waves rolled toward them. Plumes of foam broke and swirled into the air, obscuring the view, but she thought she saw it—the sloop poised just far enough away for only its masts to show above the waterline.

"No, not possible," she murmured.

She adjusted her hat brim to better shield her eyes. Surely she saw only mist or spray, and her anxiety over British ships in the area was making her imagine too much. She imagined a great deal while walking through the mist—knights and castles, children and a man to love her, rising from the fog—her dreams conjuring images where none existed. So why shouldn't she summon the sight of British war vessels from foam along the horizon? It was all her father's doing, his legacy to her, as her midwifery skills were her mother's—the stories of romance and danger, love and adventure, clouding her reason.

She was not—she could not be—seeing a sloop riding motionless across the path they were taking. It had gone. It wouldn't remain in the area in the middle of the day, and the cove to which they headed wasn't large enough for even a two-masted runner like a sloop. It was nothing more than a fine place to swim, fish from shore, or tie up a smack or rowboat.

"Raleigh," she said just loudly enough for him to hear her. "Do you see anything around the headland before the cove?"

He glanced at her, then toward the northern horizon. "A lot of foam. There must be a storm brewing out at sea somewhere, but we'll be all right."

"You don't see masts?" she persisted.

"I don't—" He muttered something, then swung toward her. "Take the wheel. Just keep us on this heading."

Before she even grabbed the wheel from him, he sprinted forward and swung onto the jib boom.

"Be careful." The wind snatched her words and tossed them over the larboard rail.

Raleigh balanced with the aid of a forward stay, a precarious perch on the slender strip of wood. The single sail bellied out in the rising wind and blocked him from view. But rising above the canvas, she saw the sloop's masts looming larger, nearer.

"God, please—" She stopped herself before she prayed.

She didn't want Raleigh snatched away from her again, not before she knew if she forgave him, if she still loved him, if the future held marriage and children with him. If she prayed, the opposite might happen. She might make God notice her, and if He had a plan for her life as Pastor Downing claimed, He might remember to implement it. Thus far, it went completely opposite to what she wanted. Or needed. And right then, she needed that sloop to vanish.

"We need to luff," she shouted to Raleigh.

But of course they couldn't. They needed at least another person to help man the sail to tack into the wind. With the wind behind them now, they skimmed over the water like a flying fish headed straight for a net. Without an anchor, they couldn't even remain where they were, a mile from shore.

Tabitha's fingers tightened on the wheel. She fixed her gaze on the compass, then the sea, then the compass again. If she adjusted their course a fraction to the northeast, they could sail past the sloop, head for the next inlet. If the sloop was anchored—

That was it!

"Raleigh!" Tabitha put every bit of her lung power into the call. "I have an idea."

A moment later, he ducked beneath the boom and reached her side. "Let me help." He took over the wheel.

Not until she held only the taffrail did Tabitha realize the strain she'd placed on her arms. Her hands hurt and she feared she would have blisters. She must be careful. If Mrs. Parks delivered within the next two weeks, Tabitha would need her hands.

She focused on Raleigh, on the threatening bulk of the sloop. "They have to be anchored. Otherwise, they wouldn't be staying in the same place."

"I thought of that. We can sail around them. By the time they up anchor, we'll be gone."

"That's what I was thinking." She smiled at him. "Maybe I've stayed on land for two years, but I still remember a thing or two you taught me."

"And I've learned a thing or two about the English." Raleigh was grim. "It doesn't make any sense for them to anchor there in broad daylight."

"Unless someone is in trouble or they need water?" Tabitha squinted at the masts. "We are nominally at peace with England and can't deny them emergency care."

Raleigh cast her a swift glance. "Do you trust them?"

"No. But it's daylight. They wouldn't be bold enough to impress men in daylight, not right off our shores anyway."

"Wouldn't they just." In those few words, Raleigh sounded angrier, more bitter, and yet somehow more British than she'd ever heard him.

She shivered in the wind-borne spray. "They've got to be stopped," she ground out. "If it's the last thing I do, I'll find a way."

"I didn't hear you." Raleigh leaned on the wheel, turning the smack two more points to the northeast. "What did you say?"

"Never you mind." Tabitha returned her attention to the sloop. She saw the upper deck now, the gangway, and tiny figures moving about. Five men stooped behind the stern chaser gun, but it wasn't run out.

From tales she'd heard from those who'd fought at sea against the British in the revolution, that gun could be run out in seconds. Seconds. But surely they saw she was a female. They wouldn't fire on a female. They didn't fire into American boats, only fired across them, threatened them.

Still, she had to force herself to stand straight, her head up, and not huddle on the deck as the *Marianne* skimmed past the anchored sloop so close to the stern she saw a face in the window. She gasped, blinked, looked again. The face was gone, but she would have testified in court she knew who it was.

16

Dominick spied the little fishing boat swooping past the stern of the sloop. Two white faces turned his way, blurs against the blue of sky and sea behind them, the man at the wheel, the woman clinging to the taffrail. The wind holding the sloop at anchor, its bow too close in to the cove, lent the smack its wings.

"He's a good seaman," Jennings, the sloop's commander, remarked. "We saw them earlier. They ran like a demon was after them when they saw us." He slapped his well-padded thigh and laughed, as though he'd made a good jest of it. "They all run like foxes before the hounds."

"Can you blame them?" Dominick leaned precariously out of the stern windows to get a better look at the smack. Something struck him as familiar, and he wasn't sure if the sloop's pitch, which was strong despite the sloop being anchored, or apprehension made him queasy. "We've been stealing their men right from under their noses."

"Their men?" Jennings's thick, dark brows drew together like a fuzzy caterpillar. "They're our men hiding out from their rightful duty to the king."

"Some. And is it worth it to risk war?"

"You, sirrah, are coming close to talking treason."

Dominick laughed off the very truth of Jennings's words. "Just keeping myself from being in trouble while here in America."

"A pity, that." Jennings cocked his large head to one side. "Never thought I'd see a Cherrett fall so low."

"Neither did I." Dominick twirled the glass in his hand without drinking the amber liquid. Spirits would definitely make him ill, if apprehension about the identity of that fishing boat didn't do so first. "I should have listened to my tutors at Oxford." He grinned as though making a great jest himself.

"At least you didn't kill anyone. I'd hate to have to arrest the nephew of a vice admiral." Jennings lifted the squat decanter from the table. "Another tot?"

"Thank you, no. I should be on my way. My . . . er . . . master will want me home to serve his supper."

In about three hours. Yet being away so long after Sunday's excursion was a risk, one Dominick hadn't expected to take. He hadn't known his uncle, the vice admiral, would have someone watching him so closely—closely enough the message had gotten out and a response back in two days.

He hadn't expected the message, a mere slip of paper that had appeared in his shopping basket that morning. The wording had been brief, telling him to meet the sloop that afternoon. He'd gone and received a longer missive.

Uneasiness crawled under his skin like weevils through a ship's biscuit. He didn't like his uncle's ship being in such proximity to the American coast a week before the scheduled rendezvous. Was war more imminent than anyone suspected?

If only Dominick had been able to hear the talk amongst Kendall's august guests, he might know more. He might know enough to please his uncle.

He sighed. "You'll want to be off these shores soon. We English are heartily disliked here."

"Not until the tide turns."

"Someone should have told you to bring a boat in instead of your whole ship," Dominick pointed out.

"Sloop," Jennings reminded him. "Only post captains get ships."

"Right. Two masts. Three masts. What do you call something with one mast?"

"Depends on who's aboard. If it's a captain's gig, it's honored company. If it's one of these Yankees, it's bait." Jennings laughed uproariously again.

Dominick smelled brandy fumes and realized the man was drunk at four o'clock in the afternoon. He tried not to show his contempt as he made a pretense of peering out the stern windows again so he could dump his brandy into the sea, with a silent apology to the fish.

"Please just see that the vice admiral knows I picked up my letter." Dominick set his glass in between the fiddle boards on the table. "I can see myself out. No need to rise."

Head bowed to avoid the low deck beams, he opened the cabin door. Although still reeking of bilge water, pea soup, and worse, the air flowing down the companionway ladder smelled like perfume compared to the stifling commander's quarters. Dominick heaved a sigh of relief to be getting away safe and clear.

Outside the cabin, the marine guard saluted. Dominick laughed in his butler's garb. No one saluted him, not even at home. But the marine guard didn't look amused at Dominick's mirth. Stone-faced, he called for someone to escort the guest over the side and into the boat that carried Dominick the dozen yards to shore.

Free at last to look at the letter the sloop had brought him, Dominick headed up the beach, quickly putting as much distance between the sloop and himself as he could. Catching sight of the walled garden, he paused, tempted to rest in its shadow to read his letter, perhaps wait for Tabitha. He had an excuse—to congratulate her on dealing Harlan Wilkins a blow at the village council.

Which was what the man needed.

Dominick's fingers curled into fists, crumpling the vice admiral's letter. He leaned against the wall, where the spreading branches of a cedar tree lent him some shade. He broke the seal of the letter with his thumbnail and gripped the edges of the parchment against the tug of the rising wind.

The missive began simply with, "Nephew." The rest was brief and to the point.

> Your request would take far too long. Carry on as though your suspicions are founded. If you have nothing to report by 21 June, you must wait to report until as late as Christmas. I'll be on the channel station during that time. Good luck and God be with you.

If God was with him, did he need luck?

Dominick frowned at the last line. It felt better than thinking about the rest—about having little more than a week to find answers that would either free him or find him stranded on enemy shores, a servant, for another six months at the least.

He certainly did need luck. God might be with him, but the Almighty would do no favors for a man who had rejected Him and done his best to demoralize His church, or at least those who served in the church.

Yet those men Dominick wrote about were politicians or social climbers using the church for their personal gain, not servants of the Lord. Most men who served as pastors and vicars and other servants of God were sincere in their faith. Finding forgiveness from any of the latter he had harmed would take a miracle.

And if he believed in miracles, perhaps he could work out whether or not Raleigh Trower was truly a repentant Yankee come home to hide from the British, or something worse. Dominick would be better off with faith. It had done him well for most of his life, until he chose to go his own way and his luck had run out six months ago.

Suddenly too weary to walk back to the mayor's house, he continued to lean against Tabitha's garden wall. Above the aromas of salt spray and sea grass, he caught the fragrance of roses and honeysuckle. Glancing up, he saw a trailing vine of the latter and plucked a handful of blossoms to hold under his nose.

He tossed the flowers away and started walking toward the village by the short route, not along the seashore. He didn't have time for sentimentality. He had to work for a living and, somewhere in between, spy on the very people who were giving him safe haven when his own countrymen, his own family, rejected him. And for what? Pompous and overfed drunkards like Jennings, the sloop's commander.

Dominick glanced toward the cove. The sloop remained, riding at anchor until the tide or the wind turned so the vessel could get back to sea. Closer to him, two figures walked along the landward side of the dunes, a man in plain, dark garb, the lady in flounced pale muslin and fluttering ribbons. The two people from the fishing boat. Dominick recognized the female's hat and gown. She looked a bit wet, the hair beneath the hat tumbled and shining russet brown.

Dominick paused and waited for them, a smile curving his lips. This should be interesting, meeting the blustering English traitor with her, with Tabitha, the lady Dominick knew he could never have and yet—

No, he wouldn't think he wanted her. She was a means

to an end, an excuse to spend a great deal of time at the seashore.

Which meant he needed to be rid of the supposed Yankee. If she decided to renew her engagement to Raleigh Trower, Dominick lost a valuable ally. Or, at the least, a valuable guise for his activities on the beach.

He straightened from his slouched stance against the wall and raised a hand in greeting. Trower stopped, his spine stiffening enough to be noticeable from a hundred feet away. Tabitha kept walking for a pace or two, then stopped, glanced back at Trower, and grasped his hand. Dominick didn't hear her say anything, but her gesture said it all: "Come along, Raleigh."

Dominick's insides tensed at the sight of her holding Trower's work-hardened hand. Those calluses would scratch her smooth skin. He probably stank of fish. Surely she wouldn't kiss him . . . too.

They came within hailing distance. Neither of the pair called to Dominick, though Tabitha looked at him, her brows arched in question. Odd that he'd never noticed how those brows, a deeper brown than her hair, came to little points on the outer corners like wings. It lent her eyelids an upward curve, as though they smiled perpetually.

He felt as though he were back on the sloop, dipping and swaying from the waves slipping beneath the hull. His mouth went dry, and he couldn't think what he should say, how to explain why he stood leaning against her garden wall, other than the words he would never speak in front of Raleigh Trower, or possibly even to her.

I couldn't go another day without seeing you.

It was a lie. Of course it was. He could, he would, go the rest of his life without seeing her and not suffer for it.

Much.

That last thought roused him from his paralysis, and he sauntered forward, smile firmly in place. "Where's your boat?"

"How do you know we were in a boat?" Trower demanded.

"I recognized Tabitha's hat ribbons." Dominick bowed to her. "How are you, my dear?"

"Wet and weary." She smiled and didn't look weary. With her cheeks a bit pink from sun, she looked more beautiful than the shiniest diamonds of the first water of London Society.

"I didn't know you were a sailor, Tabitha," Dominick said. "But you looked right at home on that floating slop bucket. I mean fishing boat."

"And you looked right at home on that British sloop," Trower shot back.

"Me on a boat?" Dominick shuddered. "I dislike small spaces."

"We saw you," Trower persisted. "No one else around here has hair like yours."

"But the English aren't from around here, are they?" Dominick looked at Tabitha. "Do you think you saw me, my dear Tabitha?"

"She isn't your dear Tabitha," Trower interjected.

"Is that for him to say, my dear?" Dominick continued to address Tabitha.

"As far as I know," she said, freeing her hand from Trower's and crossing her arms over her middle, "I'm no one's dear anything."

"But you are," Trower exclaimed. "Tabbie—"

She silenced him with a glance.

Dominick suppressed a chuckle. "Forgive me my familiarity, madam." He bowed. "I use the term as an honorific, not an endearment."

And he was a liar of the worst order.

"So, regarding my alleged presence aboard that sloop," Dominick continued, "why, do you suppose, would I be aboard one and then remove myself?"

"You're passing information to them," Trower said without hesitation.

"Information about . . . ?" Dominick gave the other man an encouraging smile.

"Don't act the fool, Mr. Cherrett," Tabitha snapped. "You know as well as we do what's going on around here."

"He possibly knows more about it than we do." Trower took a step toward Dominick. "Were you setting up the next shipment of young men for your country?"

"That's quite an accusation, Mr. Trower." Dominick kept his tone neutral as he glanced at Tabitha to see what she thought of her former fiancé's bold query.

She gazed back at him with clear, blue-gray eyes, their directness telling him precisely what he did not want to hear—she wondered the same thing.

Heart feeling as though Trower's hobnail boots had trampled on it, Dominick heaved a sigh. Now was the time to apply the adage of: when caught, tell as much of the truth as possible.

"All right. I was aboard the sloop. But it was neither arranged nor to pass information about how the Navy can acquire more human fodder for their guns." He held Tabitha's eyes without a blink. "The commander of the sloop put in to take on some fresh water, as they had a leak in a main water butt. I admit I headed their way when I saw them."

"You were headed that way before you saw them," Trower said. "I saw you when we first set out to sea."

Oh, he had been careless.

"I was out for a walk, yes. That's how I saw the sloop put in to the cove."

Tabitha broke eye contact, and his tension eased. She was beginning to believe him.

"Believe me, Mr. Trower," Dominick pushed forward with his advantage, "if I were a spy, I wouldn't meet my contact in broad daylight."

"Then why did you deny being aboard?" Tabitha asked. "Since you're here, it's obvious you weren't trying to run away from your indenture."

A glance at her face showed more concern than suspicion. Dominick smiled at her. "You have such a kind heart, Tab—Miss Eckles. At least I believe you understand my motives. I didn't want to give the appearance of improper behavior. I am a man of honor. I gave my word not to run away before my indenture ends, and I will stand by it regardless of the circumstances."

"Tabitha, you don't believe him, do you?" Trower sounded frustrated.

"Well, yes, I do." Tabitha glanced from Trower to Dominick. "If I were nothing less than enslaved in England, I'd take any chance I could to talk with my countrymen."

"But he could be passing information to them," Trower persisted.

"I could, but you have no proof of it," Dominick said.

"Unless someone else vanishes in the next few days," Trower said, his eyes narrowing. "How would that look?"

"Very bad for me," Dominick admitted with complete sincerity. He felt like praying for God to protect him. But God wouldn't protect a man who was getting only what he deserved. Possibly getting far less than what he deserved. "I'd say you'll just have to trust me," he added.

Trower laughed. Tabitha looked . . . sad, or as weary as

she'd claimed she was. A pucker had formed between her winged brows.

Dominick reached out his hand and smoothed the line with a forefinger. "You look in need of rest, my dear." He spoke in a soft voice. "I mustn't keep you any longer."

"Don't touch her," Trower ground out between clenched teeth. "She's not a strumpet to be toyed with."

"I beg your pardon, Miss Eckles." Dominick bowed to Tabitha yet again. "I meant no disrespect. I meant the gesture as one from a concerned friend, is all."

"No offense taken, Mr. Cherrett." Tabitha's cheeks had turned the color of strawberries. "Raleigh, calm yourself. Mr. Cherrett and I are—" She hesitated.

Dominick held his breath in anticipation of her completed statement as to what he was to her. A yard from him, Trower appeared as though he were about to explode.

"Friends," Tabitha finished.

"You're friends with a redemptioner?" Trower turned on her, his countenance purple beneath his sunburned skin. "How could you?"

"I don't think that's any of your concern, Raleigh."

"It's my concern if he's betraying all of us."

And it was Dominick's concern if Trower took some action to make Dominick appear as though he were betraying the locals.

"We've enjoyed some badinage, is all." Dominick tried, probably too late, to defuse the situation. "To say we're friends is pure generosity of spirit on Miss Eckles's behalf."

"Do you always kiss mere acquaintances?" Trower demanded.

Oh, no, he didn't, and the way Tabitha's lips looked at that moment—thin and tight—Dominick wanted to kiss them again, change their conformation to something much softer.

He settled for the thought—for the moment—and a rueful confession. "I felt like a friend at that moment, as she'd given me words of encouragement in my despair, and I was wishing a friend Godspeed on her journey. Perhaps I was a bit too familiar, but I hold Miss Eckles in high regard and the moment overcame my good sense."

Trower held his fisted hands at his hips as though ready to strike at any moment.

Dominick sighed to himself. If only he were as good a spy as he was a liar, he'd have his information now instead of creating a worse enemy with every breath.

"And speaking of Godspeed . . ." He bowed to both of them this time. "I'd best be on my way."

Not waiting for them to respond, he spun on his heel and strode toward the village.

"Wait just a minute." Footfalls thudded behind him.

Dominick kept going.

"Raleigh, don't," Tabitha called.

"Can't stop to chat now." Dominick waved a hand. "Master's waiting and all."

"I said stop." Trower grabbed Dominick's jacket and spun him around.

Though shorter, Raleigh was indeed stronger, or at least his fury at the moment lent him strength. His fist shot upward. Dominick swayed to the side, his hands shoved into his coat pockets. No one would accuse him of retaliating against a free man, earning him a taste of the lash.

The blow merely grazed his jaw. He raised one brow in query. "How may I help you further, Mr. Trower?"

"I don't know what your game is, Cherrett." Trower's words emerged roughly, as though each one was formed of emery grit. "But you're going to lose."

"Dear me, and I've already lost so much." Dominick grimaced as though he smelled something foul.

Tabitha ran up and caught hold of Trower's arm, a protest on her lips.

Dominick took the opportunity to beat a hasty retreat. As he loped toward the village, he weighed his options. He could continue his courtship of Tabitha and increase Trower's animosity. Or he could forget an alliance with Tabitha and give up on finding answers by June 21.

17

Though the sun blazed from a now cloudless sky, the breeze off the ocean held a chill. Tabitha rubbed her arms and tried not to watch Dominick walk away.

It proved difficult. He had a nice way of walking, relaxed, covering a great deal of ground in a short time without appearing to move with speed. All the while, his perfect posture never wavered.

Raleigh, next to her, emitted a noise like a growl. "I want that man out of here."

"Why?" Tabitha turned her attention to Raleigh. "He can't do anything. He's a bondsman."

"You don't seem to care about that." His blue eyes held accusation. "You called him your friend. That's beneath you."

"Raleigh," Tabitha said, keeping her tone level, "I am merely a midwife, little more than a servant. However respected midwives are in most communities, here I'm not."

"Because of him."

"I beg your pardon?" Her spine went rigid enough to make Dominick's seem hunchbacked.

"Don't pretend you don't know what I'm talking about." Raleigh's face darkened. "You know as well as I do that your association with someone like Cherrett is one reason the council talked about stopping you from practicing here."

"If Wilkins didn't have reasons for wanting to discredit

me," Tabitha bit out, "my chance encounter with Dominick on the beach on Sunday would not have mattered. My reputation has never been in question."

"Your chance encounter." Raleigh's upper lip curled. "Seems Mr. Cherrett has a lot of chance encounters. You on Sunday and the sloop today. I expect the next chance encounter will be with American men for the British to impress."

"Are you really accusing Dominick of being behind the abductions?"

"Can you honestly say you haven't thought of it yourself?"

Raleigh held her gaze. Tabitha couldn't look him in the eye and say the notion had never occurred to her. It had. It did. She called him friend in her desire to learn the truth and reinstate her good name in the community, or at least make the town beholden to her.

"I thought so." Raleigh smiled. "You know he's the most likely person within twenty miles."

"Except he's only been here for a few weeks." It was her only difficulty in believing Dominick guilty of helping steal men from American shores. "The disappearances have been going on for nearly a year."

"And escalated since he arrived."

"Then we should both befriend him. Maybe that way we could ferret out the truth."

Raleigh grimaced. "I'll die before I befriend another Englishman."

"Raleigh." Tabitha stepped back from the wake of his vehemence against the English. She didn't trust the British, but Raleigh's response was vitriolic. "Would God want you to talk that way about another person?"

Her question emerged somewhere between a challenge and a taunt. Unkind. Unfair. Laden with her own guilt for painting all persons of one nation with the tar brush because of the actions of their government.

"No." Raleigh bowed his head. "Forgive me. I am in the wrong in speaking that way. It's just that the sight of him looking at you like you . . . like you're . . . one of your candied flower petals, makes me sick."

Tabitha laughed and uncrossed her arms. She no longer felt the chill of the breeze. She suspected that Dominick looked at every female as though she were the prettiest, sweetest, kindest lady alive. It was part of his charm. It was only one of the dozen reasons to stay away from him.

But she wouldn't.

Her awareness of Dominick's flirtatious nature and her own susceptibility to it would protect her. She knew her mission. In the meantime, though, she realized she needed to protect Dominick from Raleigh. The latter's jealousy was palpable. He could cause trouble for Dominick if she didn't persuade him otherwise.

"Raleigh." She laid her hand on his arm and gently nudged him toward the garden gate. "Don't cause trouble for Dominick—"

"You're calling him Dominick."

"Yes, and I call you Raleigh."

"We've known each other all our lives."

"And, as you keep reminding us, Dominick is only a bondsman." Tabitha used the tone she applied to anxious fathers and children—a little too much like the coating of one of her candied flower petals. "I call Patience by her Christian name too."

Raleigh grunted and reached for the gate latch.

Seeing movement in the garden, Tabitha stayed his hand. "Please, listen to me a moment."

"You won't persuade me not to do something about that bondsman." Raleigh set his hands on his hips.

"Did you ever witness a flogging when you were impressed in the British Navy?" Tabitha countered.

Raleigh's sudden pallor answered before he mumbled, "Yes, too often."

"You know that's what will happen to Dominick if you tell Mayor Kendall about Dominick's morning excursions. Can you condemn a man to that?"

Raleigh's silence was answer enough.

"I can't either, which is why I didn't make a scene over him kissing me. He was being impudent, is all."

Raleigh's jaw hardened. "What if he's behind these abductions?"

"Then he'll get caught. And if he's not, this town may punish him, even find him guilty anyway, simply because he's English." Her stomach felt sour. "I myself hold being English against him, but I know men like Wilkins will do something foolish like hang him without a trial. I'm a healer, Raleigh. I can't be responsible for something like that, whatever my suspicions—not without proof."

"I don't think getting proof will be difficult."

Tabitha hoped not. She wanted things settled, and settled quickly.

"Then you won't say anything until then?" she pressed.

"All right, just for you." Raleigh smiled. "If you go to church with me next Sunday and the Midsummer Festival after that."

"Raleigh, if I go to church with you, everyone will think we're courting," Tabitha protested.

"Why aren't we?" He took a step closer to her. "You can't know I've changed until you spend more time with me."

"I know. It's why I went fishing with you today. But not church. Not yet." She gave him an encouraging smile, though at that moment, his nearness, with the odors of salt spray and perspiration she had once found manly and appealing, made her feel trapped in an airless room. "Please, don't force me to trust you again. It's not possible."

"I know. I'm sorry." He didn't move back, but his chin lost some of its forward thrust. "I'm just so anxious to be settled here at home."

"As anxious as you were to leave?" She didn't like the bitter taste of the words on her tongue. Even less did she like the hurt expression on his face. "Raleigh, I'm—"

"No, don't apologize." He bowed his head. "I deserve that. But will you at least come to the festival with me?"

Tabitha fumbled with the latch to the gate. "I can't."

"Why not?"

"You offered me marriage after the last one we attended together. I don't want people to think we've renewed our engagement."

"We could—all right. I'll leave it alone. But you'll dance with me there, won't you?"

"I'll dance with you there. Now, I really need to go help make supper."

"Thank you for today." Raleigh's face softened as he took her hand and kissed it. "I'll do whatever I must to persuade you things will be different between us this time. I learned my lesson."

"Give me time." She reclaimed her hand. Completely unaffected by the warmth of his lips on her skin, she entered the gate and latched it behind her.

She didn't need to look back to know he watched her all the way to the house. Instead of the tingle of excitement she'd received when knowing Dominick watched her, the hairs on the back of her neck rose. She felt like a cat petted the wrong way.

Never in the past had Raleigh been so jealous of other

men, so possessive of her. She had made it clear since he returned that she would not easily renew her engagement to him. Right now she felt no more for him than the affection she felt for any of her other childhood friends. Affection. Exasperation. And something else that didn't go along with friendship—apprehension.

Two years at sea had hardened him, not just physically, but in his demeanor. She read it in the pugnacious thrust of his chin, a certain missing warmth in his rich blue eyes. He was quick to judge.

But then, so was she. She'd judged Dominick guilty on nothing more than the grounds of his being a British subject. She could add his nighttime wanderings too, but he hadn't been in the vicinity of the missing men.

He had, however, been on that sloop. It looked bad for him. As she stepped over the threshold and through the open kitchen doorway, she wondered if maybe Raleigh was right and she should tell Mayor Kendall about the incident. Yet Kendall would not be amused to have his bondsman, his precious butler, shown to be a spy in their midst. If it were untrue, she would have damaged Dominick and tossed doubts on Kendall's judgment of men for nothing. At the moment, Kendall was her ally amongst the men of the council. No, she would find her proof, then report Dominick Cherrett for the cheat and liar he was.

She decided to seek Dominick out as soon as she could, if he didn't come to her first. An opportunity arose the next day with a request from Mrs. Lee to look in on the four-footed mother and babies. Noting the date on the calendar, Tabitha decided to call on Marjorie Parks as well.

"You're going to deliver soon," she told the young mother. "Do you know when your husband will be home?"

"He's been gone over eight months." Sadness filled Marjorie's eyes. "I want him home for the birth, then just to stay. It's too dangerous being a sailor these days."

"It's not all that safe on land," her mother-in-law declared. "British ships coming right up our waterways, indeed."

"Like they want a war," Marjorie said. "That's what Donald said before he left and the disappearances were just starting, that someone wants a war."

"Why?" Tabitha kept her hand on her childhood friend's abdomen, loving the sensation of the baby's movements.

"Some men make money off of wars," the elder Mrs. Parks said. "They become privateers like Mayor Kendall's father in the last war with England. They build ships. Prices of goods increase . . . Lots of reasons."

"Appalling." Tabitha stepped away from Marjorie. "You look well, my friend. I'll expect the baby in no more than two weeks."

"I hope you're right." Marjorie smiled. "It's uncomfortable in the heat."

"I'll be waiting for your servant to call on me."

Tabitha left for the Downings'. This time, all the ladies gathered around the mother and puppies in their new home—a three-sided box beneath the trees. The ladies cooed and giggled over the tiny, spotted creatures clambering over one another for attention and nourishment. The puppies squeaked and wagged their tails. Momma spaniel gave a canine grin to the assembly and licked Tabitha's hand.

"They're doing well," she assured Mrs. Lee. "What concerned you?"

"I thought maybe their eyes weren't focusing." She stood. "Come into the kitchen with me. I'll get you something to drink."

Tabitha started to refuse, but a pleading look from the younger woman caused her to keep her mouth shut until they reached the house. "What's really wrong, Mrs. Lee?"

"Oh, do please call me Phoebe. Mrs. Lee is my mother-in-law, and it makes me feel old."

Tabitha laughed. "You don't look old."

"I know. I look about sixteen." She grimaced. "My aunt says that's an asset for finding another husband, but I don't want to go through marriage again, thank you."

Tabitha waited for more.

Phoebe pulled glasses out of a cupboard, retrieved a pitcher from the pantry, and poured lemonade. "I made it an hour ago, so it's still cool. As cool as my heart." She laughed.

Tabitha arched her brows and sipped the tart drink.

"I've shocked you, I know." Phoebe toyed with her glass, head bent. "The thing is, Miss Tabitha, I want your help."

"I . . . beg your pardon? Are you . . . that is, does it involve a female issue?"

"Not like you think." Phoebe brushed shining curls off of her face. "I want you to take me on as an apprentice."

The glass slid from Tabitha's hand. She caught it before it broke on the floor, but lemonade spilled. "I'm so sorry."

"No matter. I startled you." Phoebe rushed to gather a cloth and started wiping up the spill. "I should have warned you, but I was afraid I'd go coward, when I've been wanting to ask you since before I came here. In fact, it's why I came here."

"Miss Phoebe, do you know anything about what I do? I mean, you were married, but you have no children . . ." Tabitha ran out of words.

"I have no children," Phoebe bit out, as though the honey of her voice had turned to frozen wax, "because of an incompetent midwife. She killed my baby, nearly killed me, and, I fully believe, killed my husband. But she is all that county has, and I want to rectify the situation."

"I see." Tabitha blinked back tears, seeing too much, understanding as much of the pain of that kind of loss as could any woman who hadn't borne a child. "Couldn't you sponsor a woman to be trained?"

"Yes, ma'am, I could." The hardness of Phoebe's voice remained. "But only I can judge whether or not I'm competent." She relaxed and smiled. "But I've taken you unawares. You don't need to answer me now."

Tabitha could have answered. Her midwifery was a skill she intended to pass along to her daughter. Never had the women of her family passed the trade to someone outside the family. They hadn't needed to. They had always borne at least one daughter by the time they were seventeen or eighteen.

Until she came along.

"I'll give it thought," she said.

"Please do." The anguish in the other woman's eyes wrenched at Tabitha's heart.

Phoebe Lee understood loss too.

Tabitha didn't feel like finding an excuse to go to Mayor Kendall's in search of Dominick after that. Instead, she crossed the alley and entered the graveyard, where three generations of Eckleses and her maternal grandmother had been buried. Simple stones marked each grave. Tabitha dropped to her knees between Momma's and Grandmomma's headstones, where she'd planted a rosebush.

Beyond the low wall, the village sounds of children and dogs, hammering and rumbling wagons, seemed distant. Around her, magnolia trees scented the air, and the dogwoods, now in full leaf, lent cool shade. Bees hummed from flower to flower. Life amidst death.

"How did you two have such faith through all you suffered?" She traced the date of her mother's death—June 3, 1807. Momma had smiled when she died. So had Grandmomma. They'd gone in peace, with a comfort she had failed to bring them in life.

"And I'm still failing you. Family tradition may die with me. Raleigh was my last hope over two years ago. I don't know how to change that now."

She caught movement from the corner of her eye and turned her head.

Dominick stood on the far side of the wall a dozen yards away. Sunlight gleamed on his dark hair, bringing out highlights of bronze and cinnabar, gilding his cheekbones as though he were some golden statue. The sight of him made her heart leap, but he was no hope for the future. He was a flirtation for now, a means to an end.

She rose and crossed the grass to meet him. "I thought about coming to see you."

"But changed your mind?" He glanced at the tombstones. "I thought I was a better interlocutor than that."

"You are." She laughed and her sadness dropped away. "I want to apologize for Raleigh's behavior yesterday."

"It's not your place to apologize for him. He doesn't like me." He ghosted his fingertips across her cheek. "With good reason, I think."

Every muscle in her body tightened, yet it didn't feel awful, as it should have. "You're rather sure of yourself, Mr. Cherrett," she managed with dignity.

"Yes, my mermaid, I am. Shall I walk you home?"

"Do you have another rendezvous with a British ship?"

"A sloop, my dear. Ships—"

"Have three masts," she finished with him, laughing. "In all seriousness," she added, "that was foolish of you to go aboard that sloop. There are grumblings about you, you know."

"I know." He too turned sober as he offered his arm. "We make an excellent pair. Raleigh Trower is telling people I'm involved with abducting sailors and fishermen from this shore, and Harlan Wilkins is telling people you're incompetent. Has it damaged your patients' trust in you?"

"Not thus far." Tabitha curled her fingers over the tensile strength of his forearm. She caught the eye of a few people crossing the square, all of whom glanced at Dominick and arched their brows in question or shook their heads in disapproval. She supposed she should release her hold on him; it looked too intimate.

But she didn't.

"I'll be more discreet in the future," Dominick said. "Though I admit discretion is not one of my strong points. When I was a boy, I once admitted that I liked to read. My classmates threw me into the mill pond, and I got a thrashing for getting my clothes wet."

"That's awful. Why would someone do that?"

"They didn't want me showing them up with the schoolmaster."

"I meant the thrashing."

Dominick laughed. "Ah, that. Well, I think I was expected to at least kick off my shoes before I went in. Fortunately, I could swim, but the shoes ended up at the bottom of the pond. So, alas, did my little New Testament."

"You carried a New Testament around with you when you were a boy?" Tabitha stopped at the edge of the cobbles and stared up at him.

"I did." He gazed past her toward the sea a half mile away. "I had a deep faith in God."

"Had?"

"But now . . ." He turned away from her. "I've probably irrevocably damaged my relationship with God."

"Do you still have one, a relationship, I mean?" She felt an odd twinge, rather like envy in anticipation of him saying yes.

He didn't answer until they walked along the edge of the water, where a narrow path of hard-packed sand made the going easier, if one didn't mind a few drops of water spraying the clothes or face. Tabitha didn't mind the water. The silence between them stung.

It remained until they stood parallel to her cottage. Then he turned to her and took her hands in his. "I don't know. The Bible says I do, but I can't forget what I've done. Every morning, my servitude here reminds me that I am worse than the son in the parable, who said he would work in the vineyard but didn't."

"I should think you're more the son who said he wouldn't work in the vineyard but did." She offered him a tentative smile.

"No, my dear, that's you." He folded her hands together between his. "You claim you have no relationship with God, but then I find out how you give to others, knowing you may never receive a farthing for your efforts. You comfort and encourage everyone from Mayor Kendall to those urchins who run wild in the square."

Her cheeks heated despite the sea spray. "Where did you hear such nonsense?"

"From Letty, from Japheth, from one of those urchins in the square." He drew her hands toward him, pulling her closer. "The village council will listen to Harlan Wilkins because he is possibly the second-richest man in town next to Kendall, but they won't act against you no matter what he says, because their wives and children think so highly of you."

She tried to shrug off the praise. "They don't associate with me a great deal, not in a social sense."

"Because you're a heathen, my dear." He grinned. "If you want to be invited to the parties, you must go to church."

"I can't pretend a faith I don't have."

"And I . . . respect you for that. But I can't help but wonder if you're pretending not to have faith." He nudged her chin up with their clasped hands and held her gaze. "I recognize the symptoms, since I have them myself."

"Maybe." She licked her suddenly dry lips.

His gaze dropped to her lips. For a heartbeat, she thought he intended to kiss her, and she caught her breath. Then his focus flicked past her, and he stepped away. "Not now."

Tabitha turned her head. A man silhouetted against the lowering sun stood without a hint of motion, like a cat ready to spring on a mouse.

18

The smell of long-dead fish assaulted Raleigh's nostrils as he slipped into the shed a hundred yards behind his house. So did another scent, something crisp and clean and familiar.

His contact, his puppet master on American soil, had arrived before him.

Raleigh swallowed against a surge of sickness at the back of his throat. In just a few minutes, he would learn who the man was or was not. It was a risk. If he spoke the wrong words, this man might kill him. Raleigh would die knowing who his contact was, but it wouldn't help Tabitha or bring her back to him. If he learned who the man was not, it could free him to launch a full broadside of attempts to win her back, instead of letting his guilt add its weight to her rebuffs. Seeing Dominick Cherrett in intimate dialogue with Tabitha on the beach that afternoon, about to kiss her, had given him the impetus to take the risk, to send a message to his master and request this meeting.

Now that he stood no more than a half dozen feet from the man, he realized that his desire to shove Cherrett out of his way and pursue Tabitha in earnest had driven him into precipitate action yet again. He hadn't trusted the Lord to take care of matters in His way, in His timing. Now he couldn't go back. The other man was moving toward him with a whisper of fabric.

"What do you want?" The voice was little more than a murmur, muffled and unrecognizable.

"I want—" Raleigh's heart nearly stopped. "I want to—I want out of this game." It hadn't been his prepared speech, but he spoke his heart.

The other man laughed. "The option is a bite of the cat-o'-nine-tails aboard a certain frigate on the American station, or even hanging."

"They can't do that without a court martial," Raleigh protested. "I'd have to be condemned for desertion."

"You have been." Satisfaction rang even through the murmur. "I got word yesterday that they held one in your absence."

Tuesday, the day Cherrett went aboard the British sloop. Not proof, but too much of a coincidence for him to risk pursuing his plan for Dominick Cherrett. Who else in Seabourne could learn of British Navy doings?

"I thought that sloop put into the inlet for a reason," Raleigh said.

Stillness and silence from the man.

Not stillness and silence from outside. Something bumped against the shed wall, a light tap like a windblown twig or a metal button.

The wind was calm.

"Did you invite someone along tonight?" his companion demanded.

"No, I—"

A hard hand curled around Raleigh's shoulder. "If I go out there and find evidence of someone being here, I may save your captain a rope."

"Go ahead." Raleigh found the words fluent on his tongue. "I left a letter saying if anything happens to me, it's Dominick Cherrett's fault."

"Did you indeed." The man chuckled deep in his chest.

"I did." It lay on his pillow.

"Then I'll just have to find it," the other man said. He moved with the speed of a striking snake, and the world went black.

Two lights still burned in the seaside cottage, one upstairs in the front, facing the ocean, one on the lower floor, spilling over the herb garden. Dominick circled the house once, glad there wasn't a dog to bark and alert the ladies to the fact that he wasn't certain if he should knock on the front door or the back. Never in his life had he been the one required to seek out medical assistance. And he was wasting time, while a man's head oozed like the insides of a soft-boiled egg thrown against a wall.

He chose the front door. The shiny brass knocker gleamed in the moonlight, drawing his eye, drawing his feet up the flagstones to lift the dove-shaped knocker for a smart rap. In the quiet night, the bang reverberated like thunder. A bird woke in a nearby tree and muttered a complaint.

Inside the house, footfalls sounded, light and quick. The door sprang open. "How may I—Dominick, what are you doing here at this hour?"

"Seeking medical assistance." He didn't smile. He wanted her to know he wasn't making up a tale.

She still gave him a dubious scan from head to toe. "You look all right to me."

"I am, but Raleigh Trower isn't."

"Raleigh?" Her hand flew to her lips, her eyes widened, and color drained from her face. "What? Where is he?" She peered past Dominick.

He stared past her face. He didn't want her to read his expression, a telltale twitch or blink that might betray the inner pang she'd set off with her reaction to news of Raleigh's injury.

"I didn't want to move him." Dominick shoved his hands into the pockets of his coat. "Will you come with me?"

"Of course. What do I need?"

"Bandages. Perhaps stitching things."

"Wait here." She spun on her heel and raced up the steps.

"Shall I come with you?" Patience emerged from the kitchen to call up the steps.

Dominick couldn't hear Tabitha's response, but Patience's lips thinned and she glanced toward him, as though she didn't like it.

"The wind's kicking up," Dominick said.

"All the more reason I should go too, besides it not being decent, her out alone with you." Patience yanked a cloak off of a rack by the door. "She won't wear this if I'm not here to make her put it on in the rain."

Tabitha appeared at the top of the steps. "I don't want to get ill, so I promise to wear it. As for the decency of the matter—where is he, Dominick?"

"A shed behind his house."

"Then you fetched his family?" Tabitha raced down the steps, heels clattering, and snatched the cloak from Patience. "His mother knows what to do about most injuries."

"Yes, but—" Dominick glanced toward Patience, took the cloak from Tabitha's hand, and whirled it over her shoulders. "I'll take good care of her, Miss Patience."

"Humph." She grabbed the edge of the door. As he and Tabitha headed down the flagstones to the gate, he felt Patience's gaze boring into his back.

"How bad is he?" Tabitha asked.

Outside the wall, the wind hit them full force, cold and damp and smelling of the sea. They walked along the landward side of the dunes but could hear the sea, its roar a beast threatening to devour the land.

"We'd better hurry." He grabbed her hand and picked up their pace.

"Because of the weather or Raleigh's condition?" she demanded.

"I don't know how bad his condition is. Bad enough I thought he needed more care than I could give him." Or wanted to, after what he'd heard Trower say about him. "There's a lot of blood, Tabitha. From his head."

"You didn't go to his family," she said.

"I made him as comfortable as I could, then came here. It seemed . . . safer that way."

"Of course, you wouldn't want them to know you're out this late." She looked up at him. "And why are you out this late, and with Raleigh?"

"I had a yearning to see the sea during a storm. Thought it might remind me of home."

Which wasn't precisely a lie. He did miss the stormy English Channel.

"And just happened to be at the Trower house?" Be it the truth or not, Tabitha's tone said she didn't believe him.

"No, I didn't just happen to be there. I saw him skulking around town and thought I'd follow him to see why he was out on such a night."

"When he could ask the same of you? Dominick, you'll have to do better than that. You wouldn't risk having him tell Kendall about your own wanderings."

"If he were going to tattle on me, he already would have." He squeezed her fingers. "Then I'd let my uncle—" He bit his tongue for the slip, cleared his throat. "I'd let my acquaintances in the British Navy know there's a deserter right here."

"You wouldn't."

"Thank you for your faith in me. Of course I wouldn't, but he doesn't know that."

"Oh, you two." Tabitha made a growling noise not unlike the sea's. "I should knock your heads together."

"From the look of it, someone already knocked Trower's head into something."

"Someone? You two didn't fight?"

Dominick felt like she had knocked his head into a wall. "No, Tabitha, we didn't fight. Why would we?"

"Maybe because he was watching us earlier?"

"That wasn't Trower. That was Wilkins."

"You're sure? Why would Wilkins—of course." Tabitha's sigh sounded as gusty as the wind. "More evidence to discredit me. I wish it had been Raleigh and you were there tonight to tell Raleigh . . . something."

"I followed him out of curiosity, is all. He doesn't even know I was there, nor will he."

Nor would either of them know of his little excursion to the Trower house after he wrapped strips of his shirt around Trower's head and before he raced to Tabitha's house.

Dominick hesitated, then said, "He was talking of how to destroy me."

"Dominick, no. He wouldn't."

"He was, but you'll have to take my word for it unless we find to whom he was speaking."

"I don't want to believe Raleigh would do that, or that you'd make it up." Tabitha stroked her thumb over his knuckles, and he flinched. "This knuckle is swollen. What happened?"

"I struck it against the shed wall trying to help him. Not that he deserved my help after trying to incriminate me." Dominick spoke through gritted teeth. "But you seem to think that condemns me guilty of striking him with it."

"It seems . . . suspicious. I mean, did you see anyone else who could have done so?"

"Would you believe me if I said yes?"

"I—" Her hand tightened on his. "I want to. But who would he be meeting out here in the middle of the night?" She gestured with the hand holding her satchel.

"You ask an excellent question, Madam Midwife." They reached the shed and Dominick pushed open the door.

The metallic stench of blood mixed with mildew and fish swirled out to greet them, along with a thud and a groan.

"Raleigh?" Tabitha darted into the outbuilding. "Raleigh, can you hear me?" Concern, affection, and a hint of anxiety gentled her tone. "That's a nasty bump, Raleigh. Are you in pain?"

"Stupid . . . question." He slurred his words like an intoxicated man. "Never . . . Who's with you?"

"Dominick." Tabitha paused. "Did he do this to you?"

Dominick leaned his head against the door frame, wondering if Raleigh Trower would tell the truth or an outright lie. He expected Trower to take the latter action, claim Dominick's guilt—a guilt that would likely get him sent to Kendall's plantation along the James River if he was lucky . . . sent to prison if he wasn't.

"I—" Trower's indrawn breath was audible from six feet away. "I don't know. I didn't see him."

"But he was here. He came to fetch me," she concluded.

"I d-don't know anything," Trower mumbled.

Dominick still did not relax.

"If he came to fetch you for me, I expect he is the culprit," Trower continued.

"But we'd have to prove it, even for a bondsman, since he's Mayor Kendall's servant," Tabitha mused aloud. "Maybe he didn't mean this to happen. You're still bleeding."

"I feel like a stuck pig. Is my father out fishing?"

"No, not tonight. It's gotten too rough." Fabric rustled. "I'll fetch him out here. Dominick stayed to help carry you."

"Don't want him touching me," Trower grumbled.

"Good, I'll leave," Dominick said. "Perhaps I should have let you drain of blood like that stuck pig, instead of using my own shirt to help stop the bleeding. One of my three good shirts, I might add, and fetch Tabitha, and—"

"Stubble it, Dominick," Tabitha broke in. "If you were where you belong, this wouldn't have happened."

"You presume." Dominick straightened from the door frame. "I'll be on my way."

"And no one the wiser regarding you being here? Do I tell them his attacker fetched me before running off?"

"Tell them what you like." He turned his back on her.

"Dominick—thank you." She touched his arm. "You did take a risk coming to me, whatever the cause of his injury."

"I did no one but Trower a favor if you think I had a hand in it." Heart feeling as though it would rise up and choke him, Dominick departed.

Outside, the night had turned more wild than before. As he broke into a run on his way back to the village, he couldn't hear his own footfalls above the surf, nor his own breath over the wind. He barely saw the ground beneath his feet or obstacles in his path. He smelled only his own wet wool and sandalwood, the sea, the memory of Tabitha's roses. He felt only the rough wool of his coat against his scarred back, the slap of rain against his face, the ache in his heart.

He hadn't come to America to fall in love. That was sheer folly. Love distracted the mind and caused mistakes. And no woman worth having would love a man in his position, as she saw it. Matters would be worse for the future of his heart, with the truth of his purpose in America stirred into the mix.

She thought she knew that truth. She knew too little, just enough to make her knowledge dangerous to him. He knew only enough to realize his danger. Yet how could he speak against Raleigh Trower without sounding spiteful? Without giving away what he was still trying to deny himself—how much he cared for her?

How much he loved her.

He couldn't. If he survived this night's work without being punished in a way that would remove him from his useful position, he would have to take Tabitha into his confidence to protect himself. To protect her.

Gravel crunched under his feet, and he slowed. He'd reached the walkways along the village streets and didn't want to draw attention to his presence. A few lights shone through windows along his way. A shadow moved behind the panes of the parsonage's front parlor. On the other side of the square, a cat posed like a statue against the illuminated windows of Wilkins's house.

Dominick skirted the parsonage and slipped between the church and graveyard on his way to Kendall's back garden a hundred feet beyond. The darkness there proved complete, and Dominick slowed further, his hands in front of him to meet the gate before he crashed into it with his entire body. He'd never returned in such complete blackness and feared losing his way amidst the gravestones.

He sensed rather than saw the walls rising up on either side of him, enclosures for the gardens of an empty house on one side and the mayor's on the other. His hand trailing the rough bricks of the wall, he followed the line.

He caught the smell of wet wool and spirits an instant before his hand struck something hard and unyielding, but wearing a coat of wool, not a coating of moss.

Another person.

He jerked his hand back, but not fast enough. Fingers coiled around his wrist and yanked him forward.

"Who is this?" Harlan Wilkins demanded.

19

Tabitha moved a candle so she could look into Raleigh's eyes. They contracted from the sudden flare of light, his lashes dropped over the deep blue eyes, and he groaned a protest.

"Looking to see if you're concussed." She smoothed the soft brown hair away from his brow, stopping when her hand met the bandage she'd wound over the stitches. "You can rest now." She started to turn away.

"Wait." He caught hold of her hand. "Tabbie, what did he tell you?"

"You need to rest. We'll discuss what happened later."

"Now." He sounded like a petulant child.

She spoke to him in soothing tones. "Raleigh, you have a badly bruised jaw and a banged-up head. You need to rest."

"I'll rest when I know what he's been telling you about me." He tried to smile. With one side of his face swollen and purple, it looked like a monster's grimace. "Please."

"All right." She returned to the chair on which she'd been sitting while repairing the damage to his skull. "It will only take a minute. He told me nothing more than that you were unconscious in a shed."

"Did he—did he admit to doing this to me?" Raleigh touched his jaw and winced.

"No."

She'd presumed he had and as much as accused him of it.

He hadn't denied it. Neither had he confirmed her assumption. He'd simply been angry with her for thinking the worst. Angry with Raleigh for trying to ruin him.

But Raleigh wouldn't do that. He might feel he was in competition with Dominick for her attention and interest, but he was neither vindictive nor mean-spirited.

At least the Raleigh she'd known as a child, as a young woman, as his fiancée, hadn't been. No, he'd simply been irresponsible enough to abandon her because he wanted an adventure.

"Did he do this?" she asked as she had earlier. "Are you quite, quite sure?"

"I—" He rolled his eyes toward her, then closed his eyes again. "The build was much the same."

"The build?" Tabitha leaned forward, her hands clasped on her knees. "Let me be clear on this. You're accusing a man, a redemptioner—so the consequences are far worse than if he were an ordinary citizen—of striking you down in the dark, but you only think so because of his height and . . . what else? Shoulder breadth?"

A nice shoulder breadth, perfect for laying her head upon in apprehension and despair.

Her insides twisted. She didn't know why she'd thought that. She had Raleigh. She could rest her head on a broader shoulder, a sturdier shoulder, in more ways than one. Raleigh was an American—home to stay, he claimed—a man with an occupation and kindness.

Yet his kindness had come into question tonight, as in the past. A kind man wouldn't have abandoned her. A kind man wouldn't be accusing another man on such flimsy evidence.

"Didn't you talk to him?" she demanded, voice harsh. "You can recognize his accent in a few words."

"Yes, he talks like some lordling." Despite his deformed features, Raleigh's sneer was apparent. "We had a lieutenant like that. He was the younger son of some minor peer of the realm and talked to the rest of us as though we were filth on his shoes."

"I don't usually talk to the filth on my shoes," Tabitha responded. It sounded like something Dominick would say. With an effort, she managed not to smile, since she couldn't imagine why she would want to at that moment. "Then you should have recognized Dominick's accent."

"Tabbie, why are you so friendly to him?" Raleigh held out his hand to her. "He's no good, you know."

"I don't know." She rose and began to pace the parlor into which they'd carried Raleigh, with its carpet rolled up and its chairs under cheap muslin coverings, preserving them for guests' use only. "I'm afraid you're right. He doesn't obey the curfew, which makes him look suspicious for a bondsman. And him being English makes matters worse. But then I think maybe I only don't know whether he's an honest man because he is English and my basis is unfounded."

"But there are bad things happening around here," Raleigh reminded her. "Men are disappearing right off our beaches or soon after they go to sea. I was one of them."

"And Dominick could be involved with the disappearances." Tabitha paused at the window.

Outside, the night raged with wind and rain. A quarter mile away, the surf slammed into the beach with such force, its boom was barely distinguishable from the thunder that accompanied the lightning flashes. Inside, the parlor and house lay quiet save for an occasional murmur of voices, the clink of crockery from the kitchen, the creak of a floorboard. Shivering in the lowering temperature, Tabitha fingered the crocheted lace of the curtains. Raleigh's grandmother had been an Acadian who'd evaded deportation to Louisiana when England took over Quebec, and she had made them herself.

England, a nation with the audacity to think it should conquer the world, wouldn't hesitate to send a spy into the heart of a seaside village and rob the country of its young men. The men that fledgling land would need if hostilities flared into war.

"Tell me what happened tonight." Tabitha faced Raleigh, turning her back to the wild night. "How did you encounter . . . this person who struck you down?"

"I was in the shed." Raleigh's words grew slurry again. "You know, we have another anchor in there. Gotta get it to the *Marianne*."

"You were looking for the anchor at ten o'clock at night or thereabouts?" Tabitha arched her brows in disbelief. "In the dark?"

"I haven't been sleeping well of late. Tuesday upset me. The sloop. That man fawning on you. You refusing to go to the festival with me."

Tabitha dropped onto the nearest chair, weary in body and spirit. "Raleigh, you're not being honest with me. Dominick said he saw you in the village. Please start from the beginning and tell me what really happened."

"May I have some laudanum?" Raleigh responded. "I hurt all over."

"And you don't want to talk to me." Tabitha remained still, torn by her desire to force the truth from Raleigh and the responsibility she had as a healer not to withhold aid from any human.

"Nothing to tell." Raleigh's words were barely discernible. "A man came in and said a few unpleasant things to me and struck me."

"But you didn't recognize his voice?"

"It sounded kind of muffled, like he didn't want me to recognize him. Now, may I please have that laudanum?"

"All right."

Tabitha retrieved the squat green bottle from her bag, measured two spoonfuls of laudanum into a glass, and took it to the sofa. She knelt beside him and slipped an arm beneath his shoulders, raising him just enough for him to drink with as little discomfort as possible.

"Thank you." He curved his fingers around hers. "I love you so much, Tabbie. Please forgive me."

"I prayed for you tonight. I haven't prayed for anyone in two years. But I wanted you to be all right so badly, I didn't know what else to do."

"Does that mean you still love me?" Hope flared in his eyes, even as the drug began to make them glaze.

"I—" A door seemed to slam on her throat, cutting off her ability to say yes.

Dominick's face flashed before her eyes, not laughing and teasing as she usually thought of him, but angry, perhaps even frightened. He claimed Raleigh had been trying to harm him.

"I need time, Raleigh." She released her hand from his, brushed her fingertips across his brow, and rose. "I'll stay in the house for the night in case you take a turn for the worse." She left him before he could stop her again.

In the kitchen, his family huddled around the table. The room smelled of wood smoke, coffee, and the ever-present fish. Her mouth watered for a cup of the coffee, but her nose wrinkled at the fishy scent. She would need to go crabbing soon so she didn't lose her taste for seafood. It was a staple of her diet there beside the ocean, and she'd never minded the odor until today.

Dominick always smelled like sandalwood, exotic and clean.

She shoved that disloyal thought aside and smiled at the Trowers. "He'll be just fine."

"Would you like me to walk you home then?" Mr. Trower asked, his face lighting with a smile.

"I think I should stay here rather than make you go out in this." Tabitha pulled out a chair. "And in the event Raleigh needs me."

"He always needs you, child." Mrs. Trower rose and went to the hearth. "Coffee?"

"Please." Tabitha ignored the immediate response that sprang into her head. *If he always needed me, why did he leave me?*

"I want to know who came and fetched you," Mr. Trower said. "Why won't you tell us?"

"It doesn't matter." Tabitha crossed the kitchen to take her coffee from Mrs. Trower. "He probably saved Raleigh's life. If he'd lain out there all night, he'd have likely caught a lung fever in this weather."

"He's likely the man who hit him," Felicity suggested. "Did Raleigh tell you?"

"He isn't saying either way," Tabitha admitted. "But we shouldn't be leaping to conclusions."

Yet she had, and now she felt heartsick over it. Her near accusation had hurt Dominick, had told him she didn't trust him. He might decide she was someone to avoid in the future. That possibility left her feeling hollow, frightened.

"Him not saying either way just says he was up to no good." Mr. Trower sighed. "Likely a meeting for a bout of fisticuffs to settle some spat with another young man."

"And why would Raleigh be doing that?" Mrs. Trower demanded.

Mr. Trower glanced at Tabitha and winked. "Maybe over a pretty girl."

"Nonsense." Mrs. Trower slapped her hands onto her ample hips. "The only other young man looking Tabitha's way is that redemptioner. And he'd be a fool to be out at night."

"No sense in young men when it comes to a pretty girl." Mr. Trower went to her and slipped his arm around her shoulders. "Do you remember Roger Tarr and the celebration of the end of the war?"

Mrs. Trower blushed and lost ten years off her looks as she smiled up at her spouse of twenty-six years.

Tabitha turned away. Her eyes burned. The fire blurred in the mist of tears glazing her vision. She tried to picture herself gazing up at Raleigh like that in twenty-six years, but the image wouldn't form. If she married him, it would be for security and children, not for love and devotion.

Most women married for security and children. Most women didn't have a skill they could practice to support themselves, and had to marry to survive. Most women, at the least, trusted the man they married, trusted him to stay, trusted him to be honest.

If Raleigh wasn't lying to her, he was withholding a great deal of the truth. She knew Dominick was withholding a great deal of the truth. But lying? She supposed he might construct a claim that Raleigh wanted to harm him in order to win her sympathy or make her distrust Raleigh.

She wished he hadn't been successful.

And for that reason, if nothing else, she needed to attempt to protect Dominick from the consequences of the night, if others continued to suspect he was involved.

"Mr. Trower, Mrs. Trower? Girls?" Tabitha faced the couple. "We really don't know who struck Raleigh. I think we should keep speculation to ourselves or risk spreading possibly unfounded gossip."

They nodded. She'd struck the right note, playing on their Christian principles about gossip to keep them quiet.

"But if it was Mr. Cherrett," Mrs. Trower said, "he's out after Mayor Kendall's curfew on redemptioners."

"Yes, and the mayor will believe you if you tell him," Tabitha pointed out. "But should a man be whipped on suspicion alone?"

"All right," Mr. Trower said, "we won't say anything to Mayor Kendall."

"Or anyone else," Fanny added.

"And we'll tell Raleigh not to make hints and the like if he isn't going to just come out and say what happened," Mrs. Trower said.

"Not that we did such a good job of instilling parental obedience into him." Mr. Trower sighed. "If we had, he wouldn't have run off to the sea when we told him not to."

Tabitha stared at the couple. "You knew he was going to abandon me?"

"I had my suspicions." Mr. Trower shuffled his feet. "It was Raleigh's place to tell you."

"Yes, yes, it was."

But she would have preferred to have known he hadn't just vanished.

Sighing to relieve the heaviness around her heart, she strode to the door into the parlor. "I'll see if he's sleeping. We should probably take turns sitting up with him in the event he takes a turn for the worse."

Raleigh was still sleeping. Mr. Trower took the first watch, then his wife. When Mrs. Trower woke Tabitha, who was asleep on a settee by the kitchen hearth, daylight struggled to break through the rain, and the girls were up and preparing to perform outdoor chores beneath oiled cloth capes.

"He's awake," Mrs. Trower said. "Go on in and I'll bring you some coffee."

Tabitha smoothed as many wrinkles from her gown as she could and retied the ribbon confining her hair to a queue at the base of her neck. Felicity gave her a cloth and basin of water. After washing her face and hands, Tabitha returned to the parlor.

Raleigh looked considerably better in the feeble gray light. Color had returned to his face, diminishing the depth of the bruise's purple.

He gave her his lopsided smile. "You stayed."

"I always stay with a seriously injured or ill patient until I'm certain things are well in hand."

"So I'm just a patient?" He grimaced.

"If you weren't, I wouldn't be alone in here with you." She perched beside him on a chair. "How does the head feel?"

"Like someone pounded it into a wall."

"And your jaw?"

"About the same. A few teeth are loose."

"They should be all right if you leave them alone. Eat soft food and chew on the other side."

"Yes, ma'am." He feigned meekness.

Tabitha sat erect. "Will you tell me the truth this morning?"

"Tabbie—" He met her gaze. His eyes held sadness. "I can't. I'm too ashamed of myself."

"I see." But she didn't. She felt more confused than ever. "So you didn't plan to meet Dominick last night?"

He started to shake his head, winced, and mumbled, "No. I just thought—I thought I might see him. And I won't say anything else. He shouldn't have been here is all I will say, and I'll see he's punished for stepping foot on my property, especially after dark."

"Even if fetching me might have saved your life?" Tabitha pressed him as she had his parents.

"I suppose he didn't want to hang for murder if he didn't fetch help." Raleigh curled his upper lip. "That's not heroic."

"He could have left you and no one would have been the wiser." She leaned forward, holding his gaze. "Raleigh, if you're ashamed of what you wanted to do last night, do me a favor and don't tell Mayor Kendall or anyone else Dominick was out here."

"No, I won't do that." Raleigh drew back. "Not even for you. The man has overstepped his bounds once too often."

"Raleigh, please."

"Why? Why should I help the man you prefer over me, a man who isn't worth looking at you, let alone touching you?"

"Because you don't want him telling people you intended to harm him. I'm beginning to believe he is telling the truth about that. But if you protect him this time, I'll say nothing of your reprehensible behavior."

"And if you promise to make him leave you alone," Raleigh returned, "I'll do you the favor of keeping my mouth shut about his being here at night."

Tabitha glared at Raleigh. He glared back. They'd reached a deadlock she knew would destroy any hope of a future together if one of them didn't yield ground.

20

He'd lost her. In one bold attempt to get rid of Dominick Cherrett and possibly free himself from the chains still tying him to the British Navy like a sheet securing a sail to the yards, Raleigh had gambled and lost the lady he loved, his chance to destroy Dominick Cherrett, and nearly his life.

"I won't say anything," he promised on a sigh. "The man will dig his own grave."

"Then let him. Don't do it for him." She looked so sad, Raleigh's throat closed. He swallowed and changed the subject. "Did you really pray for me last night?"

"I did."

"And God listened to you. I'm all right."

"Maybe." She rose. "The rain is letting up. I need to get home. Send someone to fetch me if anything happens."

"Can you fix my heart?" He tried to smile, though the attempt made his jaw hurt like ten toothaches.

"That's between you and God." She left then.

He heard her say a few words to his family, then the door closed. The hammer of rain against the window masked the sound of her footfalls.

She shouldn't be out in this weather, getting drenched because of him. She should have stayed. But she wanted away from him, from his lying tongue, his dishonesty, his betrayal of his faith.

"Jesus, what have I done?" He flung one arm over his eyes.

"I just want this nightmare to be over. I want to settle with Tabbie and have a comfortable life now."

But he had betrayed her trust—again. Worse, he had plotted to harm another human being. In that, he had turned his back on the faith he so wanted to be good at. He could never help Tabitha want to go to church, not because it was expected of her in the small town, but to worship a God she believed in and trusted. If he talked to her about God now, she would laugh in his face. Her brushing away the answered prayer for him told him that he had helped shatter her faith, and his current actions didn't make matters any better.

"Dear Jesus, can you ever forgive me?"

His crime, his sin, seemed too much for even God's grace to handle. Raleigh knew what the chaplain aboard the ship had told him, but he couldn't imagine that the godly man dreamed of anyone being so depraved as to deliberately want to harm another person.

Yet the chaplain was aboard a man-of-war. He dealt with men who wanted to harm the enemy every day. And Dominick Cherrett was the enemy. England and America weren't officially at war, but Great Britain had been taking actions that would lead to war if not stopped.

Reconciling his actions with his faith didn't seem possible. He needed forgiveness, and he didn't know how to ask for it if he had no intention of repenting—yet.

"Lord, I didn't intend to get myself into this fix. If the British hadn't impressed me . . ."

No, he couldn't blame the English captain, who was following orders. Raleigh had been born in Canada, even if he had come to his father's Virginia home a mere six months later. And they hadn't made him desert and get caught again. He'd worked his way into a position of trust on the word of the chaplain, then broken that trust.

As he'd broken Tabitha's trust in him.

The Navy could have hanged him for deserting. At the least, he should have been flogged. But his captain had been merciful and cunning. Or maybe just cunning and ambitious. Raleigh justified his actions with the excuse that his father needed him at home. If this was the only way he could get free of the Navy, he could leave for the West. But he figured that discovering the identity of his puppet master, his spy master, was faster and less harmful to others.

But he'd made a mess of it, outright accusing Cherrett. He still thought it possible. Raleigh couldn't deny that Cherrett had been out in the night, skulking around the shed. An innocent man would have been tucked up in his bed with a storm brewing. Raleigh needed to discover what Dominick Cherrett had been up to. Proving he was a treacherous blaggard might be the only way that Raleigh could destroy the regard in which Tabitha held the man.

Finding the identity of the traitor might be the only way to regain her trust and regard for him, Raleigh Trower—the man who had let her down too many times.

Dominick didn't know the expression "to cool one's heels" was literal. But after four hours in the cold confines of his bedchamber at the top of the house, avoiding a place where the wind forced rain through the tiny window, chilling one's heels seemed a more appropriate commentary on his state.

He was a prisoner. Wilkins had made certain of that. He had dragged Dominick to the house and presented him to Mayor Kendall, whom Wilkins had just left.

Which didn't account for Wilkins lurking in the alley behind the house.

Dominick spent much of his time pondering that inconsistency—and other matters like Raleigh Trower's intention to destroy Dominick and Tabitha's belief that Dominick had struck down her beau.

He flexed his bruised finger. He wished he had been the one to strike Trower. The man wanted him punished, wanted him set up to take the blame for a crime he hadn't committed.

When he had committed so many for which he had gone unpunished.

Dominick thought perhaps he should have laughed at the irony. He held his head in his hands as he perched on the edge of his narrow bed, and felt the burden of the past six months pressing down on him like a roof beam. The parson had talked about forgiving seven times seventy. Dominick needed more than four hundred and ninety forgivenesses. An infinite number couldn't redeem him, and now he was unlikely to redeem himself.

"I am too much a sinner for even your grace, God," he murmured into the darkness of predawn.

The skin on his back tightened, preparing already for the bite of the lash. Sickness knotted his middle. Not again. He couldn't endure that again. He'd rather hang or end up weeding tobacco twelve hours a day.

He doubted the former would be his fate. He hadn't run away, after all. And he could get used to the back-breaking field labor.

But he'd never see Tabitha again.

If Kendall exercised his right to whip Dominick, would she come to tend his wounds? Or would she refuse because she thought he had harmed another man?

It shouldn't matter. He'd already lost her to Trower. The man had abandoned her, but lifelong ties mattered. He had a family to love her, and his freedom.

Dominick's family would despise her, and he wasn't a free

man until he completed his mission. Away from the coast, he would never succeed. In four years, Tabitha would be wed to Raleigh and likely a mother. Besides that, Dominick's family would never accept her, would find further reason to reject him—too many of those reasons justifiable.

He wasn't supposed to fall in love. Yet he had. He loved her, adored her, wanted to see her face when he woke and before he went to sleep. He ached for the soothing lightness of her touch and the sound of her melodious voice.

But he had rejected God, all for the sake of having his own way. Not having Tabitha in his life was simply one more consequence of his actions.

And other consequences were coming. Above the drum of rain on the roof, he heard the tread of feet on the narrow staircase to his attic room. Footfalls too heavy to belong to one of the twins, too light to belong to Kendall. Unless the mayor had sent up the man who kept up the garden and horses and other outdoor chores, Dominick would find Letty on the other side of his door when it opened. He braced himself for the lash of her tongue.

The key grated in the lock. Dominick rose, bantering words forming on his tongue.

The handle turned. The door swung in. Letty's tall, narrow frame filled the doorway.

"I told you that you were going to get caught," were the first words from her mouth. "I hope you've got a strong back. Kendall doesn't take lightly to his servants disobeying him."

"I'm sure he doesn't." Dominick rolled his shoulders. "Will you, hmm, say a prayer for me?"

"My dear boy, I say a lot of prayers for you." Letty's sharp features softened. "There's something wrong with you being here. You were never cut out to be a servant."

"Call it penance." He took a step toward her, toward the

clearer air of the stairwell. "And speaking of penance, what is my next one to be?"

"I don't know. Mayor Kendall just sent me up to fetch you down to the study."

"Without restraint?" Dominick raised one brow. "Isn't he afraid I'll knock you down and run?"

"He said you have too much honor."

That made Dominick laugh, a hollow bark of mirth. "If I had honor, Letty, I wouldn't be here. But there's enough left for me to stay."

He couldn't even hope for redemption if he fled.

"And we mustn't keep the mayor waiting." He kissed Letty's cheek and edged past her to descend the steps at a decorous pace.

She followed close behind. Her breath rasped in and out of her nose, as though she suffered from a head cold or she'd been crying. When they reached the ground floor and illumination from curtains drawn back allowed as much light from the gray sky as from the candles, Dominick noted Letty's red-rimmed eyes.

She had been crying.

"Not for me," he said.

"For your soul," Letty responded. She patted his shoulder and turned toward the kitchen. "Go on in. He's waiting for you."

Dominick hesitated, drinking in the aroma of coffee and frying bacon, then knocked on the door to the study. "Mayor Kendall?"

"Come in." The voice resonated through the wood.

Dominick entered, his legs not quite as sturdy as he wished. Once inside the door, he stopped, gazing across the square of carpet to the big desk and the man who sat behind it.

Kendall's eyes appeared sunken, the flesh around them

bruised. His complexion was pale, and he didn't smile or blink or look directly at Dominick. "Close the door," he said.

Dominick did so, then leaned against it, his arms crossed over his chest.

"You don't fool me with that casual stance, lad." Harshness edged Kendall's tone. "Your eyes give you away. You're nervous and you have every right to be."

"No casual stance intended, sir. I didn't think I could walk any further."

One corner of Kendall's mouth twitched. "Impertinent to the last, aren't you?"

"Yes, sir. I mean, no, sir. No disrespect intended."

"This morning."

"Sir?" Dominick made himself straighten. A lock of hair fell over his ear, and he realized he should have retied his queue. "I never intend to be disrespectful."

"Or get caught at it, at any rate." Kendall's lips thinned.

Dominick kept his own lips closed.

"Come sit down before you fall down." Kendall gestured to a chair by the fire. "It's cold for June this morning."

The kindness lent Dominick some comfort, and he crossed the room on steadier legs. Once around the chair with its high back, he saw the tray on the low table at the hearth. Two cups resided atop the silver, and steam puffed from the coffeepot.

"Help yourself and pour me a cup," Kendall directed as he rose from behind the desk and took the other seat before the fire.

For the first time since running into Wilkins outside the garden gate, Dominick's back muscles ceased twitching. Without spilling a drop, he poured coffee and the right amount of milk into Kendall's cup first and then his own. As much as he longed to feel the warmth of the china between his fingers, he waited for the mayor to lift his mug before taking up the delicate crockery and cradling it like a precious gift.

When a man was chilled, tired, and worried, it was.

"Now"—Kendall leaned back against the brown velvet of his chair—"tell me why you were wandering about in the middle of the night, against my express orders."

"I like walking in the rain?" Dominick offered.

"Mr. Cherrett, I'm giving you an opportunity to defend your actions, instead of exercising my right to flay the skin off your back. Give me the courtesy of the truth."

"But, sir . . ." Dominick stared at the brown liquid in his cup. "Sir, there's a lady involved."

"How involved?" The coldness of Kendall's voice should have frozen the raindrops on the window. "You are not in a position to wed, so if you've compromised a young woman—"

"No, no, sir, nothing like that." Dominick's ears felt hot. "I'm not that depraved. She's far too good for me and has feelings for another man. But I don't trust him and wished to . . . well, spy on him is the only way to say it."

His words rang with complete sincerity, as he knew they would. They were, as far as they went, the truth, if not the whole truth.

"Is that a fact?" Kendall glared at him.

Dominick met his gaze without flinching or wavering.

Kendall gave a brisk nod. "So what did you hope to learn by spying on him? Is he playing her false and you wanted to expose him?"

"Yes, sir."

Again, Dominick spoke the truth, even if it wasn't quite the truth Kendall meant in his question. Trower wasn't cheating on Tabitha with another female; he was simply behaving in a manner unworthy of a man she would marry.

"Did you fight with this man?"

"No, sir."

That would mean even more trouble if he had, or if Kendall doubted him.

He suddenly wished he held the coffee in his left hand, with his right hand dangling over the side of the chair. But he held his cup in his right, the bruised knuckle glowing purple in the light.

"You have a bruised knuckle," Kendall pointed out, "and you had blood on you when you came in."

"I did, sir, but not from fighting. I know better."

"That's not what I understood from the captain of the ship that brought you to America."

Dominick shuddered. "My circumstances in England were much different. I was a free man there."

"And you are little more than a slave here." Kendall leaned forward and his tone harshened again. "Not only that, Cherrett, you are English at a time when few Americans trust the English, especially around here. If I hear that one man disappeared last night, I will have little choice but to presume you were the culprit and have you treated accordingly. Some men would likely circumvent the law and hang you."

"I'm not involved with stealing Americans for the British Navy, sir."

"And who would believe that? You're caught out in the middle of the night and have blood on your clothes. That's condemnatory behavior right then and there."

Even the coffee's heat failed to stave off the chill now.

Dominick nodded. "I know, sir."

"What you don't know is that Harlan Wilkins wishes to be mayor instead of me. The fact that my bondsman was out and about in the middle of the night is a weapon he can use against me."

"I thought you two were friends." The coffee he'd consumed turned to a whirlpool in his belly.

"Of course we are." Kendall grimaced. "As much as two rivals can be. It's too small a town not to be friends. And if my bondsman is found to be an English spy, my political future ends right here."

The man had been good to Dominick, barring the uniform and powdered hair. He wanted to reassure Kendall that he had nothing to fear, but he couldn't be certain Kendall wouldn't see through his protestations.

"I expect the one of us who finds this spy," Kendall said, "will win the next election. If it's me, I'll have no difficulty getting the senate seat in three years."

Dominick set down his coffee cup. "So what will you do to me, sir?"

"Lock you in your room every night and revoke your permission to attend the Midsummer Festival." The answer emerged so quickly, the mayor must have had it planned. "And if you get out again, I will have you whipped in the town square as an example to other redemptioners. Do you understand?"

Dominick nodded. He couldn't speak. His stomach churned, and he tasted bile.

"Then go get yourself some breakfast and rest." Kendall stood. "After that, please pack my bags for at least a week of travel."

"Yes, sir." Dominick shot to his feet. "This is a sudden journey."

"Some unexpected business has raised its head." Kendall smiled, but it wasn't directed at Dominick, and it wasn't pleasant. "And don't think you can take advantage of my absence to break my rules again. Letty is more than capable of keeping you under her thumb."

"Yes, sir, she is." Dominick edged to the door.

"And Cherrett," Kendall called after him, "be more discreet with Tabitha. She's a dear girl who doesn't deserve to have lost as much as she has. Leave her alone to resume her betrothal to Raleigh Trower."

Dominick froze, staring.

Kendall laughed, head thrown back. "Don't look so surprised. It's my duty to know what goes on in my town."

Then why didn't he know who would betray America by selling her young men to the enemy?

The answer was obvious, sickening, making Dominick feel as though he'd been hit as hard as Trower had been. He should have thought of it, of the ambition that would make Kendall need money. He'd been blinded by the man's kindness to him and the high regard in which everyone held him.

Even now, as he retreated to the kitchen, his back intact, Dominick dismissed the new idea as preposterous. Kendall wanted to run his country, not destroy it. Should war come, a war that would surely destroy the United States of America as a nation, Kendall would hold no power. On the contrary, he might be in danger as a leader of a conquered nation.

Unless he held friends in high places. High British places.

Dominick staggered to a chair and dropped into it like a stone tumbling off of a cliff. He speared his fingers through his hair, dislodging it further. He needed rest before his brainbox exploded with more ridiculous notions.

"I'll fix your hair for you." Dinah slipped up behind him and gathered his hair into her hands. "Oooh, it's soft."

"Stop that." Dominick jerked upright, dislodging her fingers with a painful yank on his scalp. "I'm in enough trouble without Kendall thinking I'm trying to ruin his kitchen maid."

"I just never knew a man's hair could be so soft." Dinah gazed at him with big, limpid eyes.

"You, missy," Dominick scolded, "need to pay more attention to your Bible. Modest behavior is a virtue."

"And since when do you refer to Scripture?" Letty stomped in the back door, her apron full of eggs.

"Perhaps this morning's work has given me my faith back." He spoke with flippancy yet felt an odd tug at his heart, as though he wasn't being entirely facetious.

God had spared him a flogging. Yet without the freedom to move around at night or get to his rendezvous on June 21, the same night as the fete, he was likely to serve out his indenture without redemption at the end.

Unless the evidence he sought lay under his very roof.

21

The storm was going to ruin her roses.

Tabitha stood at the kitchen window and frowned at the streaks of rain down the multiple panes of glass. The scarlet of her roses shone against the gray background like blood, something she'd seen too much of during the night.

Raleigh's blood staining Dominick's shirt, staining the cloth of the sofa, staining her hands. Head wounds always bled profusely and made them look worse than they were. She'd seen many in her life. Mrs. Wilkins's had been the latest before Raleigh's.

The most recent and the worst.

Tabitha shuddered in memory of that terrible wound. She'd tried to stitch it, but the woman had writhed so much in her pain, Tabitha couldn't keep the skin together or aim her needle. In the end, it hadn't mattered. Mrs. Wilkins died, and Harlan Wilkins set out on a trail of vengeance toward Tabitha.

As Raleigh had Dominick?

She couldn't believe it. No, she didn't *want* to believe it. Whether or not she *could* depended on whether or not she believed Raleigh had changed in his two years away. Lately she couldn't seem to believe in anything, not Raleigh's goodness, not Dominick's honesty, not God's interest in her.

Weary, feeling as though she carried a load of bricks on her shoulders, Tabitha leaned her brow on the cold windowpane and wished for the sweetness of the roses, their fresh scent beneath her nose, their delicate flavor under her tongue.

He looks at you like one of your candied flower petals. Raleigh's words echoed in her head, and her cheeks grew warm despite the rain-chilled glass beneath her brow. Something about that remark was unseemly, yet her mind drifted to that brief kiss, stolen but not demanded back. Worse, not regretted. Worst of all, enjoyed.

She couldn't possibly think of marrying Raleigh and have such indelicate thoughts about another man. It was disloyal, a kind of treachery.

And so foolish. If she feared Raleigh leaving again, she was unwise to care about another man who would most certainly leave. And Dominick was up to no good.

So was Raleigh. She had no doubt of that. He wasn't being honest with her. But she would try again. She would try to get Dominick to be honest with her about the night's events. Surely one of them would be, with enough encouragement. A little bribery to soften them up? Food worked with men. At least the married women she knew said so.

Her gaze strayed to the pantry holding the wooden box lined with precious paper and the even more precious candied violets from her efforts in May.

Candied violets.

Her cheeks warmed further as light, quick footfalls pattered into the kitchen.

"Miss Tabitha, are you ill?" Patience exclaimed.

Tabitha faced the maid fully. "No, why do you ask?"

"You're all flushed like you've been taken with a fever. And no wonder, coming in soaked like a drowned rat this morning." Patience pulled out a chair at the table. "Sit yourself down and I'll make you a nice cup of chamomile tea."

"Thank you. I should try to sleep." Maybe the tea would soothe her, quiet her head. She turned to her maid and companion. "Patience, how did you bear to become a redemptioner after being a free woman most of your life?"

"It was do that or starve after my husband died." Patience spooned chamomile leaves into the teapot. "And you and your family made it possible to survive it."

"But do you miss home?"

"Nearly every day." Patience's head bowed over the tea preparations. "Sometimes it's like a hole in my heart to be gone."

"Then why don't you return?" Tabitha began to pace the kitchen. "You're free now."

"God wants me to stay with you."

Tabitha swung around. "How could you possibly know a thing like that?"

Patience shrugged. "I just do. I prayed about it when I worked out my time and had a peace about staying."

"But . . . why would He do that to you?"

"Because I promised to serve Him." Patience faced Tabitha, a smile on her face. "And if keeping you safe and having someone to take care of you is how He wants me to serve Him, then it's what I'm doing."

"But why me?"

"'Cause you're all alone. God loves you too much to let you stay alone."

"If He loves me so much, why did He cause me to be alone in the first place?" Tabitha lashed back.

"I don't know, Miss Tabitha. I wish I did." Tears brightened Patience's eyes. "But He has His reasons. We just have to trust Him."

"The pastor says I have to trust God to trust others. But I can't. I—" The knocker pounded on the front door. "Oh, dear." Tabitha headed to the door. "I'll get it, Patience. It could be one of the Trowers."

Which would mean Raleigh had taken a turn for the worse.

Heart racing, she strode to the door and flung it open.

A bondservant who looked no older than fifteen all but fell into the entry on a gust of rain-laden air. "It's her time, Miz Tabitha. Mrs. Parks's pains been going all night and she said to come for you."

"I'll just be a moment. Go into the kitchen for something hot to drink."

"Yes, ma'am." Leaving a trail of mud across the shining floorboards, he headed toward the warmth of the kitchen.

Tabitha raced up the steps, burden and heart lifting at the prospect of bringing a new life into the world, a life that was welcome. Even if the father was at sea more than at home, this baby would be loved and cared for by mother, grandparents, siblings, and a host of other relatives. It was the best kind of birth, a far cry from Sally Belote's lying-in.

"Calm yourself, Marjorie." Tabitha spoke in soothing accents. "Everything is all right."

"But Momma says it's two weeks early," the young mother cried between close contractions.

Momma's predictions were one reason why Tabitha had cleared the birthing chamber of female relatives—they'd been in the way. Their intentions were good, their presence a hindrance.

"I say it's not," Tabitha responded, "and I am the midwife."

"Momma—" Marjorie groaned through another spasm

of her body, then continued, "The last one was late. There's just got to be something wrong."

"Everything is well." Tabitha washed her hands yet again and examined the woman to ensure she still spoke the truth.

She did. This lying-in was progressing as it should. The woman's pains were powerful, but not too much so. The baby lay in the correct position. When necessary, Marjorie's body dilated, and little blood showed.

"We can't predict these things too closely," Tabitha assured her.

"I can." The response emerged in a wail as a more powerful contraction racked the mother's body.

"Oh?" Tabitha looked again. "Wonderful. I can see the head."

"My husband's a sailor. He was home for only three days last September."

"Ah, yes, of course." Tabitha straightened to smile at Marjorie. "That's really all right then. It's not too early." She moved around to the side of the bed and wiped the other woman's perspiring brow with a cool, damp cloth. "Only a few—"

Marjorie's shriek interrupted Tabitha. She scooted to the end of the bed without a show of haste and lifted the sheet. "Yes, I see the crown. Now push."

"I can't. It—" More of the baby's head appeared along with a gush of fluid. The shoulders caught. Marjorie screamed.

"Easy, easy." Tabitha never raised her voice in the birthing chamber, no matter what the circumstances. "Another push . . . There."

The wrinkled, red, slimy infant slid into her hands.

"A beautiful boy." Quickly, but with movements so practiced she looked as though she worked with deliberate slowness, Tabitha wiped mucous from the baby's mouth and nose, then gave him a quick smack on his bottom to set him breathing. All the while, she kept up a flow of talk. "Look at those shoulders. He's going to be a big one. And those feet. My, are they ever big. There."

The baby's first mewing wail filled the room. For a moment, Tabitha held the infant close to her heart, never failing to marvel at the perfect fingers and toes in miniature. Her heart filled. Her womb ached with emptiness.

Then the mother, grandmother, and two of Marjorie's sisters burst into the room. The mother whisked the baby from Tabitha's hands and wrapped it in cloths warmed by the fire. One sister began to wipe Marjorie's brow. The other sister poured a glass of water for the new mother, and the grandmother began to sing a psalm of praise. Love and joy filled the chamber as Tabitha took care of the least pleasant part of the birthing process—the afterbirth, cleaning up the new mother, and removing the oiled cloth spread out to protect the bed.

Then she was done. After only three hours of work, her mission was complete. Marjorie slept, her mother, mother-in-law, sisters, and grandmother protecting her and the newborn, who slept beside her.

"I'll take my leave now." Tabitha stood by the door, loath to interrupt the tableau. "If you have any difficulties, please send someone for me immediately."

"We will, Tabitha." Mrs. Denton, Marjorie's mother, followed Tabitha into the hall and paid her. "As always, you did well."

The baby began to cry.

"I must go. Thank you." Mrs. Denton vanished into the bedroom.

Tabitha crossed the corridor to the room the ladies always

provided for her. She washed and changed into the clean gown she always kept packed in her satchel. Then she hefted her bag and headed downstairs to let herself out the front door, to her solitary walk home, to the mist.

It lay like a chilly blanket over the village, droplets suspended in the air. Though she heard other people walking, a dog bark, and some chickens cackling, she felt the mist settling on her like her earlier burden—the staggering pain of her empty arms—isolating her from the world around her. This was the part of her work that hurt, the aftermath of the joy of birth. The new mother took her infant from Tabitha's arms. Mothers, grandmothers, sisters, aunts, friends surrounded both of them.

And Tabitha went home alone.

She could marry Raleigh. She could marry him tomorrow and go home to him—if he didn't take it into his head to wander again and leave her alone. Too many men did. Burdened by family responsibilities, they headed out to sea or off to the wilderness in the West. Raleigh might do that. She didn't yet trust him not to.

She doubted that she needed to trust God to trust others. Not true. She needed Raleigh not to lie to her, or at least tell her all of the truth. Or she needed to start a new life somewhere else, where everyone didn't know her past, her follies, her failings. She needed to be far away from Dominick Cherrett and his tug on her heart.

She reached the square, and there he was, looming out of the mist, as he had that first night they met. He carried a basket in one hand and caught hold of her arm with the other.

"The mermaid midwife far from the sea." His grin flashed through the gloom. "What are you doing out and about on such a day?"

"A lying-in." Her voice was rough from so much talking over the past three hours. Her chest felt constricted, over full; the rest of her felt hollow enough to echo. "And what about you?"

"Delivering extra eggs to the parsonage." He moved his hand from her arm to her face. "Are you all right? You couldn't have enjoyed much sleep."

"I didn't, but there's such joy in bringing new life into the world, my fatigue leaves me."

She was discovering a new joy too, one born of a gentle hand against her skin, a voice she would recognize anywhere, a soft question about her well-being. Simply being near this man, despite all she knew, despite what she suspected.

"Are you all right?" she asked, wanting to prolong the interlude. "No trouble about last night?"

"Ah, well, a bit." He laughed without humor. "I got caught."

"Dominick." She grasped his hand. "What happened? He didn't . . . no, you wouldn't be here. What happened?"

"It's too cold out here to talk. Can you come in for some coffee?"

"If Letty doesn't care."

"Not Letty. She loves to feed people." He tucked her hand into the crook of his arm and headed around the side of Mayor Kendall's house. "I'll wager you haven't eaten."

"I had breakfast when I got in this morning."

"Morning was eight hours ago. My dear, you're going to blow away on a strong wind if you don't feed yourself better." He paused to open the gate. "After you."

She hesitated. "Dominick, I'm happy to come in for some coffee, but I want to talk to you about last night."

"Of course you do." He slipped his arm around her shoulders and guided her forward. "Are you going to rake me over some very hot coals, or am I forgiven?"

"For what should I forgive you? You didn't strike Raleigh, did you? Someone else was there."

"Ah, so you believe that now. Why?"

"Because Raleigh dislikes you so much but won't outright accuse you."

"But you still have doubts about me, don't you?"

"I—yes. You were still there."

"I was. I want to tell you why. I need to—" Quieting, he took several more steps, then stopped in the middle of the kitchen garden. "My dear, I want—" He stopped speaking again.

"What is it?" She gave him an encouraging smile.

"You. How I feel about you." With the aroma of mint and thyme rising on the mist around them, he slid his fingers into her hair, tilted her head back, and kissed her.

Unlike before, this was no mere brush of his lips on hers. It was long and deep and hungry. The world spun while she told herself to stop him. She dropped her bag and cupped his face in her hands while telling herself she should smack both his cheeks. She leaned toward him while telling herself she should run in the opposite direction.

"There." He raised his head but kept his hand in her hair. "I shouldn't have done that."

"Then why did you?"

"Why did you let me?"

"I—" She licked her lips, tasting something sweet like strawberries and cream. "I always feel lonely after attending a lying-in."

"I thought a birthing was a joyous occasion." His tone teased her as his fingers toyed with her earlobe.

She swallowed, trying to concentrate. "It is, but then I have to give the baby to the mother."

"I see." He released her, leaving her colder than the mist. "Then you should marry Raleigh Trower."

"You kiss me, then tell me to marry another man?"

She should have been angered. She wanted to weep.

"I can't marry you until I'm free, and that looks like it'll be too far off."

Four years with only a hope and perhaps nothing at the end, waiting for another man, a man who would leave.

"Yes, four years is too long." Regret constricted her heart.

"But perhaps it could be sooner." He stroked the side of her throat. "If you help me."

She stepped back. "I won't help you run away. The consequences are too great."

"And I would be a rascal to ask such a thing of you. But—" He glanced toward the house, where yellow light reached through the mist. "Kendall has left for Norfolk for a few days. May I call on you . . . in the daylight?"

"Noon tomorrow. The tide will be coming in. We can do some crabbing."

"Letty would like that." He kissed her again, lightly this time. "Trust me, please."

"That's probably asking too much right now." She smiled to soften her words.

He didn't smile back. "Perhaps you should forgive Raleigh for abandoning you at the altar, so you don't tar us all with the same brush."

"I'm not—"

But maybe she wasn't trusting anyone, wasn't trusting God, isolating her heart from caring too much. Even falling for Dominick was a way to protect herself. He was impossible to form an alliance with, since she knew he would leave eventually.

She had fallen for him, though. Fallen hard enough to

hurt every time she looked at him, though that was such a pleasure.

A shiver raced through her. “Perhaps I am.”

“That’s my girl.” He retrieved her bag and gestured toward the house. “After you.”

She preceded him into warmth and the fragrance of brewing coffee and baking sugar buns. Three pairs of eyes turned toward her, flashed to Dominick, then back to her. One of the identical blonde girls clapped her hand over her mouth and emitted a giggle. Tabitha realized why. Dominick had pulled down her hair.

“I—I just came from a lying-in,” she stammered.

“I encountered her while delivering eggs and cream, dear Letty.” Dominick kissed the cook on the cheek. “I hope this means something delectable for our supper.”

“You should go to bed without any, naughty lad that you are.” She turned her green eyes on Tabitha. “Did he tell you what happened last night?”

“I promised her coffee—and the tale before she walks home.” Dominick drew a chair out from the table. “Sit, Madam Midwife, and I’ll do the honors.”

While the two young women watched and hid snickers behind their hands, he brought Tabitha a cup of coffee and a sugar bun. Before he sat, he gave the twins a stern look. “Don’t you two have dusting or something useful to do?”

“No, Mr. Cherrett,” Dinah said. “Not with the mayor gone.”

“What about your sewing?” Letty turned from the fire and a bubbling pot of something savory. “You have only a week until the festival.”

“Ah, the fete.” Dominick sighed. “My dear Tabitha, I regret to tell you I am no longer allowed to go. It was part of my punishment.”

"I'm so sorry. All the young ladies will miss you."

And she wouldn't attend now either. She could go with Raleigh or on her own, but the idea of the festivities without Dominick there to flirt with her, lead her into a reel, or walk her home through the night, left her flat.

"Least of all you?" His dark eyes dared her.

She laughed. "Least of all me, as I won't be there."

"I am gratified." He reached for her hand beneath the table and squeezed her fingers. "Now then, I'll tell you what happened last night after I left the Trowers' house."

He told her of running into Wilkins, of the brief scuffle he allowed Wilkins to win so as not to compound his crime with striking a free man, of being locked in his chamber the rest of the night. He told her the details of his punishment.

"And I know which side my bread is buttered on, where the mayor is concerned," Letty put in. "He will be locked up at night."

"She is such a trusting soul." Dominick's gaze fell on the older woman. "She knows I'll acquiesce like a lamb."

"You will or pay the consequences," Letty said.

"I'm glad, Dominick." Tabitha held her cup. "If you're confined, you can't be accused of working with the enemy on these abductions, should any more occur."

"Or should someone decide I should be made to look guilty," Dominick responded.

Tabitha nodded, then pushed back her chair. "I need to get home. I haven't had more than two hours of sleep since six o'clock yesterday morning."

Dominick rose. "I'll walk you home, if Miss Letty says I can."

"It might look like dusk out there, but it's not, so go ahead. I'd feel better if she weren't alone in this fog."

Tabitha thanked Letty for the refreshments, then exited the house. Carrying her bag, Dominick strode beside her through the garden and into the alley. By silent consent, they took the back way around the graveyard and out into the square beside the church.

"Shall we avoid the beach today?"

"I think we should. It'll be full of flotsam after the storm." She took his arm. "Raleigh regrets what he intended to do, you know."

"I thought he might. But it doesn't change the fact he tried, and with whom?"

"He won't say. And you're saying too little."

"I have every intention of being honest with you, Tabitha . . . tomorrow. Not today. Voices carry in the fog."

And so they did. When she stopped listening to Dominick, she caught snatches of conversation from pedestrians she couldn't even see. She heard the footfalls before the form loomed up before them, blocking their path.

"You keep low company, Miss Eckles," Harlan Wilkins said. "Haven't you learned your lesson about associating with the bondsman?"

"A man's worth is in what he does, not the station in life he holds," Tabitha said through stiff lips. "Mr. Cherrett has proved himself worthy of my regard through his actions."

"You're just another foolish female then." Wilkins snorted.

"Like Sally Belote?" Tabitha shot back.

The muscles under her hand went rigid. Wilkins emitted a sound like steam hissing from beneath the lid of a teakettle. It erupted in an epithet.

Tabitha felt her face flame despite the cold mist. She kept her mouth shut. She'd said too much already.

"I'm watching you, Cherrett," Wilkins growled. "I won't have an English bondsman wandering about at will in my town."

Then he was gone, disappearing into the fog.

"That was probably not a wise remark, my dear." Dominick began walking again, his footfalls swift and light beside hers. "You have thrown down the gauntlet."

"No, I think I've taken it up. He threw it down when he campaigned to have me blackballed with the council." Tabitha ground her teeth. "But I shouldn't have spoken in front of you."

"Perhaps you should let Mayor Kendall know what Wilkins did to that girl."

"I've already broken my vow of confidentiality to my patient with you, which was wrong of me. Of course, it's not wrong if I'm called into court by one of the interested parties." They rounded a corner. She caught a whiff of sea air, which promised the fog would blow away by morning, and took a deep breath. "Wilkins knows that."

"But you're protecting a blaggard of the worst sort." Dominick sounded frustrated.

"But now no one will believe me. They'll think I'll be lying out of revenge."

"Perhaps he'll be happy with that and let the matter drop."

"Maybe." Tabitha suppressed a yawn. "So have you read any of the Shakespeare?"

"I've read it twice. Prospero's speech at the end, when he gives up his magic, speaks to the heart."

"Do Englishmen have hearts?" She meant the question to tease.

He paused on the path and his expression held no humor. "I used to, but I do believe you have it now."

"Dominick." She tried to laugh. It was more of a gasp. "You don't mean anything of the kind."

"I do." He drew her to him. With his lips against hers, he murmured, "I love you."

22

Dominick bounded down the steps and into the kitchen. "No uniform. No powder," he crowed. He felt as free as he would until he completed his mission.

Letty frowned at him from the table, where she kneaded bread. "I don't like this, Dominick. Tabitha Eckles deserves better than what you can give her right now."

"He kissed her in the garden," Deborah called from the pantry.

"Tell me you didn't." Letty glared at him.

"A gentleman doesn't tell anything." He raised his voice so Deborah could hear over her racket of rattling jars. "And neither does a lady."

"I'm not a lady." Deborah poked her head into the kitchen. "I'm an indentured maid servant. And you're not a gentleman."

Dominick laughed and tugged one end of the bow of her cap beneath her chin. The ribbon untied and the cap slid over her eyes. With a shriek, she retreated back into the pantry.

Letty thumped the mound of dough onto the table with unnecessary force. "Tell me you didn't kiss Miss Eckles."

"A man, gentleman or not, doesn't lie to a female." Dominick began to gather the things to make his own tea, a skill he'd acquired since his new life began.

Behind him, Letty sighed. "Are you coming between her and Raleigh Trower?"

"If I am, there's no harm done to her." Dominick measured tea leaves into the china pot. "He's not good enough for her."

"And you are?"

Dominick's hand shook, scattering leaves on the table. "Only if I can redeem myself."

"Oh, Dominick." Letty reached across the wooden surface and laid her flour-caked hand over his. "You can't redeem yourself. Only God can redeem you."

"No, no, I rejected Him." Dominick used his need to fill the teapot with hot water as an excuse to turn his back on Letty. "I need to earn my forgiveness."

"You can't. You can only get it free for the asking."

How he wished that were true. His heart ached for a freedom that had nothing to do with the sale of his indenture, free of the burdens of the past and present.

"My sins are too many." He ladled water from the boiling kettle into the teapot. The tannic aroma of tea drifted to him on a cloud of steam. He inhaled it like life itself. "Add kissing Tabitha to them. I am a rake, a rogue, and a roué, but I love her with all my heart."

"For all the good it will do her," Letty grumbled. "You're not free to wed, and she doesn't deserve to have to wait for you."

"I know." Dominick concentrated on pouring his tea. Even if he were a free man, he wasn't in a position to offer Tabitha marriage. "But a man can wish."

"I wish you'd tumbled head over heels for someone else." Dinah stomped into the kitchen, a chamber pot in hand.

Everyone covered their noses and backed away.

"Wash before you come to the table," Letty admonished her.

"Mr. Cherrett deserves to wear this for flirting with Miss Tabitha." Dinah tramped out the back door.

"Will you save us some crabs for our supper?" Deborah asked.

"Presuming I catch any."

"You'll need bait," Letty said. "I have some chicken parts from the bird I'm preparing today."

Dominick shuddered.

"I'll wrap them up well. Tabitha will have her own, I'm sure. She knows how to catch crabs as well as anyone in these parts, but a little extra never hurt."

In the end, Dominick agreed to take the bits of the chicken no one wanted to eat. Wrapped separately but in the same basket were several little seed cakes, a bottle of lemonade, and a bowl of strawberries dusted with sugar.

Whistling for the first time since his plans to avoid the church went awry, Dominick set off down the alleyway, swinging the basket and not caring that he couldn't carry a tune. It was that sort of day—the air warm in the sun and cool in the shade, a light breeze off the ocean, and the aroma of roses and honeysuckle perfuming the air.

He increased his pace. Not until several ladies smiled at him did he realize he had ceased whistling to grin. He didn't stop just because he might look foolish. He hadn't felt so good since his world had split apart in January. In a few minutes, he would see Tabitha. In an hour or two, he would tell her as much of the truth as he dared. In the moments after that, surely he would have her agreement to help him.

He reached her gate. A heartbeat before he laid his hand on the latch, the portal opened and she stepped onto the dune. A wide straw hat shadowed her face. A plain blue dress fluttered around her ankles, and she carried a basket in each hand, one covered, the other open to reveal ropes and an iron hoop.

Dominick gave her a flourishing bow. "Though the sun

is so bright the shadows are hiding, and the sky so blue it makes the soul ache for heaven, your actions, my lady, have a clandestine appearance. Are you running away?"

"Or toward." She peeked up at him from beneath the ridiculous hat.

"Hark, is this serious Miss Eckles flirting with me?" He slipped his hand beneath her chin and tilted her head back. "I do believe she is. Behold, the maiden blushes."

"Dominick." Her lips smiled, but her eyes were serious. "Patience worries about me spending the day with you. She says you'll break my heart."

"And what do you say?" He stroked his thumb along her lower lip.

She dropped her lashes over her eyes. "I say that she's probably right, but it's past time I stopped avoiding risk."

"Oh, my dear." Dominick feared she would break his heart. He brushed his lips across hers, then took one of the baskets from her. "If there is any way I can find, I will keep your heart safe."

"But not from you."

"Most definitely not from me." He smiled into her eyes. "I want it with me." He spoke the truth. He simply knew not how he would make desire become reality. "But on to fishing before the tide is wrong. Where are we going?" he asked.

"That jetty." She gestured down the beach.

"Doesn't that . . . er . . . belong to the Trowers?"

"Yes. That's the *Marianne* moored there. His father must have brought her in last night."

"We're not going out on her, are we?"

"For crabs?" Tabitha laughed, warming the chill between them. "No, we're going to work off the side of the jetty. The land shelves into deep water where the boat is moored. That's where I find the best crabs."

"Letty sent along some chicken innards for bait."

"I wondered what was in that basket. I brought some too, as well as some chicken pieces for us and some bread rolls and water, in the event we don't catch enough crabs to eat."

"I have strawberries and lemonade."

"Oooh." She licked her lips.

He closed his eyes for a moment, then set out across the sand at an arduous pace.

She caught up with him, and they reached the jetty with little conversation and a bit of panting between them. From over the dune, he caught a glimpse of the Trower house, little more than a chimney puffing pale smoke into the cloudless sky.

"Is he well?" Dominick asked.

"I presume so. None of them have contacted me." Tabitha walked onto the jetty, her footfalls ringing hollow beats against the wooden planks. She set her covered basket at the far end near the prow of the fishing boat. "Bring yours here too. The shadow of the *Marianne* will keep the food and bait cool."

Dominick obeyed, then looked at the other basket with trepidation. "Why do we need bait?"

"To lure the crabs to us. Watch." She drew a thin rope from her other basket, tied a slimy chicken liver to it, and lowered herself to the jetty so that she lay on her belly, her head and shoulders over the edge of the jetty. "Grab the net and join me."

Dominick removed his coat first and rolled up his shirtsleeves, then did as she bade. Below them, the water was crystal blue over white sand. Flotsam from the incoming tide lay about—a bottle, pieces of wood, a hunk of glass the color of the sea. Amongst the litter, multiple-legged creatures roamed.

"They're hunting for food," Tabitha explained. "We're going to lure them up to it. When one grabs it, you take the net and scoop it up."

"That's all there is to it?" He felt vaguely disappointed that he didn't need to do something requiring more of a show of skill.

She laughed. "It's not as easy as it looks. They wriggle to get away, and they have pincers that hurt if they catch a finger. And don't forget the pilings. The barnacles on them will rip the skin right off you."

"Charming." He turned his head to look at her. "This is amusement for you Virginians?"

"It's a good excuse for lying about in the sun." She grinned at him, the earlier gravity gone, and his heart melted as though it were beeswax in the sun.

God, is this more punishment for my sins? To love a woman I can't have?

But if he won his freedom, he could.

If he gave up his family.

No, he wouldn't think of that. Not now. He would concentrate on the day, the rose scent of Tabitha, the rhythmic movement of the water swirling around the jetty pilings, the sparkle of sunlight on blue water. The warmth of sunlight on his back. The heat eased tension in his damaged muscles. His eyelids drooped.

"Now," Tabitha whispered.

Dominick's eyes flew open. Below him, a hideous crustacean gripped the chunk of chicken liver.

"Slowly," she admonished.

Dominick nodded, afraid to speak, and lowered the net into the water. The crab released the liver. Dominick rolled to his side, sent the net spinning in an arc, and caught the crab on its retreat.

"Hurray, you did it!" Tabitha flung up her arms. Water flew from the line and onto Dominick's face.

He wiped it away with the sleeve of his shirt. If he ruined this one, he'd need to spend some of his precious store of coins on a new one. But surely seawater was harmless to linen.

He smiled. "Now what do I do with it?"

"Put it in the basket where the net was and hang it from a plank of the jetty. See how that one sticks out? The crabs will stay cool and damp that way."

"But we only have one." He gazed at the spiny, buglike creature. "And it's no beauty."

"But it is. It's enormous. And we'll get more."

And they did. While the sun poured over them like melted sugar syrup and the wind kept them from growing too hot, they took turns dangling the bait into the water and employing the net to scoop the hapless feeders into their clutches. After a while, they switched sides of the jetty. While doing so, Dominick glanced toward the dunes and caught a glimpse of a man standing a hundred yards away. With the sun behind him, the man's features were indiscernible, but Dominick suspected, from the breadth of the shoulders, it was Trower watching them again.

"We're being watched," he said.

Tabitha glanced inland. "It's Raleigh. He should be in bed."

"Do you want to go speak with him? I can rest here."

"No." She shook her head. "Raleigh can come to me when he's ready to tell me the truth about the other night."

"When I'm done talking to you, you may already know." Dominick smoothed a lock of hair off of her cheek, soft hair on softer skin. Just a little kiss on her brow . . .

She swallowed and drew away. "He can still come to me. Will you fetch your bait? I'm all out."

He did so, nearly gagging at the smell. "Do I want to eat a creature that eats this?"

"You eat chickens, and they eat bugs."

"True, but I don't have to watch them do it."

"You didn't watch the chickens when you were—but of course you didn't."

"No, I watched my father eat lesser beings for breakfast, spit them out at noontime, and feed them to the goats for dinner. Now, hand me that line."

They caught a half dozen more crabs before Tabitha spoke again. "You don't like your father very much, do you?"

"I used to." He remembered running to his father to show a perfect list of sums and anticipate the praise he knew was coming. "When I was young enough to think he could do no wrong." He dropped the baited string into the water. "I've had enough of crabbing. May we eat something besides these water bugs?"

"If you like." Face sober, Tabitha scrambled to her feet. "Let's take the baskets of food to the sand."

They retrieved the food baskets from the shade of the fishing boat, and each carried one ashore. Dominick set his basket in a hollow of sand and retrieved the lemonade, two glasses, and the bowl of strawberries. The dusting of sugar had brought out their juices. He would feed them to her so she didn't stain her fingers. If only—

Behind him, Tabitha screamed. Dominick spun around in time to see the triangular head and catlike eyes of a snake rear up from the other basket.

23

Tabitha froze. Her breath caught in her throat and her heart congealed in her chest. Six feet away, Dominick crouched, his gaze fixed on the snake.

It hung from the side of the basket, swaying its triangular head. Inside the basket, its tail twitched. The cloth wrapped around the food whispered a warning of death.

Dominick raised his arm. His hand disappeared beneath his fall of hair and emerged curled around the handle of a long, glittering knife.

"You can't." Tabitha's voice emerged more like a squeak. "Water moccasin bites are usually deadly—"

The snake lunged. Steel flashed. Blood spurted, and the snake's severed head lay on the white sand beside a knife with an eight-inch blade, a mere inch from the toe of Dominick's right boot.

"What kind of bondsman carries a knife like that?" Tabitha asked with a calm that pleased her. Then she gathered up her skirt, raced a dozen yards down the beach, and fell to her knees to be sick in a tide pool. She'd eaten little that day, but her stomach rebelled as though she'd downed a banquet. She doubled over, racked with pain and silent sobs.

"Hush." A strong arm encircled her shoulders. Warm breath and a swath of satiny hair brushed her cheek. "It's dead and no harm done."

"But it was there." She gasped for breath to control herself. "It was in my basket."

"Probably the smell of the bait. Here. Drink."

Cool glass touched her lips. She reached up and curled her fingers around the bottle. He didn't let go. Together they tilted the container. The sweet tartness of lemonade washed over her tongue and down her throat, refreshing, nourishing, cleansing. She swallowed once, twice, then he took it away.

"Not too much. Water would be better, but the only stuff we have is in your basket, and I didn't think you'd want that."

"No." She shuddered. "Where is it?"

"I'm afraid I dumped it all in the ocean." His dark eyes smiled into hers. "Basket, food, and our serpentine visitor. Or what was left of him."

"Yes, his tail." The lemonade threatened to come up. She gulped. "You killed it so fast. How—I mean, the knife . . ." Her voice gathered strength. "What is a redemptioner doing with a knife and skill like that?"

"It's not the usual skill and habit for a gentleman either." He raised the bottle of lemonade to his own lips, and for the first time she realized his hand trembled. "I thought I might need such a weapon against an unsavory man, not a monster. What did you call it?"

"A water moccasin. Some call them cottonmouths." She looked into his eyes so he could read her gravity. "I've seen them be aggressive toward people, and if he'd bitten one of us . . . My mother got called to treat a bite . . . The man died." She shuddered. "Do you understand what I'm saying?"

"Perhaps it crawled in the basket in search of food."

Tabitha dropped her gaze to the bottle in his hand, where sunlight reached through the green glass to flash off of liquid unstable enough to sparkle like rippling waves.

He tucked the flask into a pocket of wet sand. "Or perhaps someone put it there."

"That basket was covered. It couldn't have gotten in on its own."

"Now, really, Tabitha, how could someone have done that without us knowing?"

"Too easily from the boat. We were making enough noise ourselves to cover up any another person might have made, and you know it."

"I know it." He sighed. "I hoped you wouldn't come to the same conclusion."

"I have." She knelt there in the sand and grasped both his hands. "Dominick, someone tried to kill one of us." She strove for a light tone. "Since it was my basket, probably me."

"Who would want to harm you?" He freed his hands and cupped her face in his palms. "Who would want to destroy such beauty and kindness?"

"Who would want to harm you?"

Light flamed in Dominick's dark eyes. "The dozen people coming this way don't look particularly friendly."

Tabitha jerked away from him and turned. Indeed, what looked more like a score of people swarmed down the beach or over the dunes toward them.

Raleigh, his face pale, walked amongst them, leaning on his father's arm. He released it and straightened. "Tabbie, are you all right? We heard a scream."

All eyes swiveled past her to Dominick, curious, wary, hostile. She felt rather than saw him rise, and struggled to stand too, but she entangled her foot in her skirt.

"You need to modify your dress before you break your neck," Dominick murmured as he grasped her elbows and set her firmly on her heels.

She wished she could lean back against him. She couldn't,

not with so many people in front of her appearing ready to accuse Dominick of something.

"There was a snake," she said. "A water moccasin. He killed it." She gestured down the beach to the lone basket remaining beside a triangular dark blot—the snake's severed head. "It was in my basket."

"Tabbie." Raleigh surged toward her, head forward, rather like the snake had done. "Come home with us. Momma will make you a dinner. You"—he glared at Dominick—"can go back to your master."

"Only if Tabitha tells me to." Dominick's arm tightened around her. "Otherwise, she and I have matters to discuss."

One or two onlookers remained beside the tide pool. The rest had wandered down the beach to inspect the snake's head. Someone exclaimed, "A clean cut."

Tabitha shivered to think that the hand resting on her right arm, just below her shoulder, had held a knife that could sever the head of a human without much difficulty. A good man to have as one's friend, as one's protector.

A dangerous enemy, bondsman or not.

"Does your master know you carry a knife capable of cutting off the head of a snake?" Raleigh demanded.

"I can't see where it's any of your concern," Dominick drawled. "Now, if you'll excuse me, I'd like to retrieve my basket, our crabs, and my coat."

He strode off down the beach toward the jetty and the larger crowd. Tabitha felt cold where he'd been close to her, despite the blazing afternoon sun. She wanted to watch him, ensure that no one annoyed him or caused him trouble. But she sensed he had deliberately left her alone with Raleigh, and for that she loved him more than ever.

"How did a snake get into your basket?" Raleigh asked.

"I have no idea. It was covered." Tabitha glanced at the others nearby. "Good afternoon, Mr. Parks. How's that new grandson of yours?"

The middle-aged gentleman beamed. "He's right fine, Miz Tabitha. My boy'll be proud when he comes home."

"If he comes home," Raleigh muttered.

Tabitha shot him a warning glare.

"We need to be honest about this with men like him around." He jutted his chin at Dominick. "He struts about like he's the mayor instead of a slave. Who else would be causing trouble for men in these parts?"

"Raleigh, stop it." Tabitha cast an anxious glance at the onlookers then Dominick.

She desperately wanted to believe Dominick was not an English spy come to cause trouble in the seaboard states to foment war. No one else seemed to think ill of him at the moment. Someone had picked up the snake's head, and others gazed at it and Dominick with admiration. As for Dominick himself, he was smiling down at Phoebe Lee. Her laughter rang up the tide line, and the ruffles on her pink parasol fluttered in the breeze.

The idea of that elegant young lady a midwife made Tabitha curl her lip.

"Think it's more like trouble for the females in these parts he's causing," Mr. Parks said with a chuckle. "That's the parson's niece. She's quite a flirt, even for a widow."

"He's just trouble all around." Raleigh's jaw muscles bunched. "Please, Tabbie, will you come up to the house?"

"Is your head bothering you?" She circled him to inspect the bandage. It was clean and secured in a band around his head.

Her action drew attention to Raleigh. Several people surrounded him, asking him what happened.

Tabitha slipped away with a quiet, "I'll visit tomorrow," and made her way down the beach to Dominick's side.

Phoebe turned her attention to Tabitha. "Miss Eckles, so good to see you again. Have you thought any more about my question the other day?"

"No," Tabitha said a little too crisply.

"I see." Phoebe's face fell.

"I mean, no, I haven't thought about it," Tabitha hastened to add, "not no, I won't do it."

Yet the idea made her feel hollow inside, as though she had already lost the only man she wanted to marry and provide with daughters—and sons.

"Do please take it into consideration." Phoebe ducked her head. "I'm quite serious." She tilted her face toward Dominick. "And I'm serious about you proving you can cut a rosebud off a bush at twenty paces without damaging it."

Dominick tucked his arm through Tabitha's. "Perhaps Tabitha will allow us to use her garden. She has some lovely roses."

"I'm so pleased to hear that." Phoebe smiled. "I was afraid maybe you just grew herbs and things."

"I grow those too," Tabitha said, "but I have had a weakness for candied rose petals ever since I was a little girl and my father used to buy them for me, so I make them for myself."

Phoebe's eyes widened in surprise.

So did Dominick's. "I don't think I've tasted candied flowers since I was a lad. May I indulge just a taste of one?"

Tabitha blushed, forgetting the snake, forgetting Raleigh's accusations, forgetting Phoebe Lee. Dominick didn't care about anyone or anything but her in that moment.

"We should get these crabs somewhere to be cooked before they spoil," he said.

"Ugh, crab." Phoebe gave a delicate shudder and twirled her parasol. "I see my uncle wants me to leave with him. See you in church on Sunday, Mr. Cherrett." She glided toward Reverend Downing, the frills on the bottom of her skirt and edge of her parasol flirting in the breeze.

"Am I permitted to ask what she wants from you?" Dominick asked.

"You can ask, but—" Tabitha caught sight of someone preparing to throw the snake head into the sea, and broke off. "Why would someone do that to us?"

"Who?" Dominick asked. "The why, I'm afraid, is easy."

Tabitha began to walk up the beach toward home, wanting to run and hide behind her garden and her house door, with the locks turned. "It was in my basket. But the only true enemy I think I may have is Harlan Wilkins."

"Ruining his fine reputation in this town may be enough." Dominick walked faster than usual, as though he too wished to run. "Or others' reputations. Surely he's not the first man to father a child out of wed—I'm sorry. This is no discussion to have with a lady."

"I'm not a lady," Tabitha pointed out. "That is, my parents taught me good grammar and manners, but I work with the less delicate aspects of life, not to mention the things I learn in private."

"But you don't talk about that."

"No, but I know their secrets." She glanced back at the dispersing crowd on the beach. "There's a woman back there whose third son is not her husband's. She suffered a difficult labor and thought God was punishing her for betraying her vows, so she confessed to me. Now she doesn't speak to me for fear I'll talk out of turn, though she's been an admirable wife since, by all appearances. At least her other three sons look like her husband."

"So God's punishment worked." Dominick looked thoughtful. "Have her other lying-ins gone well?"

"They have, but I don't think God cares enough to punish us like that. The most generous, thoughtful, and God-fearing women I know have suffered difficulties in bearing children. Why would God punish them? Women suffer because of Eve, the Bible says, and after that, God forgot about us."

"The Bible tells us just the opposite." Dominick slowed. "God pays far too much attention to us and wants to be too much a part of our lives."

"Why do you think that?" She tried to read his face, but his hair had come loose and hid his countenance from her view.

He shrugged. "He took a personal interest in my life."

"And you're being punished by coming here as a bondsman?"

"I can redeem myself here." He paused when they needed to cross the dunes to her house. "Would this woman want to silence you? She was close at hand."

"After five years? No. But what about you? It was in my basket, but you might have been gentleman enough to serve me. Does someone want you dead?"

"Besides Raleigh?" He grinned. "Don't say it. I don't believe he wants me dead, just . . . gotten rid of."

"No, I think I was the target. We can't forget the knife at my throat."

Unbidden, her gaze shifted to the fall of his hair hiding the knife sheathed down his back.

"You still believe it could have been me?" Sorrow filled his eyes. "You know I couldn't hurt you."

Maybe not cut her skin, but he would break her heart. She couldn't respond.

He shook his head. "We still need to have that cose."

"Cose?" She didn't know the word.

"Talk. Chat. After we eat, please."

"Of course." She felt a little hunger now. "Patience is waiting for the crabs. We can cook them and bring them back down here." She smiled. "Since our alfresco meal was ruined, we may eat all of these ourselves."

"We still have the strawberries." His voice had grown rough.

Tabitha glanced at him and her mouth went dry. He was looking at her lips. "Come—come up to the house. We'll share the strawberries with Japheth and Patience."

"Of course." He headed over the dune, his stride long and loping, covering the ground with an appearance of unhurried grace while moving quickly. His carriage made him appear what he was—a man of rank, privilege, education, and possibly wealth once upon a time. Such men did not carry on more than a flirtation with a woman of her background, however well educated her father. She sullied her hands in her work. She saw the deprivations of human nature. The Eckleses and Blackburns, and all her other relatives who had come from Great Britain to the new world, wouldn't have associated with the likes of Dominick's family except as servants. Dominick's current status didn't change that. If he'd been American-born, perhaps. But not an Englishman.

Yet she followed him across the sand, as she feared she would follow him anywhere. When he left, she might have to pursue him.

At the moment, he led her to her own kitchen door and Patience and Japheth snapping the first beans of the season.

"We've brought you crabs," Tabitha announced.

Dominick held up the dripping basket. "Just tell me where to put them."

Patience jumped up so fast she knocked over her chair. "I've a pot keeping hot. Just a bit more wood here, and we'll have a fire hot enough to boil." She glanced from Tabitha to Dominick. "You look flushed, child. Is everything all right?"

"Yes. Perhaps the sun."

Or the proximity of the man beside her, smelling of the sea and the sandalwood that sailors brought from the East or rich men purchased from merchants.

"I seem to have lost my hat," she added, her hand flying to her bare head.

"I'll run back and look for it," Dominick said, and was gone.

"The water's boiling," Patience announced.

Tabitha retrieved the basket of crabs, hefted it over the pot, and dumped its contents. Patience followed her with salt and herbs. In moments, the rich aroma of boiling seafood with peppercorn, thyme, and sage filled the kitchen. Steam rose from the pot and swirled through the slanting rays of the sun.

The afternoon had sped by, between the pleasure of crabbing with Dominick and the horror of the snake. In too short a time, Dominick would have to leave, and he still needed to tell her how she could help him gain his freedom.

His freedom to return to his country, his family, the life where he belonged. A life where the sons went to Oxford and an eastern shore midwife didn't belong.

She would be a fool to help him, even if, as he said, he didn't intend to run away from her. Of course he would. He had no reason to stay.

But he came back this time. As Tabitha began to pull the first of the crabs from the water, he reappeared in the doorway, her hat in his hand. "It was lying on the jetty." His gaze traveled to the shellfish. "How do we eat these creatures?"

"I'll show you." Tabitha scooped a dozen crabs into a clean

pot and handed it to him. "I'll fetch the basket." She tossed a smile over her shoulder at Patience. "You and Japheth eat without me. I'll be back by dusk."

Walking beside Dominick back to the tide line, she thought she probably would enjoy herself. Regardless of what he told her, she couldn't think it was anything so terrible she couldn't enjoy his company for a few more hours.

They settled on the sand with the sun slanting from behind them and the limpid blue of the sea and sky stretching out forever ahead of them. The beach appeared deserted except for the gulls hovering in anticipation of food from the humans, and a blue heron fishing out to sea.

"Dorset is beautiful," Dominick said. "It's lush and green, and we have the sea. But this is more peaceful than the channel."

"You haven't lived through a hurricane. When I was a child, we lost our roof to one. A tree fell and came right through it. I've hated storms ever since."

"Yet you came out night before last without hesitation."

"It's my duty to do so." She began to crack open a crab with her fingers. "Some people use small hammers, but my fingers are strong enough to not need one. Just squeeze the body."

"I'm supposed to eat that?"

"No, not that. That's his innards. Here's the meat." She plucked the soft, moist flesh from the shell and held it on her palm. "Go ahead."

He took it, tasted it, then smiled. "More?"

"Crack your own. I'm hungry." She proceeded to open a claw and draw out the flesh.

Dominick sighed and picked up his own crab. For several minutes, they cracked and ate in silence. They tossed the discarded guts and shells to the edge of the water, where the gulls swooped in with shrieks of glee and pecked the matter clean.

"I suppose I can't put off my tale forever," Dominick said at last.

"No." Tabitha returned a strawberry to the bowl, no longer hungry. "Now, are you going to tell me that you're a spy for the British government?"

24

Raleigh sat on the jetty, his head in his hands. He felt so dizzy he feared he might tip forward and land face-first in the water. Both his father and his mother had encouraged him to go home and rest, as Tabitha had instructed him to do, but he knew the waves of pain rushing through him bore little relationship to the blows he'd taken on the jaw and head two days earlier.

Tabitha, his Tabbie, had walked down the beach with the lordling servant.

It was all his own fault. He hadn't trusted in the Lord to bring her back to him and had tried to be rid of the competition for her attentions, her affections. Now he was injured and had angered the man who was perpetrating the disappearances, thus making learning his identity more difficult. And Tabitha now knew that Raleigh's faith in God was a fraud. No man whose faith was sincere would wish to harm another, whatever the provocation, whatever the odd circumstances surrounding the man.

And this wasn't the first time he hadn't trusted in God to get him out of a difficult situation. He'd prayed for release from the Navy, then taken matters into his own hands.

No wonder Tabitha considered him to be untrustworthy. He was.

"God, how can I make things right?" he murmured, watching the waves lapping at the soles of his boots. "How can I get Tabbie to forgive me and trust me again if I behave this way?"

Gulls screamed overhead, seeming to mock him with maniacal laughter.

Below him, the incoming tide carried Tabitha's basket, a reminder of the danger she'd been in. Either danger to her or to Dominick Cherrett. Everyone knew a snake wasn't likely to crawl into a covered basket, regardless of the contents, with humans so close by. Yet any person who dared trap one to sneak into the basket showed determination or courage. Too easily the serpent could have turned on its captor before being used as a weapon. If Cherrett hadn't possessed and been so skilled with his wicked-looking knife, he could have been dead now. But the creature had been in Tabitha's basket.

"No one would want to harm Tabbie," Raleigh declared aloud. "No one."

"What did you say?" Footfalls echoed on the jetty, and a shadow fell across the sunlit water. "Do you think that snake was meant for Tabitha?"

"It was in her basket, but, no, no one could want to hurt her." Raleigh swallowed against the dryness in his mouth. "No one would risk killing her."

"Unless her work has given her secrets someone wants to protect." Father crouched and fished the half-submerged basket from the water. "They took a great risk."

"Too great a risk to harm someone so . . . necessary to the community." Raleigh glared at the now empty basket as though it were to blame. "Now, Cherrett, he seems a likely target for that kind of hatred."

"Because he's English?"

"Because he's above himself and an interloper. And what about him having a knife like that. Seems . . ." His eyes crossed with his effort to think of the right words to describe the inappropriateness of a bondsman in possession of a knife not much less than a pirate cutlass.

"You should come in, son." His father's voice was gentle. "This much sun can't be good for you with that injury to your head."

"I'm all right."

Another lie. He wasn't all right. His head ached. His jaw ached. His stomach ached.

"Giving yourself a brain fever isn't going to bring her back." His father sat on the edge of the jetty beside Raleigh. "She's made her choice for now. It's an unwise choice. He can't marry her."

"But it is my fault." Raleigh straightened and looked his father in the eyes, the same blue eyes that he saw in mirrors. "If I hadn't accused Cherrett of being the one to hit me, she might not have chosen to feel sorry for him."

"You know it goes back further than that, Raleigh." Father's mouth set in a stern line. "You abandoned her without a word. A woman doesn't get over that kind of hurt and humiliation easily."

"No, but I've—"

He stopped before he said he'd changed. He wanted to believe it. He wanted to be that man the ship's chaplain said he could be. But he proved again and again that he was untrustworthy for man—or woman—and, worst of all, not good enough for God to take care of him.

"I think I would have had a chance if not for Dominick Cherrett." Raleigh pounded his fist on the rough planks of the jetty. "What does she find to attract her in that man?"

Father laughed. "Ask your sisters. I believe he holds a certain manly charm."

"I didn't know I was so ill-favored," Raleigh grumbled.

"I can't say, since you favor me."

Raleigh chuckled at that and felt a bit better. Sobering, he asked, "What can I do, sir?"

"You know we have to leave things up to God. When we try to take matters into our own hands, it only causes trouble."

"Oh, yes, I know that all too well." Raleigh scrambled to his feet. "So how do I win her back?"

"Start courting someone else."

Raleigh stared at his father. "Make her jealous? Does that really work?"

"If it doesn't, then you didn't have a chance to win her back in the first place." Father grinned. "And if it does, you've shown she's just trying to make you jealous, or maybe punish you, for leaving her. After all, didn't she get friendly with this bondsman after you returned?"

"Well, yes." He and his father headed off the jetty and up the sand toward their house. "But who? Not many females around here would make Tabitha wonder if I'm serious about them instead of her."

"Mrs. Lee?"

Raleigh snorted. "She's a rich widow from a fine family. She'd never look at a fisherman."

"She was certainly looking at a bondsman."

"He was the hero of the moment." Raleigh shrugged. "Tabitha was looking at him the same—" He stopped and caught his breath. "Do you think he put that snake in there so he could display his skill?"

"And risk Tabitha's life? I don't think so."

"Maybe he didn't know the snake was poisonous." Raleigh warmed to his notion that the entire incident was a ploy by Cherrett to win Tabitha's attention. "They don't have many poisonous snakes in England."

"It's a possibility." Father looked thoughtful. "But he didn't seem like he needed that kind of risk to—but never you mind all that. Whatever the reason, it's behind us. It was likely a terrible coincidence that the snake got into the basket. If it was mere heroics that won Tabitha's attention today, it won't last for long. She's a practical woman, and you're a man of some property, as my son."

And he'd have more if his mission succeeded, property he'd intended to use to lure Tabitha back to him when the time was right. He'd thought the time was right when he'd learned some men on the council thought she should lose her license to practice midwifery in the district. She needed a man to support her. Cherrett couldn't do that. He couldn't even marry her, and he would leave when his indenture was over.

A pity his indenture wasn't over now.

Lost in thought about this possibility—how to get Dominick Cherrett out of his indenture—Raleigh increased his stride and reached the house ahead of his father. His head felt better, less achy and muddled. The sky looked a little brighter.

"Lord, have You forgiven me after all? Now I can—"

No, he could do nothing. As much as he wanted to take matters into his own hands, he must leave the future in the hands of the Lord, or he would never be free from his mistakes.

"Lord, please show me You have forgiven me." He stepped onto the back porch, where Momma sat mending one of his socks.

She smiled up at him. "I'm glad you came back. Tabitha said you needed to rest for several days. Is everything all right?"

"Now it is." He blinked in the dimness beneath the overhang of the eaves. "I think I'll rest now. Father will tell you everything that happened since I left."

"All right then, you go rest. The girls picked some flowers for your room."

"What sweet sisters I have." Raleigh started into the house.

"And someone sent you a parcel," Momma called after him. "I laid it on your bed."

Raleigh stopped. His heart skipped a beat. "A parcel? Who?"

Momma shrugged. "It has only your name on the wrapping. You'll have to open it up."

"I will." Trying not to look in too much of a hurry, Raleigh mounted the steps to his bedchamber under the roof beams and closed the door behind him.

The parcel lay on the quilt, a brown stain against the muted blues and greens of the squares. Hands trembling, he took out his penknife and slit the binding string. The brown paper fell away to reveal a Bible with a slip of paper poking out of the top margin. The thin paper rattled between his fingers as he turned the pages to the marked passage and read the message—all the more obscene for being created out of Holy Scripture—from the thirteenth chapter of Matthew, the twenty-eighth verse. "He said unto them, An enemy hath done this. The servants said unto him, Wilt thou then that we go and gather them up?"

Dominick rested on his elbows and stared at the horizon. A platoon of dark clouds marched between sea and sky, stark against the crystal blue. The sun behind them blazed with heat. Wind blowing off of the sea held an edge of chill.

"Another storm's coming," Dominick observed.

"Not until after sundown." Tabitha touched his shoulder. "That's not all that far off, so talk, if you still intend to."

"I still intend to. I just don't know how to start." He lay fully on his back, his arms folded behind his head. He glanced at Tabitha a yard away, sitting with her legs curled to one side and modestly covered with her skirt. He smiled. “You look like a mermaid.”

“Stop that mermaid foolishness. Someone tried to kill one of us today. It’s no time for frivolity.”

“Then why are you hiding a box of comfits in that basket of yours?” He reached one arm toward the basket.

She whipped it out of reach. “After you talk to me.”

“You may not want to share after you hear my story.”

“Which is why I’m not wasting them on you now.”

“Oh, Tabitha, I do love you.” The words slipped out as though his tongue belonged to someone else. He didn’t try to snatch them back or pretend he hadn’t once again confessed something so serious aloud. He watched her.

She didn’t move. She didn’t speak. Her hat brim shielded her eyes. A slow flush creeping up her throat to her cheeks was the only indication that she might have heard him at all.

“I wouldn’t have kissed you as I did yesterday if my feelings weren’t deep,” he pressed further.

“Like kissing me, Dominick,” she finally said in a low, flat tone, “giving me pretty speeches of devotion won’t change my mind one way or the other if you ask me to do something abhorrent to my nature or my country.”

“All right, so you intend not to make a commitment until you know everything.” Dominick sat up. “And after you know . . .” He sat cross-legged, his elbows on his knees, his chin in his hands. He fixed his gaze on the sea, its endless, churning power. “Then let me get the worst of this over straight off. Raleigh Trower is absolutely correct. I am a spy. An English spy.”

She gasped. Other than the sharp inhalation of breath, she neither spoke nor moved. This time not even her face betrayed her.

Dominick opened his mouth to comment on her lack of reaction, then realized she was in what must be her midwife mode—calm and still and ready to hear anything. After Sally Belote's confession, not much else could shock her. She might have even heard worse in the course of her occupation.

"I'm much worse than that." He made himself smile. "Well, that depends on one's perspective. I am not a spy for the crown, as you might think. My king didn't send me, nor anyone in the government. I have no military rank or anyone at Whitehall who even has a high opinion of me. But I have an uncle who is a rogue vice admiral in the Royal Navy who offered to send me to his plantation on Barbados or come here to spy out a spy."

At this, she arched her winged eyebrows, and the corners of her mouth twisted up in a mocking smile. "Are you sure this isn't an adaptation of some lost Shakespeare drama, Dominick? If so, you'd best be advised that I am not impressed with tall tales."

"You don't believe me?" Dominick jerked upright. "Tabitha, I've stretched the truth a time or two since we've met, but this, I promise you, is nothing less than factual. When I found myself in a spot where leaving England for a bit seemed like the better part of valor, my uncle said I could redeem myself this way."

"Redeem yourself from what?" She leaned toward him. "What could have been so dreadful that a man with an Oxford education would become a servant for four years to accomplish it?"

"I . . . uh . . ." Dominick scooped up a handful of sand and watched it trickle from his fingers. Thus would go any love for him Tabitha might have had. "I wounded a man in a duel."

She jerked as though he'd struck her with the rapier that had sent his challenger dropping to the grass. Her face paled, and one hand fluttered in the air, as though she wanted to grasp an elusive stronghold.

He caught her hand in his and breathed a sigh of relief when she didn't pull away. "It was a fair fight. He challenged me. But dueling is illegal and the authorities got wind of it, so we both had to get away for a while."

"Four years is a rather long while," she said dryly. "Four years of enforced servitude. Was that what your uncle had planned for you on Barbados too?"

"No, I'd have been free there, but I couldn't have made amends. Here . . . if I can find out certain information, my uncle will buy my indenture. I could be gone in weeks."

"Gone." She tugged her hand free and tucked it beneath a fold of her skirt. "And you want me to help you so you'll go away from me all that much sooner?"

"For the good of both our countries, yes. That is—Tabitha, I want to stay, but I've no work here and you Americans are a bit hostile to me."

"And your father won't want me showing up on his doorstep alongside his precious son."

"I'm not a precious son to him." He shifted his shoulders, feeling the stiffness settle in. "Perhaps I can make him accept me back into the fold and restore my allowance if I succeed here, but unless I do what he wants, he will never care what I do."

"And what is it he wants you to do?" She tilted her head. In a flash, the sun shone beneath the wide brim of her hat and showed the bright sparkle of her eyes. "Let me guess. You'll need a wife with money and position."

"I want a wife with character and beauty."

"Dominick, I can never go to England. You English wouldn't accept me. I'm barely tolerated in regular social circles here, let alone the sort you enjoyed."

He jumped. “What sort do you think I enjoyed?”

“The sort that would think Wilkins and Kendall unacceptable despite their money.”

He couldn’t deny it without lying, so he said nothing.

“Is your family wealthy or highborn?” she persisted.

He sighed, picked up part of a broken crab shell, and began to draw the Cherrett family crest in the sand. “You may as well know. My father is the fifth Marquess of Bruton.”

“Worse than I thought.” Her voice sounded strangled. “But you’re a younger son. You really are just plain Mr. Cherrett, aren’t you?”

“No.” He couldn’t look at her. “I’m Lord Dominick. In England, my wife will be known as Lady Dominick.”

“And even for a younger son, Lady Dominick must come from a good family, have been presented to the queen, and know how to use a fan, not how to tie off an umbilical cord.” Her tone held no emotion at all. “I’ve never even owned a fan.”

“I never fell in love with one of those ladies.” He erased the leopard rampant and reached out to her. “Believe me, Tabitha—”

“I believe you.” Her face was set, white beneath the brim of her hat. “But how long does love last when the bride you met on a misty beach, instead of a smoky drawing room, is an embarrassment to you in front of your peers?”

“You couldn’t be—”

“I couldn’t not be.” She ducked her head, hiding her expression from him. “I suspect you’ve merely been toying with me to convince me to help you end your indenture.”

“I have—”

“No, no excuses.” She held up a hand. “I’m still your friend, and I’ll hear you out.”

“I don’t deserve your friendship, but I thank you for it.” He took her hand in his, gripped her fingers as though they were his only lifeline, and stared at the water. The tide was ebbing now, yet heavy breakers told of a storm out to sea. His insides felt as though some of those breakers slammed against his ribs. "My father wanted me to be a vicar. It's tradition in my family for the third son, if there is one, to go into the church. I objected. I have no vocation for serving God as someone under my father's direction must serve Him."

"How could even a marquess direct a man of the cloth?" She looked bewildered.

"In England, a landowner holds the living." He grimaced. "Men flatter him to get placed there, if it's a good one."

"And you didn't want to flatter your own father?"

"I didn't have to. It was expected of me." The sun felt like a burden cloaking his shoulders, and he shifted them as though he could shrug off the weight. "My father would have told me what to preach on Sundays and whom to invite to dinner or whom to visit in the parish. I watched this all my life. He uses the vicar for his personal advancement, not for the advancement of the kingdom of God. As a good son, I should have obeyed him, but I couldn't let God be used that way."

"I can't even imagine thinking of God that way." She sounded wistful.

"I felt very much as though God were a part of my life. I threw it away with everything else in my life." His throat felt thick. "You see, the man I wounded in the duel was a vicar's son, defending what his father did against my accusations of corruption." Dominick laid one hand over his eyes. "He'll always walk with a limp because of me. I'll never forget his face . . ." He shook himself like a wet dog and tried to smile. "So when my uncle offered me a way to find redemption, I took it."

"I thought redemption comes only through God." Tabitha

laughed without humor. "Here I am talking to you about God."

"Talking wisely about Him. Redemption does come from Him, but I—" No, he couldn't tell her more, not everything, from the beginning of his crimes against God's people to the humiliating end. Shame burned through him, and he released her hand to clasp his knee. "Barbados would have been too easy for me. I'd have been the owner's emissary and treated like someone special. I couldn't let myself be pampered and petted and left to live in luxury, and only be out of England with little consequences other than hot weather. So I took my uncle's second choice—a maximum of four years of bondage if I failed."

"And redemption if you succeed at what, Dominick?" Her voice held an edge. "Selling the young men of my country to your Navy for this endless war with France?"

"Quite the opposite, my dear." He breathed a bit easier for the moment. "I'm here to work *against* whoever is selling men to my country's Navy. If I can prove who it is, my uncle will buy out my indenture. I'll be a free man, and I can return to England with my honor restored for catching men who are surely going to drive our countries to war within the next year, as things stand now."

She looked ghostly in the gloom that was growing from the clouds rushing toward shore. "Aren't you . . . aren't you working against your own country?"

"Only if the man perpetrating the abductions is part of the British government's own plan for war." He could smile fully now. "Which he isn't."

"How can you be sure of that?" She hugged her arms across her middle, as though she were cold or her belly hurt. Her hat brim masked her eyes again. "Do you . . . know who it is?"

"No, not for certain. But my uncle would know if England wanted war with America." He tamped down his eagerness to explain more and enlist her aid. "But someone in the Navy is working with him, and who that is, my uncle doesn't know."

"And you're supposed to find out everything."

Dominick nodded. "But I've discovered I can't do this on my own."

She gave him a sidelong glance. "I expect you've always known you can't do this on your own, and the spinster midwife was an excellent ally."

"No, Tabitha—"

"Never mind protests." She gave him a half smile. "Why do you think I can possibly help?"

"Because I suspect I know who the perpetrator is, and with your assistance, I can find proof."

25

Tabitha stared at Dominick, taking in every feature, memorizing each detail, from his long-lashed dark eyes to the strong cheekbones and jaw, to the hint of russet in the swath of satiny brown hair falling over his shoulders. This mental portrait was likely all she would have of him—whatever pretty speeches he made about loving her—if she helped him.

If she helped him, he would leave like all the rest.

Her heart an aching mass in her chest, she rose without speaking and began to clean up the remnants of their meal. Her eyes burned. The clouds sweeping over the sea blurred around the edges, and the lowering sun blazed with a halo around the center gold.

She felt sick. From the corner of her eye, she saw Dominick watching her, and wanted to throw the basket at him, pelt him with strawberries and gull-picked crab shells. She wanted to shout at him, "I am not going to help you leave me alone and be bride of nothing but the mist."

Instead, she gathered up the basket and started for the house without a word, without a backward glance. "How could You be so cruel to me again, God?" She sobbed the words aloud, thinking maybe the Supreme Being would hear her. She was too far away for Dominick to catch her quiet wail above the surf and wind.

She thought.

His hand closed over hers on the basket handle. "Tabitha, look at me."

"Why should I?" She blinked against the mist in her eyes. "I'll never forget your face."

"All right, then answer me this question of logic." His voice held a note of humor, as though he were about to laugh, and she wanted to shove her fingers into her ears. "You are a logical woman, practical and even scientific."

She shrugged.

"I'll take that as a yes." He removed the basket from her hand, switched it to his other side, and clasped her fingers. "If God doesn't care about you, how can you blame Him for everyone leaving you?"

"If God is all love and forgiveness, how can you think you have to earn your redemption?" She glared at him. "Dominick, this is going to get you killed." She saw the dark, triangular head, the catlike eyes, and pressed her hand to her stomach. "It almost did. That snake was meant for you, and the person didn't care if he got me instead this time. That means someone knows and—Dominick, you've got to run away. I'll help."

Maybe they could go together.

"There's land and freedom beyond the mountains." A plan began to form in her head. "No one will find you, not this person wanting to start a war, not Mayor Kendall, not—"

"Shh." He slipped his arm around her waist and held her against his side. "I can't run away. I have a mission to fulfill. I need to show my family, my country, and God that I can do something important, something right."

"And you will." She pulled away from him. "You'll succeed, if you're not dead, and then you'll go back to England to receive your honors and the embrace of your family. And I'll . . . be here . . ." She gave her head a vigorous shake. "How can you even ask me to help you leave me one way or the other?"

"Don't you want to help find out who is causing these disappearances?" They had reached her garden, and he turned to face her, his back to the gate. "The village, the entire eastern shore, would be grateful to you. Mayor Kendall would shower you with so many honors Wilkins wouldn't be able to touch you—if he isn't the man we're seeking."

"Dominick, no. He wants to be a senator."

"Which takes a great deal of money. Or do you think this person is doing it out of the goodness of his heart toward England's struggle with France?"

"No, but—" She felt out of breath, as though she'd been running.

The sky was darkening, from the setting sun in the west and cloud cover in the east.

"You need to go," she said with a heart full of regret.

"I know." His lashes dropped over his eyes. "Will you help me if I promise I won't leave you behind?"

"You expect me to believe Lord Dominick Cherrett would take Midwife Tabitha Eckles back to his august family?" She snorted. "Don't make promises like that. It only makes it hurt worse when they're broken."

A glint of anger flashed through his ridiculously long lashes. "Then you'd rather see me in bondage for years and no future beyond just to keep me near you? Is that any way to show your love?"

If you can't trust God, you can't trust anyone, and if you can't trust anyone, you can't enjoy their love. The pastor's words rang in her head as though the man stood beside her.

Tabitha shook her head. "Maybe I love you too much to expect you to stay here after you're free, or to be saddled with a bride who would shame you to your family."

"You wouldn't shame me with anyone, Tabitha." He cupped her chin in his hand and leaned toward her.

She turned her face away so his lips merely brushed her cheek. "Don't use embraces to persuade me. I can't think when you touch me. I want to agree . . ." She backed away from him, her hand to her middle. "But you know that, don't you? Kiss me into senselessness, and I'll do anything?"

"Don't be silly. I wouldn't do something like that."

"Look me in the eye and tell me that, Lord Dominick."

"Of course I kissed you to win you to my side before asking for your help." He looked her in the eye, and the impact of his chocolate brown irises melting into hers was nearly as compelling as his touch. "I decided immediately to use all my charm on you—the spinster, too-often abandoned midwife—to get your help. Who better? You can go wherever you like whenever you like without anyone gainsaying you. But it all changed. Oh, Tabitha, how I got caught in my own web, hoist by my own petard."

How she wanted to believe him. Only the stiffness of her spine stopped her from leaning toward him, resting her head on his shoulder, promising him anything.

"So if God is involved in our lives, why does He make us suffer?" she cried.

"We make ourselves suffer, Tabitha." He stroked her cheek—her wet cheek. "I railed against His church. You rejected Him. He didn't make us do those things."

"And now we have to pay for our actions?" She shook her head. "I don't see that as God loving me like a parent."

"Parents—" He stopped, and a look of pure pain contorted his features. "I hope God loves us more than parents do. If He doesn't, I'm doomed."

"Your father wasn't loving?" she asked tentatively.

He emitted a bark of humorless mirth. "Quite the opposite. But if I succeed here, he might . . . not be ashamed of me."

"Then you can't take me back to England with you for sure." She thought her own pain would crush her chest. "He would never respect you for—for caring about me."

He opened his mouth, then closed it again and shifted his shoulders as though they ached from carrying a heavy burden. "If I succeed, if I bring honor back to the family, he might allow anything."

"But I can't place you in a position to have to choose between me and your father." She took a step backward. "You'd better go. The sun is about to set."

"I don't want to go. I can talk Letty around if I'm late. Kendall's gone."

"But I don't want you to stay." She picked up the basket, turned her back on him, and walked away. If Dominick wouldn't move from her gate, she could enter from the front. She hoped for his sake he would leave. He might think he could talk females around to his side with a smile and flicker of his eyelashes, but Tabitha wasn't so certain Letty would divide her loyalty between master and fellow servant. Asking her wasn't fair.

At the corner of the wall, Tabitha glanced back. Dominick was gone. Disappointment stabbed her, foolish female that she was. Of course he wouldn't come after her. He'd courted her, with one goal in mind—to get her help. Once he had it, once they succeeded, he would leave. Nothing in Seabourne, in Virginia, in America, could hold back a man who wanted to redeem himself to either his earthly father in England or his heavenly Father.

She didn't blame him. She had let him court her so she could learn if he was up to something. She had succeeded. The knowledge did her no good. He wasn't trying to harm the local inhabitants; he was trying to help them, if he was telling the truth.

She believed him. He wouldn't ask her to work against her countrymen. That was too risky. He knew asking for her help at all jeopardized his relationship with her, if he cared for her as anything beyond the flirt of the moment and as someone he could make an ally. In telling her, he compromised his safety. He trusted her enough not to betray him.

He trusted her, but she didn't believe a word he said about his feelings for her. She could talk about how he wouldn't take her to his family because his father would despise her, and when he denied it, she as good as called him a liar. Oh, he cared for her, but not enough to stand against his need to redeem himself with his family.

Just as Raleigh hadn't cared enough to suppress his desire to roam the world. As her father hadn't cared enough not to go out in the cold after birds' eggs and tax his weak lungs.

"God, if You're there, tell me what is wrong with me that no one will stay," she cried out to the pounding surf and howling wind. She dropped to her knees and covered her face with her hands. "I just want to be loved by someone who won't leave me."

Pastor Downing had said God would never leave, that His love was perfect. Yet Tabitha didn't sense it. She'd only seen Him take from her. With every death, with every disappearance, her heart broke a little more. She held herself from people more and more. She'd gotten close to Dominick for a reason, and fallen for him in the process. She loved him more than she'd ever loved Raleigh or any of the others who had courted her in her youth.

Then why did you send him away?

The question slammed into her head like a chunk of windborne driftwood. She gasped and covered her ears. The howl of the wind diminished, but the question ricocheted around her brainbox like a trumpet blast echoing off the mountain.

Why . . . Why . . . Why . . .

She wanted everything given to her—love, family, permanence. She hadn't gone out to fetch the egret egg for her father. She hadn't gone to the birthing in her mother's place. She hadn't loved any of the young men who had tried to court her. Now that she loved Dominick, she wasn't even sure she had loved Raleigh. She was paid for the kindness and care she bestowed on her patients. She'd even considered running away with Dominick, which would have left Patience and Japheth behind with no one to support them.

No wonder God didn't want her. She gave absolutely nothing.

Kneeling on the dune outside her garden wall, she understood why Dominick felt the need to redeem himself. What he'd done was regrettable, but not horrendous. And he'd been honest about his goal, about his desire to make himself unwelcome in the church as one of its servants. If someone challenged him to a duel, that man shared Dominick's guilt.

Tabitha's was all her own. No one had brought grief upon her except herself, not those who had gone away, not God. Her. She was the one who needed to seek redemption.

And she knew just where to start.

26

Tabitha hesitated at the edge of the town square and drew the hood of her cloak more tightly around her face, against the rain. Across from her, Mayor Kendall's house rose tall and elegant and welcoming, with its red brick, blue shutters, and light glowing behind the windows. The warmth of candle flames drew her. She wanted to go straight to Dominick and give him her decision, make it real before she lost her courage. Instead, she turned to her left and circumvented the square to the parsonage.

She intended to head for the garden and back door. As she passed the front, however, it opened and Phoebe Lee stood in the door frame, her hair shining in the gloom like a little candle flame. "Come in and get dry," she called.

Tabitha did so, her feet feeling heavier with each step. This too she must do, this commitment she must make, before she talked to Dominick. "I'm wet, Mrs. Lee."

"Phoebe," the widow admonished her. "And that's what a fire's for—to dry you. Come in. I've just made us all tea."

Tabitha reached the front steps. "I'd rather talk to you alone."

"Does that mean—" Phoebe clasped her hands under her chin, and her face seemed to hold a flame behind it. "I knew the Lord brought me here for a reason." She held the door wider. "Come into my uncle's study. There's a fire there, and he's out visiting the Parks ladies."

"Is everything all right?" Tabitha stopped on the threshold. "No one came for me."

"No, no, nothing's wrong. The younger one is just fretting over her husband being gone for so long. With good reason too." Phoebe held out her hand. "Give me your cloak. I'll take it into the kitchen to dry."

In minutes, Phoebe had Tabitha tucked up before a fire just large enough to dry her and not overheat her. She held a cup of tea, and a plate of tiny cakes stood on the table in front of her.

"This isn't necessary," Tabitha protested yet again, because she was in the pastor's house, because she wanted to forestall what she was about to say to make her future final.

"Of course it's necessary, Miss Tabitha." Phoebe flashed a heartwarming smile. "I think you've only come to call on me for one reason."

"I could be coming to say no." Tabitha tried to smile but felt like weeping.

"Are you?" Phoebe gave her a direct look.

Tabitha sighed. "I should be. In at least five and possibly more generations, no female in my family has passed her skill of midwifery onto anyone except her daughter. We started at sixteen, presuming we'd be married by eighteen or nineteen and able to carry on no matter where our husband took us. But I'm four and twenty, nearly five and twenty, and the likelihood of me marrying grows . . . dim."

"I don't know why you'd say that." Phoebe reached across the space between their chairs and touched Tabitha's hand. "You're perfectly lovely and so very kind. I'm surprised a dozen men haven't offered for you."

"A few might have." Tabitha stared at the swirling amber liquid of her tea. "They all seemed to vanish like the mist—" She broke off and laughed at her fancy. "So I accepted Raleigh's proposal and then he vanished."

"But he's back."

"And I'm wiser. I can't marry a man I don't love."

"Let me add *wise* to your other qualities." Phoebe's smile was sad. "I made that mistake, let my head be turned by a handsome face and handsomer fortune, and here I am a widow at twenty-two for my folly."

"Or his." Tabitha smiled. "You're still with us."

Phoebe laughed. "You are so right. Now please do go on before I burst with sitting still and waiting."

"Taking you on as an apprentice," Tabitha said through a constricted throat, "is an admission that I will not have a daughter to carry on the family tradition. I'll be the first female in generations who has passed her knowledge on to an outsider."

"But Miss Tab—"

"Wait." Tabitha held up her hand. "If I don't finish quickly, I may not be able to." She blinked against the glaze over her eyes. "I feel that I have a responsibility to share my knowledge for the sake of as many women and their babies as possible. So yes, Phoebe, I'll teach you, in lieu of a daughter, how to be a midwife."

Raleigh hoped the storm would give him a reprieve from his next obligation. Although the rain fell throughout the night, it dissipated by midnight. Unable to sleep, he knelt at the side of his bed and prayed.

Rather, he tried to pray—more than, "God, help me, please help," which stuck in his throat.

He couldn't ask God to get him out of the situation in which he found himself. He hadn't trusted God to get him out of the Navy. He'd made the break for himself, using his ability to swim to slip overboard one night and head for shore while the ship was anchored in Halifax. He had relatives who would harbor him—he thought.

But they hadn't been home. While he tried to figure out a way to break into their house, he encountered one of the officers from his ship attending a party at a neighbor of Raleigh's relatives. Bad luck. Bad timing. A lack of forethought. He'd been caught, and he thought what he was doing was worth saving his neck from being stretched from the yardarm.

But not anymore. If he couldn't work out the identity of his contact, he was nothing less than a traitor to his country, to his family, to Tabitha. The only good that might come from it was that he might be able to implicate Dominick Cherrett and send the Englishman packing back to England or to an American prison.

Surely Dominick was involved. He'd been lurking outside the shed, Raleigh was quite certain. Outside the shed listening to Raleigh attempt to destroy him, another despicable action. Yet if Dominick were involved with stealing men and selling them to the British, what harm could Raleigh have done to him?

Of course Dominick was involved. Raleigh's contact had known Dominick was outside. Raleigh's contact merely used the ploy of hearing someone to catch him off guard and distract him long enough to knock him senseless.

"God, I don't want to be a traitor, but I already am."

And if he didn't get out of his situation soon, he would commit the crime again.

"Help me find a way, or keep the storm here."

But the storm rolled off across the land, leaving a gentle breeze and light swells behind. It ended up a perfect night for their mission.

Listening to the silence with his stomach dropping to the pit of his belly, Raleigh rose and pushed open his casement window. Cool, sweet air blew into his face, and the chirp of a cricket pelted his ears.

No, it wasn't a cricket. No night insect chirped with such a regular pattern. It was the signal for him to come out.

Despite what the ship's chaplain claimed, God had left Raleigh to his own devices, the consequences of his folly. He couldn't blame God. Raleigh had made his choices, made his mistakes.

"I'll find a way to make up for this," he whispered to the night, to God, to Tabitha across the dunes.

He vaulted over the sill to land as light as a cat on the porch roof then the saturated ground. His footfalls made no sound, nor did the footfalls of his master. The man sneaked up on Raleigh and closed hard fingers around his forearm halfway between dunes and water.

"You're going in the wrong direction." The man's raspy whisper cut through Raleigh like a cutlass. "Into the village."

"The village?" Raleigh's tone went high, like a youth whose voice was breaking. "Those might be people I know."

"You should have thought of that before you chose life and treachery." The man laughed.

Bile rose in Raleigh's throat. He said nothing. He couldn't. If he stopped his work, the British Navy would hang him. If he went to the authorities here, the Americans would hang him.

Unless he had valuable information.

He considered swinging around and snatching the mask off his companion's face. He would learn the identity. Dissipating clouds had left behind a cleansed sky with a moon as bright as a lantern hanging low over the water. But Raleigh wouldn't live long enough to tell anyone who the traitor amongst them was. Raleigh would be dead before he hit the ground. He'd seen the man's knife.

Dominick Cherrett had a knife . . .

Raleigh kept his head down and his feet moving. He carried a knife too. Nothing like cold steel to persuade a reluctant sailor to come with them. But he wasn't very good at using it for more than cleaning fish. He'd never learned to throw, and the few times he'd wielded a cutlass in battle, he'd nearly died from the horror of steel meeting flesh.

"Why the village?" he asked after a few hundred yards of silence.

"There are some sailors celebrating their return home after a voyage to the East."

"And we're to send them back again?" Raleigh's throat closed. "Their families—"

"They should be with their families, not out drinking and carousing."

"True, but . . ." Raleigh sighed. "How many?"

"Four, if we can manage that many."

"We don't have help?"

"We've never had help."

Raleigh stopped. "Didn't you have help the other night when you hit me?"

"No, Cherrett wasn't invited along." A hint of anger colored the husky murmur. "He should be dead."

"The snake?" Raleigh dared to ask.

Silence.

"That snake could have bitten Tabitha, you know." Raleigh allowed his own anger to blossom. "She's done nothing wrong."

"Other than play the strumpet with Cherrett?" Now Raleigh heard amusement.

He clenched his fists. "She wouldn't."

"You didn't see them embracing last night. I did."

Embracing, not the brush of lips he'd witnessed, but an embrace.

Raleigh opened his mouth to ask where and when, but his companion raised a hand. “Silence. I hear them.”

They had reached the edge of the village, and Raleigh heard them too—tramping feet, two or three men, with two of them singing in off-key harmony. The singing was to the advantage of the captors. It masked any sound they might make.

“Go behind.”

The direction was unnecessary. Raleigh knew the drill. He slipped up behind the man in the rear, the silent one, whose lagging footsteps suggested he was either exhausted or inebriated. Either way, he should be easy prey. Grabbing the man’s hair with one hand, Raleigh drew the man’s head back so his throat was exposed to the knife blade.

The other two sailors kept going with their song, surely waking up the town.

The man in Raleigh’s grip choked. “No, want . . . wife . . . baby.”

Raleigh’s hand slipped. He knew this man. His baby was barely two days old. He was about to steal Donald Parks away from his beloved wife and brand-new baby.

“Take my money,” Parks pleaded. “Just let me see my wife and children.”

Raleigh’s knife clattered to the stone path. Parks spun. His hand swooped toward Raleigh’s already bruised jaw.

Other hands caught him. Steel flashed. Flesh met flesh. Parks dropped.

“I’ll tie him up,” Raleigh’s master announced. “You get one of the others or you’re a dead man.”

“Run.” Raleigh’s voice emerged barely above a whisper, but apparently the others listened. Pounding feet running for safety was the last thing Raleigh heard.

27

The minute Letty and Dominick stepped into the square, the nearest knot of people ceased talking and turned to stare. Their faces weren't friendly; they registered hostility.

"Something's happened," Dominick murmured. He paused a dozen feet from the others who had come to buy fresh fish, milk, and eggs.

Letty kept walking. "Nancy, Kitty, what's wrong?" Her voice rang out over the square like a town beadle.

Dominick didn't hear the response. He didn't need to. He guessed from the grim faces that more men had vanished the night before. He didn't understand the hostility toward him. Never before had anyone blamed him for the disappearances. He was a servant just like them. Many of them were English too, though most were Irish like Letty. Even they never blamed him for his heritage—until now.

"Who was it?" Letty asked.

Dominick dared to sidle forward to hear the answer. The name Parks sent a jolt through his middle. The man's wife had just borne him a new baby two days earlier.

Tabitha would be devastated.

Dominick glanced around, as though he would see her somewhere in the crowd. He didn't. She knew he went to the market with Letty on Saturday mornings. She would avoid it for no other reason. The night before, she had sent him away before he could leave her.

If he'd been certain she was wrong, that he loved her enough to stay in America or risk taking her to his family, he would have gone after her. But her words pounded through his head when she said them, while he watched her walk away, and as he paced the six feet of open space in his attic room behind a locked door.

He loved her. He didn't doubt that for a moment. Yet he would give her up if she stood between him and regaining his honor or gaining his father's respect.

Well, at least his father's acceptance back into the family. He needed that removal of the burden from his soul first. That took away his right to go after her or even ask her to help him, to touch her, or to expect her to seek him out. Still he looked for her and ached from her absence and the anguish she would feel over Parks's disappearance.

From some of the glances shooting his way, he might end up aching from a beating by the crowd. One burly Scot gripped a hammer like a cudgel. Dominick had his knife, but he wouldn't use it.

"You can't blame him," Letty cried. "I can vouch for him myself. He gets locked in his room at night."

"Don't the mayor trust him?" an Irishman demanded.

"He doesn't." Letty grinned. "He was sneaking off at night to court a lady somewhere out of this village." She shot Dominick an apologetic look. "Mayor thought he just might not come back at night."

"Sure it was a lady?" someone yelled. "Or some naval captain?"

"He came back smelling like roses." Letty chuckled.

Dominick's face burned.

"And then he got himself caught red-handed," Letty continued. "So he gets locked up at night, and he's too big a fella to get out his window, even if he could climb down from the attic."

"But he's English," a woman protested. "He's got every reason to steal our menfolk for their Navy."

"If I could do that," Dominick said, "don't you think I'd have gotten myself away by now?"

A few people murmured. Most looked on in silence.

"I signed my indenture papers," he said, pressing his advantage of the moment. "Just like the rest of you."

"You don't talk like the rest of us."

"I don't." Dominick nodded. "I admit I'm from an important family. Important in England, that is." He dug his toe into the stones beneath him and tried to smile. "So important they got rid of me."

A handful of people chuckled.

"Why?" Letty demanded, her green eyes narrowing.

Dominick took a deep breath. He might as well tell everyone. Once he told her, they would all find out eventually anyway. "I injured someone in a duel and my father sent me packing without a penny."

Letty frowned at him. Most of the other women's faces softened. A few of the men nodded, either in understanding of his father's actions or in sympathy. He couldn't tell. He noticed more the lowering of that Scot's hammer and lessening of hostility.

He slipped his arm through Letty's and bent to whisper in her ear, "What gives with the unfriendliness toward me? It's never happened before."

"Someone's been talking out of turn." Letty still scowled. "Dueling indeed. Over a female, I'm sure."

"No, not a female." He scanned the crowd again, seeking another face besides Tabitha's, the face belonging to the man he suspected of pointing a finger at him as the one responsible for the disappearances. "My behavior has been reprehensible, but never where females are concerned."

If his suspicions were correct, then perhaps Kendall wasn't guilty. On the other hand, he liked his English butler, so perhaps locking Dominick in his room was a way of protecting him from incidents like this one. Or to direct suspicion away from his household. Kendall, after all, was not home. That didn't mean he was in Norfolk, as he claimed he would be.

Dominick didn't see Raleigh Trower, but he did see Tabitha. A basket over her arm, she strolled into the square with her long-legged gait and paused beside a cart bearing butter and cheese. Even from across the intervening space, Dominick saw her face whiten and guessed she must have just learned the news. He took a step in her direction. He needed to go to her, offer her comfort.

Letty grasped his arm. "I need to do my shopping before all the best cream is gone."

"Yes, ma'am." Dominick followed Letty in the opposite direction without protest. It was the best course for now. Tabitha needed to come to him.

But she'd walked away from him, with too good a reason to give him the right to go after her. And she hadn't come the night before, though he'd seen her in town.

His eyes stung in the brightness of the morning sun. Even without her help, he needed to complete his mission and be gone. The longer he was around Tabitha, the more both of them would suffer.

Unless she abandoned him as easily as others had abandoned her.

How he would manage on his own, he didn't know. He must find another ally, but not through courtship. That had proved dangerous.

Basket of cream and butter over his arm, he strolled with Letty back toward Mayor Kendall's house. A few people apologized for their suspicions. Dominick shrugged it off as understandable.

"I'm English and a stranger to you all. But I don't approve of what my country is doing any more than you all do. We've been at war most of my life, and I've seen friends die. Why would I want to see more go?" He couldn't resist one more glance to where he'd seen Tabitha earlier. "And Parks should have been able to see his baby."

His words must have rung with the sincerity he intended, for the mood around him changed, grew sympathetic rather than antagonistic.

But Tabitha was gone.

Beside him, Letty was muttering and grumbling. "Who would start saying such things about you? Have you made enemies here, lad?"

"Just one that I know of." Dominick took one last look around the square for Trower or Tabitha. Neither was in sight. "Raleigh Trower thinks I've stolen his lady."

"You have." Letty opened Kendall's gate. "Not that it'll do her any good."

"She's free to choose whom she likes." Dominick stalked past her. "If she prefers me, it's because Trower left her at the church."

"And you know how to use those bold eyes of yours." Letty snatched the basket from him. "Now, get out of my kitchen. Even if you don't have anything to do with Mayor Kendall gone, I still have to cook for all of us."

"I suppose I could polish silver." Dominick removed his coat and shuddered at the thought of all that emery grit sticking to him, but an idea struck him. "Aren't there candlesticks in the parlor and Kendall's study needing to be polished?"

"Just the parlor. The ones in the study are glass and I wash those myself."

"All right. I'll attend to the ones in the parlor."

And seek an opportunity to slip into the study.

Except the opportunity didn't come. Either Deborah or Dinah seemed to flit past him the entire time he scrubbed and rubbed the brass candelabra in the parlor. The brass gleamed like pure gold when he was done with it. He hadn't gotten any closer to getting into Kendall's study, short of snatching the feather duster from Dinah and offering to apply it himself. Since she would find this peculiar, he refrained and returned to the kitchen.

The aroma of a buttery pastry and fresh coffee met his nose. His mouth watered. "Letty, my dearest lady—"

She swatted him with a flowery apron. "Don't try your sweet talk on me. I'm old enough to be your mother. If you want coffee and a tart, just say so."

"So." He grinned.

She plopped a miniature dried apple pie into his hand. Suddenly hungry, he took a healthy bite—

And choked as Tabitha strolled through the back gate.

"Greedy." Letty smacked him on the back.

He gasped from the pain of his knife sheath biting into one of his scars, and inhaled another crumb.

"It appears," Tabitha said, giving him a smart blow on his lower back, "that I arrived just in time."

"I'm all right," Dominick said.

And he was. Her nearness, her scent of violets and roses rising over the pastry, the warmth of her hand on his back, with only the thin linen of his shirt between her fingers and his flesh, felt like balm on a wound.

At that moment, it was her hand on a wound, an old wound, a scar. When she ran her fingers down and back up again, pausing and repeating the motion, he knew she'd felt the marks, the ridges down his back, even through his shirt.

"Perhaps some air would do you good," she said in her honey voice. Her hand still on his back, she nudged him forward.

"Keep the girls out of the garden, will you please, Letty, my love?" He spoke the words in a light accent and pleaded with his eyes.

She gave him a sharp nod and returned to the oven set into the hearth.

Feeling a bit weak-kneed, Dominick stumbled over the threshold and had nearly reached the bench beneath the cedar tree before Tabitha stopped him, a hand on his shoulder and her person planted on the path ahead of him. "Who did that to your back?"

Dominick offered her a twisted smile. "That father who you're so concerned will dislike me for bringing you home."

"Your father?" She looked like she had after he'd killed the snake—a bit green. "But Dominick, it must have been a—a—whip."

"A carriage whip, to be precise. When I came home after the duel . . ."

It all flashed before him, his father's face so full of loathing. The staring servants. The way the falling rain turned his blood pink on the cobblestones of the stable yard.

He made it two steps further and collapsed onto the bench. He wouldn't be sick in front of Tabitha, but it took willpower.

Tabitha sat beside him and took one of his hands in hers. She said nothing. She simply caressed his fingers one by one and in between.

He started to relax. "He'd already found out. He met me in the stable yard. He already had the whip in his hand." Dominick shivered despite the warmth of the sunshine. "It was January and raining, but he ordered me to strip to the waist, right there in front of the grooms and coachman and I don't know who else. When I refused, he ordered two of the grooms to do it for me." His body burned with remembered shame, and he stared at the brilliant red of a strawberry bush a dozen yards away. Red like blood. "My eldest brother made him stop, or he might have killed me. I'd made him angry before, but that was like nothing I'd ever experienced. Always before, he just shouted and let my schoolmasters do the caning. And in front of the servants . . ." He shook his head. His hair cascaded out of its queue and over his face.

Tabitha brushed it back, her fingers as light as petals. "Why was he so angry?"

"I'd shamed the family." He conjured up a grin. "You know how it is with us English—family, country, God, in that order. I thought I was putting God first, and in doing so, I shamed the family. So I had to be eliminated."

"What did he do after beating you?" Her fingers rested on the pulse beneath his ear. He felt it leap to her gentle caress and wanted nothing more than to bury his face in her hair and hold her close.

"He ordered me thrown off his land as I was." Dominick tilted his head to press her hand between his cheek and shoulder. "I remember landing on the road outside the gate, but nothing more until I woke up at the home of a physician in Lyme Regis. My brothers had carried me there. I stayed for a month until I had enough strength to travel. I got as far as Plymouth with the little money I had, and had some vague notion of heading to the West Indies. I'd forgotten my uncle was attached to the vice admiralty office there. He and my father heartily dislike one another, so he was happy to help me. And here I am." He straightened and looked her in the eye. "But why are you here?"

"To offer you my help."

"Tabitha." The pain of memory, of shame, slipped away. "Why? Because of Parks?" That idea dampened his joy a bit. He wanted her to have come because of him.

"No." She rose and paced to the strawberry bushes and back again, a ripe berry between her fingers. "I was on my way here when I heard the news. I had to pay a visit to Mrs. Parks first. Duty." She offered him the berry.

He took it, bit off half, then returned it to her.

She held the leaves then sank to her knees before him. "I never should have walked away from you. But I've done that all my life. I didn't do what was right, and then those I love left me. If I'd done the right things, I don't know that the same bad things wouldn't have happened, but sometimes I think it's likely they wouldn't have. And now God has noticed me and given me this chance. If I love you, then I know no other way to show it than to help you gain your freedom, even if that means losing you in the end."

Her voice shook. Tears clouded her eyes, and the blazing sunlight showed the bruises of fatigue beneath her eyes and the faint lines at the corners of her mouth and lids. In that moment, she looked drawn and older than her four and twenty years.

Dominick thought her the most beautiful woman he'd ever seen. He wanted to pull her close and kiss her senseless. Then he would sweep her away to a parson who would marry them despite his redemptioner state, so she wouldn't even leave him to walk to her home on the outskirts of the village.

"And I didn't go after you yesterday," he murmured. "What a fool. Or a coward."

"You were being the gentleman you are. I told you to leave." She tasted the strawberry, then popped it into her mouth. "If someone doesn't pick these today, they'll be ruined."

"My practical beloved." Dominick laughed and rose. He leaned down to take her hands and lift her to her feet. "I seem to do this a great deal. And if Letty weren't glaring at me . . . Time for that later. For now, my dearest lady, I want to make you promises. But I won't, if there's even the slightest hint I might break them. I've brought enough dishonor on those I wish to honor most."

"You need to honor your father first. I understand." Her lower lip quivered and a tear glistened golden like a topaz on her cheek. "I understand even more now that I know about what happened. So where do we start?"

"Right here." He gathered the tear on his finger and wished it were a topaz he could keep forever. "If you distract the ladies, I can search Kendall's study."

"Is that all?"

Dominick laughed. "I suspect it'll be more than enough."

Side by side, they strolled toward the house. Letty and the twins greeted them in the kitchen, with curious looks from the former and snickers behind their hands from the latter.

"Your strawberries are nearly too ripe." Tabitha spoke a little too quickly. "If you like, I'll help pick them and prepare them for jelly."

"No, child, it'll take all afternoon."

Tabitha shrugged. "I told Patience and the Parkses I was coming here. Someone will find me if I'm needed."

"If we're boiling fruit and sugar," Letty said, her hands on her hips, "we don't need you distracted by this male here."

"I disappear when real work needs to be done." Dominick kissed Tabitha full on the lips, to give the girls something to giggle and tease about and give Letty cause for a lecture, and beat a hasty retreat from the kitchen.

Outside the door, he leaned his ear against the panel to

listen. He was right. Dinah and Deborah were giggling and sighing, and Letty was lecturing.

"He won't marry you, child. One morning I'll unlock his door and find he's discovered a way to escape. And he won't take the likes of you back to England with him. He'll break your heart, I can assure you of that."

"That presumes," Tabitha drawled, "that I have a heart."

The women laughed.

Dominick slipped into Kendall's study. Shelves of books and a massive desk greeted him. With no idea for what he sought, he didn't know where to start.

The desk made the most sense. But it yielded nothing of importance, with one exception. Ledgers filled two drawers. A swift glance through showed neat rows of numbers, some of them in Dominick's own handwriting—household accounts and accounts from the plantation further inland. He'd seen these ledgers and knew they weren't out of order.

Neither was the desk. He found nothing taped to the underside of drawers or the top, and the measurements omitted the possibility of a secret compartment.

Two other drawers yielded quills, pens, ink, wax, and paper. A fifth drawer held labeled keys. Keys to the carriage house. Keys to the front and back doors of the house. Keys to the cellar, Kendall's study . . .

And the attic, where Dominick slept.

He slipped the key into his pocket and turned his attention to the bookcase. Again, not knowing what he sought, he simply began a methodical search through every volume, pulling them out, flipping the pages open, groping behind.

He found it on the next to last shelf, as the aroma of boiling fruit crept into the room. It was nothing more than a folded sheet of foolscap tucked behind two fat volumes of sermons. On it was a list of dates. Nothing special about that. They listed the days on which men from the eastern shore had disappeared.

But Kendall had departed the previous morning, and the last date was June 15, the night before last.

28

Within twenty minutes, if she hadn't shared a strawberry with Dominick, Tabitha believed she would never want to eat another seedy red fruit. Her hands were stained. Her borrowed apron was stained. She thought maybe her eyes were stained. But without every last ripe berry picked and prepared for preserving in the form of jam or jelly, she didn't know how she would keep Letty and the twins occupied and away from the front of the house.

"I'm likely to die of picking these horrid things," Dinah complained. "Whoever planted so many bushes anyway?"

"The gardener, I expect." Tabitha would have rubbed her aching lower back if she didn't fear staining her gown. "And they all come ripe at once. It's just like tomatoes."

"I won't touch a tomato. Momma always said they was poisonous." Deborah dropped a handful of berries into her bucket and headed for the house.

"Where you going?" Dinah called after her. "You can't leave with the work half done."

Deborah tossed her head. "I just have. I'm going to make these into a poultice with some oatmeal and slap it on my face. It's good for the complexion."

"Your complexion is already beautiful." Tabitha eyed the younger woman with her porcelain skin and not a hint of a wrinkle. Tabitha's own mirror told her the wrinkles had begun. They were faint. One needed bright light to see them, but she knew they were there. Most considered her an old maid already, beyond marriageable age. It didn't matter now. She wanted no one after knowing Dominick.

Thoughts of Dominick made her worry Deborah would go off to her chamber to apply the mask.

"Maybe I should try your poultice. Will you show me how to make it?"

"I'll even apply it for you," Deborah said, then she and Dinah giggled. "I wonder if Mr. Cherrett will want to kiss you with slime all over your face."

Tabitha's face heated from more than the sunshine. "Girls, don't talk about that. Mr. Cherrett was being . . . a wee bit forward in his behavior, and I've put a stop to it."

"I wouldn't have." Dinah sighed.

"Nor I." Deborah closed her eyes. "Don't you like him?"

"I like him fine." Tabitha ducked her head in the pretense of searching for more ripe berries. "That doesn't mean he should behave improperly."

"What's improper about kissing?" Deborah asked.

"Nothing unless it leads to . . . more." Tabitha straightened and frowned at the girls. "Do not even insult either Mr. Cherrett or me by asking. Some things are meant for marriage and marriage alone, and don't either of you forget it. I don't want to have to see you begging me to deliver a baby and stop your pain if you won't tell me who the father is."

The girls' eyes widened until they looked like they would pop out of their pretty faces.

"You do that?" Dinah breathed.

"Yes, I do that. I am required to."

The last time gave one man in the village cause to fear her or despise her, which sometimes was one and the same. He could have planted the snake. He might want to be rid of her and her knowledge that badly.

"Who did you do that to?" Deborah asked.

"That I can't tell you." Tabitha rose. "I think that's all the berries, girls. Let's get these inside and cleaned."

"That's worse than picking them," Dinah cried.

"I suppose you could go do something else . . . if you don't want any jam on your bread for the next year." Letty stood in the kitchen doorway, her hands on her hips. "You girls clean them. Tabitha and I will slice them and crush them for cooking."

After another twenty minutes of slicing and crushing strawberries, then sliding the mass into one pot for jelly and another for jam, Tabitha thought the smell of strawberries would forever make her ill. The company was lively, though. Deborah and Dinah could talk of little other than their new gowns for the Midsummer Festival. Letty reminded them of all the work they still needed to do to have them ready in time, and urged them to clean more quickly. The girls complied. Not wanting the work in the kitchen to stop until Dominick appeared to tell her his search was complete, Tabitha slowed on her slicing.

"Getting tired?" Letty asked. "We should get Dominick in here to help you."

"Where is he?" Dinah asked. "When food's involved, he's usually around."

Tabitha laughed at that, then told what she could only justify as a stretching of the truth. "Not today."

"Maybe it was having to kill a snake," Dinah suggested. "It would put me off my feed."

"He wasn't off his feed earlier." Letty gave Tabitha a quizzical glance. "Is he really off sulking somewhere?"

"I don't know where he is." That, at least, was the truth—more or less. She smashed a batch of strawberries so hard, juice sprayed over the sides of the bowl.

"They did have a lover's quarrel," Deborah crowed. "Look how she attacked those poor berries."

"You were telling me about the embroidery on your gowns?" Tabitha made the change of subject deliberately obvious.

The girls giggled.

Letty frowned, her hands still. "What is he up to?" she murmured. "He looked like you'd handed him the gold at the end of the rainbow when you two came inside. It wasn't a quarrel you were having."

"No, but I expressed my interest in helping you all with the strawberries, and he wanted nothing to do with it." Tabitha smiled. "He doesn't seem to like domestic work."

"No, but he's good about telling us when we boil his egg too long," Dinah called across the kitchen.

"He likes it runny." Deborah made a gagging noise.

Letty scolded her, though she laughed while she did so.

"Three minutes, Dinah," that young lady mimicked Dominick's accent, "or it's completely inedible."

Tabitha laughed and wished she could hug him at that moment, then fix him three-minute eggs for the rest of his life.

"And the toast," Deborah exclaimed. "He calls them fingers and—"

The back gate slammed and footfalls raced up the path. All the ladies in the kitchen swung to face the opening.

"Tabbie." Fanny Trower flung herself into Tabitha's arms. "Tabbie, Raleigh's missing."

"Missing? Where?" Tabitha took a deep breath to calm the sickening thrum of her heart. "No, don't answer that. It's a stupid question. I mean, when was the last time anyone saw him?"

"He went to bed like the rest of us." Fanny's words emerged between sobs. "Early. He and Father were going to go out fishing at dawn if the weather broke. But when Father went into Raleigh's room, he wasn't there. His bed hadn't been slept in, and his window was open."

"They stole him out of his room?" Dinah shrieked. "What kind of monster—"

"Dinah, hush." Letty's command was a whiplash. "Keep to your work," she added more gently.

Afraid she might be sick, Tabitha took Fanny's hand and led her outside. "Tell me everything you know about Raleigh last night."

"There's nothing more to tell." Fanny's pretty face was red and swollen from crying. "We hoped you might know something. But no one's seen you for hours."

"I've been here for quite a while." Tabitha began the mundane task of scrubbing her hands in the basin beside the kitchen door, seeking calm with a routine exercise. "The Parkses knew."

"No one there remembered. They're upset too."

"Yes, I know." Tabitha continued to scrub her hands. "You say Raleigh's window was open?"

"Ye-es."

"Was the floor wet?"

Fanny stared at her. "My brother is missing and you're worried about the floor being wet?"

Tabitha applied another glob of soap to her already spotless hands. "It helps us know if he left before or after the rain stopped last night."

Fanny was now open-mouthed. "How can you think of all that at a time like this? We just know Raleigh hasn't been seen since we went to bed last night."

"I'm trained to think like this."

"But you're not trained to rub the skin off your hands." Dominick appeared, set the bowl of soap out of Tabitha's reach, and lifted the pitcher of clear water. "Hold your hands out."

"You're just as bad as she is," Fanny wailed. "Who cares about soap? My brother is missing."

"Yes, Miss Trower, I heard." Dominick's mouth set in a thin line. His jaw looked hard. He didn't give Fanny a sympathetic comment such as expressing sorrow or regret.

Not like her Dominick at all.

Uneasiness added its weight to Tabitha's fear. If he didn't react with horror to Raleigh's disappearance, perhaps he knew something already. Or had learned something.

"Dominick?" she started to ask.

"Did you look for footprints outside the house?" Dominick asked.

"You don't care, do you?" Fanny glared at him. "You're one of those—those—Englishmen we all hate for good reason."

"And you think you won't be welcome in England," Dominick murmured to Tabitha. "She couldn't flirt with me enough a few days ago."

"Fanny," Tabitha said in as calm a tone as she could manage, "that was uncalled-for and unkind. Dominick had nothing to do with Raleigh's disappearance."

"How do you know?" Fanny, tears still streaming down her face, clenched her fists at her sides. "He's the enemy, isn't he? But you prefer him to my brother. If you hadn't, if you'd married Raleigh, he'd still be here."

"Only if he'd stayed to marry her," Dominick shot back. "Now, do please apologize to Miss Eckles and let us see what we can do to help find your brother."

"I don't want your help." Fanny spun on her heel and raced to the gate.

"Then why did she go running about looking for you?" Deborah asked as she emerged from the house.

"She's overwrought." Dominick shoved his hands into his coat pockets. Paper crackled, and his mouth and jaw took on their earlier grimness. "Letty, can you do without Tabitha from now on today?"

"And you too, I presume?" Letty called from the hearth. "If the girls get back in here and help stir instead of gawking like a couple of mooncalves."

"Go," Dominick ordered.

"Humph." Dinah tossed her head. "You're not our master."

"Do you want me to tell him you're shirking your duties and making Letty work harder?"

"You wouldn't," Deborah protested.

"We'd tell him you've been kissing Miss Tabitha." Dinah gave him a sly look.

Dominick tugged the bow securing her mobcap to her head. "Go right ahead. I dare you."

"You—you oaf." Hands clutching her slipping cap, Dinah raced into the kitchen.

"Your admirers disappear with the speed of our male citizens," Tabitha said.

"You don't look amused." Dominick took her hand, then released it. "Get rid of that apron, do please."

"Oh, the apron." Tabitha yanked it over her head and tossed it toward the washstand. "And I'm not amused. The hostility of too many people around here toward your being English is . . . frightening. During the revolution, people did things to loyalists. I'm afraid for your safety."

"I'm not precisely coolheaded about it myself." He tucked her hand into the crook of his arm. "Earlier, if Letty hadn't pointed out that I was locked up in my bedchamber all night, I think they would have hanged me from the nearest tree several times over."

"Then maybe you should stay here and let me help search."

"I can't." His free hand slipped into his pocket again. "I can't sit about like womenfolk and wait for something to happen to anyone else."

"Is it going to?"

"I have reason to believe so."

She caught her breath. "You found something."

He nodded, and his face worked. "Not here." He opened the gate and ushered her through.

They couldn't talk in the alley or the street or the square. Too many people milled about or rushed with apparent purpose in different directions, some across the neck to Norfolk, others toward the sea, still others to Hampton Roads. They'd gone to fetch Mayor Kendall, to look for British ships at anchor where the James and Elizabeth rivers met the Chesapeake.

"Let them get a taste of their own search and seizure," someone shouted to anyone who would listen.

"The village has gotten bolder," Dominick observed.

"No one's disappeared from right inside the village before." She tightened her hold on his arm. "And no one's ever been hostile to you before."

"Except for you." He gave her a smile that turned her knees to the consistency of the boiling strawberries.

"You frightened me."

"Nothing frightens you, my brave girl."

"There you're wrong."

Losing him frightened her. A loveless, childless future frightened her.

"Has someone set people against you? Since yesterday?" she asked.

"Either that, or the fact that I live in the village and the disappearances took place in the village, makes me someone easy to blame. But I was locked into my room, and until today, I didn't have a key to get out."

"Dominick, you didn't." She stopped to stare at him. "You took a key from Mayor Kendall?"

"I did. He had so many jumbled together in a drawer, he'll simply think he gave it to Letty and mislaid it."

"But he might work out why, and if something happens to someone else, you won't have that protection." Tabitha held out her hand. "Give it to me. I can say I took it from you for your own good, if necessary."

"If you insist." He removed the key from his pocket and slipped it into her hand. "There may be need for it."

"I would never come to your room." She glanced about, hoping no one had seen him giving her the key. They stood between the church and the parsonage. Everyone's attention seemed to be on the square.

"Even to help me?" he asked.

"I'd be ruined."

But he could be dead.

She inhaled with a sharp realization. "If there was no alternative, yes."

"Oh, Tabitha." He slipped his arm around her waist for a brief embrace. "Shall we go to the Trowers' house and see what we can find out?"

"Yes." Tabitha matched her footfalls to Dominick's long stride. "I think he must have been taken from his room, though it's at the top of the house. After all, why would he go out at midnight?"

"Why indeed?" Dominick's jaw looked like marble—hard and pale.

Tabitha's stomach felt like a whirlpool—swirling and sinking. "What did you find?" she asked.

"Nothing more than a list of dates and a name."

"Was last night one of those dates?" She posed the question but knew the answer.

Dominick gave a brief nod.

"And Ral—" She choked on the name. "Raleigh's name was listed?"

Dominick didn't answer. He didn't nod or shake his head. He turned along the landward side of the dunes and picked his way with care, yet quickly, through the rank grasses.

"Dominick, should we go to the Trowers if they're going to be hostile to you?" Tabitha asked at last.

"I don't particularly care if they are." He sounded cold.

He sounded like she thought an aristocratic Englishman would—frosty and indifferent to lesser beings. Lesser beings like her, a schoolmaster's daughter. A midwife's daughter. A spinster midwife.

Though he held her hand close to his side, she felt like a chasm was opening between them.

"Are you looking for footprints?"

"Yes."

They reached a rise of land behind the Trower homestead. The house lay nestled amidst a sea of carefully tended greenery and neat outbuildings. Chickens clucked in a fenced yard, and a cow lowed from a small pasture.

"Things would have been muddy last night," she pointed out.

"And as long as they weren't too trampled today, we might learn something." Dominick released her hand. "Do you know which room is Raleigh's?"

"Only because I know which windows belong to the other rooms." Tabitha gave the house a wide berth in the hope that no one inside would recognize her and Dominick. "What can footprints tell you?" she asked, then answered it herself. "If he was taken."

"Precisely."

"How did you know that?"

He gave her his swift and brilliant grin. "As a recalcitrant schoolboy, I had to learn how to cover up my . . . er . . . escapades."

"Did you learn the hard way? I mean, were you caught?"

"Yes, ma'am. My footprints gave me away to my elder brother, who took my nursery pudding for a month to keep his silence."

"I think you'll have to translate *nursery pudding* for me." She held up her hand. "Later. Raleigh's room is above the porch. Should I distract the others again?"

"A wise idea." Dominick looked preoccupied as he headed for the side of the house.

Tabitha approached the kitchen door. She'd never in her life seen anyone enter the Trowers' house from the front. They rarely used their parlor. But when she walked through the open door in the back, she found a nearly dead fire and no signs of cooking. Only the smell of fish hung in the air, and voices rose and fell from the direction of the parlor.

She let herself through the door. Talk ceased at her appearance. Fanny scowled at her but bit her lip, as though keeping herself from saying something rude.

"I came as soon as I learned," Tabitha said, going to Mrs. Trower. "I'm so sorry."

"Thank you for coming, child." Mrs. Trower clasped Tabitha's hand. "This must distress you greatly."

"It does."

Tabitha studied the woman's face. Although her swollen eyelids bore the evidence of previous tears, the rest of her face was calm, peaceful.

Her smile was genuine and warm as she drew Tabitha down beside her. "We've been praying for him, and I know the Lord is taking care of him."

"I admire your faith."

Tabitha wanted the Lord to take care of her and know it as certainly as Mrs. Trower did. But Raleigh's mother was a good woman, a woman who could pray, a woman without a conscience burdened by the guilt of knowing she had given too little to others. Even now, Tabitha sat with the family and a few neighbors only because Dominick was searching for clues to what had happened to Raleigh and needed to go unnoticed as easily as possible. Clues that could lead to his freedom. Freedom to return to England and away from her.

"Let us hope God chooses to listen to your prayers," Tabitha said.

"It's the English." Fanny curled her upper lip. "And Tabitha there is courting the one who's probably guilty."

"Mr. Cherrett is a gentleman, for all he's a redemptioner," Mrs. Downing interjected before Tabitha could respond. "And he couldn't have taken Raleigh because he is a bondsman."

"Never you mind her, Tabbie," Felicity soothed. "She's just jealous because he never looked at her."

"That's not true," Fanny cried. "Momma, how could she say such a thing?"

"Girls." Mrs. Trower sighed. "Fanny, go fetch a cup of coffee for Tabitha. She looks tired."

"No, thank you." Tabitha rose, afraid Fanny would see Dominick if she went into the kitchen. "I should go look in on Mrs. Parks. With the upset, she could go off her milk." She pressed her cheek to Mrs. Trower's, nodded to the other ladies, and beat a hasty retreat.

She didn't see Dominick outside. Thinking he might have

returned to the village on his own, she started in that direction. Movement behind an outbuilding caught her attention. She turned. Dominick leaned against the shed where Raleigh had been knocked down. He stared inland, his face an expressionless mask.

Tabitha joined him out of sight of the house. "You found something."

"I did." He closed his eyes and leaned his head back against the rough wood of the shed wall. "My dearest, please hear me out before you take a scalpel to my gullet."

"Hear you out about . . . Raleigh?" She shivered despite the day's heat. "Is it . . . bad?"

"I think so." Dominick faced her and took her hands in his. "Tabitha, if you're an impressed man, you have a limited number of ways to get out of the Navy. You get out by dying, because your ship is paid off—taken out of commission or destroyed—or by desertion. Yet Raleigh, who is questionably a subject—I mean, a citizen of the United States of America, at least as far as the British Navy is concerned—came home claiming they let him go. I've always had my suspicions about him, but I couldn't prove anything, and who would believe my word of concern over his?"

"A bondsman to a freeman." Tabitha nodded. Her head swam, and the hair on the back of her neck rose. "What were your suspicions? That he deserted?"

"Yes. Most men only get flogged for it, but they can be hanged under the Articles of War."

"Why didn't you think his ship was paid off?" She wanted the question to be a challenge; it sounded like a fragment of a straw to grasp.

"It occurred to me. So I asked that sloop commander about it." Dominick's fingers tightened on hers. "It wasn't. He has orders to search for deserters on these shores, but you saved

Raleigh that day by being aboard. He wasn't about to leave you alone on a fishing boat."

"How kind." Tabitha's tone dripped sarcasm.

"It was. He could have been accused of shirking his duty. But that's beside the point." Dominick held her gaze. "Tabitha, my love, Raleigh either deserted or was sent here, perhaps bribed with a promise of freedom."

"Just like you."

"Yes, except I am here to catch the man trying to foment war, and Raleigh's working with him."

"How can you be sure of that?" Tabitha pulled her hands free and crossed her arms over her middle. "Maybe he's trying to catch the same person."

"Tabitha, Raleigh left on his own last night. I found footprints in the mud leading away from the house. A single pair of footprints coming this way."

"And?" Tabitha pressed her forearms hard against her belly to keep it from jumping.

"And I found this in Kendall's study." Dominick drew a folded sheet of paper from his coat pocket.

In a glance, she saw it was a diary of sorts with a list of dates and a few names. One name appeared three times—the night before she met Dominick on the beach and Raleigh came home, the night Raleigh was attacked, and the previous night.

Thomas Kendall.

"So your suspicions are right." Tabitha's fingers flexed, crushing the edge of the paper. Her eyes blurred. "Mayor Kendall and Raleigh are guilty of betraying their country."

29

Raleigh opened his eyes. The first thing he thought was that the second blow to his head had blinded him, so dark were his surroundings. The second thing he thought was that the foul odor around him was going to make him ill. The third thing he thought was that, within the day, he was going to be a dead man.

He might not be able to see in the blackness, but he heard the creaks and groans of timber, along with the splash of water and distant shouts of men. Coupled with the stench, he knew he had been taken aboard a man-of-war, a British ship. He was indeed a dead man. He had failed in his mission. He would be considered a deserter now, his punishment hanging.

He doubled over. A moan rose to his lips, burst forth. He clasped his knees and buried his aching head in his arms.

"You're awake." A disembodied voice rose from the blackness. "I was afraid they'd killed you."

"Who is it?" Raleigh guessed the answer before he received it.

"Donald Parks. I was on my way home to my wife and child." His voice broke. "Children. When we dropped anchor in Hampton Roads, I had word that my wife had another boy. My b-boy." He fell silent. Several long, deep breaths told of a man trying to get control. "I was nine months away. It's too long. But I thought I'd made it safe home."

"I'm sorry." Raleigh's eyes burned. "I never meant—"

He couldn't confess what he'd done, what a fool he was. If Parks ever got free or was able to write home, he would tell everyone about Raleigh's treachery. Tabitha would count herself fortunate to have fallen in love with a redemptioner instead of a man without honor. He'd thought he could win her back, show her he wasn't the coward who had deserted her before making her his wife. Now she would learn the truth and think of him with contempt, loathing, scorn.

And as a traitor.

"Oh, Tabbie," he murmured past the feeling of a band compressing his ribs to squeeze every drop of life from his heart. "My dear, dear girl."

"Did you leave a lady behind too?" Parks asked.

"I did." Raleigh shook his head, fought back a cry of pain, and blinked against an explosion of fireworks before his eyes. "At least I had hope of her being my lady."

Except that wasn't really the truth either. He'd had hope until he saw a redemptioner kissing her, and her not raising a hue and cry over the man's insolence. He'd tried to win her back, but Dominick Cherrett had taken hold of her heart.

"She's in love with someone else." Oddly, the admission spoken aloud released some of the tension in his chest. "I just wish she'd remember me well."

"Remember you?" Parks sounded confused. "She'll see you when you get home, won't she?"

"Parks, we aren't going to get home. This is a British man-of-war. Once you're aboard, it's nearly impossible to get off again."

"But we're Americans. They can't keep us. They can't. They can't." His voice rose with each repetition, and he began to bang against the bulkhead. "Do you all hear me? You can't keep me! I'm an American."

"Shut up in there." Someone pounded back. "We're trying to sleep."

"But it's a mistake," Parks bellowed. "I'm an American."

"That's what they all say." Wood rasped against wood.

Light flooded into the chamber, and Raleigh moaned against the pain of the brilliance and the man behind the flame.

"This one ain't a Yankee." A booted foot slammed into Raleigh's ribs. "He's a subject of the king, and he's a deserter."

"Trower?" Donald Parks questioned. "Are you Raleigh Trower?"

"Yes." Raleigh bowed his head. "And yes, I'm a deserter too."

"But you're an American," Parks protested.

"He were born in Canada," the British seaman said. "And we'll put down on the muster book that you're from Bermuda or someplace, so's we can claim you ain't no Yankee."

"You can't." Parks lunged.

Raleigh tripped him, sending him sprawling on the deck before he could attack the seaman.

"He's a bosun's mate," Raleigh said with a sigh. "If you strike him, they'll flog you."

"He can watch," the bosun's mate said. "'Cause they gonna flog you, or maybe hang you. Depends on the behavior of your friend here. If he's good, you get flogged. If he don't cooperate, you get hanged. You got till the captain's dinner is over to think about what you want to do."

He returned to the doorway, stepped over the coaming, and closed the hatch. Blackness fell around them like a blanket, like a shroud.

"Thank you for stopping me." Parks shifted. "Can you tell me what's afoot here, Trower?"

"I can tell you a tale that will make you mind your p's and q's."

"I want a tale that will get me free."

"That's what I mean." Raleigh leaned his head back and realized they'd been locked in the bread room, probably until the ship weighed anchor and neither of them could swim to shore or bribe a provisioning boat to take them home. "I deserted once. They caught me and gave me the option between hanging and going ashore to help sell Americans to the British. One captain in particular. Roscoe." He pronounced the name like an epithet.

"You were involved in . . ." Raleigh sensed Parks moving away from him. "How could you?"

"I thought I could discover the man's identity." Raleigh sighed. "I couldn't. He was too careful. And when I tried to stop you from being taken, he put me here too. Now I'll be lucky if they only flog me half to death instead of hanging me outright for desertion."

"Just for trying to stop them from taking me away?" Parks sounded appalled, bewildered.

"For deserting in the first place. I'm listed in the book as a Canadian. That makes me a British subject. And that means they'll likely hang me for desertion."

"Then we have to escape."

"I can't." Raleigh held his aching head. "I can't go back. I've been a traitor to my own country, to America. They'll hang me too. Here I'll have the chance to beg them just to flog me and somehow make up for everything I've done. Maybe . . ." He let his voice trail off while his thoughts raced ahead.

If he went back to Virginia without knowing who had been the ringleader of the abductions, he would not only die the death of a traitor, a shame to his family, but he would leave

Tabitha thinking the worst of him. She might never love him, but he didn't want her to despise him, to think his faith in God was false.

"She'll never forgive me this time," he said to the darkness, and Parks if he was listening. "That's the biggest burden to bear, knowing I've played a role in Tabbie's damaged relationship with God, because mine's been so bad, so unforgivable."

"No relationship with God is unforgivable," Parks said. "He forgives us if we ask for it."

"That's what the chaplain aboard ship said. But I didn't trust God to get me home and ended up betraying my country."

"God still loves you."

Somewhere above them, a bell clanged eight times. Feet pounded on the deck and men shouted and grumbled. Midnight? Dawn? Noon? They would haul him up for punishment at one of those hours.

"Can God forgive me for making someone else fall away from her faith?" Raleigh asked.

"You didn't make her fall away," Parks said. "She made that decision on her own."

"But my behavior won't convince her to return to the Lord."

Parks said nothing for so long, Raleigh feared the man knew of no answer to this. The ship rocked. Raleigh's head spun. He wanted to sleep. He wanted to keep talking to the older man, whose faith seemed unshaken despite his circumstances.

"Trower," Parks said at last, "we are accountable for our behavior, but God promises that, as long as we repent and ask for it, He will forgive us."

"But I feel I have to do something to make up for my mistakes."

"There's nothing we can do to make up for the past." Parks sighed. "We'd all be doomed if we had to earn our forgiveness. Believe me, my life hasn't been a good example of a man of God. But I have freedom in my heart knowing God has forgiven me anyway." He chuckled. "Now if only I could have freedom in my body."

"If only . . ." Despite the darkness, Raleigh closed his eyes.

He knew Donald's wife. She was sweet and pretty, and her family was generous and loving. She had the new baby. Her husband shouldn't be where he was. None of them should be. Yet if Raleigh's contact wasn't stopped, he would steal more and more men until President Madison declared war. Some men prospered from war. Try as he might, Raleigh could think of no one in the Seabourne area who would profit from a war. But the frigate's captain knew, since he was working with him.

"I might not need to do anything to earn God's forgiveness," Raleigh said, "but what if I want to?"

"Then I suggest you pray hard." Parks took a long, unsteady breath. "We both need to pray for our release."

"We will." Raleigh gripped the edge of a barrel filled with ship's biscuit and maneuvered to his knees. "I have an idea."

Tabitha paused beside a birch tree and wrapped her arm around the slender trunk. Her legs felt as though they had lost their ability to hold her upright, yet she couldn't hold on to Dominick for support. What she knew she must do led to a future where he wouldn't be around for her to hold on to, as no one else had been.

"God is always with me," Marjorie Parks had said regarding living without her husband for months on end. "And he's given me my family."

Tabitha's family was gone, but she had a community. Her work might send Dominick home to England, but it would also garner her accolades in the village.

And God already cared. She was supposed to believe that.

"Yet where were You when I prayed for my family's healing or for Raleigh to come back?" she cried aloud. "Even Raleigh returning is a joke. A sad, sick joke, if he's involved." She turned to bury her face against the tree trunk and found Dominick's shoulder instead. She pushed against it. "No, I can't depend on you. You'll go too. Soon, if we're right at all."

"I'm here now, dear lady." He stroked her hair, and she realized it had tumbled down her back sometime in her rushing about. "And I'll come back for you." He kissed her temple. "No, I'll take you with me."

"Don't make empty promises. I don't need them." She placed her hands against his chest to push him away, but she clung instead. "Your conscience is bearing enough without feeling guilty over me."

"Then that gives me motivation to stay." He curved his hand around her chin and tilted her face up. "I presume you were yelling at God earlier, though, not me."

"Yes. He's supposed to be listening." She blinked against the impact of his deep brown eyes on her heart. "Part of me wants to pray you'll stay, but I'm afraid to. Whether or not I have faith in God can't depend on whether or not—" She stopped, hearing her own words.

Dominick smiled. "Whether or not God answers your prayers the way you want Him to?"

She nodded.

"If He doesn't, it's because He has other plans. Better plans."

"My family dying when I still need them is a better plan?" Tabitha pulled away.

"We can't always know why God arranges things as He does. That's faith."

"How can you have faith and think you need to atone for your past?"

"I . . . can't." Sadness clouded Dominick's face. "I know God can forgive me. But I don't know how. What I've done . . ." He looked away. "And now I've just told you two people you care about aren't who you think they are."

"You think they're involved." Tabitha stiffened her spine. "We can't convict them on a single sheet of paper you found and Raleigh disappearing. Donald Parks disappeared too. And Mayor Kendall is in Norfolk."

"Is he?" Dominick tilted his head as though listening. "He only said he was going there. He rode, so there's no servant to verify the truth of it. And Raleigh? For all we know, he's gone because he's taken Parks to his British contact."

"Dominick, you can't mean—"

But of course he did. He made a great deal of sense. Too much sense. And she could help make sense of things too.

"Whether or not Mayor Kendall is in Norfolk can be proven." Tabitha smoothed down the front of her dress, seeking strawberry stains. "I can go under the guise of visiting the new mother there, and find out."

"I'll go with you."

"If you're caught, you'll be flogged."

Dominick winced but shrugged. "I'll risk it."

"No—" Tabitha broke off. She would ensure that he didn't go, but not by trying to talk him out of it. "It's too late to leave today. We'd be benighted on the road."

"But you can't travel on Sunday."

"It's the best day to travel. The roads will be quiet and I can be assured Kendall won't leave Norfolk—if he's there."

"If you go, I'll follow you."

"You can't. I took your key."

"I'd like it back so I can look out for you."

"No."

"Do you know what it's like to be treated like a prisoner? I had more freedom as a vagabond in England than I have here."

"If God cares about you, He'll see to your welfare." She crossed her arms over her middle, daring him with her eyes.

"Oh, He cares. I have no doubt about that. He cares about what I've done . . ." He turned away. "Very well, go to Norfolk. You know where to find me if you need me."

"I'll walk back with you." She tucked her hand into the crook of his elbow. "I want some of that jam that should be finished by now."

"And to ensure I go home and stay there."

"Maybe."

"Oh, Tabitha." With a noise half like a growl and half like a laugh, he stopped, turned, and kissed her. "Just don't lose the key."

"I'll give it back to you when I return." She took his arm again and they returned to the mayor's house.

"I'll be gone for a few days," she told Letty. "Will you watch over Mr. Cherrett here? He's . . . got a wandering eye."

"Not since he met you, he don't," Dinah said with a giggle.

"Does he indeed?" Letty met Tabitha's gaze and nodded.

She understood. Tabitha could rely on her to ensure that Dominick did nothing to jeopardize his position.

A little mollified, Tabitha returned home to pack and ordered Japheth and Patience to be ready to leave at first light. They would spend most of the morning traveling the rough road to Norfolk, and Tabitha would call on Sally Belote as her excuse for being there.

In the morning, Dominick knelt at his attic window and listened to a wagon rumble out of the village. Tabitha was on her way to Norfolk. If he was right and Kendall was involved, she was walking straight into danger.

"I should be with her." He pounded his fist against the windowsill. "Lord, why am I confined here like a prisoner? I'm of no use to anyone like this."

He'd never been of use to anyone. He'd taken and taken from his father's generous, if indifferent, largess. He'd taken knowledge from his Oxford tutors, and he'd taken information from people who thought he'd befriended them. He'd used his social position, money, and brains to get whatever he wanted. He'd even taken away his father's desire to see his youngest son become the vicar of the church at Bruton-on-Aix, the family parish. He'd taken friendship and now a selfless, loving act from Tabitha.

He'd given nothing.

"Lord, You gave us so much—Your wisdom, Your love, Your life. I can never do enough to be worthy of that. Even finding out the identity of this traitor isn't enough to make up for the past."

Of course it wasn't. His father had been generous only while Dominick did as he wished. When he learned of his son stepping over the line, he treated Dominick worse than his lowest servant, worse than his horses or dogs. Only perfection pleased.

Only perfection pleased God. God wanted a cleansed heart, a repentant life.

"And I will never get there. I've sinned too much." Dominick's chest tightened and his eyes burned. "I can't earn forgiveness, even with this mission."

But the mission would help. His father might still despise him and deny him access to the family, but others would receive him. He could rejoin his friends with his head held high. His brothers would talk to him. He'd have a family again, even if it was as good as being an orphan. Most of all, he could find work as someone's steward or man of business. In time, Father might even reconsider his edict that Dominick's name must never be mentioned in his hearing. Eventually, the people he'd hurt might forget enough to forgive.

And would that be enough for them to accept Tabitha?

Thinking of her lovely, serene face, her practical and compassionate nature, and her intelligence, he didn't know how they couldn't want to be near her as much as he had from the minute he'd encountered the mermaid on the beach. Yet thinking of English society with its strictures and mores, its prejudices and adherence to lineage, its respect for wealth and loathing of getting one's hands dirty in trade, he knew they would shun her at every opportunity.

She was right. He could have his old life back in England, or he could have her.

His old life meant a position, a place, the knowledge that he belonged with a certain type of people. He would find work, interesting work. He might even earn enough respect for a position in the foreign office. Staying with Tabitha meant staying in America, where his name meant nothing. He owned no land and lacked the ability to acquire it. He was English and despised in many circles for nothing more than that heritage. He might love her more than anyone he'd ever known—related to him or otherwise—but his love might not be enough to give her the security she wanted, the life she deserved.

If I'd truly loved her, I'd have left her alone to renew her courtship with Trower.

One more sin to blot his copybook.

Yet if she'd truly loved Raleigh Trower, none of Dominick's machinations should have won her away. She hadn't rebuffed him. She accepted his friendship then his courtship. She'd even sought him out. If he left her, she would be alone in the world again.

He couldn't do that to her. At the same time, he couldn't face a life with no purpose for himself, no vocation, no profession. Without land or money in America, being a gentleman, third son of a marquess, meant nothing. He suspected being a former bondsman made matters even worse, regardless of any service to their country he had performed. It could harm her future as much as her presence in England could harm his.

Yet how could he leave her without anyone to love her? And what if she clung to him merely because Raleigh Trower was gone and Dominick was there?

Only one way to find that out.

If Raleigh Trower still lived, Dominick would find him and free him, whatever the cost.

30

Remembering how she'd been treated at the Belote home before, Tabitha rounded the house and knocked on the back door. It was closed, odd for a warm summer day, and she feared the servants were elsewhere, that everyone was elsewhere. The house lay in a stillness not common in the middle of the afternoon.

Then she heard a baby's cry, the weak mewling of a newborn. She stepped back from the house and glanced up toward the sound. Yes, an upstairs window stood open. Movement flashed in the dim interior of the chamber beyond, and the crying ceased.

"Sally?" Tabitha called. "Sally Belote? It's Tabitha Eckles."

"No," she thought someone gasped.

"May I come in?" Tabitha persisted.

Silence.

"Sally, is something wrong?"

The baby responded with a whimper.

Not caring if she offended the haughty Mrs. Belote, Tabitha tested the handle of the kitchen door. It yielded with a touch. With an exhalation of breath she hadn't realized she'd been holding, she marched into the kitchen to find it neat, the fire banked, loaves of bread rising beneath a spotless linen cloth on the worktable. For whatever reason they were gone, it appeared Cookie and her daughter Abigail would be returning soon.

But why Sally was alone with the infant and not answering her, Tabitha must find out. She remembered her way through the house and hastened up the steps to the second floor. Sally's room overlooked the back garden and field beyond—a pleasant view, but not as fine as the bay on the other side. Nor as cool. The air grew increasingly stifling as Tabitha traversed the hallway on the upper floor and found Sally's door.

Locked—from the outside.

Heart jumping into her throat, Tabitha turned the key and opened the door. Of course, she could be making a mistake. If Sally had suffered from a mental break, as women sometimes did after childbirth, Tabitha could place herself in danger. On the other hand, the child was most certainly in danger, and the girl shouldn't be alone with him.

But she was alone. Quite alone. When Tabitha opened the door, the baby was nowhere in sight. No infant lay in his mother's arms. No cradle stood by the cold hearth. The chamber, with its pastel colors and ruffles, belonged to a young woman about to launch into the world of husband hunting, not the chamber of a new mother.

Except for the smell. Tabitha caught a whiff of urine, rich mother's milk, and another odor as familiar as those of a baby, but completely unrelated.

Her nostrils flared. She clutched her neck, where the mark of the knife barely remained.

From her chair near the open window, Sally stared at Tabitha with huge blue eyes. Her mouth worked. No sound emerged.

"I heard the baby," Tabitha said. "And I smell him. Where is he?"

"Not here." Sally shook her head. "He died."

"In the last two minutes?" Tabitha closed the door, locked it, and slipped the key into her pocket. It clinked against the one to Dominick's chamber.

His prison.

"I heard him crying," she persisted.

"It must have been a cat." Sally didn't move from the chair. "We have cats in the stable."

"Sally, I am a midwife. I have been around scores of babies. I know the difference between a baby's cry and a cat's." Tabitha moved further into the room, glancing around for a hiding place, for the source of that smell.

Tobacco? Whiskey? Some herb with which she was unfamiliar?

Nothing came to her immediate attention, but the baby could be hidden in any number of locations—under the tall bed, inside the chest at its foot, inside the armoire. In any of those locations, he could suffocate in the heat of the chamber. And something had made him stop crying and stay quiet.

Her skin crawled with the possibilities.

"Where are your parents, Sally?" Tabitha asked.

"Father's at sea and Momma is at church with the servants." Sally didn't hesitate in her answer. In fact, she sounded like she was reciting.

"So why were you locked in your room?" Tabitha sidled over to the bed and perched on the edge. She took out Dominick's key and began to play with it. "It's awfully hot in here."

"I want to go shopping, but Momma says I have to stay here until I stop—until my milk dries up."

"Understandable. If you can't take the baby with you, you could make a mess of your gown." Tabitha dropped the key. "Oops."

She sank to her hands and knees. Under the guise of retrieving the key, she looked under the bed. Nothing, not even dust motes.

"So how recently did the baby die that your milk is still

coming up?" Tabitha rose and walked to the chest to sit. "You don't seem sad about the loss of your child."

"I'm not." Sally stuck out her lower lip. "He's a nuisance. That's what Momma says."

"And what do you say? How do you feel about the baby?" Tabitha examined the chest. It was so full of quilts, the lid wouldn't close properly. If the baby lay in there, he was indeed departed from the world—and recently. He couldn't possibly breathe.

Two enormous tears pearled on Sally's lashes. "I love him. He doesn't look a bit like his . . . like him, and he doesn't—" She clamped her hand over her mouth.

Tabitha narrowed her eyes. Sally sat on a chair twice her size. Despite the warm day, a blanket was draped halfway across her lap.

Of course.

"I'm pleased to hear you love him." Tabitha sprang, whipped back the blanket, and exposed a tiny form nestled on the chair beside Sally, his eyes closed, his face scrunched up, his lips working at a cloth teat. "He looks quite alive to me, Sally."

"I'm so glad. I'm always afraid." Sally began to sob into her hands. "Momma says I have to keep him quiet when people come to call. But the only way I can is to soak a cloth in sugar water with a drop or two of brandy on it."

"Oh my." Tabitha scooped up the infant. He weighed no more than a pumpkin, but his limbs were rounded and smooth, signs he was eating well enough. Still, Tabitha removed the sugar teat and examined every inch of him. And she sniffed. Perhaps the brandy was the familiar scent she'd caught. But it wasn't. The cloth needed to be changed, and the baby should have begun to cry in a stranger's arms. No harm should have been done with only a drop or two of spirits.

"No more brandy." Tabitha glanced around. "Where are clean cloths? He needs a fresh one."

"In that chest under the quilt." Sally rose and retrieved a square of fine muslin. "I'll take him. The mess doesn't bother me at all. He smells so sweet even like that." Tears continued to fall down the girl's cheeks. "I don't want to give him up, but Momma says I must because his daddy won't marry me."

"Yes, the daddy." Tabitha carried the child across the room to where Sally had spread the cloth on the floor. "Has he come by to tell you he won't marry you?"

"I-haven't-seen-him." The words emerged in a breathless rush, all running together.

Tabitha frowned. "Are you sure about that?"

"I'll take Charles now." Sally held up her arms.

Tabitha gazed at the sleeping infant—the perfection of round cheeks, peach fuzz on his head, miniscule ears. She touched the bottom of a tiny foot, and the toes curled. She knew Sally watched her, waited with arms extended, to take her child, but Tabitha couldn't let go. Her arms wouldn't open, her hands wouldn't release the precious bundle of life.

"He'll ruin your gown, miss," Sally prompted.

"Of course." Tears misting her eyes, Tabitha forced herself to give Sally's son back to her. "When did you see Harlan Wilkins last, Sally?"

"I said I haven't." Sally kept her head bent over the baby.

Charles opened his eyes and blew a spit bubble.

"Isn't he wonderful?" Sally's voice held awe. "He hardly ever cries, but he knows me more than anyone."

"I can see that." Tabitha looked away, her heart a mass of pain in her chest. "I want you to look at me, Sally, and tell me you haven't seen your baby's father."

"I haven't." The girl took a long, shuddering breath. "And it's not Harlan Wilkins. I lied about that."

"You lied in extremis of labor?" Tabitha swung toward her, staring. "Then who is the father if it's not Harlan Wilkins?"

"It's"—Sally leaned forward and kissed Charles's cheek—"Thomas Kendall."

"Mayor Kendall?" Tabitha felt like the floorboards had been yanked out from under her. "No, it can't be. He—"

Was in Norfolk. He made a number of journeys to Norfolk. His plantation was nearby, but that simply afforded him opportunity and access . . . Yet why wouldn't Kendall marry Sally? He was a widower, and she came from a good family. Surely she was more dangerous to a politician unwed than as his wife.

"No, not Kendall," Tabitha said. "It's Wilkins, and he's frightened you into lying."

"No, no," Sally cried.

Charles began to wail.

"I—he—" Sally cuddled the baby close to her chest. "No, he hasn't been here."

"Which he?" Tabitha knelt to be at eye level with the younger woman. "Wilkins or Kendall? Kendall or Wilkins?"

"Wilkin—I mean, Ken—" Sally paled. "You tricked me."

"Why did you lie to me?"

"I . . . didn't." Sally turned her head to wipe her wet face on her shoulder. "I swear I didn't."

"Not when you said Wilkins, did you?"

"No. That is—he'll take my baby away if he finds out."

"No, he won't." Tabitha stroked loosened hair back from Sally's brow. "He doesn't want that much trouble. But he won't find out. I promise you that. I never tell on my patients unless they require me to testify for them in court."

Was that why Wilkins was frightening Sally into lying?

And slipping poisonous snakes into Tabitha's basket? Just to protect his reputation? But of course, if he wanted to be the next mayor of Seabourne and maybe Norfolk if he amassed enough of a fortune—

She reined in that line of thinking. Not now. Not yet.

"Sally, listen to me," she said in a gentle but authoritative voice. When the girl looked at her, Tabitha continued. "You must stop putting Charles under blankets in this heat, and no more brandy."

"But Momma—"

"Tell Mrs. Belote I said so. And if she tries to make you, you come to me. It's twenty miles away, but there are always wagons traveling to the sea. Someone will give you a lift. Do you understand? You will harm your baby, maybe even kill him, if you continue this treatment."

"I don't want him to die," Sally wailed. Charles wailed along with her.

Tabitha hugged them both, held them for a full minute. "I believe you, child. And don't let Harlan Wilkins frighten you. If he tries again, get a message to me. I'll manage him." Slowly she rose and pulled the key from her pocket. "This is what you should be hiding. You need fresh air and sunshine."

With another long look at the baby's sweet face, she rose, then turned her back on the pair and left the room. She kept the door open behind her. She wanted Sally to be able to stay at home and receive the loving-kindness of her family. At the same time, she wouldn't be the least ruffled if she added Sally to her household. Sally and Charles.

Thinking of the joy of having a baby around, she rounded the house and climbed into her wagon. She nearly directed Japheth to take her home. Then she recalled her plan to investigate whether or not Mayor Kendall had been in Norfolk over the past few days, as he claimed, and directed her driver into town. If she obtained her information quickly, she would be able to go home, with the days so long this time of year. Part of the journey would be in the dark, but she was used to traveling at night.

Not much remained of Norfolk after the fire of five years earlier, not to mention the destruction caused by the British during the revolution. It was still the largest city within a day's travel, and the anchorage in Hampton Roads brought numerous merchant vessels to drop anchor and unload nearby. For Kendall to go there to enact legal business was likely.

To go there to enact illegal business was just as possible.

Armed with news of Raleigh's and Donald Parks's disappearance two days before, Tabitha began inquiries about Kendall at the wharves, where sailors looked at her askance, and at warehouses, where she wasn't treated much better. At the first two inns upon which she called, the landlords sneered at her. The second one went as far as to say that his establishment allowed no solicitation.

"I am not soliciting." Cheeks hot, stomach roiling, Tabitha stalked out and proceeded to the third inn.

"Why do you want to know?" the landlord asked.

To Tabitha, this sounded as good as an admission of Kendall's presence, so she was forthcoming with her identity. "I'm Tabitha Eckles, the local midwife in Seabourne." She smiled. "That has nothing to do with Mayor Kendall, though. I was simply here visiting a patient and knew he was supposed to be in Norfolk, so thought I'd look him up."

"Indeed." The landlord narrowed his eyes. "Would he expect you to call on him?"

"Mayor Kendall and I are on friendly terms, sir." Tabitha bowed her head as she recalled the previous inn experience. "Not inappropriately friendly. We have mutual concerns about the safety and well-being of the inhabitants of our village, and there's sad news—"

"He knows." The landlord covered his mouth with his hand and coughed. "That is to say, word has gotten here already."

"Of course." Tabitha smiled. "So has Mayor Kendall been here since Thursday? I mean, you've seen him?"

"For every meal, ma'am. I expect him for his dinner soon. Would you care to wait?"

Tension uncoiling inside her, Tabitha hesitated as though thinking, then shook her head. "No, thank you. If he already knows what's happened, I'll wait to speak with him when he returns home." She started for the door, then paused to glance back. "Who brought him the news?"

"A gentleman rode in early yesterday."

A gentleman? Unable to think how to ask for a description of this gentleman, but suspecting who, Tabitha nodded and departed.

"Mr. Wilkins were here calling on the mayor," Patience told Tabitha at the wagon. "I went around to the kitchen to get some water and got to talking."

"Good girl." Tabitha patted the maid's hand. "Let's be on our way home then. I'm finished here."

She wanted to get home. She wanted to see Dominick and tell him he must be mistaken, or else Kendall had another accomplice. Either situation was possible. The paper from the study seemed incriminating, yet a number of people could have hidden it there, especially if—

Tabitha's blood ran cold. Someone might have hidden it there because he suspected someone would search the study. Someone like Dominick.

The snake could have killed Dominick as easily as her. Maybe both of them were disposable, both of them a danger to the man at whom they should point their fingers.

Tabitha turned her thoughts over and over on the journey

back to Seabourne. Never had the twenty miles felt so long, so dull, so stifling. She wanted to jump out of the wagon and run all the way home. When they reached her cottage by the sea, she went into the house just long enough to set down her bag before going into the garden and out the back gate.

She was halfway to the village before she thought better of her actions. Darkness had fallen at least a half hour ago. She couldn't walk up to Mayor Kendall's house and ask to see Dominick. All too likely, he was secured for the night. All of them might be asleep for the night. Her request would cause a disruption and unwanted attention.

Feet dragging, she turned back toward home.

She caught the scent a heartbeat before an arm coiled around her waist and cold steel pressed against her throat. "This is a reminder to mind your own affairs, midwife."

Searing pain scored her shoulder. The arm released her. She reeled, fell to her knees on the sand, fumbled to find her kerchief to staunch the flow of blood oozing down her chest. It was merely a scratch. It wouldn't kill her. If she remained conscious so the incoming tide didn't drown her—

A rush of air swooped behind her. She ducked. Not fast enough to avoid the blow, but fast enough to roll away from the tide line before the second blow struck.

As darkness claimed her, she identified the smell from her garden, from Sally's room, from the house of one of her patients.

31

"Can you swim?" Raleigh asked Donald Parks sometime after the evening dogwatch rang through the ship. "And when I say swim, I mean really manage to stay afloat in the water and move."

"I grew up in Seabourne. My father made me learn." Parks sounded weary, discouraged. "But what good is swimming if we're stranded down here?"

"We won't be for much longer. They—they'll want to punish me before we up anchor." Raleigh swallowed at the thought of that vicious cat-o'-nine-tails lacerating his back.

If a rope didn't score his neck.

"That way all the hands can watch and know . . . They can see what happens to deserters."

"But I'm not a hand." Parks shifted in the dark. "I'm a prisoner."

"They'll make you a hand soon enough, and they'll want you to see me punished. Pressed men are the most likely to desert, so they'll want you to see what happens if you leave without their permission." Raleigh snorted. "As if they ever grant permission to ordinary seamen. But you're going to have to desert now or end up heaven only knows where."

"Ha." Parks didn't sound amused. "I could end up heaven only knows where if I go over the side."

"You could." Raleigh rubbed his aching temples. Too little sleep, the blow to his head, and nearly no food or water for too long were taking their toll on his ability to think, to plan, to try at least one more time to get something right. "But I don't think we're all that far from shore. They got us here too quickly for distance, and the waves against the hull sound like shore breakers more than deeper-water waves."

"They do," Parks confirmed.

"And the few times they've opened the hatch," Raleigh continued, "I've heard shore birds. But it could still be a mile or so. Can you manage that far?"

"If the tide is going in and not coming out."

"If it's going out . . ." Raleigh hesitated, not wanting to state the obvious.

Parks coughed. Or perhaps laughed. "I drown if it's going out unless I can grab something to keep me afloat."

"Maybe an oar. You might find an oar at hand if you're near one of the boats."

"And I could use it for a weapon if anyone tries to stop me."

"Yes."

But if he did strike another man with an oar and they caught him, he'd be lashed to the upright grating for flogging too.

Raleigh's empty stomach churned. "It's a big risk, Parks. Is it worth it?"

Parks remained silent for so long, Raleigh expected him to say no. Then the other man inhaled a loud, deep breath. "Yes, it's worth it. But what about you? How will you get away?"

"I won't," Raleigh said. "When I got caught trying to desert, I made a bargain with the captain. I failed to fulfill it. I'll never be trusted again."

"I'm sorry." Parks sounded as though he meant it.

"One thing, though, Parks." Raleigh chose his words with

care. "Please tell Tabitha the truth. I mean, please tell her that I helped you get away."

"I'll tell everyone."

"No, just Tabitha. Let the others think I'm just . . . gone."

"But your family." Horror colored Parks's voice. "Don't you want your family to know where you are?"

"They'll know."

"But—"

"Quiet. Someone's coming."

A few moments later, the hatch opened and a marine stood in the opening, a lantern shining into the bread room. "Captain'll see you, Trower."

Parks stood as far as the low deck beams allowed. "What about me? I want to—"

"Sit down, sailor," the marine barked. "If Captain wanted you, he'd have asked for you. Trower, on your feet."

"Yes, sir." Raleigh rose, head bent, shoulders slumped.

The marine moved aside. Raleigh stepped over the coaming and preceded him between rows of hammocks slung between the guns on this lower gun deck. Men slept in four-hour shifts. Neither the light nor the tramp of Raleigh's and the marine's booted feet seemed to disturb the men in their berths. They were too used to constant noise even in the middle of the night.

Raleigh had never gotten used to the noise. Only when completely exhausted had he slept. Perhaps he could use that as an excuse for his behavior, the agreement, the treachery.

God, let Tabitha forgive me so she can forgive others. Let her be happy. The prayer rose in his head as he climbed the ladder to the main deck and trudged to the quarterdeck companionway.

Another marine stood post outside the captain's door.

He thumped the butt of his musket on the deck and called, "Trower's here, sir."

"Come in," was the quiet response that sounded like a thunderclap to Raleigh.

And let Parks get home to his family. He doesn't deserve to suffer for my failings.

If Raleigh hadn't failed so miserably, Parks wouldn't be there.

Sure he was about to be sick on the deck, Raleigh entered the captain's cabin. The odors of tar, bilge water, and unwashed bodies diminished inside the main cabin, with its fine woods, soft furnishings, and cleanliness. The aroma of lemons wafted on the breeze puffing through the open stern windows. Raleigh took a long, calming breath, smelled his own stink, and choked.

"Do not befoul my carpet, Trower." Captain Roscoe glowered at Raleigh from behind an unlit pipe. "You're in enough trouble already."

"Yes, sir." Raleigh stared at the black-and-white squares painted on a length of canvas to form a carpet. "I failed. Now I'm a traitor to America."

"Be thankful for that." Roscoe turned jovial. "We'd hang you otherwise. As it is, you'll just get a flogging. Forty lashings at noon tomorrow."

Forty. Raleigh sank to his knees under the weight of the number. "It'll kill me."

"Not likely. Just lay you up for a week or two. Now get back below. You'll be kept locked up until after you receive punishment."

"Yes, sir." Raleigh turned and fell into the companionway.

A marine hauled him up by the back of his coat and half dragged, half carried him back to the bread room.

When the hatch closed and the marine's footfalls died away, Parks asked, "What happened?"

"Noon tomorrow," was all Raleigh could say.

Dominick began to pound on his door the instant the first rooster crowed. He needed to go to Tabitha, discover if she'd arrived home yet, and go after her if she hadn't. If he remained confined any longer like a prisoner who'd broken parole, he thought he might tear the door off its hinges with his bare hands.

A shouted protest rose from the floor below. The words were indistinct, the tone unmistakable.

"Let me out and you can go back to bed," Dominick responded, emphasizing each word with a rap. "Please, Letty."

Below stairs, a door slammed. Footsteps thudded on the steps. Then the blessed grate of a key turning in the lock sang in his ears.

Letty shoved open the door. "What's wrong?"

"I have to get out." He waved his arm around the tiny chamber. "It's stifling in here."

"So it is." Letty clutched her dressing gown to her throat. "How do you manage to look so cool when you come out?"

"Breeding." He grinned. "Or lots of canings to get the manner correct."

"Humph." Letty's face twisted. "You'd think they could have gotten you some courtesy while they were at it. Don't ever wake me up again, do you hear me? If you do, I'll use a whip on you myself."

"No, you wouldn't." Dominick kissed her soft, wrinkled cheek. "You love me too much."

"Humph," she repeated to empty air.

Dominick was already slipping past her and racing down the steps. He slammed up the bar across the kitchen door with one hand and tugged on the handle with the other. Sweet, cool morning air blew into his face. He paused to take in a healthy gulp, then sprinted across the garden and out of the gate.

On his way out of the village, he chose to walk. Seeing him out early wouldn't surprise anyone. He had been before, fetching eggs and fish and milk for Letty. But if he ran, they might think he was getting away while Kendall remained in Norfolk.

If Kendall was in Norfolk.

His leg muscles quivered with the need to bolt past the trees and onto the dunes. If she wasn't home yet, he would sit in her garden and wait. He needed to know what she had discovered in Norfolk. Time was running out for meeting his uncle.

Once past the trees, he began to run again. The sand might as well have been snow. His feet sank and slowed him. Then he reached the hard-packed sand near the water's edge and the going grew easier, his speed faster. He leaped over bits of driftwood and other debris the tide churned up. Pale streaks of sunlight reached across the sky, shimmering off the water—

And the face of the woman crumpled at the water's edge.

Dominick dropped to his knees. His heart lodged in his throat, strangling his cry of dismay. Above him the gulls spun and shrieked. For several moments he couldn't move. His outstretched hand hovered an inch from her throat, where he didn't know if he would find a pulse at all.

"I'm not dead." Her voice was rough and quiet, but not breathy.

"Thank God." Dominick doubled over and pressed his cheek to hers. "I thought . . . But what's wrong? Did you fall? Where are your servants?"

"Not . . . expecting me."

"They should know. They should be going with you. They—oh, Tabitha, what hurts? Should I carry you?"

"No. No. I just fainted when I tried to get up. And my shoulder." She shifted a bit and moaned. "It starts bleeding again if I move."

"Bleeding? What's wrong with your shoulder?" Dominick made himself straighten and slipped one hand beneath her head. The sand was damp, but he didn't know if water or blood accounted for the moisture. "What should I do?"

Never had he felt more useless than he did at that moment. If his education and rank hadn't prepared him to carve roasts and polish silver, it most certainly hadn't prepared him to manage a wounded female. The thought flashed through his mind that this was why he wouldn't survive in America as a free man. If he didn't have money, he needed practical skills like knowing what to do in an emergency. And he didn't have a bit of a notion on how to proceed.

From the sand, Tabitha chuckled, albeit hoarsely. "Dominick, you look like you're going to swoon. Sit back and put your head between your knees."

"It's the blood." He rose, walked to the water, and splashed cold Atlantic water on his face, then returned to kneel beside her. "I'm all right now. Tell me what to do."

"If you can lift me, I think I can manage from there. It's just . . . a scratch. And my head . . ."

"Just a scratch." Dominick's voice took on a brisk tone. "And a blow. How did you acquire these wounds?"

"The little matter of a knife and . . . I don't know what. But later, please. I'm freezing."

That was something he could manage. He pulled off his coat and tucked it around her. When he reached her left shoulder, he found the scratch, the stickiness of drying blood. Sliding his fingers into her hair, he discovered a swelling lump over her right ear.

"Better?" He gathered her, coat and all, into his arms and rose to his feet. "Mermaids don't weigh much, I see." He smiled down at her lovely face, so close to his, nestled against his shoulder.

She smiled back. "You Englishmen are stronger than you look." Her eyes gazed into his, dull with pain despite the generous curve of her lips. "Will you take me home?"

"I'm not strong enough to stand here holding you all day." He brushed his lips across hers. "And I want you in a condition to tell me what happened. You left for Norfolk yesterday morning and now I find you lying on the beach in Seabourne." He started walking as he babbled. "If the sun hadn't shone off your face, I'd have thought you were more flotsam."

"I nearly was." She closed her eyes. "Dominick—" A shudder raced through her and up his arms. "Do you have your knife with you?"

"Ye-es." He drew her closer and wished her house weren't another half mile away. "Why?"

"Someone tried to kill me." She wrapped her uninjured arm around his neck. "No, not some—"

He tripped over driftwood, jarring them both.

"I'm so sorry." The scarred skin on his back pulled taut. "I won't do it again. I promise. I won't—"

"Shh." She pressed her fingers to his lips. "It just . . . hurts a bit. But I don't think it's deep. It doesn't seem to be bleeding anymore."

"No, it's just sticky." He tried not to gag. "Is Patience there to help you clean it? I don't think I should."

"No, you shouldn't. Patience will do well, though. You can guard us." She grasped a handful of his hair as though it were a lifeline. "Dominick, it's not Mayor Kendall. It's Harlan Wilkins."

Her head ached. Her shoulder stung. But she was free of sand and dried salt water. Dominick sat beside her on the garden bench, and she felt safe, warm, cherished.

He looked grim as he took his knife from its sheath and laid it on the bench close at hand. "Now that you look more like a lady than a drowned mermaid, perhaps you can tell me how you've reached your conclusion despite evidence to the contrary."

"The man who did this to me"—she touched her now-bandaged shoulder, lumpy beneath her gown—"was the same one who held a knife to me the night I met you."

"It makes sense in that the method is the same, but how do you know?"

"I caught his scent. It's tobacco and whiskey and"—she gave him a sidelong glance—"sandalwood."

"Don't look at me that way. I am not guilty." He rubbed his thumb along her chin. "And that's pretty slim proof."

"I smelled it in Sally Belote's room too."

Dominick straightened, alert. "Who would have been—Wilkins."

"Yes. She practically admitted to having seen him and how he told her to lie to me about it, to say the mayor is the baby's father."

"Kendall? Never."

"Really?" Tabitha arched her brows. "You were quick to believe him guilty of treachery."

"That's different from debauching a young woman."

"True, but if Wilkins was ready to implicate Mayor Kendall . . ." She trailed off, waiting for him to reach the conclusion she had.

"He could have placed that paper in Kendall's study hoping someone would find it." Dominick nodded.

"Someone like you."

"Who might conceivably look for that paper or, if nothing else, a book." Dominick pursed his lips. "But where do you come into this? Why is he harming you? Other than this young woman in Norfolk and what you know about that."

"That would be enough, I think, but I was assaulted before then."

"Yes." Dominick nudged her with his elbow. "You accused me."

"I still could." She resisted the urge to rest her head against his shoulder and simply let him hold her, forget knives and betrayal, dangers and futures of love she couldn't have. "But maybe I know more than just about Sally. Or he thinks I do."

Dominick gave her a quizzical look.

"His wife," she said. "I was there when she died. The servants said she fell down the steps pacing about the house waiting for him to come home, but what if she fell down the steps before he left home? What if she was pushed? Or even was trying to stop him from doing something?"

"Like go out hunting victims for the British Navy?" Dominick shook his head. "That's a strong accusation without more than speculation. Unless she did say something?"

"Nothing that made sense without context." Tabitha rubbed her gritty eyes. "I don't even recall what exactly she said. Not a great deal. I thought she spoke against the pain. She suffered . . . I could do too little for her . . ." She covered her face with her hands, remembering the woman's face, her fruitless early labor, her dying words. "'Don't go,' she'd said. But he abandoned her when she needed him most. And where was God?"

"He was there, Tabitha." Dominick pulled her hands down and held them between his. "He was waiting to be invited to join you."

"I was too busy trying to stop the hemorrhage and raging against her husband. He should have been there uninvited. God should have been there uninvited."

"He was. You just didn't acknowledge Him."

"Would He have saved her life?" Tabitha challenged.

"I don't know. Man interferes with God's plans." He grimaced. "Believe me, I know that more than anyone. But Wilkins. Do you think she knew something and he pushed her down the steps?"

"It's possible. It's as likely as him being our traitor."

"But why?" Dominick rose and began to pace between rows of verdant herbs—chamomile and mint, rosemary and thyme, parsley, garlic, and comfrey. His voice drifted back to her. "Why would Wilkins or Kendall risk their lives for a few hundred pounds they're making from the sale of seamen to the British Navy?" He turned down the row of lavender, paused, and plucked a sprig. "What can either of them gain?"

"Men prosper from war." Tabitha smiled at the sight of him surrounded by delicate plants and wished for the strength to join him. "I kept thinking about this last night, when I was conscious enough to think. Mayor Kendall's father and uncle made a fortune during the revolution as privateers. Others might want war for that reason."

Dominick's head went up, his expression turned haughty. "We'll destroy you in a month."

The demeanor, the tone, and the words shouted of his birthright—British aristocracy, pride in his family, in his country. He believed, without equivocation, that England would trounce the United States in armed combat.

She wished he wasn't right.

"You have no Navy to speak of, and a handful of privateers can't take down the strongest Navy in the world," Dominick said, pressing home his point.

"But even men on the losing side make money in war." Tabitha reached down and plucked a sprig of mint from its shady corner beneath the cedar tree. "And both men have ambitions that cost a great deal of money."

"How do they make money in war other than privateering?" Dominick asked as he rejoined her on the bench.

Tabitha stared at him. "Building ships. Making weapons, making clothing. Providing preserved meats and ship's bread. I expect there are others. Ship chandlers too."

"Ah, trade. Not something I was taught."

"What were you taught?"

"Latin and Greek, history and philosophy, mathematics and reading . . ." He shrugged, then smiled, tucked the sprig of lavender into the neckline of her gown, and let his fingertips rest on the faint scar on her throat. "Wooing lovely young ladies."

"A pity you aren't a better spy." She removed his hand and raised it to her cheek. "You could be using those skills in a land where they're appreciated, instead of here, where having land or being a shopkeeper means more."

"Ah, you wound me." He smiled, but the fact that it didn't reach his eyes suggested he spoke the truth despite his light tone.

"I'm not a very good spy either." She kissed his palm, the healed gash where the knife had pierced him between thumb and forefinger, evidence of him being a poor butler. "We have no more than suspicions against two upstanding citizens of

Seabourne and a stronger suspicion against a man whose family is loved here, even if he himself isn't since abandoning me at the altar."

"Do you want him back?" Dominick asked. "I mean, if we knew where to find him and I wasn't here, would you accept his suit?"

"If he's involved, then he's a traitor too, and the answer is—"

"Mr. Cherrett?" The cry came from the garden gate. "Dominick Cherrett." Breathless, Dinah raced toward them. "Oh, sir, you're here." She tripped and landed on her knees on the path.

"What is it, child?" Dominick hastened to raise her to her feet again. "What's happened?"

"Kendall." Dinah's chest rose and fell like bellows in the hands of a nervous blacksmith. "Mayor Kendall's home and furious about you being gone since dawn."

"Then I'd best be on my way." He looked at Tabitha. "I'll return as soon as I can."

Tabitha glanced from Dinah's anxious countenance to Dominick's too-expressionless face, and stood. "I'm coming with you."

"You can't," Dominick protested. "You're injured."

"I'm coming to explain your absence." Tabitha took his arm, leaning on it more heavily than she wanted to. "So he understands you weren't up to mischief."

"It's not him being here that's the difficulty," Dinah gasped out. "It's Mayor Kendall's study. He says someone's been searching it and a key is missing."

32

The eight bells signaling the noon hour rang through the ship like the tolling of a church spire calling mourners to a funeral service. Despite the stifling heat of the bread room, Raleigh shivered like a man with ague. He knew what was coming. He'd witnessed the ceremony often enough, the ritual so rigidly adhered to in the British Navy that it held an aura of religious fervor.

Raleigh wished for religious fervor. He settled for knowing nothing he had done was beyond God's forgiveness, if not man's. Or, in his situation, woman's.

"Don't forget to tell her," he told Parks, as he had so many times that he'd lost count. "If you reach Seabourne, tell Tabitha she must forgive me and not blame God for my abandoning her."

"I won't forget." Parks's voice was tight. "And if you survive and I don't, tell my family I love them. And there's money in a bank in Norfolk. My last voyage . . . it was successful for all the crew." He sighed. "It'll be my last unless we go to war."

"If the English keep stealing our men, we will."

"Then I'll tell everyone I can what I know in an attempt to stop some of the destruction." Parks shifted, his body thumping against the deck. "It gives me a reason to live."

"We both need it." Raleigh bowed his head. "And Jesus to accept us if we don't survive."

"He's already accepted us." Parks shifted again. "If—"

The drum began, the wordless order for all hands to assemble on deck. Bile rose in Raleigh's throat. His skin crawled. Gooseflesh rose on his arms.

Tramping feet accompanied the drum rolls. Then the hatch opened and a marine stood in the opening, two more behind him.

"On your feet," the first one commanded. "The both of you."

They rose. Parks laid a light hand on Raleigh's shoulder, then allowed himself to be nudged forward through the gun deck to the main hatch. Raleigh followed. His boots felt as heavy as the cannonballs that filled those guns during battle. His head felt as though it had received a full broadside. Soon his back would feel worse. Fire. That's how others had described it. After the blow of the lead-weighted leather straps—nine of them—the fire came, blazing through flesh, muscle, bone. Most men fainted after half a dozen. The bosun's mate wielding the lash would have him cut down, and the ship's surgeon would revive him for the rest of his punishment.

Raleigh intended to faint after two lashes.

At that moment, stepping into the blazing sunshine and seeing the ship's company assembled, hats off in deference to the Article of War about to be read, Raleigh thought he might faint before the punishment began. If not for the firm hand of the marine on his arm, he might have run and jumped overboard.

A quick scan of the crowd showed him Parks, pale but docile, between two marines, and too far from the gunwale.

Raleigh steeled himself for what he must do.

The marine marched him to the foot of the quarterdeck ladder. The captain, lieutenants, and midshipmen stood above him and the assembled ship's company. The lieutenants looked solemn, the midshipmen a little queasy, the captain grave.

"Raleigh Trower," the captain began.

The ship's company fell silent.

"In your absence," the captain continued, "your court martial was conducted and found you guilty of the fifteenth Article of War, which reads as thus." He opened a leather-bound book in his hands and cleared his throat. "'Every person in or belonging to the fleet, who shall desert or entice others so to do, shall suffer death, or such other punishment as the circumstances of the offense shall deserve, and a court martial shall judge fit: and if any commanding officer of any of His Majesty's ships or vessels of war shall receive or entertain a deserter from any other of His Majesty's ships or vessels, after discovering him to be such deserter, and shall not with all convenient speed give notice to the captain of the ship or vessel to which such deserter belongs; or if the said ships or vessels are at any considerable distance from each other, to the secretary of the admiralty, or to the commander in chief; every person so offending, and being convicted thereof by the sentence of the court martial, shall be cashiered.'" He closed the book. "Do you have anything to say for yourself?"

"I am not a British subject," Raleigh intoned.

"It has been established by the North Atlantic fleet commander that you are." The captain glanced to the nearby bosun, who held a green baize bag. "Let the punishment begin."

The sea breezes grew as hot as the sun. Sea and sky, staring men and blazing sun, spun around him. He was going to lose consciousness for certain.

"None of that." The bosun threw cold water into his face.

While Raleigh sputtered, two marines grabbed his arms.

They stripped him to the waist, then tied his hands to a hatch grating that had been propped upright. He leaned his cheek against the hot metal, certain it was branding him. The sun beat on his back, and every muscle drew up tight like a turtle seeking its shell.

Lord, grant me strength—

The first blow fell. White-hot pain seared through his skin like nine pokers from the fire.

Raleigh screamed.

Only the timbers and sea and rigging made noise. In the quiet, the whistle of the lash sounded like another scream. It bit into flesh. Raleigh sank his teeth into his lower lip hard enough to draw blood, then sagged from the ropes binding his hands.

"He's gone off, the weakling," a marine called. "Surgeon?"

A knife flashed. The ropes fell from Raleigh's wrists. He slumped to the deck.

Near the bow, a shout rose. "Stop him. He's—"

A roar like thunder soared from the throats of the sailors. They tried to run to the source of trouble. Guns and stays and fellow crewmen got in their way.

No one got in Raleigh's. He rolled and sprang. His hand flashed out and snatched the cat-o'-nine-tails from the bosun's grip, and Raleigh began to wield it. Heading aft toward where he'd last seen Donald Parks with his marine escorts, Raleigh applied the whip to anyone who got in his way.

"Man overboard," someone yelled.

"Stop the deserter," the captain bellowed. "Marines, stop him."

They closed in around him, behind him. Raleigh caught their red coats, their shining bayonets. He struck one across the face with the handle of the lash and tangled another's legs with the straps. The man went down. The handle yanked from Raleigh's hand. Weaponless, he charged forward, lunged for the rail. His shoulder struck a third marine in the chest. The man stumbled. Raleigh grabbed his musket and raised it to club back the next man grabbing for him.

"Take him down," the captain shouted. "Take him—"

A gun fired. Something like a hammer slammed into Raleigh's back.

He tumbled over the railing and into the sea.

Dominick lost his ribbon somewhere between Tabitha's house and Kendall's study. His hair tumbled around his face and shoulders, and sweat plastered his shirt to his back. He wanted to slip up the steps and wash, but Kendall saw him coming and called for him to enter.

"Close the door," Kendall commanded from behind his massive desk.

Dominick did so, then leaned against it, his arms crossed over his chest. "Dinah said you wished to see me."

"I do, but not looking like you did when you walked off that transport ship." Kendall frowned. "What have you been doing?"

"I've been with Tabitha Eckles." Knowing that could be taken improperly, Dominick hastened to add, "I felt in need of an early morning walk, and found her lying on the beach. She'd been injured."

"Injured? Tabitha?" Kendall's face paled. "Sit down and tell me what happened."

Dominick sauntered across the study to a chair near the desk. He let his gaze stray to the point in the bookshelves where he'd found the list of dates and Raleigh Trower's name. At the same time, he attempted to observe Kendall's reaction to the look. Kendall kept his eyes on Dominick, his face grim and revealing nothing. Either he knew about the notations and schooled himself not to follow Dominick's glance, or he knew nothing and thought his bondsman appeared to be avoiding his eyes.

Again, nothing learned.

His own mouth set in a hard line, Dominick settled into the chair and made himself hold his hands on the arms rather than crossed against his chest, where his heart thudded so hard he feared his raised pulse showed at the base of this throat. Tabitha in danger from Wilkins. Him in danger from Kendall. The twenty-first of June far too close with no definite information available.

"Well?" Kendall prompted.

Dominick jumped. "Well what, sir?"

"Tell me about Miss Eckles. What happened?"

"Oh, yes." Dominick shifted on the hard wooden seat of the chair. "She was on the beach and was assaulted. He left her unconscious on the edge of the water, but she came to awareness early enough not to be drowned in the tide."

"And why was I not informed at once?" Kendall shot halfway over the desk. "What are you thinking, Cherrett? This is a serious incident, and I need to know at once. The sheriff needs to know at once. Does she know who did this heinous crime?"

"It's not for me to say, sir." Dominick resisted the urge to push his chair away from Kendall, though he was still a yard off. "If she wants you to know—"

"If? If?" Kendall stood upright and began to pace. "First young men disappear from my town, then a new father on his way home disappears along with a young man who has just returned, and now the midwife is attacked." He reached the window, where sunshine poured in like flames from a grate, and swung back. “I am mayor of this village. I need to know the instant something occurs.”

“You were in Norfolk, sir.” Dominick gripped the arms of the chair to stop himself from standing. He needed to remain in a subservient position at present, and he was a full head taller than the mayor. “I would have told you as soon as I returned.”

“And when did you intend that to be?” Kendall shot back.

“As soon as you returned, sir.”

“Is it?” Kendall strode forward and glared down at Dominick. “I have my doubts.”

“I . . . beg your pardon . . . sir?” Dominick shook his hair out of his face and met Kendall’s gaze. “About what do you have your doubts, sir?”

“You look like a convict off of a British Navy transport,” Kendall said, as though each word was a heavy burden. “Your hair and clothes are a disgrace, and you give me that haughty proper grammar like some Oxford don, as though I am the servant and you the master. Is it training or breeding?”

“A little of both, sir.” Dominick bowed his head, his mind filled with Tabitha’s pronouncement that he couldn’t have both his past and her in his future. “Neither has done me any good. I am the servant and subject to another man’s whims, unable to see my lady safely home at night, or even make her my wife. And it’s no one’s fault but mine that I’m here.”

“I know, Dominick.” Kendall circled his desk and subsided into the chair. “I know why you’re here.”

“Sir?” Dominick started.

“I know about the letters, the duel,” Kendall continued.

Dominick relaxed. For a moment, he’d feared Kendall knew about the mission.

"I know your family wanted rid of you and put you on a ship bound for America with no money."

So he didn't know he'd put himself on the ship because he already had no money and his father had made England unpleasant for him.

"I've kept you locked up at night for your own safety," Kendall continued. "If others learned of your background, they could make a great deal of hay out of you wandering about after hours. Wilkins flat-out accused you of being a spy. Because I know you were locked up, I know it's not true, so that protects you. I will continue to protect you, and you will pay the consequences if you break my rules again. I have no choice in the matter. I can't be seen as being gentle with an Englishman many don't trust, and you can't afford to be subject to accusations. Do you understand me?"

"Yes, sir." Dominick thought about the calendar, the date of his last chance at early release from his bond looming ahead of him, impossible to meet, and the room seemed to grow dark despite the sunshine. He needed his freedom to spy on Wilkins.

"Now," Kendall said, leaning forward and holding Dominick's gaze, "where is the key that was in my desk?"

33

As she had found necessary twice since leaving her house, Tabitha found a place to rest. Although only a few hundred yards from Mayor Kendall's, she sank onto the low wall surrounding the cemetery and inhaled the fragrance of a nearby magnolia tree. Its sweetness calmed her with a reminder of the pleasurable aspects of life, the little gifts God had given to His people as a reminder of . . . His love?

She started to lift her left hand to rub her eyes, which felt like her attacker had walked through them with sandy boots. The shallow cut pulled, and she emitted a low moan of pain, of frustration. She needed to get the key to Dominick before something awful happened to him. Patience had wanted to go, but Tabitha needed to assure herself he was all right, see him, inhale his scent, touch his face. She needed to create memories to carry with her forever.

Is that what you want from me, God? To sacrifice everyone I love until I have only You in my life?

That, of course, presumed she could have God in her life. But when people abandoned her through death and desertion, who was left but God? If He did care, of course.

She rubbed her eyes with her right hand, then rested her palm over them against the brilliance of the day. From an oak in the yard of the parsonage, a cardinal whistled and chattered, and another answered from across the square. Children played with shouts of joy and infectious giggles, and her heart wrenched. If He was all she was going to have, she desperately wanted to believe God loved her.

A hand curved around her shoulder, large, strong, gentle. "What's going through your head, my dear?" Dominick asked.

She couldn't answer him completely. In no way would she make him feel obligated to stay with her. She lowered her hand and chose a half truth. "I was just remembering something my mother used to say." Tabitha glanced over her shoulder, where a slab of pale gray granite marked her mother's grave. Roses tumbled over the stone, half obscuring the words "Honored Daughter, Wife, Midwife, Mother."

"I always loved flowers," she continued. "Momma used to tell me they were a reminder that God loves us. I don't think that's in the Bible, but it gave me comfort after Father died. I planted that first rosebush. I used to walk past here and look at it and tell myself that God loved me in spite of my father leaving us. In spite of it being my fault because I wanted to read an herbal rather than collect eggs for him. When Raleigh left, I didn't have anywhere to plant flowers. I had my garden at home, but it had always been there and didn't seem to have the same impact. Then, when Momma died so soon afterward, I planted that second bush. It blooms even better than the first, but I forgot that it was to remind me I was loved by God. I felt like He'd left me like everyone else."

"And now?" Dominick settled on the wall beside her. "Do you believe that God has abandoned you?"

She plucked at a loose thread on her dress. "I've certainly abandoned Him. But if I'm wrong, then what is left once you leave?"

"If we can't prove anything against"—Dominick glanced around at the empty square and graveyard—"him, I'm going nowhere for a long time."

"And that makes you unhappy." She observed the tightness at the corners of his eyes and the downward slant to his lips. "What happened with Kendall?"

"I was on my way to get the key." Dominick sighed. "If I don't get it to him within the hour, Kendall will send me inland to his plantation."

"And if that happens, you will remain a redemptioner for another four years and I will still be unable to see you."

"But locked up here, I can't spy on Wil—anyone. I am so frustrated at night, I can barely sleep."

"If God is with us, then shouldn't we be able to pray about it?"

"Yes, but—" He bowed his head. His hair cascaded forward in a river of shining brown, red, and gold. "You might have abandoned God, but I betrayed Him."

Tabitha brushed his hair back behind his ear so she could see his face. "How do you betray God?"

"Seven years ago . . ." He swung his legs over the wall so he faced the graveyard, his back to the town. "It all started seven years ago at university."

"Riotous living like what we hear of most students?" She spread out her skirt so she could take his hand in hers out of sight of any passersby. "Surely if God forgave the prodigal son—"

"I was worse than a prodigal." Though low, his voice held an intensity that thrummed through him. "I was showing so much promise at university, I knew I'd never convince my father I shouldn't be a vicar. So I began to write letters to newspapers, to periodicals, to print shops." He drew one foot up to rest on the wall and looped his hands around his knee. "I used my family position to glean information, then exposed every scandal involving a man of the church, from bishops to sextons. Even if I knew the man had repented, I reported the incident." He paused to take a deep breath.

"Why?" was all Tabitha could think to say, as she tucked her abandoned fingers into her pocket.

Dominick snorted. "I wanted the church to refuse to ordain me."

"You couldn't simply engage in riotous living?" Tabitha asked, then laughed. "That was a silly question. I expect the church wouldn't be surprised if a young aristocrat engaged in riotous living while a student."

"Precisely." Dominick half smiled. "And believe it or not, I didn't want to engage in that kind of behavior. Drinking to excess and gaming and . . . other forms of debauchery didn't appeal to me. I had a deep faith in God that said those things were wrong." He sighed. "A pity it didn't tell me that destroying the credibility of men serving God, most of them sincerely, was wrong too. I felt so self-righteous, so certain that all vicars and curates were like the ones my father kept around him in the livings he controlled. When I uncovered a new slip in proper behavior, I rejoiced in the man's fall from grace as more grist for my scandal mill." His tone dripped with self-loathing.

Tabitha laid her hand on his arm but said nothing. She couldn't work out how she felt about his revelation enough to express any emotion or reasonable reaction.

"Of course, no one knew who was writing the letters except for one of my Oxford tutors," Dominick continued, still using that note of disgust. "He advised me to stop, that I was hurting men who didn't deserve to be hurt. He told me God would forgive them if they asked, and it wasn't my place to force these men to confess or lose their positions. But I wouldn't listen."

"And did anyone lose his position?" Tabitha asked.

"No." Dominick shook his head, sending his hair shimmering in the sunlight. "But one man lost his wife."

"What?" Tabitha stiffened.

Dominick gave her a sidelong glance. "Despicable, aren't I? I discovered he'd had an indiscretion a few years earlier. A print shop made broadsides about it, and a few days later, his wife left him."

Tabitha caught her breath.

Dominick plunged on. "He went after her, publicly begged for her forgiveness. She gave it, and on the way home . . . on the way home . . ." He covered his face with his hands. A shudder ran through him.

Tabitha wished they were alone so she could wrap her arms around him, absorb some of his pain instead of making him bear it alone. She settled for tugging one of his hands down and holding it between both of hers in silent support.

He kept his other hand over his eyes as he choked out, "She died . . . in a carriage accident. I—I as good as killed her."

"Did you make him misstep in his marriage?" Tabitha pulled his other hand from his face. "Did you make her run off instead of staying to talk things out with him?"

"No, but—"

"Then you didn't kill her." She squeezed his hands. "Yes, you probably shouldn't have exposed their private concerns to the world, but they made their own choices."

"A pity their son didn't see it that way." Dominick's voice was dry, his face tight. "He left his mother's funeral to find out who had written that broadsheet. He exposed me for writing the letters and challenged me to a duel. You know the rest." He rubbed his hands over his face. "I have damaged too many lives and you are much better without me, but I don't want you to be—without me, that is. It's merely that . . . Tabitha, I must make up for the lives I've damaged. If I can save lives, prevent a war, even prevent more young men from being stolen, perhaps then I can find my way back to my earlier relationship with the Lord. But I can't do it as a bondsman. My uncle was wrong. But we couldn't think of another way to get me here."

"Maybe that's what God wants of you." Tabitha inhaled the magnolias and glanced at Dominick's face to remind her of God's beautiful creations. "If He is involved in our lives and we want Him to be, then it's possible He has a reason to keep you here in bondage."

"What, more punishment?" Dominick snorted. "I suppose it's nothing less than what I deserve for what I did. If I could punish myself, I would. I'd go back and go into the church rather than hurt anyone as I did."

"Would you really?" Tabitha felt a little ill. "Would you want that much to please your father? Would you serve the church now if your father still wanted that of you?"

She could scarcely breathe while she waited for his answer. If he said yes, then she knew he had made up his mind about their future. *God, I sure hope You're with me and I'm wrong about You not caring.*

Dominick gazed into the cemetery for several moments. Somewhere a wagon rolled along the cobblestones. A woman called, and the children's play ceased. For a full minute, the town lay in silence save for the humming of bees in the flowers.

His inhalation of breath sounded like a wave against the shore in the stillness. "If I could find my way back to a harmonious relationship with God, I would love to serve Him. If I could be forgiven, what better way to thank Him?"

"Then we must get this key back to Kendall." She produced the object from her pocket. It shimmered before her misty eyes. "And I'll do the spying for you."

"You want to be rid of me so quickly?" He gave her a half smile.

"I want you to be at peace so soon." Aching in every joint, she headed for Kendall's house.

Dominick fell into step beside her. "You should stay here. Letty will take care of you. You're too tired and injured to walk home."

"I want to be alone."

So that only God would witness her breaking heart.

"Take this to Kendall." She handed Dominick the key. "I'm off."

"No, wait." He caught hold of her elbow. "Tabitha, at least let me walk you home."

"You can't. You have work."

"Kendall will understand. He's not an unreasonable man."

"Any man who threatens to flog another is unreasonable. It's barbaric to inflict pain like that."

"Like my father?"

Tabitha didn't answer. She feared if she opened her mouth, she would demand to know why he would prefer to please a man who had scarred him for life and left him to die, over a woman who wanted to bring him nothing but healing. Yet what were the commonplace words her mother always told patients in extremis? *Only God is the true healer.*

So that must mean she could only pray for Dominick, not heal him herself.

She needed to go home and think about that. Praying meant admitting God was there, that she'd been wrong. And if she was wrong, she needed to repent of the sin of denying God's presence. The idea made her quiver inside.

She rested her hand on a fence rail for balance. "I need to rest, Dominick, but we can talk when Mayor Kendall will let you get away. If we're to get you free, we need to plan how I can help you . . ." She glanced at the nearby house, too close with its open windows for mentioning names.

"I shouldn't let you. It's too risky." He touched her cheek. "Perhaps there's another way, something that won't involve you. Doing so seems wrong."

"It's my choice." She touched his cheek and turned away.

"This evening before sundown, if I can persuade Kendall to let me go," Dominick said behind her.

"Your hour is almost up. Take care of that key." Tabitha made herself walk briskly away. When she rounded the corner, she slowed according to her strength. Getting home would take a while.

She pictured her future without Dominick. She had an apprentice. She could take on more. Her life wouldn't be empty. She would have a great purpose. The country was growing all the time. It needed women healers. And if war came, the women would need to take over for the men.

She wanted to accept the notion wholeheartedly. But an emptiness remained, a gap like a hole in a window, where wind and rain and cold could seep in.

"If You're there, God," she murmured as she traversed the square, empty in the heat of midafternoon, "then I need You to fill that hole. I've been seeking for others to do this, a man to give me children, and that's all fallen through. You're my last hope of anything permanent, forever, secure."

Tabitha leaned against a tree to catch her breath. She needed sleep. She needed time to let her shoulder heal, but Dominick didn't have time. She would have to start spying on Wilkins that night.

She headed for home again. Twice more she paused to rest. Her shoulder ached. Her head ached. If she slept until dark, maybe she would feel refreshed enough to carry out her plan, flimsy as it was.

She was a hundred feet from her garden when she saw a man lying on the ground outside the gate.

Raleigh. Raleigh. Raleigh. His name rang through her head with each thud of her heart, each slam of her foot on the ground.

He'd escaped. He'd returned to her. Unlike Dominick, he had nowhere else to go, and this experience would teach him not to wander. She might not love him as she loved Dominick, but he was good and kind, and they'd been friends forever.

She charged forward and dropped to her knees beside the man.

It wasn't Raleigh.

"Donald," she said in a quiet voice, "can you hear me?"

Donald Parks opened his eyes. "I . . . can hear . . . you. Just . . . tired. Swam . . . forever."

"You can sleep later." Tabitha began to examine his head and neck for signs of injury. "You need to tell me now what happened."

"Can't." His eyes closed. "Sleep."

"All right. All right." She resisted the urge to shake him awake. "I'll have my manservant carry you inside and get you out of those wet clothes. But first, tell me . . ." She had to clear her throat. "Raleigh? Is he all right? Do you know?"

"Yes, I do." Donald caught his breath. "I'm sorry, Miss Tabitha." His face worked. "He's dead."

34

"I simply wish to see if she arrived home safely." Dominick explained himself to Letty for the second time. "She was attacked last night. She's injured. But she came into town to help me, and I have to assure myself she's safe."

"You'd have heard if she isn't." Letty sprinkled salt into a cooking pot, from which the aroma of stewing venison, onions, and garlic rose on fragrant steam. "Unless she was foolish enough to walk along the beach."

"Which she just might do." Dominick paced the length of the kitchen. "I can't live with this confinement if it means I can't ensure the safety of my lady."

"Is she your lady?" Letty faced him, her hands on her hips. "Seems to me she's not a lady, as you English know it, and you won't be taking her back to your fancy family in four years, or whenever they forgive you enough to pay off your indenture papers."

"They won't." Which was something he needed to consider. "They're happy to be rid of me."

So would they be happy to see him back even if he did work out who was trying to foment war? Something else to ponder.

"And would they welcome you with a village midwife on your arm?" Letty persisted.

Dominick toed a place in the brick floor, where the mortar was chipping away. "I don't think so."

"Then why are you toying with her affections?"

"I'm not toying with them. That is . . ." He slumped onto a chair and forked his fingers through his hair. "Letty, I don't know what to do. I should have stayed away from her, but I didn't and now the damage is done. With Trower gone, I can't repair it."

"You could stay here." Letty seated herself across from him. "Four years goes by quick. Or maybe Kendall would give you permission to marry."

"And have me live a separate life from my bride, locked up at night like the horses?" Dominick gripped the edge of the worktable. "Letty, I can't wed her until I'm free, and I can't take her home with me and expect to repair matters with my family. We have no future. And—" Suddenly he couldn't speak.

"Seems to me that a family who throws you out, then won't welcome you back because you married a lovely girl like Miss Tabitha, isn't one who shows loving-kindness."

Dominick shook his head. "I don't want to have to choose." At that moment, looking into a future without Tabitha, he didn't want to complete his mission if it meant going back to a family that had thrown him out on the road like a stray dog. "Yet how can I make my peace with God otherwise?" he thought aloud.

"You make your peace with God by asking for it, not by doing something." Letty rose and gave the pot a stir. "But you know that. You hear the parson."

"The parson doesn't know how many people I've hurt. I need to make up for it."

"You can't." Letty slammed the lid onto the kettle. "There's nothing you can do to make up for any sin you commit. Making yourself suffer won't take away anyone else's suffering."

"But it reminds me not to do it again."

Yet there he was, knowing he was going to hurt Tabitha if he left for England once he obtained his freedom. England and the family that hadn't contacted him once in six months. England and the family that didn't understand that his faith in God had prevented him from serving in the kind of vicar's position his father wanted—one who would preach according to what the marquess wanted the people to believe, not what the Bible said to believe. England and a family that could give him entrée into a world he knew, a world in which he felt comfortable and welcome.

Welcome once. Yet who had contacted him other than his one Oxford tutor? Dominick had accomplished what few gentlemen had—taken the tests to obtain his degree—and only his tutors had congratulated him.

"I'm English, Letty," he said at last. "There's no place for me here."

"And what place is there for you there?" Letty asked.

"I . . . don't know." Dominick slid from his chair and began to pace again. "Gentlemen's work. A steward. A secretary. Perhaps a position in the government, if my family will sponsor me."

"Lots of maybes and ifs." Letty took flour and lard from the pantry. "Here, at least, you have people who love you for certain."

"Then that's the easy road and I can't take it. It costs me too little."

"Oh, lad . . ." Letty sighed. "Go on with you. As long as you're back in time to serve supper, there's no sense in your fretting over the lady."

"Yes, ma'am, I'll be back." He reached behind him to tighten the ribbon holding his hair in place, then darted out the door before Letty changed her mind.

Odd he'd told her staying would be no sacrifice. Surely it

was. He would have Tabitha, yes, but he had nothing else, no prospects but more servitude, no standing in society, no name that would open doors once he was vindicated. In truth, he would have no security to offer a wife.

Or was it security he sought for himself?

Dominick slid to a halt beside the church. The doors stood open, and the hard-edged notes of a harpsichord being hammered with more exuberance than skill drifted into the square. He climbed the steps and slipped into one of the pews, closing the door with a click so the musician couldn't hear. In the cool dimness, he slipped to his knees and leaned his brow on the immovable back of the pew in front of him.

The position felt strange, uncomfortable despite the padded bench beneath his knees. He couldn't remember the last time he'd knelt in a church. He couldn't remember the last time he'd prayed. He had so much to say, he didn't know where to start.

The music banged off of his ears. His conscience created havoc in his chest. Words crowded into his throat, tasted bitter on his lips.

"I do remember, God. The last time I prayed was the night before I wrote my first letter. I asked for success in convincing my father I shouldn't go into the church."

He hadn't waited for God's help. He'd begun his campaign of destruction. Perhaps he'd meant it only for himself, but he'd learned that he was hurting others soon enough to stop.

"But I didn't stop. I went my own way. I was so determined to reject serving the church, I didn't think that—that . . ."

That God might want him serving his Lord and Savior?

The thought slammed into his head on a discordant collection of notes from the harpsichord, and he caught his breath. Surely God didn't want him in the ministry. The idea was too horrendous, standing in the pulpit on Sundays while spending weekdays listening to instructions from one of Bruton's minions or Bruton himself. That wasn't serving God. And the church wouldn't have him now.

Unless he accomplished his mission and his father took him back. And if he succeeded, then he would have to leave Tabitha, or his father wouldn't help restore his son's good name.

"Lord, this choice hurts too much."

The temptation to run surged through him. He could ask Kendall to send him to the interior or sell his indenture to someone far away. He wouldn't have to risk accomplishing his mission and could avoid the choice between Tabitha and his father—marriage to Tabitha or service to God.

Honor demanded he remain, discover who wanted to start a war, and choose. To accomplish that, he needed to talk to Tabitha about how she could help him.

She would help him leave her in order to restore his honor.

The thought of that much love turned him into a creature the consistency of a jellyfish. With effort, he forced himself to his feet and out of the pew. As he exited the church, he thought someone called his name. He didn't look back. Staying in the quiet safety of the sanctuary felt like too much of a temptation. He had to reach Tabitha's house and return to Kendall's before dark.

He hastened on his way, raising a hand or giving a nod to people he passed. Other than a few who had blamed him after Parks's and Trower's disappearances, he seemed welcome in the town, even liked. It was a pretty place there by the sea, a much warmer and kinder sea than the English Channel near his home. His former home. He didn't even mind the heat that much, except at night in his stifling attic. It was better than the freezing garret he'd stayed in for the week before a ship left for the other side of the Atlantic, before his uncle had found him.

Most of all, he liked the little cottage on the outskirts of town, where a wall protected the garden from the wind off the sea. The garden where roses vied with herbs for the lady's favor. She healed with the herbs. She ate the roses.

The notion made him smile. He was still smiling as he let himself inside the gate and trotted up the path to the kitchen door.

"Mr. Cherrett." Patience swung around to greet him, spraying a stream of steaming water from a kettle. "We wasn't expecting you."

"I know." He stepped over the threshold and reached for a towel to mop up the water before the woman slipped. "I didn't mean to startle you, but I had to ensure that Miss Tabitha arrived home safely and is resting."

"She's safe enough, sir, but she's not resting." Patience began to pour the kettle's contents into a washbasin. "Mr. Parks came crawling in about an hour ago."

"Parks?" Stooping, Dominick lost his balance and sat in the water. "How? I thought he'd been taken."

"And so he had." Tabitha's low voice drifted from the doorway. "He got away, thanks to Raleigh." She stepped gingerly over the spilled water and offered Dominick her hand. "He probably died so Donald could get away." Her voice was flat, her eyes red-rimmed.

"Oh, my dear." Dominick scrambled to his feet and drew her to him.

A sob shuddered through her. He stroked the tail of hair tumbling down her back and murmured nonsense sounds while she wept.

Patience slipped out of the room, balancing the washbasin of hot water.

"Can you tell me what happened?" Dominick asked at last.

Tabitha nodded and pulled away. "They got picked up the other night and were rowed out to a frigate about a mile offshore. Donald was semiconscious and Raleigh completely gone. They were locked in a storage room, and the guards kept telling them Raleigh would be hanged for desertion."

Dominick winced. "They didn't?"

"No." Tabitha smoothed his hopelessly wrinkled cravat. "The captain said he needed men so he would only flog Raleigh instead."

"God have mercy on him." Dominick's back muscles tightened, and nausea filled his belly. "Was it . . . harsh?"

"It never got past the second blow." Tabitha told Dominick what she knew of the events that followed. "Donald glanced back long enough to see someone go over the rail."

Dominick heaved a sigh of relief. "So Trower could still be alive."

"It doesn't seem likely if—if he was shot."

"But if he was running, he might have jumped into the sea and not fallen. It's difficult to strike a moving target with a musket."

"You think it's possible?" Tabitha's eyes lit her face like moonbeams on a dark night, then clouded again. "But they'd probably hang him now that they've likely worked out that he helped Donald escape."

"Not yet. That takes a court martial, even for an impressed man."

"So if he wasn't killed in the escape, he'd still be—" Tabitha closed her eyes. "Why would I even hope he'd be alive? He'll never get off that man-of-war now that they've gotten him back."

"Would you want him here?" Dominick posed the question, though he didn't want the answer. "Do you love him still, my dear? Could you . . . could you build a future with him?"

"Love him still?" Tabitha wiped her eyes on a corner of her apron. "I'm not sure I ever loved him as more than a dear friend of my youth. But we were so comfortable together before he left, we could have had a comfortable future." She ducked her head, her lashes hiding her eyes. "If I didn't have you, if circumstances were different when he returned, I could still have a future with him. But circumstances are as they are."

"And can change." Dominick cupped her face in his hands and kissed her long and hard, then released her and strode to the door into the rest of the house. "I need to talk to Parks, if he's at all well enough and his wife's not with him."

"She's not. He wants to be well enough to walk in his door, the silly man. So he's sleeping, but you can wake him if it's important." The intensity of her gaze suggested she knew it was.

"It is." Dominick set his jaw. "I need to know where that frigate is anchored. That captain is the key to all of this, if he's receiving abducted men, and it's time he was paid a visit from Lord Dominick Cherrett."

"Dominick, you can't. You won't be home by sundown." She grasped his arm. "Wait."

"And have them sail, if they haven't already?" He shook his head. "I have to take the risk, for Trower's sake, for yours, and for mine."

"But Kendall will punish you."

"I'll risk it." Dominick shuddered at the thought of pain ripping across his back. "It's worth the risk to end this warmongering once and for all."

"But Dominick, I'll—" She snapped her mouth shut so hard he heard her teeth snap together. "Please, don't do it. I—I'll go."

"Do you think a British naval captain will talk to me or you?"

The question was cruel, condescending. He knew it before he saw the pain twist her features. It couldn't be helped. She'd be a fool to take the kind of risk he intended. If this captain was involved with the abductions, he was dangerous. He would do away with a village midwife. But Dominick doubted the man would risk harming the son of a peer of the realm—however disgraced that son—or the nephew of a Vice Admiral of the Red.

"If I don't return," he added more gently, "you'll know where to send someone to rescue me or to go after the frigate. Try to get a message to my uncle. A boat will put in at the inlet north of here on June 21."

"You could be halfway to Barbados by then." Tabitha twisted her hands in her apron. "You can't risk it."

"I can't avoid risking it. If I don't, I'll suffer four more years of servitude and have accomplished nothing. Young men will continue to disappear from these shores, and we'll have war inside a year."

"Then let me go with you. If Raleigh is merely injured, he'll need medical assistance. And—and you—" She gazed at him with wide, blue-gray eyes. "Please."

Now he was the fool for considering her request for a moment. But as he looked into her eyes, he heard himself saying, as though his voice belonged to another man, "Can you row?"

"Yes, of course. But we can take the *Marianne*. It'll be faster and safer."

"You know how to handle her?"

"Of course," she repeated.

"But your shoulder."

"I can handle a single-masted fishing boat." Her pointed little chin set.

Dominick's insides melted. Somehow he would stop her from going with him. "I'll talk to Parks while you change your dress." He slipped out of the kitchen and rounded the stairway to enter the parlor.

Donald Parks lay on the settee with his feet propped on a chair to accommodate for his height being longer than the furnishings. His eyes were closed, but he opened them at Dominick's footfalls across the floorboards.

"I don't know you," he said.

"No, we haven't ever met."

"English." Parks started up. "You can't make me go back."

"No, I can't." Dominick laid his hand on the other man's shoulder and nudged him down. "Officially, I'm a redemptioner belonging to Mayor Kendall. I am also a spy trying to stop a war, and you can help."

"You're a what?" Parks looked as though Dominick had struck him across the face. "Mister . . . um . . ."

"Officially, it's Lord Dominick." He smiled. "But you can call me Cherrett, if you don't have other choice names for an Englishman."

Parks smiled through cracked lips. "What do you need to know?"

Dominick told him, and Parks answered to the best of his knowledge. By the time Tabitha raced downstairs in canvas boots and a woolen cloak over her gown, her hair tied up in a knitted cap, Dominick had all the information he could glean from the American.

"You need to think about what you're doing, Dominick," she said. "The sun is beginning to set."

"If I have the answers to the disappearances, everything will be all right."

He hoped.

He glanced at Parks. "Shall we send someone to notify your family of your return?"

"Please." Parks raised himself on one elbow. "I don't think I look as bad as I did earlier, do I?"

"They're not going to care." Tabitha touched his brow as though he were a child with a fever. "I'll send Japheth before we leave."

"She shouldn't go with you," Parks said.

"I know. But if I don't take her, she'll go on her own." A twinge of envy twisted inside him. "She needs to save Trower."

"I need—" She broke off and headed for the door, calling for Japheth.

Dominick followed. In moments, they were heading out across the beach toward the jetty and Raleigh Trower's boat. Dominick thought of reasons why she shouldn't go, from her injured shoulder to the risk of confronting a man with armed marines and hundreds of sailors at his command. Dominick's rank should help save him, but if things went badly, not even he could protect Tabitha.

He stopped her at the jetty. "You can't go."

"You can't stop me." She caressed his cheek. "I have to do this for—for Raleigh."

"Yes, Raleigh." He gritted his teeth.

He was willing to get her former fiancé back for her, if he still lived, but he wasn't willing for her to go after him. But she was right. He couldn't stop her. If he took the *Marianne*, she would find another boat. She was safer beside him than alone.

He hoped.

"All right, but do everything I say." He grasped the painter and drew the little craft closer to the jetty. "Climb aboard."

She obeyed and leaped aft to loose the sheets. Her face glowed in the slanting sunlight. Sunlight that spelled trouble for him if he failed to return before it faded. Sunlight emphasizing her beauty. His heart bounded toward her before he loosed the painter and jumped aboard.

"Hurry," she called.

He hurried. He hadn't been aboard a sailing boat since the brief peace of 1802, when Englishmen felt secure sailing the channel for pleasure. But he had enjoyed that year of freedom before he left Dorset for Oxford and had spent every minute he could on the water.

He raced to hoist the sail while Tabitha took the tiller. Slowly, agonizingly, the craft turned on the ebbing tide and light breeze and headed out to sea.

"Wind," Tabitha cried from the wheel. "We need more wind."

"We're not going all that far, though it may take a bit to find the frigate, if she hasn't upped anchor. In which case we won't find her at all in the dark."

"We have to try. But Dominick—"

A shout sounded from shore. She glanced back, then leaned over the wheel as though she could make the fishing boat move faster, a groan escaping her lips.

"What is it?" Dominick shoved the belaying pin into the rail and ran back to her. "Is it your wound?"

"No, it's Harlan Wilkins. He saw us."

35

The *Nemesis* rode at anchor miles down the coast from where Donald Parks had gone over the side. By the time they found the frigate, full dark had fallen, and Tabitha could barely stand upright.

"We were right." She feared the weakness of her voice reflected her pain and fatigue. "They must have been searching for him, figuring the tide currents would bring him this way."

"I didn't think the captain would risk Parks getting away." He rested his hand on her shoulder. "Or Raleigh."

"Yes, Raleigh." Tabitha sagged against the taffrail. "How do we approach them without getting fired upon?"

"I'll hail them, if you can take the wheel."

"Of course." The now often-spoken words had lost some of their conviction.

Dominick stepped away from the tiller but remained at her side, peering down at her through the starlight. "I shouldn't have let you come. You're about to faint on me."

"I'm not such a weak creature." She smiled at him. "But maybe the captain is gentleman enough to offer me a chair, if he lets us aboard."

"Tabitha—"

"Who's there?" a voice cried from the prow of the frigate.

Dominick cupped his hands around his mouth. "Lord

Dominick Cherrett." He dropped one hand to the wheel. "Hold her steady. I'll lower the sail." He dashed forward.

Lights flared along the rail of the *Nemesis*. Faces shone in the yellow glare.

"Did you say Lord Dominick Cherrett?" a marine called.

"I did." Dominick sounded calm, confident, every bit the aristocrat he was. "Toss us a line and lower a bosun's chair. I have a lady with me."

"A lady?" the marine repeated.

A quiet chorus of laughter rippled over the water.

"What's a Cherrett doing out here?" The marine now sounded suspicious, and no rope was forthcoming yet.

"That, sirrah," Dominick responded, "is your captain's concern, not yours."

"Is that so?" The marine leaned over the rail and spat. "Well, the captain won't be concerned if we don't let you aboard just because you're claiming you're a lord. Mebbe you're one of those tricky Yankees come to cause us more trouble."

"And perhaps my uncle, Vice Admiral Landry, will be interested in your insolence," Dominick returned.

The marine straightened. Shadows moved around the lights, and murmurs drifted through the night.

"A bit of a conference," Dominick said to Tabitha. "They aren't quite certain I'm telling the truth, but now they're wondering if they should risk letting me aboard in the event I am."

"You shouldn't have called me a lady." Tabitha tugged at her worn gown. "They'll be expecting elegance."

"What they're expecting is what I tell them to expect."

Tabitha stared at him. Confidence, determination, even occasional haughtiness she'd seen in him. Outright arrogance, as he demonstrated now, was entirely new and disconcerting.

"Should I behave a certain way?" she asked.

"Be your wonderful self." Grasping a stay, Dominick stepped onto the gunwale and called out, "Throw us a line now, or I'll tell my uncle how uncooperative you all were."

"We have to notify the captain before we can let you aboard," the marine informed them. "But we're dropping a line to you now. Can you catch it?"

"I'll give it a good try," Dominick muttered.

As he spoke, a rope sailed across the lantern light, straight at Dominick's head. He ducked. The rope struck the deck of the *Marianne* with a resounding thud, and Dominick dove after it.

"Come help me, Tabitha?" he asked, keeping his voice quiet. "We need to moor against them, or we'll drift too far leeward and not be able to return."

"Which might not be a terrible event." Tabitha moved to the deck to join Dominick in hauling the fishing boat closer to the frigate's side. Although several sailors lined the rail of the ship towering over the *Marianne*, none of them offered to assist. Tabitha used only one hand, so the going proved slow. By the time their bow bumped the hull of the *Nemesis*, men in officers' uniforms had shooed the sailors from the rail.

"I'm Avery, the first lieutenant," one man announced. "You are Lord Dominick Cherrett requesting permission to come aboard with a . . . er . . . companion?"

"I am." Dominick finished securing the line. "And don't ask me to explain why I'm here. I'll tell only the captain."

"But of course." Avery spoke to the men around them, then turned back. "We're lowering a bosun's chair."

The canvas sling landed on the fishing boat's deck. Dominick settled Tabitha into it, brushed her cheek with his thumb, then grabbed for the mooring line and began to climb. Tabitha wanted to watch, to admire his strength and agility, but the tug on the rope of her makeshift chair sent her spinning around and up. Lanterns flashed one second, starlight the next. Nausea struck. She closed her eyes. When the motion of the chair stopped, her head kept spinning.

"You look a bit green, my dear." Dominick's hands steadied her. "Didn't you enjoy the ride?"

"Next time I climb." She resisted the urge to collapse against him.

Dominick chuckled, held her for a moment until she nodded that she was steady on her feet, then tucked her hand into the crook of his elbow. "Take us to the captain, Mr. Avery."

"Aye, sir . . . er . . . my lord." Avery raised his hand. For a moment, Tabitha thought he would salute. But he dropped it to his side and headed aft.

Dominick led her after the lieutenant. Men fell into step behind them, lining the deck on either side of them. On the far side of the men, guns hulked against the rails. She counted thirty-six. Thirty-six guns that could destroy an American vessel in minutes, that had damaged American shipping. War would bring disaster to the country.

The knowledge that she and Dominick were doing what they could to prevent it kept her feet moving, her head high. She knew the men stared, wondering what sort of female she might be, speculating she was the type to be out at night with a man. If they failed in their mission, everyone would believe Wilkins in the end and her reputation would be irredeemable.

If they failed in their mission, Dominick would suffer even more.

Lord, please be with us, she found herself praying. *Please don't abandon us now.*

They walked toward a man in a smart blue coat with gold

epaulets and white breeches. He stood at the head of a ladder, his hand on the hilt of a sword, with two marines flanking him behind, their hands on their muskets. God and two of His archangels? On a British man-of-war, she knew she wasn't far off. She and Dominick were in his power now that they stood on his deck.

She kept her smile in place as they reached the captain. The captain didn't smile back. He frowned at Dominick. "Who are you and what do you want?"

"You know who I am," Dominick returned. "Who are you?"

The marine beside Dominick punched him in the back. "You be respectful when you address Captain Roscoe."

Dominick said nothing. He stared at Roscoe, who stared back. Tabitha held her breath, wondering who would blink first. Around them, the ship and crew seemed to hold their breath too. Even the wind seemed to have ceased whispering through the rigging. Not a spar or timber creaked. Only the sea hissed, a snake coiled around the hull.

Tabitha's heart began to pound hard enough to make her throat hurt.

Then Roscoe relaxed. His shoulders remained straight, but his face lost its rigidity and he smiled. "I do believe you speak the truth. Now, how may I help you?"

"We've come to inquire about a local man named Raleigh Trower." Dominick glanced around, as though expecting Raleigh to step from the shadows between the great guns. "He was once in the British Navy, and we thought perhaps he . . . rejoined the service."

"Indeed." Roscoe sighed. "Then I regret to tell you, you have come on a fruitless journey. No one has joined our service for months. We are not on British soil, after all."

"How odd." Dominick glanced at Tabitha. "Didn't Donald Parks say it was the *Nemesis* where he left Raleigh?"

Tabitha swallowed against a dry throat but still couldn't speak. She kept her gaze on Roscoe, watched him pale beneath his sun-darkened skin. If he chose, he could forget Dominick's class rank and do away with both of them. Donald was, of course, their insurance of safety. She must cling to that.

She wanted something more substantial than a man so exhausted he couldn't stay awake for more than a few minutes at a time. She clung to Dominick's arm, but suddenly he wasn't there. Without so much as another glance in her direction or a word to anyone, he slipped into the shadows and vanished.

Tabitha clutched air for a moment, then clasped her arms over her middle.

Shouts arose from the men. The captain bellowed an order and marines sprang into action, charging in the direction Dominick had vanished. No one so much as looked at Tabitha. She stood in the middle of a sea of men with ocean around them, and knew her vulnerability, her weakness.

"Lord, I have only You," she whispered. "I've neglected You and blamed You and don't deserve anything from You, but You made promises. Please keep them, if I'm not too much of a sinner."

Oh, but she was. She was angry and bitter and unforgiving. She trusted no one.

You need to trust God so you can trust others, the pastor had said.

"I don't know how to trust You, God," she nearly whimpered. "But I will try, if You can forgive me enough to help."

A running seaman bumped into her. She lost her balance and fell. He kept going, intent on a disturbance somewhere else on the ship.

Tabitha stared at the deck, bright in the many lanterns'

glow. Bright except for the dark splotches leading from the larboard rail to somewhere on the starboard side, the direction Dominick had taken like a trail of bread crumbs. Except this was a trail of blood droplets.

Donald had heard a shot.

On her hands and knees, Tabitha darted along the trail, dodging seamen and skirting ropes, keeping the marks in her sight.

They disappeared in the darkness of a hatchway. Tabitha scrambled down the ladder. Not enough light remained to guide her if more blood splotches led the way, but a glow further down the passageway and raised voices guided her forward. Guided her into a cabin with canvas walls, a hanging cot surrounded by naval officers, marines, and Dominick, and another man lying in the midst.

"Raleigh," Tabitha cried out and shoved her way to his side. "You're injured." She dropped to her knees beside the cot and glared up at the men. "Where's your surgeon?"

"Here, ma'am." A stooped gentleman with flowing white hair stepped forward. "You'd best go now. This is no sight for a lady."

"I'm a healer, a midwife." She took Raleigh's hand in hers. It was cold, the nails turning blue. A glance at his face showed blue lips with a trace of bubbling blood at the corners. She didn't need her medical knowledge or a surgeon to tell her that her lifelong friend was dying.

She stared up at the officers and Dominick through tear-misted eyes. "How did this happen?"

"He was shot in the back," Dominick said in a voice cold enough to turn June into January.

"He was eluding punishment," the captain interjected, "aiding and abetting the escape of a crewman, and attempting to escape himself. It's just—"

"Nothing of what you do is just." Dominick turned on the man and grabbed his lapels. "You are aiding and abetting the abduction of American seamen, and only your cooperation will save you from—"

"Dominick, careful," Tabitha cried.

Two marines grabbed Dominick and flung him away from the captain.

He struck the bulkhead, grunted, then shot upright again. "Anyone who lays a hand on me will answer to Vice Admiral Landry. Do you understand?"

The cabin settled into a tableau of frozen faces and silence. Above, feet pounded and men called. Raleigh's breath rattled in his throat, and brighter red blood trickled from his mouth.

Tabitha dropped her head onto his chest, heard the death rattle emphasized, and didn't attempt to stifle her sob.

"As far as I'm concerned, Captain Roscoe," Dominick enunciated in that deadly chill of a voice, "you have murdered this lady's fiancé."

"He is not an American." Roscoe sounded defensive, tense. "My lord, I swear to you—"

"Never mind what he says, Captain," another man called from the passageway. "He's not a lord. He's a runaway redemptioner."

Tabitha choked on a sob. Her head shot up in time to see Harlan Wilkins stroll to the doorway of the cabin. "Don't think you can get away with this, Cherrett. Kendall knows and has given me permission to take you ashore for punishment."

"No." Tabitha tried to rise. "You can't—"

Dominick gave his head a barely perceptible shake and raised a finger to his lips.

Roscoe glared at him. "Did you lie to me, man?"

"No." Dominick smiled. "And neither did—what's your friend's name?"

"Wilk—how am I supposed to know the name of a Yankee?" Roscoe snapped.

"A thought." Dominick stepped toward Wilkins. "I suppose you have reinforcements, so trying to escape is pointless, unless Roscoe thinks it's better to protect the son of a peer of the realm than help him save his own neck."

"A disgraced son." Wilkins snorted. "Or did you think none of us knows?" He turned to Roscoe. "He can't do anything to harm you, Captain Roscoe. He can't deny that he's a redemptioner, and after his master is done with him for attempting to run away, you'll be long gone from these shores."

With Tabitha aboard.

She bit her lip and hunched beside the cot. She could choose between helping to ease Raleigh's last minutes or hours on earth, ensuring he reached the shore of the land he considered home rather than being dumped into the sea, or stay with Dominick and prevent him from receiving another flogging he did not deserve. She couldn't leave her old friend alone. She couldn't see Dominick hurt again, scarred worse than he already was.

She couldn't bear the idea of Wilkins getting away with his crime.

She lowered her head to Raleigh's chest again. The rattling grew fainter under her ear.

Above her, Captain Roscoe cleared his throat. "I didn't realize he was a redemptioner, marquess's son or not. I think you need to remove him from my ship, Wilkins. We need to sail."

"So you do know his name," Dominick said. "Do you think my knowledge can't harm you?"

"Who listens to a redemptioner against an upright gentleman like Mr. Wilkins here?" Roscoe's tone was dry, his face sneering.

"Kendall might have, but not any longer." Wilkins's voice held a note of joviality. "And I need to get this servant back to his master. A whipping should teach him he's not a lord's son anymore, ha-ha."

Tabitha's fingers convulsed around Raleigh's. She sucked in her breath. She couldn't stay. She had to go after Dominick, save him, and expose Wilkins for what he was—a traitor to his country, a debaucher of women, indirectly a murderer who completely ignored his victim lying on the cot, his lifeblood dripping out of him.

And Dominick was leaving peacefully, without a fight. A quick glance up told her he submitted to the two men who grabbed his arms and twisted them behind him before they marched him toward the companionway ladder. In fact, he smiled as though he held a delicious secret.

Except pain tightened the corners of his eyes and darkened the irises.

Tabitha touched her lips to Raleigh's cheek. "I love you, my friend. Go to God in peace. I'll tell everyone you're a hero. You helped—" Her throat closed. She started to rise.

His fingers tightened on hers and his lips parted. "Tabbie, don't go."

She looked at his once dear and healthy face, now gray and somehow distant. She heard Wilkins and his men departing with Dominick. Her heart felt ripped in two. She might be able to help Dominick. If she stayed, she could give Raleigh comfort in his last minutes.

"Please." He gasped for breath. "So I know . . . forgiven."

"You are." She bent, kissed his brow, then raced up the companionway after Dominick. No one tried to stop her as she raced for the *Marianne*. She needed to sail it alone for only a mile. Surely she could manage that.

36

Dominick gritted his teeth against the pain of two burly strangers twisting his arms behind him. He knew it was nothing compared to the pain to come, flesh bared to the night, bared to the bite of the whip.

His stomach rolled. He swallowed and smiled over his clenched teeth. He had Wilkins. He had Roscoe. Wilkins could claim Dominick was running away, but he knew Wilkins was a traitor. Roscoe could sail away, but Dominick knew when he would make contact with his uncle, Admiral Landry, who possessed the power to stop the man. With Tabitha's help—

Dominick jerked against his restraints as though someone had punched him in the middle. Tabitha was still aboard the *Nemesis*. If Roscoe sailed, she would be captive, unable to return, unable to stop Wilkins.

He'd wanted her to remain quiet until Wilkins condemned himself in front of her too, but not to stay. Not to remain with Raleigh.

How could he ever have thought of leaving her to another man? It was a mistake, just one more in too many. No matter what happened in the next few hours, weeks, years, he wanted Tabitha at his side, his friend and his wife, his lover and the mother to his children. He couldn't give her up for a renewal of prestige and the possibility of a good position received from his family's largess. They would survive in this strange new land with God's guidance and help, with the wits and talents God had given to them, with the community around them.

If Tabitha survived the night.

If he survived the night.

Dominick bowed his head and prayed for Tabitha's safe return to Seabourne. He thought about praying for release from punishment for a crime he hadn't committed, but he had disobeyed. He wasn't back on Kendall's property by sundown. He deserved the lashing, however ill the prospect made him feel.

"Don't go puking on the deck," one of his captors commanded. "We'll make you clean it up."

"After you get your whipping." The other guffawed.

Dominick kept his head bowed, his body relaxed. Talking to these men would get him nowhere. Talking to Wilkins was likely to get him dumped overboard. Dominick would appeal to Kendall. He was a good man, a fair man. He said he would mete out punishment for disobedience and could never garner respect if he didn't carry through.

But the lash!

Dominick swallowed against the burning at the back of his throat. He had eaten nothing since sometime the day before, or he feared he would have fouled the wooden planks at his feet. His head spun and his heart ached.

"Please bring her back to me," he murmured to the wind. "I'll find a way—"

Or perhaps he should let God find a way for them to be together. When Dominick chose to find a way to direct his future, he made amok of it.

"All right then, Lord, I give this up to You." He spoke a bit louder than he'd intended.

His jailers laughed. "Look, he's saying his prayers."

Dominick smiled. He wished for peace. He felt a tension like the inner workings of a clock. He tried to twist around to see if another boat followed, if anyone was bringing Tabitha ashore. His captors held him fast. All he could do was look ahead to the pale line of sand and the glimmer of light from the village a quarter mile beyond.

The fishing boat cruised up the Trowers' inlet and tied up at their jetty. Wilkins leaped to the dock and strode off toward Seabourne. The rest of the men tied a rope to the one binding Dominick's wrists behind him, and led him onto the sand and over the dunes. They walked swiftly, too quickly for a man off balance on sand. Twice he landed on his knees. Both times the men laughed and dragged him to his feet again. His shoulders burned by the time they reached the square. A well-lit square filled with people, including Kendall, Letty, Dinah, and Deborah.

He was going to be punished in front of anyone who wanted to watch.

He raised his head and stared Kendall in the eyes. What he read there took his breath away. It wasn't anger or contempt or, worse, anticipation. It was pain, raw and open.

"I trusted you," Kendall said. "I gave you freedom I've never given a servant after years, let alone months."

"I wasn't running away. I'm trying to stop these men from stealing American seamen and selling them—"

"I found him aboard a British frigate," Wilkins interrupted. "He'd convinced the captain he was the son of a lord and should be helped."

"A captain you knew by name," Dominick shot back. "A captain who knew you by name. A captain who had an American aboard." He returned his attention to Kendall. "Have you talked to Donald Parks?"

"He was abducted." Kendall looked bewildered, taken aback.

The crowd around them had fallen quiet, watching, listening.

"He got away," Dominick said. "He—"

"Isn't with his family." Wilkins sneered at Dominick. "If the man got free, why isn't he with his family?"

"So men like you can't silence him." Dominick glanced around for the Trower family. Not seeing them, he added, "Like they silenced Raleigh Trower."

"What happened to Raleigh?" Kendall asked.

A murmuring rose like the wind.

"He's—"

"Lying." Wilkins raised his voice. "Trower took his boat out fishing, is all. You can go see for yourselves the *Marianne* is gone. And this redemptioner here"—he flicked a finger against Dominick's nose—"was trying to run off with Tabitha Eckles. You can testify yourself, Letty Robins, that he and the midwife have been carrying on like the morally corrupt aristocracy this man comes from. Tell them, Letty."

"It's true." Letty's eyes blazed and a white line shone around her lips. "I told him to steer clear of her, but he insisted he had to see her. He promised me he'd return, but he lied to me. I trusted him, and he lied to me."

Dominick stared at her. "Letty, I fully intended—"

"Then you expect me to believe that she led you astray?" Letty cried.

"No, no." Dominick closed his eyes.

"Where is Tabitha?" Kendall asked.

Dominick shook his head. "I don't know. That is, the last time I saw her, she was kneeling beside Raleigh's cot."

And he'd never seen anyone grieve as she had. She might claim she didn't love Raleigh as a wife loved a husband, but she loved him as a friend.

"I'm afraid they'll keep her so she can't verify what I say," he added.

"Or to ensure your English friends rescue you?" Wilkins jeered. "Mayor Kendall, you can't believe this man any more than you can believe that incompetent midwife."

The last two words struck Dominick with understanding. Of course. Wilkins was discrediting Dominick's character as he had nearly succeeded in discrediting Tabitha's, to protect himself from Sally Belote's claim of paternity, from what Tabitha might have worked out from a dying woman's ramblings. When he failed with Tabitha, Wilkins tried to kill her.

He wouldn't fail with Dominick—he read it on Kendall's unhappy face. Everyone knew through Letty and the girls that Kendall had declared he would whip Dominick then send him to the interior part of the state if he disobeyed the curfew again. Without Kendall accepting Dominick's excuse for why he hadn't been home by sunset, the punishment would be carried out, or Kendall would be shamed as a man who could be a leader, a mayor, a senator.

"I am telling the truth." Dominick made one more effort to convince Kendall as he looked the man in the eye.

Kendall turned away and gestured to his groom. The man held a carriage whip. A whip much like the one Dominick's father had used.

For a moment, the square turned black. He heard nothing. The warm summer wind felt more like a January frost. And the smells were the same—horse manure, damp wool, his own perspiration. Only a lifetime of training kept his back straight, his head high.

"Take him to the fence in front of my house," Kendall said. "And bind his hands to it."

"I'm innocent," Dominick said in as clipped a tone as he could manage. "I do not deserve this punishment."

He leaned against the gate as the same two men cut the ropes around his wrists and retied him to the top bar of the gate. What he was about to endure was nothing to fear. Like the beating his father had given him, it was only man's punishment and didn't matter in the end. Jesus had taken the true punishment for Dominick's wrongdoing. Man's punishment meant nothing but temporary pain. Because of Jesus's pain, Dominick could be free in his heart, whatever his body suffered.

"Remove his coat and shirt," Wilkins commanded.

Dominick didn't need to ask how they would manage that with his hands tied. A tug on the back of his neck and sting against his skin, followed by ripping, told of a knife blade parting the fabric. Night air touched his skin.

The crowd gasped. His scars tightened.

"Proof he's a reprobate," Wilkins all but crowed. "He's been whipped before."

"I am forgiven and innocent in Your eyes, O God," Dominick whispered to the brick front of Kendall's house. "I can do nothing, but in You I can do all things."

"That's right," one of his captors from the frigate said with a chuckle, "say your prayers."

"Fifteen lashes," Kendall pronounced, then sighed.

Twenty-five fewer than his father had given him.

He tensed, awaiting the first blow. He didn't look to see who would wield the lash. He didn't want to, he didn't need to know.

"One," someone shouted.

The crowd fell still enough for Dominick to hear the whistle of the whip sailing through the air.

And footfalls clattering across the cobbles.

"No, stop!" Her beloved voice rang across the square.

The crack of the whip rang in his ears. His body jerked.

He tasted blood from where he'd bitten down on his lip to keep from crying out.

"Two." The shout soared through the night.

The whip whooshed.

"Stop!"

Something hurtled against his back. Something—someone—soft and warm and smelling of the sea and roses.

The whip cracked. She cried out and jerked against him.

"Stop!" he shouted.

Others took up the call. But the whip fell again. Tabitha screamed and slid along his body to the ground.

With a roar, Dominick wrenched the bar from the gate and swung around. Wilkins raised his arm. The lash hurtled to its full length.

Hands still bound to the rail, Dominick lunged. The bar and his head struck Wilkins in the middle. Merchant and whip, bondsman and bonds, landed on the cobbles in a tangled heap.

37

The gate latch clanged. On her knees before the roses, Tabitha glanced up, heart leaping with hope.

Red hair shimmering despite the overcast day, Letty strode up the flagstone path and waved a folded sheet of vellum under Tabitha's nose. "I expect you've been waiting for this."

Even over the fragrance of the roses, Tabitha caught a whiff of sandalwood and snatched the letter from Letty's fingers. It was merely folded with the edges tucked in, not sealed. She yanked it open and read:

> My dear, now that my right arm has healed enough to write and my uncle has dropped anchor in Hampton Roads, Kendall is allowing me to see you. His coachman will bring you to Norfolk, and Letty will be your chaperone. Please do not delay.
>
> Your, Dominick

Tabitha stared at the penultimate word. An error or a deliberate statement? No matter. He had written.

She tucked the missive between her stays and chemise.

Letty laughed. "That can't be comfortable."

"It's more comfortable than having him twenty miles away and no one telling me if he's all right or not."

"He felt the same way." Letty touched Tabitha's left shoulder. "Is that healing all right?"

"All of me is healing all right." She rose, albeit stiffly. "Though I think part of me will always mourn Raleigh."

"Even though he was a traitor to our country?" Letty asked.

"He more than paid the price for trying to get his freedom." Tabitha blinked back tears that still came quickly to her eyes, weakness from a wound that came too close to going septic. "Donald Parks is with his family and a free man because of Raleigh. And we don't know how many others are free now."

"Or may get freed, if the politicians can work things out. And speaking of politicians, the mayor and vice admiral and your gentleman are waiting for you. You'd better get some things packed and your clothes changed if we're to make Norfolk before dark."

"Of course." Tabitha dashed into the house, calling for Patience.

In less than an hour, she was seated beside Letty in Kendall's well-sprung coach. The road between Seabourne and Norfolk proved somewhat better in a carriage than in Tabitha's wagon, but the hours of travel still took too long. After three days apart, she yearned to see Dominick. Simultaneously, she wished she'd never seated herself upon the luxurious cushions. Lying in bed while someone else tended her wound, then creeping about her garden while her strength returned, she could pretend all would be well with Dominick, that he would stay with her because his uncle never came. Her excuse for him not visiting her was genuine. Afraid his bondsman was permanently injured because he couldn't move his right arm, the mayor had taken Dominick to Norfolk to a physician. Dislocated, the diagnosis returned. Painful but not ultimately serious. Dominick would be well soon.

"Well enough to return to his duties," Dinah had reported with a sniff. "He might have exposed Harlan Wilkins for a blaggard and a traitor, but he's still a redemptioner."

"He won't be when his uncle gets here," Tabitha had responded as a counter to the girl's condescension.

Now the uncle had arrived and she'd been summoned. No doubt they needed her testimony of what had occurred aboard the *Nemesis*.

"I'm surprised they haven't gone on to Richmond," Tabitha said. "Wouldn't the governor want to know about all of this? Or the Navy, such as it is? Or even President Madison?"

"They've sent dispatches to all of them." Letty pulled needles and yarn from a basket at her feet and began to knit something fluffy and pink. "As soon as the doctor tells Dominick he can travel, I expect they'll be heading up to Washington City."

"Before he returns to England?" Tabitha stared out the window as she spoke. A falling mist made the trees look like sentries along the road. "Kendall will sell his indenture, won't he?"

"I wouldn't know." Letty pursed her mouth.

Tabitha smiled. Letty, so loyal to her master, wouldn't divulge such information to anyone who didn't need to know. She would be a good cook and even housekeeper for a budding politician.

"So what are you knitting?" Tabitha changed the subject to the mundane.

They discussed the merits of a knitted blanket over a quilt for a baby, and other inconsequential matters. Tabitha fidgeted. The mist made the light too poor for reading. It slowed the coach. A four-hour journey took six. Then the first lights of Norfolk broke through the gloom and she began to fuss with her hair, tucking a strand behind her ear, then pulling it out again to curl against her neck, tilting her hat to the left, then tilting it back to the right. Her blue sprig muslin gown looked too cheerful for a lady mourning the death of a friend, even if that friend had betrayed his country. The men would think her irreverent. The vice admiral would find her dowdy and out of fashion, wholly unsuitable for his nephew.

When Tabitha began to untie and retie the ribbon around the high waist of the gown, Letty tucked her knitting into the basket and grasped Tabitha's hands. "You're going to wrinkle it."

"I look like what I am—a nobody from nowhere, an insignificant—"

"The most respected woman on the eastern shore, Tabitha Eckles. Now, lean forward and hold up your shawl." Letty smoothed the bow against Tabitha's back.

She winced.

"I declare that man could have stopped the lash from striking you," Letty grumbled.

"He certainly could have the second time." Tabitha recalled the sight of Dominick's scarred back and shuddered. "How could a father do that to his son?"

"Some people just have anger inside them when others cross them." Letty leaned forward. "We're here."

"It's a house." Tabitha had expected an inn.

"It's the mayor's house. The Norfolk mayor, that is."

Tabitha's heart began to race. Only Letty's presence stopped her from flinging herself out of the carriage and racing to the door, calling Dominick's name. Letty, and Tabitha's desire not to shame him for even being friends with her.

What felt like an hour later but was likely only a quarter of that time, the coach stopped, the door opened, and a servant in crimson livery held up his hand to assist her to the ground. "They're waitin' in de parlor, Miss Eckles. But here's Molly to help you freshen up before you go in."

"Thank you." Tabitha spoke in a breathy voice unlike her own.

She needed water to quench her dry throat. She needed a new gown, something of silk and lace from London, though she'd never cared about what she wore in her life. She didn't even own any jewelry.

Her legs felt like year-old carrots as she climbed the steps to the house and then another flight to a small, brightly furnished bedchamber, where all the necessities for recovering from a long journey awaited her.

"They said as how you were to eat if you're hungry," Molly said. "They already dined. The Englishman will sail on the ebb tide, so they couldn't wait any longer."

Englishman or Englishmen? Tabitha couldn't ask. She couldn't dream of eating.

"I'll go straightaway then."

On legs that now felt about as strong as sea grass, she descended the steps and followed the manservant into the parlor. Part of her mind told her it was full of men. She saw only one. He stood at the hearth, one arm propped on the mantel, his hair shining in the candlelight. He turned as her slippers whispered across the floorboards. Their glances touched, held, locked. Neither moved.

"So this is the brave young lady." A hearty British voice rang through the room.

Tabitha jumped.

Dominick lowered his arm and turned. "Yes. Tabitha, let me present you to Mayor Bland and Vice Admiral Lord Landry."

Another lord. Tabitha suppressed a sigh and held out her hand, decided she'd better curtsy instead, and completely forgot where to place her feet so she didn't lose her balance.

The vice admiral caught her hand between both of his and saved her from toppling over. "You are even lovelier than I was led to believe, my dear." He smiled, and Tabitha decided

Dominick must take after his mother's side of the family. The smile was the same, the brown eyes as deep and warm. "And I was expecting a great deal."

"Completely exaggerated, I'm sure." Tabitha's cheeks burned. "I—I'm just a village midwife."

"And quite the bravest female I've ever had the privilege of meeting." The vice admiral led her to a chair. "Fetch her a cup of that tea, Dominick. You're still a redemptioner as far as I know." He let out a full-throated laugh.

Tabitha dropped onto the chair, her gaze flashing to Dominick, then Kendall. "Still? But I thought—"

"I'd give up my English butler because he's a hero?" Kendall shook his head. "It's all my friends from Richmond and Charlottesville could talk about after they left, I understand. And now he's even more valuable to me."

"I see." Tabitha schooled her face. "The price is too high?"

"No price is too high to free my nephew from bondage," the vice admiral pronounced. "This man won't name one."

"I'm moving to Richmond and want him with me," Kendall said.

"But Seabourne needs a mayor." Tabitha leaned forward. "And Dominick deserves his freedom to return to his family unless—" She glanced at Dominick.

He smiled. "Uncle assures me that the rest of my family and most of society has forgiven me, now that word of my father's treatment's gotten out. That hasn't endeared me to him, I'm afraid."

"His own fault if he's no longer respected for not putting family first." Vice Admiral Landry curled his upper lip, then smiled. "All I need is for Kendall here to name the price. We want Dominick home."

"What do you want, Dominick?" Tabitha asked.

"To go for a walk with you." He crossed the room and stood behind her chair, his hands on her shoulders. "Ask your questions, gentlemen. We've a scant few hours before the tide runs out and the ship leaves for England. We can discuss me later."

"Yes, yes." The vice admiral sipped from a glass of ruby-colored liquid, cleared his throat, and began.

Somewhere during answering questions about all her encounters and suspected encounters with Wilkins, including matters to do with the claim of his fatherhood, someone pressed a cup of tea into Tabitha's hand. Later, a plate of tiny sandwiches appeared in front of her. She consumed all of it without thinking. Her voice grew hoarse and her body limp.

"Just tell me once more," the vice admiral began.

"No, Uncle, that's enough." Dominick broke in. "She needs air."

Tabitha raised a hand. "I'd like to know what's going to happen with Wilkins."

"There'll be a trial, of course." Kendall cleared his throat. "Probably in Richmond, since everyone on the cape is too angry to give him a fair hearing."

"If it goes that far." Dominick's eyes gleamed for a moment before he dropped his gaze. "He doesn't like the jail, I understand, and just might confess."

"But Dominick can't testify as a bondsman, and I'm a female," Tabitha pointed out. "Where are your witnesses?"

"Roscoe will testify." The admiral compressed his lips into a thin line.

Kendall reddened. "And I understand there's a paternity matter you can testify on."

"Hardly proof of treason," Tabitha said.

"But enough to persuade him he's perhaps better off in prison than leg-shackled." Dominick grimaced.

Tabitha shuddered. "I suppose now I know that Mrs. Wilkins wasn't just rambling the night she died. I think he pushed her. She likely found out about his activities."

"We think so." Kendall blinked. "Poor lady. She was a lovely young woman."

"I tried to save her." Tabitha's stomach knotted around the meal she'd consumed. "Can we ensure he pays for the upbringing and welfare of his child before he loses all his assets?"

"With your testimony," Kendall said, "he'll lose a paternity suit. I . . . ahem . . . anticipate no difficulty in having the town council reinstate their confidence in your ability as a midwife, my dear."

"Yes, yes." The admiral cleared his throat. "If she still wants to practice."

"She will." Dominick took Tabitha's hands in his and lifted Tabitha to her feet. "She's told you her story three times already without a word changing. Now, Mayor Kendall, Mayor Bland, with your permission . . ."

"Be back by sundown." Kendall smiled as he spoke.

Dominick laughed and drew Tabitha's hand through the crook of his elbow, then held her fingers against his forearm. "With this mist, who can say when sundown is?"

"It's not a nice evening for a walk," the vice admiral called. "Take her into the dining room. It should still be warm in there."

Dominick ignored him, and Tabitha willingly followed him into the cool dampness of the misty evening.

"What do you want?" she asked.

"To take a walk with you." Dominick led the way down to the beach. "To talk about our future."

Tabitha's heart skipped a beat. "What . . . future?"

"What it holds for us." He paused at the water's edge,

where the surf made the mist lift and swirl like the gauzy gowns of dancers. "My uncle will pay whatever price Kendall requests to set me free so I can return to England. Once this news reaches the *Navy Gazette*, few people will care about the scandal I caused, except maybe my father. My uncle is afraid, though"—he rested his hands on her shoulders—"that you will be a hindrance to me finding a good position in the government or even a private house."

"I thought as much." Tabitha blinked salty mist from her eyes. "But I—"

He touched a finger to her lips. "So I turned him down."

"You what?" She grasped his lapels. "Dominick, you didn't."

"Kendall said if I'll stay and work the full term of my indenture, he'll give me permission to marry you right away." He smiled. "If you'll have me. Will you give up being a midwife and come to Richmond?"

"I—I—" Her head spun. "I promised Phoebe Lee I'd take her on as an apprentice because I thought I'd never have a daughter."

"I hope you have daughters." He touched his lips to hers. "But you don't have to disappoint Mrs. Lee either. Kendall was teasing you back there. He has no intention of leaving Seabourne now. He'll even let us live in your house."

"Dominick, is this possible? I mean—" She didn't know what she meant. She couldn't think of anything but the joy of him staying with her.

"I mean we can spend the rest of our lives together, have a family."

"But your upbringing, your position." She shook her head. "How can you give all that up?"

"It'll take me longer than we have here tonight to explain it all. Suffice it to say that God has shown me another path, one not based on my family name but on the gifts He has given me. I'm not really going to be Kendall's butler. I'll work as his factor and man of business, and we'll see where God takes us from there."

"And He will take us if we let Him." Tabitha laughed from sheer joy. "Oh, Dominick, is this real?"

"Quite." As he drew her to him for a lingering kiss, the sun broke free and banished the mist.

Acknowledgments

Though she works primarily alone, no writer is an island, or if she is, many causeways link her to the mainland of humanity. Here I'd like to thank those paths back to sanity.

Therese Stenzel for starting the authors' promotional group HEWN Marketing and agreeing that my English hero qualifies me for influencer support.

Debbie Lynne Costello and Kathy Maher for their Crown Marketing Group specializing in nineteenth-century American Christian fiction. Your friendship is even more valuable.

Kathy Cretsinger deserves special thanks for understanding my post-edits angst and agreeing to read the manuscript. Your phone call saying you loved the story came just when I needed it most. And your suggestion for a fix was insightful too.

A few blessed beings will likely see my gratitude in every book, primarily my editors for not telling me I'm a dolt, and the members of my household, both two- and four-legged, for accepting my weird hours as normal.

Without brainstorming from my talented critique partners, Louise M. Gouge, Marylu Tyndall, and Ramona Cecil, I doubt this fledgling idea that had been in the back of my mind for ten years would have turned into a full-blown novel.

As always, in addition, my agent Tamela Murray deserves that I do something humbling like clean her house every day for a month, for giving this story such swift and intense attention.

Finally, I wish to extend a special thanks to staff and professors in the Virginia Tech history department, especially Professor Roger Ekirch for allowing me to run with my project on midwives' role in society, and Ms. Janet Francis for corralling her undergrads to give me research assistance. Matt and Mike, I hope you're faring well, wherever your lives have landed you.

The role of midwives in history began to fascinate **Laurie Alice Eakes** in graduate school, and she knew that someday she wanted to write novels with midwife heroines. Ten years later, after several published novels, four relocations, and a National Readers Choice Award for Best Regency, the midwives idea returned, and *Lady in the Mist* was born. Now Laurie Alice writes full-time from her home in southern Texas, where she lives with her husband and sundry dogs and cats.

"If you're looking for an awesome writer and a story charged with romance, you don't want to miss *A Hope Undaunted*."

—Judith Miller, author of *Somewhere to Belong*, Daughters of Amana series

Kate O'Connor is a smart and sassy woman who has her goals laid out for the future—including the perfect husband and career. Will she follow her plans or her heart?

a division of Baker Publishing Group

www.RevellBooks.com

Available Wherever Books Are Sold

"Laura Frantz portrays the wild beauty of frontier life."
—Ann Gabhart

Facing the loss of a childhood love, a dangerous family feud, and the affection of a Shawnee warrior, it is all Lael Click can do to survive in the Kentucky frontier territory. Will an outsider be her undoing?

Available Wherever Books Are Sold

"You'll disappear into another place and time and be both encouraged and enriched for having taken the journey."

—Jane Kirkpatrick, bestselling author

This sweeping tale of romance and forgiveness will envelop readers as it takes them from a Kentucky fort through the vast wilderness to the west in search of true love.

Available Wherever Books Are Sold

"Fans of Amish novels may find Gabhart's well-researched historical fiction to their liking."
—*Publishers Weekly*

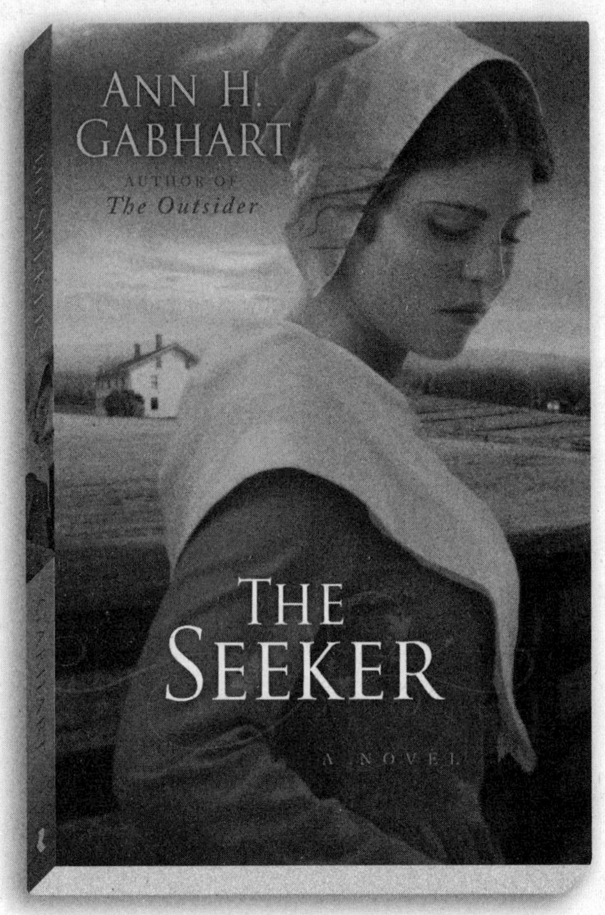

Ann Gabhart weaves a touching story
of love, freedom, and forgiveness.

Available Wherever Books Are Sold

Be the First to Hear about Other New Books from Revell!

Sign up for announcements about new and upcoming titles at

www.revellbooks.com/signup

Follow us on twitter
RevellBooks

Don't miss out on our great reads!

a division of Baker Publishing Group
www.RevellBooks.com

Sign up for announcements about new and upcoming titles at

www.revellbooks.com/signup

Follow us on

RevellBooks

Don't miss out on our great reads!